Cynthia Harrod-Eagles won the Young Writers' Award with her first novel, *The Waiting Game*, and in 1992 won the Romantic Novel of the Year Award with *Emily*. She has written over sixty books, including twenty-eight volumes of the Morland Dynasty – a series she will be taking up to the present day. She is also the creator of the acclaimed mystery series featuring Inspector Bill Slider.

Apart from writing her passions are music, wine, horses, architecture and the English countryside.

Visit the author's website at www.cynthiaharrodeagles.com

Also in the Dynasty series:

DYNASTY

28

The White Road

Cynthia Harrod-Eagles

sphere

SPHERE

First published in Great Britain by Time Warner Books in 2005
This paperback edition published by Sphere in 2006
Reprinted in 2006, 2007

The moral right of the author has been asserted.

A CIP catalogue record for this book
is available from the British Library

ISBN: 978-0-7515-3345-3

Papers used by Sphere are natural, recyclable products made from
wood grown in sustainable forests and certified in accordance with
the rules of the Forest Stewardship Council.

Typeset in Plantin by Palimpsest Book Production Limited,
Grangemouth, Stirlingshire

Printed and bound in Great Britain by
Clays Ltd, St Ives plc
Paper supplied by Hellefoss AS, Norway

Sphere
An imprint of
Little, Brown Book Group
Brettenham House
Lancaster Place
London WC2E 7EN

A Member of the Hachette Livre Group of Companies

www.littlebrown.co.uk

AUTHOR'S NOTE

After some consideration, I decided it might cause complications if my fictional characters joined real regiments. So while the various military actions described in this book really happened, the West Herts are my invention. The York Commercials likewise never existed, but they are based on genuine 'Pals' units.

THE MORLANDS OF MORLAND PLACE

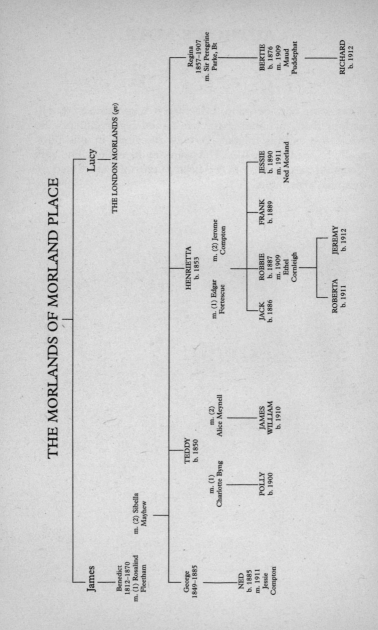

James ——— Lucy

THE LONDON MORLANDS (*qv*)

Benedict
1812–1870
m. (1) Rosalind
Fleetham
m. (2) Sibella
Mayhew

George
1849–1885

TEDDY
b. 1850

HENRIETTA
b. 1853

Regina
1857–1907
m. Sir Peregrine
Parke, Bt

NED
b. 1885
m. 1911
Jessie
Compton

m. (1)
Charlotte Byng

m. (2)
Alice Meynell

m. (1) Edgar
Fortescue

m. (2) Jerome
Compton

BERTIE
b. 1876
m. 1909
Maud
Puddephat

POLLY
b. 1900

JAMES
WILLIAM
b. 1910

JACK
b. 1886

ROBBIE
b. 1887
m. 1909
Ethel
Cornleigh

FRANK
b. 1889

JESSIE
b. 1890
Ned Morland

RICHARD
b. 1912

ROBERTA
b. 1911

JEREMY
b. 1912

THE LONDON MORLANDS

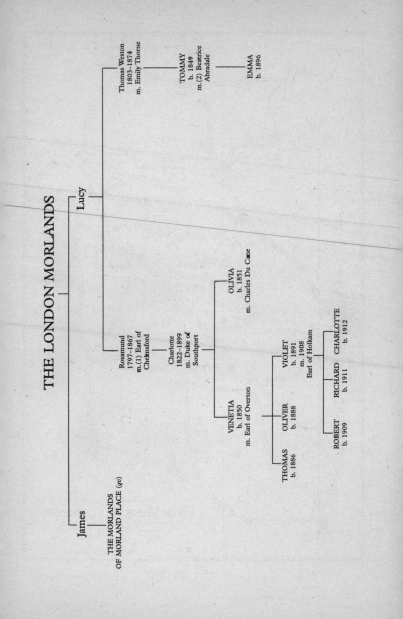

James

Lucy

THE MORLANDS
OF MORLAND PLACE (qv)

Rosamund
1797–1867
m.(1) Earl of
Chelmsford

Charlotte
1822–1899
m. Duke of
Southport

Thomas Weston
1803–1874
m. Emily Thorne

TOMMY
b. 1849
m.(2) Beatrice
Abradale

EMMA
b. 1896

VENETIA
b. 1850
m. Earl of Overton

OLIVIA
b. 1851
m. Charles Du Cane

THOMAS
b. 1886

OLIVER
b. 1888

VIOLET
b. 1891
m. 1908
Earl of Holkam

ROBERT
b. 1909

RICHARD
b. 1911

CHARLOTTE
b. 1912

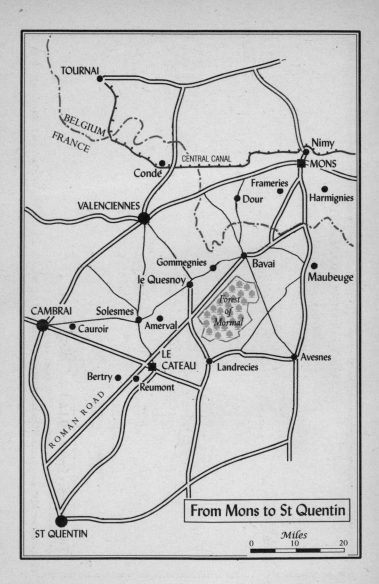

TOURNAI

BELGIUM
FRANCE

Nimy

CENTRAL CANAL

MONS

Condé

Frameries

Dour

Harmignies

VALENCIENNES

Gommegnies

Bavai

le Quesnoy

Maubeuge

CAMBRAI

Solesmes

Forest
of
Mormal

Cauroir

Amerval

LE CATEAU

Avesnes

Bertry

Landrecies

Reumont

ROMAN ROAD

ST QUENTIN

From Mons to St Quentin

Miles

0   10   20

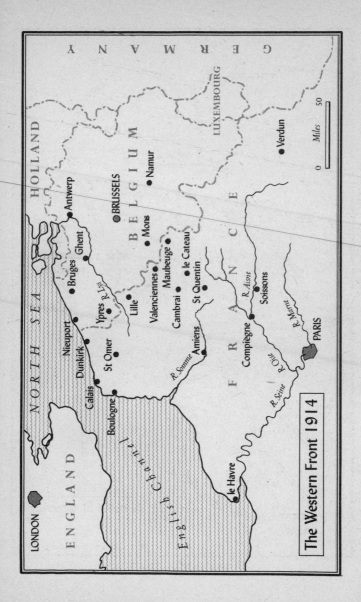

The Western Front 1914

BOOK ONE

Exhilaration

Laughing by and chaffing by, frolic in the smiles of them,
On the road, the white road, all the afternoon;
Strangers in a strange land, miles and miles and miles of
them.
Battle-bound and heart-high . . .

Robert Service: *Tipperary Days*

CHAPTER ONE

3rd August 1914

Jessie moved restlessly to the morning-room window and stared at the bright August day outside. 'It doesn't feel a bit like Bank Holiday Monday,' she complained.

Ned looked up from the newspaper. 'I'm not going to work,' he pointed out. 'The servants are all off. And the weather's perfect. What more can you want?'

'I just said it doesn't *feel* like it. No-one talks about anything but war. And there's nothing special happening at Morland Place. We always used to have a cricket match or a river trip or *something*. But Uncle Teddy hasn't arranged anything at all, not even a family luncheon.'

'I'm sure we'll be going over there anyway. And I'll lay any money that your mother has arranged enough food for a banquet, never mind a luncheon.'

Jessie smiled at that. Her mother Henrietta still lived at Morland Place and acted as housekeeper, since Teddy's wife Alice didn't care to. Alice had always been indolent, and since her miscarriage, her health had been rather delicate. Henrietta remembered the standards of hospitality that had prevailed at Morland Place in her childhood, and was glad that Teddy's wealth allowed her to uphold them.

'Well,' said Jessie, 'nothing was said, but I *did* think we'd go over there later. It would seem very odd not to, don't you think?'

'Very odd,' he indulged her. 'You don't imagine you need to persuade me, do you?'

Ned was the illegitimate son of the late George Morland,

3

elder brother of Teddy and Henrietta. Teddy had adopted the orphan Ned, had given him a name, an education, and finally a business of his own with which he could support himself respectably. Though Teddy had since acquired two children of his own, his affection for Ned had never wavered. Ned owed him everything, loved him as a son and called him 'Father'. Had Teddy not taken him in, he would have been put on the parish, and a very different – and possibly very short – life would have faced him.

There were still some old-fashioned folk in York who would not forget Ned's origins; but for most people it was enough that he had been to Eton, owned a successful business, and behaved like a gentleman. For another section of society the important thing was that he rode well to hounds (on fine Morland-bred horses), was a good shot and gave good dinners. Finally, he had married his cousin Jessie, who was a gentlewoman and a good hostess. What more could a reasonable person demand?

'But I suppose,' Jessie sighed on the heels of his last remark, 'if we do go it will be just war, war, war. I wish we'd hurry up and get into it, so we could talk about something else.' She looked across at the back of Ned's newspaper. 'I suppose it *is* going to happen?'

For answer he folded the paper and smacked it into a square to show her an advertisement. It was a notice from the German consul in London. She read aloud, '"Germans who have served, or are liable to serve, are requested to return to Germany without delay, as best they can."'

'A mobilisation order, in effect,' Ned said.

'I wonder *The Times* printed it,' Jessie said, with a touch of indignation. 'Isn't that aiding the enemy?'

'There are thousands of Germans living in this country, and it's probably a good thing to get them to go away of their own accord, rather than have to round them up and imprison them. In any case,' Ned reminded her, 'they're not officially the enemy until we declare war, and we haven't declared it yet.'

'When will we?'

'Very soon.' He tapped the paper. 'It says in here that the

4

Germans have declared war on Russia, and both countries have mobilised. Germany has invaded Luxembourg and is on the brink of invading Belgium. It can't be more than a day or two at the most. We'll be at war tomorrow, or the next day for certain.'

Jessie was silent. She had heard all the talk among the servants and in the streets, and knew that the majority of her fellow countrymen had been anticipating the war with elation. Everyone seemed eager for 'a scrap' and longed to 'teach Germany a lesson'. But though it was impossible for her not to feel some of that pleasurable excitement, simply by contagion, the war was not entirely welcome to her. She had inherited from her father his half of a horse-breeding business, to which Uncle Teddy had added the other half as a wedding present. And three months earlier she had received a visit from the army's local horse procurer, John Forrester, who had been conducting a census. If the threatened war did break out, 120,000 horses would immediately be 'conscripted', and that meant most or all of hers.

Some of her animals had been specifically bred for the army; but there were also the polo ponies – her speciality – and the hunters, and her own personal horse, Hotspur, who had been given to her by her father, and Ned's hack, Compass Rose. How could she bear to part with them? Suppose they got wounded – or killed?

Ned had a shrewd idea what she was thinking, and said gently, 'If Forrester comes for them, there'll be nothing you can do about it. In a war, everyone has to do their bit.'

'I know,' Jessie said. But that didn't make it any easier.

Ned thought that when the war did come, there would be more serious things to worry about than the horses, but he did not say so. He thought she was looking more than usually pretty that morning, with her cheeks a little flushed from agitation and her eyes bright. He loved her so much, and he sought to turn her thoughts to happier channels. 'Do you want to telephone to Morland Place and see what time we should go over? Father may have organised something after all.'

'Oh, yes, I'll do that,' Jessie said, pleased. She liked telephoning. She very rarely had the chance to do it, so it was a novelty to her. She was very proud of the fact that Maystone Villa, their house in Clifton, two miles from Morland Place, had had the telephone from the beginning: Ned had installed it because of his business. And now Uncle Teddy had had it put in, after years of talking about 'doing it one day'. Her face fell a fraction as she thought about that. Didn't it prove that he thought war was imminent?

Before she could go into the hall and make the call, however, the front-door bell rang. For a moment neither of them moved; and then they remembered that the servants had the day off, so Daltry, Ned's man who acted as butler, would not be answering it.

'I'll go,' said Ned.

Jessie waited, listening without interest, until the sound of the visitor's voice at the door made her eyes widen. It was a voice she knew very well and had not been expecting: their cousin, Sir Percival Parke, or Bertie, as he was always known – he hated the name Percival.

Ned appeared in the doorway. 'Look who's here!' he said, with pleasure.

Bertie was beside him. He was a tall, broad-shouldered man, rather tanned at the end of this long, wonderful summer, his fair hair bleached several shades lighter by the sun. At thirty-eight he was in the prime of life, and everything about him seemed vigorous, from his brisk movements to the very curl of his hair. Ned, though handsome in his own way, looked somehow soft and pale beside him.

'I hope I'm not intruding?' Bertie said, advancing into the room.

Jessie went quickly to embrace him. 'Of course not,' she said. 'We had no idea you were in Yorkshire.'

'I supposed I should have telephoned first, but I always forget you have the thing.'

'You're welcome at any time,' Jessie said. 'Come and sit down.'

Bertie settled himself in a chair at the table, and looked

vaguely around. 'Have I interrupted breakfast?' he asked, of the uncleared table.

'We finished ages ago!' Jessie laughed. 'It's August Bank Holiday Monday – servants' day off,' she reminded him.

He smiled. 'It's the gypsy life I lead – I forget things like domestic routine.'

'Talking of gypsies,' she said, 'what *are* you doing up here?'

'And why aren't you staying with us?' Ned added, with mock sternness.

'I only came up yesterday, and I was occupied until a very late hour, so I took a room at the Station Hotel rather than disturb you. I had one or two things to see to at the Red House.'

'You haven't got a tenant for it yet?' Ned asked.

'No, it's still empty.' The Red House was Bertie's inherited property at Bishop Winthorpe, about ten miles away. His wife Maud had never liked it, and had finally persuaded him to move to a new place, Beaumont Manor, near Cheshunt – so much more convenient for London, which was her first love. She had wanted him to sell the Red House, but he had not quite liked to do that. He had hoped to rent it out instead, but though he had let the grazing land easily enough, no-one seemed to want the ugly old house – to which he had such a perverse attachment. 'However, as things are,' he went on, 'a use may be found for it soon, in one of many ways.'

'As things are? What do you mean?' Jessie asked, puzzled.

'A telegram found me at the hotel this morning. It had quite a round trip. It was sent to me at Beaumont, and the servants sent it on to Maud in London, and she sent it to York. A miracle of modern communication.'

'Never mind how it arrived. What *is* it?'

'Mobilisation.'

The word brought a cold pang to Jessie's stomach. She stared. It was Ned who spoke. 'You've been called up?'

Bertie nodded. 'The decision to mobilise was taken last night, apparently, and it will be officially announced at four this afternoon. But some of us more experienced reservists had the word early. I'm to report to barracks at Sandridge tonight.'

'It's definitely war, then?'

'The Germans are massing on the Belgian border. The Government sent a note to Germany demanding assurance that they will not violate Belgian neutrality. But of course they will. We'll be at war tomorrow.'

'Oh, Bertie!' Jessie cried.

Bertie said. 'It's a relief to come and tell it here. Everywhere else I've been, people are waiting for the war in high excitement. York is full of young men longing to "have a go" at the Germans. You'd think it was part of the Bank Holiday celebrations. There'll be rejoicing tomorrow when war's declared.'

Ned eyed him shrewdly. 'Don't tell me *you*'re not the least little bit excited. Come, Bertie! Not a tremor somewhere?'

Bertie grinned reluctantly. 'Of course there's a little bit of me that's glad it's come. Action rather than inaction – what man doesn't prefer it? It'll be a glorious thing to trounce the Bosch. They've been asking for it ever since South Africa. And it's a relief that the waiting's over. I haven't been able to settle to anything for weeks. But of course –' the smile faded a little '– I fought in South Africa and I know war isn't really exciting and heroic. It has its moments, but mostly it's a dirty business. Still, it has to be done. We can't let Germany trample over the whole of Europe.' He met Ned's eyes seriously. 'If we don't drive them back – if they overrun France – it'll be us next.'

There was a brief silence, and then Jessie said, 'Sandridge? Where's that?'

'Near St Albans. I'm gazetted to the West Hertfordshires.'

'That's not your old regiment, is it?'

'No. Experienced reservists are being sent where they're needed, to fill spaces in the regiments that are going out first. In the army you go where you're sent. Obedience first and foremost.'

'Don't joke,' Jessie said. 'You won't like being a new boy, with no old friends about you.'

Bertie shrugged. 'They're short of experienced line officers. My own regiment had enough. But I shall be in the first wave of the British Expeditionary Force, which is an honour.'

'I suppose you'll have to be on your way, then,' Ned said, 'if you have to report tonight. Where's your kit?'

'At Beaumont. I shall have to call there to collect it, and arrange one or two things, but at least it isn't far then to Sandridge. I telegraphed as soon as I had the news, for them to look it out and have my horses sent on.'

Jessie saw the little frown of concentration as he thought ahead, saw how it altered his face. His carriage was different, too. Already he seemed a soldier rather than her cousin, a man of authority and purpose. It was this, rather than anything he had said, that brought the reality of war home to her. It was going to happen. And he would be going away, to face danger and perhaps death. 'When will you go overseas?' she asked, in a small voice.

'I can't say. But very soon, I imagine.' He looked from one to the other. 'I wanted to call in and say goodbye. And I'd like to take my leave of Aunt Hen and the others at Morland Place. Are you going over there today?'

'We were just talking about it. Have you transport?'

'No, I took a taxi up from the hotel.'

'We'll drive you, then,' said Ned.

Edward 'Teddy' Morland, as the younger son, had not expected ever to inherit Morland Place. He had his own property, commercial and industrial, in York and Manchester, and had always thought of himself as a town bird. George was the countryman, a squire born, interested only in the land, in hunting and shooting and farming.

But George, with the aid of an expensive wife, had run up debts and come close to ruin. The tragic loss of his only son had sent his wife to an early grave, and George himself to drink. By the time he died, the Morland Place estate was in a bad way. Most of the land had been sold off, and the house – a moated manor house with its foundations in the fifteenth century – was dilapidated and part-damaged by fire.

At first Teddy had offered it as a home to Henrietta, with

her husband Jerome Compton and their children, when Jerome had suffered bankruptcy. Later, when Teddy's first wife had died, he had moved in himself with his baby daughter and adopted son Ned, and the two families had co-existed happily ever since. Over the years Teddy had used profits from his commercial ventures to restore the house and buy back the lands, and had found that he was not a town bird after all, but as much of a squire as his brother. Perhaps there was something in the blood, he thought. He hoped, anyway, that he would be a better caretaker of the Morland inheritance than George had proved.

Though he had a new wife, Alice, and a son by her, James William, he could never have too many people around him. Family was his delight. Two of Henrietta's sons, Jack and Frank, had moved away and gone to seek their fortunes in the south, but the middle boy, Robert, worked for a bank in York, and when he had married Teddy had persuaded him and his wife Ethel to live at Morland Place. They had added two children to the nursery. Teddy's only regret when Ned married Jessie was that they could not be persuaded out of moving to Clifton – though Jessie was at Morland Place most days, one way or another.

It was, of course, the servants' day off at Morland Place as well, and they had all been eager to go into York and see what fun might be going. But the family had remained in the dining parlour, lingering over breakfast coffee, and then migrated only as far as the drawing room, to smoke and talk.

The talk was of war, of course. 'The sooner the better,' was Robbie's view.

'It can't be much longer,' Teddy said. 'If they invade Belgium, that will be that.'

'Why is that so important?' Ethel asked, sugaring her coffee. 'I don't see why we should go to war for Belgium. I don't know anyone who has ever been there.'

'My dear child,' Teddy said patiently, 'we're all solemnly bound to protect Belgian neutrality – us, France and Germany. We signed a treaty. If Germany breaks it, we shall have no alternative.'

'We must protect gallant little Belgium, dear,' Robbie said. It was a phrase he had seen in another newspaper that morning, and thought rather appropriate. Tiny Belgium had bravely refused to give safe passage through her territory to mighty Germany's armies.

'In any case, the real target is France, isn't it?' said Lennie Manning. He was a distant cousin from the American branch of the family, who had been staying for the summer. 'Germany wants to add France to its empire. That can't be allowed.'

'What will you do, Lennie, if war comes?' asked Polly, Teddy's daughter. At fourteen she was just the right age to have a crush on her handsome cousin. He was eighteen, between school and university, and was expected back home at the beginning of September to prepare to go up to Yale.

Henrietta looked across at him. 'I suppose you'll go home at once?'

'Lord, no!' Lennie said. 'And miss all the fun? Not for anything! Oh – unless you want me to go, I mean. If I'm in the way . . . ?'

'Not at all,' Henrietta said. 'We love to have you here.'

'You're welcome to stay as long as you like,' Teddy added.

Lennie sighed with relief. 'Thank you, sir,' he said, and thought that if things got exciting he could always delay his return by a week or two.

'If I were you,' Polly said, 'I wouldn't go back at all. If there's a war, you could go and fight in it.'

Lennie met her eyes and his own widened as the idea took hold. What a glorious thing that would be! The chances of getting into a scrap like this at home were just about zero. The good old USA hardly even had an army, and there was no-one over there to fight anyway. 'That's quite a thought,' he said. 'I wonder if I could? But I don't suppose Pa and Granny would approve.'

'I should think not, indeed,' said Henrietta, foreseeing family complications.

'Though I don't know so much about Granny,' Lennie said, on second thoughts. 'She paid for my trip over here, after all, and she might think it was a lark. She was quite a wild thing when she was young, if you can believe her stories.'

'I don't know whether foreign nationals are allowed to join the British Army,' Robbie said.

Polly wrinkled her nose. 'Is that what you are? A foreign national? It doesn't sound very nice. But you aren't one, Rob,' she went on. 'You could join all right.'

'I'm a married man with two children,' Robbie said. 'Anyway, they won't want volunteers. It's trained men they need. War is a matter for professional soldiers these days, not amateurs. What with the standing army, the reserve and the Territorials, they'll have all the men they need.'

'Unless the Germans invade us,' Teddy said, 'and then every man will have to stand-to and defend our homeland.' He smacked his fist into his palm. 'By George! If they invade us, they'll find us a tougher nut to crack than they think! What a glorious fight that'll be! If I were younger – if I were your age! But there's plenty even an old fellow like me can do. If they should come to Yorkshire, they won't take Morland Place, not while there's a drop of blood left in my veins!'

Polly was quite taken with this bellicosity. 'It's a fortified house, Daddy. We could pull up the drawbridge and hold out here for weeks. There's your sporting guns we could shoot them with. And if we collected stones I'm sure I could learn to use a slingshot. You can kill a man easily with a slingshot if you hit the right place. I read it in a book. And we could pour boiling oil down on them from the barbican – oh, couldn't we? I've always wanted to pour boiling oil!'

'They're sure to have artillery,' Lennie pointed out, though reluctant to spoil her dream.

'The walls are very thick,' Henrietta said. 'The house was besieged in Cromwell's time – was it? Or some time in history, anyway, and they didn't manage to knock it down.'

'I wish I'd got on and had the portcullis mended,' Teddy said, 'when little Emma Weston was visiting. You remember, she wanted to see it lowered. I was very sad to disappoint her when it wouldn't move. I must speak to the estate carpenter about it first thing tomorrow.'

In this atmosphere, Bertie's arrival with his news acted

as a shake to a bottle of champagne. Excitement erupted, and everyone crowded round and bombarded him with questions. Only Henrietta had reservations. She had seen him off to war once already, wondering if he would come back. Now – very soon, it seemed – it was all to do again. Since his mother, her younger sister, had died, she had taken the place of a mother to him. She called him her 'extra son'. She felt tender towards him; proud, of course, but afraid and tearful.

To her Bertie played down the danger, told her old soldiers like him were too canny to get into trouble, promised letters and souvenirs, said it would all be over by Christmas. But the others had no doubt that this was a great and glorious moment. Teddy was pleased and proud, Robbie eager with questions; Polly was wild with excitement, Lennie frankly envious.

There was to be a cold luncheon, and when the men were settled around the table, smoking, and talking about the political and military situation, Henrietta caught Jessie's eye and beckoned her outside. 'I think we'd better bring luncheon forward, dear, so that Bertie can sit down with us,' she explained.

'Shall I get Ethel to help?'

'No, leave her be. She thinks she might be in the family way again, so she ought to rest as much as possible.'

Jessie followed her mother across the hall, hearing behind her the lift of words above the murmur of voices, like the word balloons of cartoon artists: '. . . great war between Britain and Germany . . .', '. . . almost ordained . . .', '. . . that fellow Le Queux . . .', '. . . glorious cause . . .'

'Why are they so pleased about it?' she asked, as they went through the green baize door to the kitchen passage. It flapped behind them and closed the last three inches with a sigh that was as much a characteristic sound of the house as the ticking of the long-case clock or the ringing of the house bell. 'Only Bertie's going, but you'd think, to hear them, they were all going to fight the Kaiser, hand to hand.'

'Men are always excited by war,' said Henrietta. 'I suppose that's why we keep having to fight. To them it's a glorious adventure – and of course it must be exciting to travel to a foreign country and see new places and have a change from the everyday things they do all the time.'

'I suppose so,' said Jessie. 'If I had to go and work in a bank every day like Robbie, or go to the mill like Ned . . .'

'And besides,' Henrietta went on, 'one has to stand up for what is right. The Germans are very wicked people, and they have to be stopped. What would you think of a man who wasn't ready to fight to protect his country and his wife and children?'

The last words brought Ethel's putative condition to Jessie's mind, and she said out of the thought, 'Does Robbie know?'

Fortunately Henrietta's mind worked in a similar way, and she said, 'Oh, yes. She told him first thing. He's very pleased, of course. We all are.' The next question was inevitable. 'I suppose there's no news for you and Ned?'

Jessie turned her head away. 'Don't you think I'd have told you right away if there was – war or no war?'

'Never mind,' Henrietta said, with quick warmth. 'It will happen in God's good time.'

Jessie acknowledged the words with a nod, but said nothing. Ned so much wanted children, and it was the one shadow in his life that they had been married going on three years with only a single miscarriage to show for it. Jessie's mind was divided. She wanted children, of course she did, but she dreaded it too. It would put an end to her present way of life. There would be months of inaction to endure, when every particle of her cried out to be on horseback, while her business at the stables went undone, or was badly done. And at the end of it, there would be the pain of childbirth (which she couldn't bear to imagine) and more months of inaction – and then, in all probability, the whole thing to go through again. A woman's life was a miserable thing, she thought, compared with a man's. He had all the fun, could go anywhere and do as he liked, could have children *and* a business, all without suffering and without giving up *anything*. So really, she thought, it was not entirely bad that God's good time was being delayed like this.

The wonderful cold collation that Henrietta deemed necessary for a servantless luncheon reflected the bounty of early August. There was a roast turkey-poult, a poached salmon in its jellied liquor, crayfish in a curried sauce, and a galantine of duck. There was a magnificent pork pie – a speciality of the cook, Mrs Stark, with its crisp, golden raised crust decorated with her favourite pastry device, a wheat-sheaf, and the fragrance of its filling rising through the hole in the lid. There was a pea and potato salad, French beans with garlic and almonds, a great bowl of lettuce and young spinach mixed, plenty of crusty bread and Home Farm butter. There was a dish of gooseberry fool scented with Henrietta's own elderflower-water, and a wonderful array of fruit – plums, of course, and greengages, figs, Bon Chrétien pears, and a dish of the little Alpine strawberries that grew round the edge of the beds in the kitchen garden.

The feast, accompanied by some of Teddy's best bottles brought up from the cellar by way of celebration, was eaten early, and then, much too soon, Bertie stirred, put out the cigar Teddy had pressed on him, stood up and said he was afraid he must go, to collect his bag from the hotel and catch his train.

'I'll drive you,' Ned offered.

'No, let me,' Jessie said quickly. 'You stay here and talk to Uncle Teddy. You haven't seen him all week.'

'She wants to show off her driving,' Ned said to Bertie. 'Will you feel safe?'

'It won't be the first time she's driven me,' Bertie said.

In the motor-car, there was silence at first. Jessie was very conscious of Bertie beside her: the side nearest him seemed to feel him, as if he were a furnace radiating heat. She was remembering, against her will, the time she had driven him home to the Red House and he had kissed her and told her he loved her. But he had already been married to Maud then – and now she was married to Ned, and there was a double barrier between them. They had sworn to be nothing but cousins to each other after that; but now, on the eve of his departure to war, Jessie's feelings were stirred up and her thoughts in a tumble. It was obvious that Bertie's were too.

He breathed rather fast, and there seemed a flush to his skin under the tan. Though he was too much a soldier to fidget, she felt his restlessness like electricity on the air.

'Just this little time, then,' he said at last, 'to say goodbye.'

'Don't say it like that,' she begged.

'Like what?'

'As though it's—' She couldn't finish.

'Jessie,' he began.

She stopped him with a flicker of a look, sideways, away from the road ahead just for a moment. 'Bertie, you won't get hurt. Promise me.'

'As I told your mother—'

'Yes, I know, but that was just for her. Tell me the truth. You won't get hurt?'

'I'll certainly try not to,' he said. Already they were turning onto the main road. The distance from Morland Place to York station was so damnably short. 'I came through the South African war without a scratch, didn't I?'

'You were *wounded*,' she said fiercely.

'Well, but here I am, fit to fight another day. Jess, I want to ask you something.'

She gave him another glance – longer, wary. 'What is it?'

'Can I write to you? Can I send you my letters home?'

'You'll write to Maud,' she suggested, stiffly.

'Yes, of course, but those will be the sort of letters one writes to one's wife. There's so much one can't say in them.'

'Such as?'

'Such as the truth,' he said. 'You asked me for it just now. The truth one can only write to one's . . .' He paused so long she thought he wouldn't find the word, but at last he said, 'One's friend.'

'Friend,' she repeated. Well, there was nothing to object to in that, nothing to fear, nothing to feel guilty about. Here was Micklegate Bar and the city wall, up ahead of them, and she swung the big motor left and down towards the station, and in a moment was pulling up outside the Station Hotel. She set the brake and turned a little in her seat to look at him. His handsome, firm face was so familiar, it was like her own reflection in the looking-glass. His blue eyes

16

seemed almost transparent to her, as though she could look right in at his thoughts. How was it that Ned – with whom she had grown up, to whom she was married – never seemed like that? Ned was always and definitely *other* from her, even in his familiarity – a solid and opaque separateness. That was exciting at times, disconcerting at others. She could not fathom him. But Bertie she knew absolutely.

'Can I write to you?' Bertie asked. He knew that there would be times of fear, of loneliness, of boredom – many of those – in between the moments of action when one was too busy surviving to be afraid or to think much. It was in those inactive moments that he would need her. Writing to her would bring her close to him. 'And will you write to me?' He saw her doubtful look, and knew that she was afraid of being disloyal – to Ned, whom it was so damnably impossible not to love. 'As a friend,' he added at last.

'Yes,' she said then; and hearing how bare and ungracious it sounded, and catching the shadow of the thought she would not think, that he might be badly wounded, that he might die, she put out an impulsive hand to him and said, 'Oh, Bertie!'

He caught the hand and took it to his lips, and kissed it. She felt the warmth of his breath and the soft roughness of his moustache and closed her eyes in the pain of memory. But when she opened them, he was smiling, a very ordinary, cousinly smile. He put her hand back on her lap and patted it, and said, 'Thank you for that. And thanks for the lift. Now I must be off. I'll write to you when I get to France.' He opened the door and got out and, turning back to close it, saw her woebegone look. 'Cheer up. Perhaps it really will all be over by Christmas.'

She made herself smile. 'I'm sure it will. Take care of yourself.' He nodded and walked away. She watched him disappear into the hotel entrance, and then drove off.

When he had received his telegram, Bertie had at once sent off two of his own, one to Beaumont with instructions about his kit and horses, and one to Pont Street, to Maud.

He had married her on his return to England, after a long

spell abroad, when he had come home to wind up his deceased father's affairs. He and his father had not got on. Things had been so bad at home he had run away, first to the war in South Africa, and afterwards to India, where he bought and bred horses for Richard Puddephat, Maud's father, who was an army procurer. Bertie had been already over thirty and without any intention of marrying, or any expectation of ever finding anyone to love. Richard, he sometimes thought, had taken advantage of his confused state of mind. England was so wildly different from India; and he was a newly succeeded baronet, burdened by feelings of grief and guilt about his father, and struggling with all the complications of winding up an overstretched estate. Almost before he knew it, Bertie had found himself pledged to marry Maud, a girl he hardly knew and had never thought about before.

Of course, a gentleman could not go back on a pledge of that sort. But Maud was pretty, well-bred, agreeable, and seemed to want to marry him; and Richard, besides, had wanted a son-in-law to take over his business. Bertie was content with the arrangement. It was only later, when his head cleared, that he doubted the wisdom of tying himself to a girl he felt nothing for. It was later still that he fell in love with Jessie.

He thought now, though, that he had loved Jessie all along without realising it; and that if he had remained in England while she grew up, he would have married her as soon as she was old enough. The thought of what he had missed was enough sometimes to throw him into black despair. Maud had no affection for him nor he for her. She was a cold woman, with a commonplace mind, and no interest in anything beyond dressing nicely and standing well in society. She had married him to get an establishment, and to be Lady Parke; but since he had married her for reasons just as far divorced from passion, he could not blame her, nor even dislike her. Simply, he was indifferent to her. He did his duty by her, they got along cordially when they met, and they did not mind if that was not often. He spent his time at Beaumont, raising cattle and breeding horses; she preferred to stay mostly in London, where she was generally accompanied by her father, who had lived with them since their marriage.

So when he had received his telegram, it had been necessary to wire to Maud in London to say that he would not have time to go to Pont Street before reporting to barracks, and that if she wanted to say goodbye to him, she would have to meet him at Beaumont. He was not sure, as the train rattled him southwards through the golden August countryside, whether she would be there or not.

King's Cross was packed, as was Liverpool Street and everywhere in between, with travellers, returning day-trippers, and reservists and territorials on their way to report. There were many anxious-looking foreigners, loaded with shabby luggage, hurrying to Victoria for the boat-train – German butchers and barbers, waiters and cooks and musicians making a last-minute escape. There were bewildered Americans who had hastily cut short their continental tours, and now found themselves safe in London, but somewhat at a loss as to what to do next, and frequently without important pieces of luggage, left behind in the panic.

There seemed to be mounds of luggage everywhere and a distinct lack of porters, but Bertie threaded his way through it all, moving easily with only his overnight Gladstone to carry. The York train had been late and he caught his connection with only minutes to spare. There wasn't a seat to be had, and he settled himself resignedly in a corner of the corridor. More and more people crammed in in the last moments before the train pulled out, and it was with difficulty that Bertie unfolded the evening newspaper he had picked up at the W. H. Smith kiosk.

The announcement of the mobilisation was on the front page; and the headline news, in large black letters, was that Germany had declared war on France. As he read he caught the eye of a man standing next to him – who could hardly, in fairness, avoid reading the newspaper over his shoulder. He was taller than Bertie, some years younger, clean-shaven, with tightly curly brown hair and mild brown eyes like a puppy's. He smiled placatingly, and nodded towards the headline. 'Now we're for it, eh?'

'Yes,' said Bertie.

'It'll be us next.' The man eyed Bertie's moustache and general bearing. 'Military man, sir?'

'Reservist,' said Bertie.

The man grinned. 'Me too. Some lark eh? Got m' telegram this afternoon. Wife in floods, two boys fit to explode with excitement. They're in a compartment back there. Taking them up to my parents, then it's off to barracks. You?'

'The same,' said Bertie. He couldn't help warming to this open-faced, friendly man. 'I'm going home to pick up my kit, and then I've to report to Sandridge.'

The frank eyes opened wide. 'Sandridge? Not the West Herts, by any chance?' Bertie nodded, and the man struggled to extricate his arm from the press of bodies and offered his hand. 'Pennyfather,' he said.

'Parke,' said Bertie, and they shook.

'Well, what a joke,' said Pennyfather. 'I say, it'll be nice to have a friendly face there. I was rather dreading being a new boy again. Not even my own regiment, and I understand the regulars are middlin' savage towards us reservists – think we're pretty poor fish! Though I must say, you look fit enough. Took you for a regular at first sight. And the 'tache is a good touch, if you don't mind my mentioning it. I must grow one myself. Wish I'd thought about it sooner, but somehow I really never thought it would come to war. All the papers said Asquith and Co. hated the idea, so I thought we'd get off in the end.'

'We were always bound to defend France.'

'I suppose so, but I never really thought the Germans'd do it. They must be mad. We'll have to teach 'em a lesson they won't forget.' The brown eyes were serious now. Pennyfather went on, 'I heard a bunch of chaps on the platform talking about volunteering. In high feather, longing to "bash the Bosch". Talking about having to get in quick because it would be all over by Christmas.'

It was plainly meant to be a question. Bertie shook his head. 'I remember before the South African war, everyone said exactly the same thing. Perhaps they've said it before every war there ever was. But it never *is* over by Christmas.

A chap I know who's close to Kitchener says the old man talks about three years, perhaps four.'

Pennyfather sighed. 'I suppose he ought to know. I didn't *really* think – but I let my wife latch onto it, poor little beast. It'll be hard for her, bringing up the boys on her own. They're four and five – just the age to take a lot of handling. Better she doesn't know I may be gone four years.'

Bertie thought of his own little son, and deemed it best to turn their conversation to easier channels. 'Are you sporting at all? I was wondering whether to take my guns with me. I won't mind so much missing the shooting this year if we can bag a brace or two in France. Help to eke out rations, you know.'

Pennyfather grinned. 'Anything to break the monotony. I don't own any guns, but I like to shoot when I get the chance. What have you got?'

They talked comfortably of guns and sport until Pennyfather's stop approached and he had to 'go back and gather the memsahib and the brats'. They shook hands and looked forward to meeting again at Sandridge. Bertie caught a glimpse of him on the platform, ushering a slight, dark-haired woman like a soft little bird, and two sturdy, excited boys in identical suits and caps; and then the train pulled away. He was left feeling strangely comforted, and not dreading the transition nearly so much.

He had expected to have to take a cab from Cheshunt station, but the motor was there waiting for him, so he guessed Maud had come down after all. When he entered his house she came into the hall to meet him: tall, fair, hand-some, composed, her hair immaculate, her gown of lavender crape stylish and simple. She smiled and kissed him, and said at once, 'Your horses went off this morning. Reynolds went with them to see them settled. Salmon has started packing for you, but he's not sure what you'll want to take, so you'll need to speak to him. And Hobbs was asking whether you'll be taking the Purdeys. Will you have time for a little supper before you go? I've ordered something cold to be got ready, but if you haven't time, I can have it packed in a basket if you like.'

Sensible, efficient Maud, he thought: good wife, good housekeeper, always to be relied on, calm and capable. He chided himself for not always keeping her good qualities to the forefront of his mind. His discontent was not her fault, none of it. It was not in her nature to be warm, and she had not the intellectual gifts to be a companion to him. We are all what we are, he thought. Maud is the perfect wife according to her own lights, and I must never allow her to think she fails me in any way.

So he smiled and said, 'You seem to have thought of everything. Thank you, my dear. Give me ten minutes to speak to Salmon, and then I'll have supper – if you will sit down with me.'

'Certainly, if you like,' she said. Her pleasant, unemphatic smile did not change by a minim, but he thought she was pleased that he wanted her to join him. He ran up the stairs to speak to his manservant, and pick out the books and personal items he wanted packed, and check that all his kit was present and correct, then hastily washed the railway grime from his hands and face and went down to supper.

There was a fine round of cold roast beef, with potato salad and a half-bottle of claret, the last of the late raspberries with cream, and then cheese, and coffee. A good, simple meal, he thought – and wondered ruefully how often he would think of it in France once the action started.

As if she had read his thoughts, Maud said, 'I did wonder whether you wanted to take some foodstuffs with you. I don't know when you will be going overseas . . . ?'

'I don't know either,' he said. 'The supply situation should be much easier than it was in South Africa. As long as the Royal Navy keeps the Channel free, we ought to be able to get everything we need. But it might be a good idea to take a few luxuries – coffee, brandy, cigarettes and so on.'

'If you'll excuse me, then, dear,' Maud said, rising, 'I'll go and see what we have in the store cupboard and have it packed up. Salmon doesn't go with you, does he?'

'No, I'll have a soldier servant assigned to me.'

'Well, I certainly hope he'll be more careful with your boots than Salmon is,' Maud said, with mild severity. 'They should be put onto trees as soon as they're taken off, not left for hours until the leather's cold.' And she left him.

He sat down again, and continued his supper. He would have liked to linger over the excellent cheese, but time was hurrying on and he must leave two hours for the journey in the motor, in the dark and through country lanes. He wiped his mouth and rose, just as Maud came in, followed by a nurserymaid with their son Richard in her arms.

'It won't hurt him to be woken up for once,' she said briskly.

'You brought him down from London with you,' Bertie said wonderingly.

'I thought you'd want to say goodbye to him,' said Maud.

It was thoughtfulness of a high order. 'Thank you,' said Bertie humbly, and reached for the sleepy boy. Richard could hardly wake up, and his head nodded against his father's shoulder. He was getting heavy. Bertie kissed the smooth, silken cheek and smelled the cleanness of his baby skin and the softness of his long, fair curls. His heart twisted painfully. When would he see the boy again? He was a little over two years old now. When Bertie came again, he would probably be out of dresses and into suits, and his baby curls would be cropped.

He met Maud's eyes. 'I hope he doesn't get to be too much of a handful,' he said, for something to say. His heart was too full for more apposite words.

'Father will help me with him,' she said. And then, 'They say it will be all over by Christmas – but it won't, will it?'

'No,' he said. 'I don't think so. But I should get leave around then.'

She nodded sensibly. 'Well, that's not so long.'

It was time to go. He kissed the boy again and handed him, asleep now, back to the nurse, who carried him away. Maud followed him out into the hall where his small mound of luggage waited, including, he saw, his gun case, and a hamper, which he supposed contained the luxuries Maud had gone to seek. 'Thank you,' he said.

She raised her eyebrows. 'For what?'

'For being such a good wife.'

She seemed unimpressed by this. 'It's my job,' she said.

At the door she kissed him goodbye, unsmiling now. She did not say, 'Promise you won't get killed.' She did not ask him to write. She didn't even say, 'Take care of yourself.' She kissed his cheek and then stood back, calm as a statue. And she said, 'Goodbye.'

The barracks gave the impression of a kicked ants' nest with the sudden influx of reservists, who all had to be medically inspected, kitted out, allocated a rifle and then accommodated and fed. The normally immaculate barrack rooms were marred with footmarks, strewn with items of kit and personal belongings. The barrack square was a scene of such disorder as it had never before witnessed, thronged with people queuing for the quartermaster's store, the mess hall, the armoury, to see the MO or the adjutant, hurrying back and forth with messages, or wandering purposelessly in a manner calculated to give an NCO an apoplexy.

Cooper, the servant assigned to Bertie – a slightly under-sized, thoroughly crafty-looking regular, the sort who would turn an innocent inside out and shake the last farthing out of him – was impatient of it all. 'Some o' the reservists turned up Sat'd'y morning,' he confided in disgust. 'Didn't wait to get their telegrams. Tchah! Got nothin' better to do with their Sat'd'y nights! Dunno how we're supposed to fit 'em all in. Doubling up? Trebling up more like! And three sittings at mealtimes – the cooks are going mad. Some of the officers are being boarded in the town for the time being, sir, but I wangled a room for you all right. It's small, but all the better for that in the present circs, sir, else you wouldn't be able to keep it to yourself. And it ain't for long.'

It was fortunate that Cooper had decided he approved of Bertie. Though scornful of most human beings, he was a countryman born and had been a groom before he joined the army, and he loved horses. By the time Bertie arrived he had already inspected Kestrel and Nightshade, and thoroughly admired them.

'Nicest bits o' blood an' bone I've seen in many a long while, sir,' he said. 'Some of the young gentlemen hasn't got no 'orses at all, o' course, an' what *they*'ll get given out o' the pool is hanyone's guess. Roarers, borers, stargazers – any old rubbish. And there's a reserve lieutenant brought such a screw of a chestnut as you've never seen – blood weed, all flash and no bone, sort that's forever throwing out a splint. Break down the first hard march, it will, and *then* where'll he be? Tchah! Some crooked dealer saw *him* coming a mile away, an' no mistake.'

He approved of Bertie's kit, too, especially the hamper of luxuries, which made his eyes brighten. 'You was in South Africa, wasn't you, sir?' Bertie concurred. 'Thought so. I can tell a proper campaigner, sir. Don't you worry, sir, I'll look after you all right. Hanything you want, you just let me know. I know wangles that'd make your eyes pop, sir – all at your service!'

Bertie was glad to hear it. It was important to have a servant who was on your side. He could make life miserable for you in so many ways if he took against you. Cooper would 'wangle' a good deal for himself out of the relationship, Bertie had no doubt, but as long as he, Bertie, came out ahead, that was all in the budget, and a price worth paying.

In the tiny dark room that was to be his until they went abroad, Bertie changed into uniform, finding it just a little snug, for all that he thought of himself as fit. Then he went along to the officers' mess. The colonel, to whom he had reported on arrival, was there, and called him over cordially. 'Ah, Parke, come and meet some brother officers. Gibson, a drink for the captain – brandy? Whisky? Or there's a fair-to-middling port.'

'Whisky, sir, thank you, if you don't mind.'

'Good show. I'm a whisky man myself. Whisky, then, Gibson. Now then, names: Penkridge, the adjutant, you've met. And these are Yerbury, Athersuch, Fenniman and Harcourt-Miller.'

Over the murmur of greeting, Yerbury said, 'Parke? Not Sir Percival Parke by any chance? I served under you in South Africa, sir. You won't remember me – I was just a boy.'

But Bertie did – just. He managed to scrape up a memory. 'You were wounded up above Lydenburg,' he said, shaking hands. 'I'm glad you seem none the worse for it.'

'I heard you were wounded too,' Yerbury said.

'Just a scratch,' Bertie said.

The colonel and the adjutant had turned away for private talk, and as Bertie's drink came, Fenniman said, '*Sir* Percival?'

'Baronet,' Bertie said, knowing it would have to be got over sooner or later.

'Been in India at all?'

'On business, not with the army. I've only served in South Africa.'

'Well, thank God for that,' Fenniman said. 'Some of these Indian officers are the limit.' He screwed an eyeglass into one eye, inspected Bertie briefly and offered his hand. 'Glad to have you aboard. Quite worried when they said they were sending us reservist officers from outside the regiment. No knowing what we'd get.'

'It's Cartwright's fault for breaking both his ankles,' said Athersuch. 'Silly ass. He was playing rugger with a wastepaper basket in the corridor – slipped and went feet first into a doorframe. Going a hell of a lick.'

'And then that other feller – what was his name? – Daniels? – came down with the measles. The adj was in a perfect panic, thinking of it spreading through the whole barracks,' said Fenniman, taking out a cigarette case and offering it around. 'I was glad to see the back of him. He wasn't a gentleman.'

'You really are the most frightful snob, Fen,' said Harcourt-Miller languidly.

'Not at all. Just can't be too careful who you share a mess with these days,' said Fenniman. He nodded to Bertie. 'Now I guessed you were all right as soon as I heard you'd brought your guns with you.'

'How on earth do you know that?' Bertie asked in astonishment.

'Oh, you can't keep anything a secret in this place,' said Harcourt-Miller. 'But, as a matter of interest, Fen, how did you know?'

'My servant told me. "The new reserve gentleman's right down your alley, sir," he said.' Fenniman seemed to be an accomplished mimic. 'He got it from your servant, apparently. Who've they given you?'

'Cooper,' Bertie answered.

'Oh, I know him. He'll look after you all right, as long as you keep an eye on him. You know what these old sweats are like – give them an inch and they'll take a mile. But he'll be invaluable when we get to France. Chaps like him can always get their hands on anything you want.'

'Any idea when we'll be embarking?' Bertie asked.

'The grapevine has it that it'll be at the end of the week. Not much time,' he added gloomily, 'for sorting out the muddle. Incorporating a whole battalion's-worth of reservists is no easy task – saving your presence, Parke.'

'So we've just one more chap to worry about,' said Athersuch. 'Reservist from outside the regiment. Name of – what was it, H-M?'

'Pennyfather,' Harcourt-Miller supplied.

'Oh, I met him on the train,' Bertie said. He looked mischievously at Fenniman. 'You'll like him. We talked about shooting.'

The others laughed. 'He's got the measure of you, Fen,' said Harcourt-Miller.

'Laugh all you like,' said Fenniman. 'I tell you, we have to try to keep this war exclusive while we can. That's why we've got to win it before Christmas. Once they start letting volunteers in the whole show will go to pieces. Can't have the officers' mess cluttered up with people with frightful accents eating peas off their knives. That's why we're doubly grateful to you, Parke – not just a gentleman but a veteran. A lot of our fellows are four- or five-year men, no battle experience. We need you experienced chaps to help us trounce the Hun before they throw this war open to all-comers.'

Bertie gathered from the faint gleam in Fenniman's eye that he was not entirely serious. But he said, 'The Germans outnumber us three to one. It may not be as easy as you think to trounce them.'

'Oh, rot!' said Athersuch. 'Two-thirds of the German army is made up of conscripts, yokels who were holding a pitchfork a week ago and think of nothing but getting back to their fields.'

'Exactly,' said Fenniman. 'The BEF will be made up of real soldiers. We'll show 'em how it's done. Christmas dinner in Berlin, and we'll use the Kaiser's head for our regimental football game on Boxing Day. Hullo-ullo-ullo. Who's this?'

Bertie turned and saw Pennyfather coming hesitantly in. He saw Bertie and smiled with relief. Fenniman saw the exchange and called out, 'Come and join us, Pennyfeather! You see, we know who you are. We know all about you – Parke here's been spilling your darkest secrets.'

'But we're prepared to love you all the same,' Athersuch said, 'as a brother officer and a gentleman. Gibson! Where is the man? Oh, Gibson – a drink for Mr Pennyfeather.'

'It's Pennyfather, as a matter of fact,' said Pennyfather.

'A small distinction, but his own,' Harcourt-Miller drawled.

'I knew a chap called Pennyfeather at school,' said Athersuch.

'Never knew you went to school,' said Fenniman.

'I was at Winchester,' Athersuch said.

'What infernally bad luck for you,' said Fenniman, with elaborate sympathy, and the others laughed.

Bertie sipped his whisky and looked round the handsome, wood-panelled room, decorated with portraits of colonels and representations of famous battles, moth-eaten flags and silver sporting trophies; listened to the chat, the banter and the laughter and felt the warmth of companionship that was starting up all around him. It all seemed instantly familiar. He was glad to be back.

CHAPTER TWO

When, in the increasing expectation of war with Germany, the Royal Flying Corps had first been thought of in 1912, it had been envisaged as a single organisation serving the aeronautical needs of both services. There was to be a Central Flying School, a Royal Aircraft Factory, and an Air Committee to co-ordinate the two wings, the military and the naval. Colonel Seely, the Under-secretary for War, was in charge of it all, and was chairman of the Committee.

Unfortunately Asquith, the Prime Minister, was not 'air-minded'. His interest in flying was as small as his expectations of it were low. Also he had not sufficiently taken into account the traditional, entrenched and bitter rivalry between the two services. No unified command structure was set up, and the two wings of the RFC were not only separate but growing ever further apart.

The military wing was wholly run and controlled by the War Office, the naval wing by the Admiralty. Each trained and disciplined its own men, ordered its own machines, undertook its own research, devised its own battle plans, and refused to co-operate in any way with the other. The Air Committee, which was supposed to co-ordinate the efforts so as to prevent wasteful duplication and downright dangerous disagreement, had been given no executive power by Asquith, and could do nothing but advise and plead. The meetings were ineffectual and were held less and less often, as senior War Office and Admiralty officials refused even to turn up for them.

'And now that Churchill's created the RNAS,' said Jack Compton to his fiancée Helen Ormerod, 'the separation is complete, and we shall never have a proper air force.'

Winston Churchill, the First Lord, *was* air-minded – Jack had taken him up in an aeroplane once and had been impressed by his keenness, and his grasp of the potential of aeronautics. But now Churchill had announced the creation of the Royal Naval Air Service, which effectively abolished the naval wing of the RFC.

'He wanted to run the whole show himself,' Helen said.

'He always does,' Jack grumbled. 'He always thinks he knows better than other people, and if they disagree with him they're simply wrong.'

They were sitting on a bench in the garden of Helen's parents' house, Fairoaks, on the evening of Tuesday the 4th of August. On the lawn nearby, Helen's mother's dachshunds were playing a chasing game with Jack's disreputable-looking mongrel, Rug. The late golden light, slanting between the trees, gilded the grass and lit a trembling cloud of tiny insects that hung over the lily pond. Now and then it lit a fire in the diamond of the new engagement ring on Helen's left hand as it rested in Jack's right.

'Well, I suppose the navy's requirements for an aeroplane do differ from the army's,' Helen said, trying to be reasonable.

'Only in the matter of floats,' Jack said, 'and they can be fitted to pretty well any machine instead of wheels – or even as well as. The trouble is that there are limited resources and only a small number of companies building aeroplanes. Having two rival schemes is bound to lead to waste and delay.'

'Sopwith's does pretty well out of the Admiralty,' Helen reminded him.

Jack was a designer and tester at the Sopwith Aviation Company, and had shares in it too, being an old friend of the owner, Tom Sopwith. Jack was one of the pioneer flyers – his certificate was No. 23.

'We do, of course,' Jack acknowledged. 'And so do others. Churchill does believe in ordering aircraft from lots of different factories, and somehow he always manages to find the money for them. And that will lead to development. But neither wing will ever tell the other about any advances it makes. And besides, flyers need their own special training, not to be trained as soldiers or sailors and then have a bit of flying tacked on at the end.'

Helen eyed him sympathetically. 'You're restless,' she said. 'I know these moods of yours when you want to change the world.'

He grinned reluctantly, and squeezed her hand. 'Only certain bits of it.'

'Yes, like the minds of certain people high up in the Government and the War Office. You're not so different from Mr Churchill after all.'

'Oh, but I'm much handsomer – don't you think?'

She signified her opinion by kissing him, and their embrace continued until a sharp chorus of barking warned them that someone was coming. They parted hastily to see Helen's younger sister Molly approaching.

'Oh, grue!' she called cheerfully. 'Kissing again! I'll be jolly glad when you two get married and I won't have to see you being soppy all over the place.' The dogs raced to her and jumped up for her enthusiastic caresses.

'At least I don't let dogs lick my face,' Helen observed, straightening her cuffs.

'I don't *let* them, they just do it,' Molly said, finding a biscuit in her cardigan pocket and breaking it scrupulously into three for her admirers. 'Anyway, dog-lick is all right. I read a story once about an explorer who fell down a cliff and had a terrible injury and his dog kept him alive for weeks until he got rescued by bringing him rabbits to eat, and licking his wounds so they didn't get infected.'

'Did you come out for a purpose, or just to annoy us?' Helen asked.

'Oh – Mother sent me,' Molly remembered. 'Supper's ready. And there's a visitor.' She made a face. 'Colonel Morton. Dull.'

Helen laughed. 'He's not dull, he's very nice.'

'Well, old anyway.'

'Go on in and tell Mother we're coming,' said Helen.

Molly started to turn away and then turned back. 'You're not going to start *kissing* again, are you?'

'None of your business if we are.'

Jack managed to hold in his laughter until Molly, with the dogs at her heels, had rounded the rhododendrons out of sight.

'That terrible child!' Helen said. 'I'm sure I wasn't as abominable when I was her age.'

'I'm sure you were adorable,' said Jack.

'Darling, I was never *that*,' she said frankly. 'But I was much more strictly brought up. I wasn't allowed to say what I liked, the way she does.'

'Stop wasting valuable time and kiss me,' Jack said. When they broke apart a moment later, they both said, in chorus, 'Grue!' and went laughing, arm in arm, down to the house.

Dusk was coming on fast, and the pink-shaded lamps were lit in the dining-room. The Ormerods were quite modern in their thinking and had both electricity and the telephone.

'It's so warm I've left the French windows open,' said Mrs Ormerod, 'but I may have to close them if the moths come in.'

'Moths don't hurt you,' Molly said.

'I really can't bear the way they bang themselves against the lights.'

'That hurts them more than you,' Molly said logically. 'May I have wine, Mother?'

'Certainly not. Not until you're eighteen. Or seventeen at least,' Mrs Ormerod said vaguely. Molly was the child of her later life, and she had never had the energy to be strict with her as she had with Freddie and Helen.

Mr Ormerod, carving ham at the end of the table, said, 'I wonder when we'll get news of the ultimatum.'

German troops had crossed the border into Belgium at half past eight that morning. The Belgian government had appealed to France, Russia and Britain for help, and the British ambassador in Berlin had handed an ultimatum to the German government: unless Germany withdrew the troops by midnight – eleven p.m. British time – a state of war would exist between them.

'The German government will take it right up to the last minute,' Colonel Morton said. 'Why should they answer before they have to?'

'You don't think they'll agree to withdraw?'

'Not a chance of it,' said the colonel cheerfully. 'We shall have a scrap all right.'

'Will you go, Colonel?' Molly asked. 'To the fighting, I mean?'

'Oh, I think I'm a bit senior for that sort of show, m'dear,' he twinkled at her, 'but I shall find a way to make m'self useful, don't you worry. What about you, young man?' he addressed Jack. 'You must be fairly bursting to be off and have a crack at the Hun.'

'Jack's an aeroplane designer,' Helen said. 'His work is important.'

'Aeroplanes? Oh, I don't think they'll play much of a part, you know,' the colonel said kindly. 'Scouting, perhaps – carrying messages – but we've got the cavalry for that sort of thing. They're used to the job. Much better leave it to them.'

'What about artillery spotting, Clive?' Mr Ormerod suggested. 'I've heard it said they could be useful there.'

'Balloons are better for that,' said the colonel. 'More stable, more reliable. Trouble with your aeroplanes, Mr – er – Compton, is that they fall out of the sky all the time. Always going wrong. And you can't keep an aeroplane still in the sky the way you can a balloon. No use trying to spot for the artillery if you have to keep flying round in circles just to stay aloft!'

Helen's hand squeezed Jack's knee comfortingly under the table, but he was a long way from growing angry over comments like these, when uttered by an old soldier past his campaigning days.

'How about bombing, sir?' he said calmly.

The colonel smiled indulgently. 'Now, young man, I think you're trying to catch a fish! You know as well as I do that an aeroplane can't lift any kind of load. Hard enough to get it off the ground with one man inside, never mind a couple of hundred-pound bombs. If it was airships, now, rigid airships – a great pity we didn't go into developing them the way the Germans have. Those Zeppelins of theirs, they have regular mail and passenger services the length and breadth of Germany, you know. Wonderful machines! They'd have no difficulty in lifting any load you cared to tax them with.'

'I read a wonderful book, once, Colonel,' said Molly, putting butter on her potatoes, 'where the Germans flew their airships right across the Atlantic and attacked America. It was called *The War in the Air* and—'

'Don't talk so much, Molly,' Mrs Ormerod quelled her. 'And that's quite enough butter.'

'Even an airship can't travel that far yet,' Jack said, 'though the day will come . . .'

'In any case,' said Mr Ormerod, 'surely the Hague Convention banned the dropping of bombs from balloons. Wouldn't that apply to airships too?'

'It's a moot point, sir,' Jack said. 'In 1911 the Italians dropped grenades from a Blériot during their North Africa campaign, and they claimed that an aeroplane was not the same as a balloon, so I dare say the same argument could be made.'

'By Jove, you're very well up in your military history,' said the colonel.

'I regard it as aeronautical history, sir,' Jack replied.

'Ah, I see. And what future do *you* envisage for aeroplanes?' he asked, a trifle indulgently. 'Surely they'll never be more than toys for rich and idle men?'

Jack thought a moment, and said, 'It's only five years, sir, since Blériot flew across the Channel. Six years ago, no-one believed even *that* was possible. Newspapers were still claiming that no-one would ever get an aeroplane off the ground. Blériot flew at twenty miles an hour and only just high enough to clear the waves, and people said then that that was the limit. But now we have aeroplanes that can fly at many thousands of feet from the ground, and at speeds of seventy miles an hour. If we can do all that in only five years, who knows what the future will bring? Achieving what now seems impossible must be measured in months. After all, how many centuries did it take to develop our modern guns?'

Molly applauded at the end of this speech, and Mr Ormerod laughed and said, 'Bravo! There's one for you, Clive. Answer if you dare!'

The colonel looked stubborn. 'It's an achievement, I grant you that, and your aeroplanes *may* be useful to the two services one day—'

'You've said yourself, sir,' Jack went on, 'that the Zeppelin's an amazing machine. Our own efforts to develop a rigid airship have come to nothing. The Germans are well ahead of us in the air, and I assure you that they are working on new and better aeroplanes even as we speak. *They* will not assume that it's impossible to drop bombs out of an aeroplane – and if they do build them, we had better have the means to combat them.'

Mrs Ormerod had not really been listening, for she had seen a moth enter through the open French windows and was watching it dance round one of the wall lamps; but she caught the last part and said sternly to Jack, 'You are not suggesting, I hope, that the Germans would do anything so horrible as to drop bombs out of the air on people? What a dreadful idea. I cannot believe any German would do anything so uncivilised. I had a German governess when I was a girl and she was a most superior person; and we met some very nice people at Baden-Baden – what was their name, George? The Wolfstocks or Wolfsteins or something of the sort. Most refined and educated people, though not from Berlin – some other city, whose name I can't recall. You remember, we almost thought their eldest son might do for Helen.' She nodded to the company at this unanswerable proof of German acceptability. 'Molly, push the bell, will you? Oh, never mind, here's Barker now. Barker, close the French windows. And please remove that moth from the light in the alcove.'

Colonel Morton had a friend at the War Office who had promised to telephone him at eleven at the Ormerods' house

– he had not the telephone at home. Molly was sent reluctantly to bed – 'Oh, not fair! When it's something life-or-
death like this, I ought to be allowed to know, seeing as Jack
says we're all going to be bombed in our beds.'

Helen promised sportingly to come up and tell her the
news if she was still awake. Then the others settled down
to talk and smoke, and Mr Ormerod sent Barker for his
best brandy. Everyone kept away from the topic of war for
the time being – Mrs Ormerod had seemed very alarmed
at Molly's parting remark about bed-bombing. The conversation ranged unconvincingly over a number of subjects that
did not stick, until Mrs Ormerod, peacefully sewing one of
her squares of petit-point, got onto the subject of Helen's
forthcoming wedding, on which she could conduct a mono-
logue without help from anyone.

She had got as far as 'The Voice That Breathed O'er
Eden', and Mendelssohn, definitely, because that other piece
– Wagner, was it? – sounded somehow so vulgar, like something a German band might play in the street, and, oh dear,
one didn't seem to be able to get away from Germans this
evening, but there was no doubt they were very cultured
people, despite those ghastly bands of theirs, and the
German waiter at the White Hart was the most civil and
pleasant creature – and now she came to think of it, Mr
Ormerod's tailor was German, wasn't he, George?

And then the shrill of the telephone's bell broke into the
gentle murmur of her flow.

Barker came in and said, with the air of having touched
the thing only with his fingertips, that there was a call on
'the instrument' for Colonel Morton. He conducted the
colonel out into the hall where the instrument lived, and a
few moments later Morton returned and said to the
company at large, 'Well, that's that. No satisfaction from the
German government, so we are now officially at war.'

There was silence, and Jack, looking round, noted with
interest that everyone was perplexed, that even the colonel
appeared a little pale, that however much they had thought
they expected it, the reality still came as a shock. They were
at war. This was it – no escape now. It was a grave respon-

sibility, and no slight task, given Germany's military power. But Right was on their side, and determination and strength of character, which had always come to England's aid when she needed them.

As if he had heard Jack's thoughts, Mr Ormerod said, 'We settled with Napoleon when he thought he could rule the world, and by God – sorry, m'dear – we'll settle with the Kaiser! Even if we have to do it single-handed.'

'Bravo, Daddy,' said Helen. She turned bright eyes on Jack, and it was at that moment he knew that he had to go and fight. He felt the blood surging through his veins and a man's strength in his muscles. Morton and Ormerod were too old, but he, and every other young man, had a part to play. It was his duty to help protect his country, to make the world safe for his wife-to-be and their future children. It was more than his duty – it was his deepest desire.

On Wednesday morning Venetia, Lady Overton, woke in her bedroom in her house in Manchester Square to find she was not alone. She sat up with a start, her hand flying to her throat, and then realised it was her husband who was sitting beside the bed watching her.

'Beauty!' It was the nickname of his youth, which only she used now. 'You startled me. What are you doing?'

'Waiting for you to wake up,' he said.

'Well, why didn't you climb in beside me?' she said pleasantly. 'That would have woken me.'

'I've only just got back from the War Office. I've been working all night.'

'I guessed you would.' She had had a telephone call from him last evening to say that war had been declared. 'What time is it?'

'Just after seven.'

'I suppose it isn't worth your while coming to bed now,' she said regretfully.

'I'd probably just fall asleep,' he said, 'and I'd rather like to enjoy my wife's company for an hour or two. I haven't seen very much of you these past weeks.'

'An hour or two? When do you have to go back?'

'I shall probably have to go back for a few hours this afternoon, but otherwise I'm free until tomorrow. You know that Kitchener's taken over from Haldane as Secretary of State for War?'

'You said you thought it would happen. How does it affect you?'

'Oh, not at all. Mine wasn't a party appointment, and Kitchener sent me a very kind note asking me to continue. He mentioned you, by the way – obviously retains a fond memory of your dealings with him in South Africa.'

'Bosh!' Venetia said. 'K doesn't care a jot for any woman – though he was surprisingly pleasant when Millie Fawcett and I had dinner with him in Pretoria. Not charming, you know, but he spoke to us sensibly and actually listened to what we said. Most refreshing.'

'Don't I always listen to what you say?'

Venetia leaned forward, caught him by the lapel and pulled him towards her. 'You,' she said, 'are a very superior specimen of the male sort.' And she kissed him.

'Mmm,' he said, straightening up. 'Well, at all events I think Kitchener is disposed to like me for your sake, and wants me to stay on. Of course he's bringing his own personal staff, so I shall have to go in this afternoon and show them where everything is, but I'm to have the rest of the day off.'

'Quite right, when you've been working through every night for the past week.'

'So I thought I'd have a bath and change my clothes and then take you out to luncheon.'

'Don't you want to sleep?'

'If I sleep now, I won't wake up until tomorrow,' Overton said. 'Don't worry, my love, I'm an old campaigner, I shan't drop off into the middle of the turtle soup and shame you. And then tonight, perhaps we might take in a show – what do you think?'

'Dear me, how gay,' Venetia murmured. 'Well, there is a concert at the Albert Hall I should like to hear, if that suits you.'

'Admirably,' Overton said. He stood up with the effort of a very tired man.

'You look worn out,' Venetia said, with concern.

'I shall do very well when I've bathed and shaved. I'll go through and ring for Ash. Don't wait breakfast for me.'

'Of course I'll wait breakfast for you,' Venetia said, swinging her legs out of bed and reaching for her robe and the bell at the same time. 'I wouldn't miss seeing you eat a proper breakfast for worlds.'

Their leisurely breakfast was interrupted by a number of telephone calls, as various friends and acquaintances rang to share the news about the declaration of war, speculate about what would happen next, and discuss which of their relatives would be going to France, and how soon. Consequently they had not long finished eating and were still sitting over the newspapers when Burton came in to announce a visitor.

'At this hour?' Venetia said, before a glance at the clock on the morning-room mantelpiece showed that it wasn't 'this hour' any more.

But Burton was already standing aside for the visitor and announcing her, and Venetia jumped up in her usual energetic way at the welcome sight of her sister Olivia.

'Dearest!' she said, enveloping her in a hug that had Burton backing hastily out. He had very firm views about how a lady should behave in front of servants, even with close relatives. He had once interrupted Lord and Lady Overton kissing each other *in the drawing-room*, and the memory still chafed.

'You look so lovely,' Venetia said, stepping back to admire her sister. Olivia had always been the beauty of the family, and she had kept a great deal of it into old age, with a fine-boned, elegant look that went well with her serene expression. She was simply but beautifully dressed in an olive-green coat and skirt, a much tucked and frilled cream silk blouse, a large hat covered with black marabou, and a fur piece over her shoulders (Olivia had a fur for every different season). Venetia discovered from kissing her that she smelled delicious, of one of the French perfumes her husband, Charles Du Cane, imported from Paris for the wife of whom he was so proud.

Olivia had never had the ambition and energy that distinguished Venetia from most of her sex. She had been a lady-in-waiting to Queen Victoria, and deeply devoted to her, but after the Queen's death she had been content simply to be happily married, keep house, entertain and do good works, as gentlewomen had done since time immemorial. Venetia thought that her daughter Violet looked a lot like Olivia, and had a similar temperament. It was odd how often children resembled an aunt or uncle more closely than their own parents.

'You're as beautiful as ever,' Venetia said. 'Darling Livvy!'

'You look very well too,' Olivia said.

'Bony as an Irish yearling,' Venetia corrected.

'I think she's beautiful,' Overton said, coming to kiss the visitor. 'Olivia, my dear.'

'Come and sit down,' Venetia said. 'We're shockingly late with breakfast this morning, as you see. Why did that fool Burton go away? I wanted him to clear. Beauty, would you ring for him? Livvy, come and sit over here, away from the ruins. The wreck of a meal always looks so dispiriting, doesn't it?'

There was a window-seat at the other end of the room from the breakfast table, with two armchairs drawn up to it and a low table between them. With the sunshine pouring in, it made a pleasant group for conversation.

'So what brings you to London?' Overton asked.

Olivia slipped off her fur and adjusted her cuffs, saying, 'The war, really. Charles had to come up to see his bank about something, and I wanted to see you. I don't quite know why, but I felt I needed family at a time like this.'

Venetia said, 'It's absurd, but I understand what you mean. The very word "war" is unsettling – makes one feel that everything is about to fall apart. I've been as nervous as a cat all week. It's a relief, in a way, that the moment has come at last.'

Olivia nodded. 'I suppose it will be quite exciting for you. War will bring out the best in your sort of woman – the active, busy sort, I mean.'

Overton said, 'I hadn't thought about that, but I'm sure

you're right. Venetia will plunge into something – several somethings, probably. It's the end of our plans to retire to the country, isn't it, darling?'

'You've too much to do at the War Office to retire,' Venetia retorted. 'But I suppose I will do something. War means casualties. The army's peace-time medical facilities won't be enough, and if the young male doctors go off to field hospitals, someone will have to do their work at home.'

Olivia laughed. 'I'm glad to hear you don't think of going to France yourself! Charles said he wouldn't put it past you.'

'Livvy, darling, I'm sixty-four! I shan't be going anywhere – a little light organising at home is all I'm fit for now. Oliver will do all the doctoring for this family.'

'How is he getting on?' Olivia asked. She was fond of her nephew – named, as she was, after her father – though she sometimes did not understand his lively sense of humour.

'He's still working with Mark Darroway in Soho, and gaining a great deal of useful experience there, and at the Southport. I think he enjoys that sort of thing much more than his practice work, but of course it's the practice that pays his salary.'

'Will he be going to France?'

'Certainly not,' Venetia said sharply. 'He has far too much important work to do here. There are plenty of others who spend their lives holding patients' hands and delivering rich women's babies who can go.'

Overton met Olivia's eye and smiled. 'You can't expect detachment in a mother. Has the war caused excitement in your part of the country?'

Olivia and Charles lived in Northampton, on the edge of the Ravendene estate, which had been her and Venetia's childhood home. Both their brothers had died without issue, and the Southport dukedom had passed to a distant cousin, but he was very kind and gave Olivia the run of the house and grounds, which was pleasant for her.

'Goodness, yes,' she said. 'I've never seen people so exercised. You'd think we were going to be in the front line, the way people have been preparing. And last week I had a deputation of ladies from the neighbourhood asking me to head a branch of the Red Cross, if war should be declared.' Her cheeks were pink at the thought. 'I'm not sure quite what the branch would do, but I must say it will be pleasant to feel one is doing something, however small, for the war effort. And the duchess called yesterday to ask if I thought it would be a good thing to have an open day in the park to raise funds. I said I thought it was a splendid idea, and then she asked me what the fund ought to be in aid of.'

Overton suppressed a snort of laughter at the order of priorities, and Venetia, throwing a quelling glance at him, said, 'There will be so many good causes. Perhaps the most immediate would be support of servicemen's families. The reserve will be called up – won't it, Beauty?'

'Yes,' he said, recovering himself, 'and it can cause considerable hardship when the family breadwinner is taken away.'

'But they get an allowance, don't they?' Olivia said.

'A separation allowance, yes, but it's never enough,' Venetia said.

'Well, I shall mention it to the duchess when I get home. I rather think she wanted something to do with *wounded* soldiers but, as you say, this is an immediate need, and there aren't any wounded yet. She could always have another event, a fête or a sale of work perhaps, for the wounded later on.'

'Yes, darling, she could,' Venetia said gently.

She had misjudged Burton, who reappeared at that moment not only with a footman and a maid to clear the table but with fresh coffee and the drawing-room service, together with a plate of macaroons for Lady Olivia.

They were still chatting comfortably half an hour later when more visitors were announced. This time it was the Overtons' daughter Violet (who was married to the Earl of Holkam), accompanied by Emma Weston. Emma was an orphan whose father, the MP Tommy Weston, had been a friend of Venetia's youth, and had left charge of Emma to her, jointly with an uncle on the mother's side. As the uncle lived in a remote part of Scotland and rarely left it, Emma naturally much preferred to stay in London. Venetia considered herself too old to undertake the day-to-day chaperonage of a vigorous eighteen-year-old, so Emma stayed with Violet, who was a very social creature and enjoyed having a young female companion.

'Aunt Olivia!' said Violet. 'How lovely. It's like a party. And what are you doing at home, Papa, at this time of day?'

'Isn't this war exciting?' Emma cried, before Overton could answer. 'Lord Holkam went out and volunteered *first thing* this morning, and war was only declared last night. I call that splendid!'

Violet said, 'I'm very proud of him. He's going to be in uniform almost before anyone. Of course, he was in the Officers' Training Corps at Oxford, and Freddie Copthall says anyone with that background will be wanted. But Holkam didn't wait to be called.'

'Everyone says the war will be over by Christmas,' Emma said, 'so it makes sense to get in as quickly as possible.'

'And Freddie says the best regiments will be filled up very quickly,' Violet added. She reverted to her earlier question. 'What are you doing at home, Papa?'

'I stayed home to take your mother out to luncheon,' Overton said. 'Would you two young ladies like to join us?'

'Oh, thank you,' said Violet, 'but we're lunching at the Ritz with Freddie and the Damerels and Peter Hargrave. And we've to call on Betsy Desborough first, so we can't stay long.'

'I quite understand,' Overton said sadly. 'You would find us old people terribly dull company.'

Violet said, 'You're not *old*, Papa. And we love your company. Why don't *you* join *us* at the Ritz?'

Overton caught his wife's eye and laughed. 'Ah, I'm afraid we'd find you young people far too stimulating.'

After a quarter of an hour, Violet and Emma stood to go. 'When are you going down to the country?' Venetia asked.

'It was to be next week, but now with the war starting I don't know. I don't think I want to leave London with all this going on.' Violet waved a hand gloved in lavender suede to indicate the general excitement. 'Probably I shall go down and see the children at the weekend, and then come back. Goodbye, Aunt Olivia. It was lovely to see you.'

'You must come and visit us,' Olivia said. 'Make Holkam bring you down when the shooting starts.'

'That would be lovely,' Violet said, returning her kiss. Both of them, Venetia noted, had forgotten that when the shooting started, Holkam might be in France. Old habits of thought were hard to shake off.

Olivia remained talking to Venetia until her husband called to collect her, and they departed to visit some relatives on the Du Cane side. Venetia and Overton ordered the motor to come round, and drove off to Claridges, where they might hope to have a quieter luncheon than at the Ritz. The streets of London seemed to be packed, and their chauffeur – appropriately named Driver – apologised to them as the traffic ground to a halt for the second time.

'The restaurants all seem to be full, as well,' Overton remarked, looking out of the window.

'It's always like that in war-time,' Venetia said. 'Don't you remember in the Boer War everyone became very social and gave parties, the theatres were packed every night, and you had to book tables in restaurants?'

Overton watched the milling crowds with a grave expression. 'I wonder which of our young men will go away?'

'Holkam, for one,' Venetia said. 'Perhaps it will mellow him.'

Claridges was full, too, but the Sandowns were entertaining a small party and as soon as the Overtons appeared in the doorway sent the head waiter over to invite them to join them.

'It's a celebration,' said Lord Sandown, 'in honour of our grandson, who's in the reserve and goes to join his regiment tomorrow.'

'Venetia, my dear,' said Lady Sandown, leaning across the table to be heard against the well-bred din of a full dining-room, 'I must come and see you tomorrow. *Everyone* is starting up committees, and I must make sure I get the best people on mine. Now *promise* me you won't join anything until I've had a chance to speak to you. That odious

Desborough woman is telling everyone you will be on hers because dear Violet is so friendly with her son and daughter-in-law. If it's not too bad that she's stolen the Worsleys already, and Claudia Worsley and I were at school together!'

At the Ritz, there were similar crowds, a similar din, and a great deal more champagne. Given the greater youth of the clientele, the manager had taken a chance on putting in extra tables, with the result that everyone was elbow to elbow, but Emma thought it added to the fun, and meant that conversations spilled over from one table to another. Violet was telling Freddie Copthall and the Damerels about Holkam's volunteering, and how proud she was. Emma was enjoying the attentions of Peter Hargrave, with whom she had *almost* decided she was in love, and of Billy Wentworth and Kit Dawnay. The three young men vied for her attention and flirted with her in a very flattering way, and when she expressed her admiration for Holkam's immediate volunteering, hastened to assure her they would be joining too, as soon as was practically possible.

'You'll look divine in uniform,' Emma said to them generally, though it was Peter's broad shoulders and slim hips she was particularly imagining. 'Which regiment will you choose?'

A lively discussion of the best regiments, and whether there was more glory in the cavalry or the line, followed. And then young Lord 'Des' Desborough, husband to Betsy, lounged across from the next table and said, 'Oh, Miss Weston, pardon me for interruptin', but I was particularly charged by m' mother to ask you to be on her committee.'

'What committee is that?' Emma asked, pleasantly aware of the glares her companions were directing at the interrupting lord.

Desborough looked blank. 'I don't think she mentioned,' he admitted at last. 'But it's bound to be somethin'. At all events, she particularly wants you to join it – and Lady Violet, if you can persuade her.'

'Don't do it, Miss Weston,' Kit Dawnay urged. 'The Dowager Lady Desborough's committees are always desperately dull. *My* mother will be setting one up, and she'll have much more lively people on hers. Go away, Des, you shan't have Miss Weston. She's too good to be wasted on things that will bore her half to death.'

Emma let them fight over her, fluttering her eyelashes at one and then another, and thought that the war looked like being a very wonderful thing.

Venetia and Overton enjoyed the concert very much – they hadn't been to anything for months – and then decided in favour of supper at home rather than going to another restaurant. Every street still seemed to be packed, and London did not look like going to bed for hours yet. 'But I'm too old for so much gaiety,' Venetia had said. 'All this noise and chatter and whirligig gives me a headache. What I should really like is a plate of sandwiches and a glass of whisky in our nice quiet library at home.'

'That sounds wonderful,' said Overton, and took up the speaking-tube to say to the waiting chauffeur, 'Home, Driver.'

Burton opened the door to them with the news that the War Office had telephoned earlier for Lord Overton and, on being told that his lordship was not at home, had asked that the message be given to him that Lord Kitchener would be greatly obliged if his lordship could find it convenient to telephone him at the War Office as soon as he returned, as a matter of some urgency.

'I'll bet that K didn't use half so many words,' Venetia murmured. 'Go, my darling. But join me for supper if you can.'

As Overton went away to the telephone, Venetia noticed that Driver was still hovering in the doorway, despite Burton's frowns and barely disguised shooing movements.

'Could I have a word, my lady?' Driver said, craning round Burton's disapproving bulk.

Venetia almost said, 'At this time of night?' but then reasoned that Driver would not be daring Burton's odium if it were not important, and said instead, 'Certainly, if it can't wait.'

'I'd rather say it as soon as possible, my lady.'

'Very well. Thank you, Burton.' Under her level look, Burton admitted the chauffeur, closed the door behind him, and stalked away.

'It's just this, my lady,' said Driver, nervously, twisting his cap round and round in his hands. 'I've really enjoyed working for you, and I never thought to look for another position, not ever, as long as I gave satisfaction—'

'But?' Venetia encouraged him. 'Spit it out, man. You've given satisfaction, if that's what you want to know.'

'Oh! Thank you, my lady. I'm right grateful to you – for that and for giving me the job in the fust place. Like I said – well, not to put too fine a point on it, seeing how late it is – well, I thought I ought to say straight away that I mean to volunteer. That is, if you don't mind too much, my lady.'

She ought to have guessed it, given that they had been talking about nothing but the war all day. She was a little dismayed, because he was a good chauffeur and a good servant, but she could not, of course, stand in the way of a man's patriotic duty. 'Are you sure it's what you want, Driver?'

'Oh, yes, my lady. Me and a couple of pals, my lady, we was talking about it on Monday night, and saying if war was declared, we'd go together and volunteer first thing.'

'And *why* do you want to?' she asked, out of curiosity.

'Why, to fight the Hun, my lady, and teach him a lesson.'

'And protect our native land?' she supplied.

'It's a sacred dooty, my lady, that's how we see it. If old England needs us – well, for King and Country, and – and—'

'I understand,' Venetia said. She could see beneath his patriotic fervour and fierce disapproval of Germany another longing, which had afflicted men since the dawn of time: the longing for adventure. And who could blame them? If she had been a domestic servant, or even a chauffeur, would she not have wanted to exchange dreary familiarity for a sojourn in a strange land, with a lot of vigorous fighting and some jolly songs thrown in? 'Go, with my blessing, Driver,' she said. 'Have you decided which regiment you want to join?'

When Overton finally joined her in the bedroom, looking tired out again, she sought to distract him from whatever Kitchener had been saying with a counter-irritant. 'I have bad news for you, my love.'

Overton blinked. 'Bad news? How's that? How can you have had news since we got home?'

'Our chauffeur brought it. He's leaving us. He's going to volunteer.'

'Our chauff— Good heavens. Well, dash it, that's damned inconvenient.'

'Oh, we shall manage. Philips can drive you, and I'll take taxi-cabs. I could hardly refuse to let the fellow go.'

'No, no, I see that. Patriotic duty and so on,' said Overton. 'I wonder who will be next. Lord, I hope Burton doesn't leave us!'

'I don't see Burton as the type.'

'No, perhaps not. When is Driver leaving?'

'He's going to volunteer first thing tomorrow.' Her lips twitched with laughter as she remembered the last part of her interview with him. 'He's going to join the Service Corps.'

'Oh? Not going into a line regiment?'

'No,' said Venetia. 'He's going to be a driver in the Service Corps. The Service Corps, apparently, needs drivers.'

Overton began to smile too. 'And they're taking ours?'

She nodded, the giggles spilling over. 'Our Driver is going to be a driver.'

In a moment Overton caught it from her, and they clung together, breathless with ridiculous laughter. It was not so very much of a joke, Heaven knew, but sometimes laughter was what was needed, and it only took an excuse.

CHAPTER THREE

It was on the Wednesday that Jack was visited at work by Major Kennet of the RFC. He was in his tiny office in the busy Canbury Road works, going over a rigging plan with one of the foremen, when a smart military figure appeared in the doorway.

'Could you spare me a moment?'

'Of course,' said Jack, feeling his pulse increase a little at the sight of that uniform. 'Is that all clear now, Hooper?'

'Yes, sir, thank you, I'm all straight now.'

The foreman departed, and Jack, at a loss to offer a chair since there was only the one, behind his desk, came round to shake Kennet's hand. He had met him once before at the Royal Aircraft Factory when he had delivered a machine there. 'What can I do for you?' he asked. New orders for aeroplanes were not usually addressed to him, and development plans were always discussed with Tom Sopwith.

Kennet didn't waste time. 'I have Sopwith's permission to address you. I want to ask you to join us in the RFC.'

'Join you?' His mind was lagging a little behind, and he thought he was being offered a new job – in design, presumably. 'You mean at the RAF?'

Kennet smiled. 'No, no, it isn't your engineering skills I'm after, it's your flying skills. You're one of the best flyers in the country, and I've seen something of what you can do at air shows and such. Look here, the British Expeditionary Force will be embarking for France very soon, and its RFC contingent will be following close after. We're hoping to send

49

four squadrons and we're getting together every serviceable aeroplane we can lay hands on. Frankly, it'll be rather a motley collection. We're short of ground crew and we're also desperately short of experienced pilots – chaps who can take any machine up and keep it up long enough to do a job. Now, *you* know all our aircraft types inside out. You could fly any of them – and you could also be frightfully useful with advice on the ground.'

'You're asking me to join the RFC as a pilot?' Jack said, catching up finally.

Kennet positively grinned. 'Got it at last! You look bemused. I know war was only declared yesterday, but we've all known for weeks it was coming. Hadn't you thought at all about going into uniform?'

'Yes, I'd thought about it, of course, but I hadn't got as far as working out the details. What made you think of me?'

'As I said, I've seen you fly. And Hugh Trenchard thinks the world of you – says no-one else could have got him through his test in time. He telephoned me last night at Brooklands and suggested it would be worth my while motoring over to see you. Rather noble of him – he'd dearly like to have you at the Central Flying School, but he knows our need is greater. We've no doubt we'll get plenty of chaps volunteering now the word is out, but it'll take time to train them and we need flyers right now. What do you say? Are you game?'

Jack felt the rush of blood tingling through his veins. Here was the call to the great and glorious cause! Here was duty to be done, and he was being asked personally to join the spearhead. He felt honoured, and humbled. 'Of course,' he said. 'Of course I'll come.'

'Splendid! I knew you would.' Kennet shook his hand vigorously. 'I'll get the paperwork started, then. You'll have to undergo basic training, of course, but that can be crammed into a couple of weeks – less, perhaps. Have you done any shooting?'

'I've gone after rabbits as a boy, but I haven't had a gun in my hands for years.'

'Oh, you'll do all right. If you can shoot a rabbit you can shoot anything.'

Jack laughed. 'I didn't say I'd ever actually *got* one.'

'You've handled a gun, that's the important thing,' Kennet said firmly. 'And, of course, you won't need any flight instruction. You'll be gazetted second lieutenant and we can have you off to France in no time.'

So exciting had all this talk been that it was only now that Jack remembered Helen, and he was struck cold that he should have forgotten that they were to be married at the end of the month. 'When will you want me to start?' he asked.

Kennet cocked his head at the change of tone in his voice. 'As soon as possible. Does that pose a problem? I've spoken with Sopwith and he's happy to release you at once.'

'I've a fiancée,' Jack said. 'The date is set for the twenty-ninth.'

'We can't spare you until then,' said Kennet. 'A few days, perhaps. But ideally we'd like you to come tomorrow.'

Jack thought. 'Could I telephone you later today and let you know?'

Kennet agreed, wrote down his number, and departed; and Jack put away his papers, tidied his desk, and went to find Tom Sopwith to ask if he could leave now to go and speak to Helen.

As he drove crunching over the gravel of Fairoaks' drive, the front door opened, and Rug, standing with his paws up on the dashboard as usual, gave a single bark of greeting as Helen appeared, neat in a blue serge skirt and white blouse. As he stopped the engine and climbed out, she called, 'It's all right, we know. Major Trenchard telephoned Daddy this morning.' Trenchard and Ormerod were old friends.

She linked her arm through Jack's and turned with him through the door into the hall. 'Daddy said he'd been going to suggest it himself.' She stopped, looking up at Jack's face. 'You did say yes? You are going?'

Before he could answer Molly came thundering down the stairs, jumping the last three, to rush up to him crying, 'Going to the war, oh, you are so lucky! I wish I was a man.

51

Men have all the fun. It's not fair!' Then she stopped, stared, and said in a shocked tone, 'You are *going*?'

Jack gave a shaky sort of laugh. 'It must be a family trait.'

'Will you take Rug? Can I have him, if not? I mean, look after him until you come back? You'd like to stay with me, wouldn't you, old Ruggy-wuggy?' she crooned, rubbing the dog's cheeks between her hands in a manner that made his tail almost revolve in ecstasy.

'Molly, Mr Compton and I would like to have the opportunity to speak privately,' Helen said patiently.

Molly stared. 'Mr Compton? Mr *Compton*? You don't expect me to call him that when he's going to be my brother?' She turned to Jack. 'You don't mind if I call you Jack, do you?'

Mrs Ormerod appeared from the kitchen passage, looking harassed. 'Is that Mr Compton? Oh, I thought I heard your motor-car. Such a fuss this morning! The grocery order arrived not half filled, and when I telephoned to Pemberton's they said that ladies have been coming in all morning and buying up everything in the shop. Because of the war, they said. I didn't know there was any need to stock up, did you? But if everyone else is doing it, perhaps I ought to go out in the motor and try to buy some things. What do you think, Helen? Pemberton said it was sugar and coffee they were taking first, and you know what your father would be like if he didn't have his coffee at breakfast. One can hardly speak to him before the second cup,' she explained, with a faint smile, to Jack. 'Molly calls him Mr Bear – very naughty and silly, Molly dear. You really must show respect to your elders. When I was a girl – oh, Helen, don't keep Mr Compton standing in the hall. Will you have some coffee, Mr Compton? Or is it late enough for sherry?' She glanced at the clock. 'Good heavens, is it that time? Sherry, then – and you'll stay for luncheon?'

'Mo*ther*!' Molly cried in exasperation. 'Jack hasn't come here to talk about shopping and lunch. He's going to war – you *are* going, aren't you?' She put in a final, desperate appeal to Jack. 'Oh, do say you are!'

Helen took charge. 'Mr Compton and I want to speak privately. Mother, do take Molly away.'

'Of course, dear. Go into the morning-room. You won't be disturbed there – Ellen's dusted it already. I'll see you at luncheon, then, Mr Compton. I'm sure the turbot will stretch. Molly, take Rug into the garden, there's a good girl. The young people won't want him interrupting their talk. Soap, that was another thing Pemberton said was being bought up. Oh dear, I do hope there won't be shortages. But the grouse will be in next week, that's one blessing. Your father is very fond of game.'

Alone at last, with the morning-room door firmly shut against Molly's disappointed, enquiring face, Helen sighed. 'Soap, turbot, sherry, grouse! It's like trying to conduct a love affair at the music hall. Now, Jack Compton, tell me all – and quickly, before someone else comes to interrupt us.'

The morning-room was quiet, and dim now that the morning sun had gone round. It smelled of furniture wax and carpets, and very faintly of soot – a fine sprinkling on the paper fan in the grate showed that the warm weather had dislodged a little fall since the maid had done her daily round. The only sound was the light, fast ticking of the little French clock on the overmantel and, from beyond the lace drapes, where the sash window was open a little at the top, the insistent chirping of sparrows on the roof.

Helen faced him expectantly, and she seemed suddenly clear to Jack, close and vivid like something seen in that strange silvery light one experiences before storms. Her dear face: the steady, warm eyes, the unexpectedly full and passionate mouth, which counterbalanced the strong nose and chin and broad forehead, hinting at the hidden side of her practical and forthright nature. He loved her so much, and had – oh, stupidly! – wasted so much time that they could have spent together. And now war had come, and how could he bear to leave her with the promise of that mouth unfulfilled? The clarity with which he was seeing her now seemed to portend something: he felt that something was going to be decided here, now, in this room, that would change the course of their lives.

'Major Kennet came to see me at the works this morning,

to ask me to join the RFC. They are desperately short of experienced pilots,' he began.

'That much we know,' Helen said, a shade impatiently. 'You haven't yet said that you accepted the invitation. Your reticence suggests you have doubts.'

'Not doubts,' he said. 'I want to do my duty. I feel I ought to go. And as they've gone to the trouble of asking for me individually, by name—'

Helen grinned. 'Humbug! "Duty" indeed! You're as excited as a schoolboy at the thought of it – or if you're not, there's something wrong with you! Freddie telephoned this morning, bewailing the fact that he was never in the Territorials, and asking if Daddy thought they'd be taking volunteers, and whether he could use his influence to get him in. So don't try and tell me you're not bursting to go. What's the trouble? Didn't you say yes?'

'I asked Kennet if I could telephone him later. I had to talk to you first.'

She stepped closer, putting her hands up on his shoulders. 'You don't think I'd try and stop you? I shall be as proud as Punch to have you in uniform. What woman wouldn't?'

'But, you see, they want me to go right away, and there's our wedding to think of. By the end of August I'd be in France and I wouldn't be able to come back for it.'

Helen dropped her hands. 'Well, yes, that is something to think about. Poor Mother has invested so much time and effort in this wedding, it will break her heart not to have it. I think,' she added ruefully, 'that she thought she'd never get me off her hands. She could hardly believe it when you offered for me.'

'I wish you wouldn't talk like that,' said Jack. 'It was my blithering stupidity that kept you waiting. I'm lucky that you didn't lose patience with me and go off with one of your other suitors.'

She laughed. 'Who were so many, of course! Mother was always having "little talks" with me, and telling me not to drive men away by being "too clever". "Men don't like girls who express opinions, dear," she'd say – and you proved

54

that, right enough, with your Miss Fairbrothers, and the other witless angels.'

Jack put his head in his hands. 'Don't remind me,' he said, with a theatrical groan.

'Oh, I must have a little fun with you, for my pains! But, dearest, to be serious, what's to be done? About the wedding, I mean.'

'I've been thinking about it on my way over, and it seems to me that there are two possibilities. Kennet said they really wanted me tomorrow but that they could give me a day or two. Either we could get married straight away by special licence, or we could put it off until either the war is over or I have leave. Everyone's saying it will be over by Christmas, but even if it isn't, I should think I'd be bound to have some leave by then, or if not, soon afterwards. Even if it's only a week, it would be enough to have a proper wedding, the sort you deserve.'

Helen was thoughtful. 'If we do it right away, it would have to be a small affair. Mother could never change all the arrangements in time. My gown's nowhere near finished, and even if the church and the rector were free, the guests would hardly be able to come at such short notice. And then there's the reception to think of.'

'Just so,' Jack said.

She sighed. 'For myself, I really don't mind. I'd marry you in a register office if I had to. But Mother has her heart set on a grand occasion – and of course it would break Molly's heart. She's so looking forward to being my brides-maid, and her dress isn't even started yet. On the other hand,' she looked at him with longing, 'the idea of your going away, of having to wait – oh, Jack! Even the end of August seems too far away.'

'Yes, I know,' he said. 'I feel that too.' He gathered her in his arms and held her close. To go away without having made her his, without having tasted the intimacy he had longed for for so long – it would be very hard. To marry tomorrow and have one day together, he thought, would be worth everything. But it must be her decision, and he would not press her. She had waited for him even longer than he had waited for her.

She drew back at last with a sigh. 'I think we must wait,' she said. 'If it were just the two of us – but we have to think of the family. We'll tell Mother it must be postponed until you have leave.'

He nodded. 'I'll let you know the moment I hear.'

'And you'll go tomorrow?'

'I'll telephone Major Kennet this afternoon and say I'm ready whenever he wants me.'

'We'd better go and face them, then,' Helen said, turning towards the door. She gave a tight smile. 'At least Molly will be so glad you're going to the war it will outweigh the disappointment of a put-off.'

He caught her arm and turned her back. 'Kiss me first. Molly's sure that's what we've come in here for, so we might as well be guilty as charged.'

Now the smile was a proper one. She laid her lips to his, her arms crept up round his neck. She was nearly as tall as him, which made it comfortable. Jack felt his senses rouse at the touch of her, and Christmas suddenly seemed aeons away.

'My soldier hero!' She laughed softly as they broke apart.

'Your knight of the skies,' he agreed. 'And of course you'll be "the girl I left behind me".'

He took her hand and they went out to find the family.

'You'll look so handsome in uniform,' Helen said. 'As soon as you've got it, you must have your photograph taken and send it to me.'

On Thursday Jessie was riding over to Morland Place on Hotspur, her mind full of the amazing scenes she had witnessed in York that morning. As 'war fever' gripped, the shops were besieged by people stocking up against future shortages. It was the middle class who were doing it, those with motors that could be loaded and chauffeurs who could help carry. Flour, sugar, coffee, sacks of potatoes, whole cheeses, whole hams, tinned food – she had seen them being carried out in tottering piles to waiting motors, to the resentful muttering of onlookers. Already a word had been circulated for these opportunists – 'hoarders'. The mayor had published a plea in the local newspapers that morning, insisting that there would be no shortages and asking people not to buy more than their usual amounts. In one paper, a letter to the editor had fulminated against hoarding as 'unpatriotic' and had, predictably, called for hoarders to be gaoled.

There was a further problem: the banks had not reopened after the Bank Holiday. By government decree, they were to remain closed until Friday while paper money was printed and distributed, which was to take the place of gold sovereigns and half-sovereigns for the duration of the war. This had given rise to a temporary but severe shortage of currency. Those who had gold were unwilling to part with it, and the only paper money at present in circulation was the five-pound note, far too large a denomination for everyday transactions. In York that morning Jessie had overheard the reaction of a cab-driver to the suggestion that he should accept a white 'fiver' in payment of his fare – which would have involved his parting with his entire stock of silver and copper in change. While this was probably the intention of his passenger, the cabbie had had vociferous views on the subject, and on the character of a man who would try such a trick. He threatened to give the man in charge if he did not come up with suitable coinage to pay his reckoning, and as a large crowd had gathered, which was noisily in support of the cabbie, the man had at last been obliged to part with a half-crown and weakly wave away the change to be allowed to escape.

The poor, who normally dealt only in copper and silver, were not much affected: it was the better-off who found themselves caught out, and Jessie noticed that prices had shot up since Tuesday as a rounding-up process took care of the lack of change. She was not worried herself about possible food shortages, since there would always be plenty of produce available at Morland Place from the home farm, but she did wonder about forage. She was very glad that, on the advice of Uncle Teddy, seconded by Ned, she had bought in extra oats, bran and linseed last week, though it was before her usual time of ordering, so that her corn bins were all full. The glorious summer weather had meant the hay harvest had been good; but now war had been declared the army would have first call on that, and by the time winter set in she wondered if there would be anything left in stock, and what it would cost. The earth, probably. Coal prices had gone up steeply, too, though they were usually low in August, and she hadn't ordered their quarter's fuel yet – the coal cellar was almost empty. And Purvis the chauffeur, who had been a reservist, had been called up, which left all his jobs to Daltry, who already had enough to do.

She was riding Hotspur without much attention, so that when a pheasant rattled out from under the hedge across his path and he shied in surprise she was almost unseated. It brought her attention sharply back to the present: to the dusty summer track, the dark green of the hedges and trees, the lavender of the warm afternoon sky, lightly fretted with high wisps of cloud; to Brach, her big Morland hound bitch, coming out from the hedge, grinning guiltily (now Jessie knew who had flushed the pheasant) and then turning to halt with her ears sharply pointed. Jessie heard the sound of pounding hoofs, and a moment later someone burst out onto the track up ahead from the side lane that led to Woodhouse Farm.

It was a hairy-footed chestnut vanner being ridden bareback and in a rope halter by Jimmy Banks, one of the farm's grandsons. Having little control over his mount he had difficulty in stopping it plunging through the hedge opposite, and there was a moment of skidding and whirling as the ginger nose went up in the air and the rider tugged ineffectually at the rope, trying to turn the hot and excited horse in the right direction.

'Hi!' Jessie called. 'Are you all right?'

The vanner, stubbornly refusing to turn in the direction the rider evidently wanted, had reared in protest, sending Jimmy sliding towards its tail; but at the sound of Jessie's voice its ears shot forward, and it turned in relief at the sight of another horse, trotted up to Hotspur and stopped, nose to nose, legs trembling and breath coming in offended snorts. Jimmy had managed to haul himself back into position by the mane, and now broke into panting speech.

'Eh, Miss Jessie, thank the Lord! I was going to Morland Place for the maister, but mebbe you can help. It's our grandad, miss. The requisition officer's come and wants to take away our 'osses, and Grandad won't let him. He's fair framin', miss, and he swears he'll kill him before he lets him take our Daisy and Boxer. He's got his gun out, miss. Our grandad's as gentle as a lamb, miss, but he loves them 'osses like his own children, and I don't know what he might do. Dad sent me off to get help on Ginger, and the officer tried to stop me. I think he thought I were going to hide him somewheres. Oh, miss, will you come?'

Jessie was in motion before he had finished, setting Hotspur into a canter, and the vanner whirled and followed, reluctant to be parted from this new friend. It surged up alongside, eyes bulging, and matched Hotspur's stride, its great hoofs cutting sods out of the grass verge. The lane was narrow and Jimmy's leg was scratched all along the hedge, while Brach, crowded out, ducked under it and cut across the corner of the field to avoid being trampled. It was not far to Woodhouse. Jessie pulled Hotspur down to a trot as she reached the gate, and turned into the yard to find the tableau much as she had imagined it when Jimmy told his story.

There in front of the stable stood Grandad Banks, old Ezra, who was in his eighties but still hale, the sort of gaunt, rangy Yorkshire farmer who never seemed to age much after sixty. In his black work trousers, tied at ankle and knee with binder twine, his big hobnailed boots, his collarless shirt and eternal, battered black waistcoat, he looked to Jessie exactly as he always had. His hair was silver and stood out round his head, lit from the side by the sun in a rather Old Testament manner. His white beard was jutting belligerently with the determined gritting of his jaw, and he held his shotgun aggressively at the ready, guarding the stable door.

Held at bay by this formidable figure was the requisitioning officer – not Forrester, but his deputy, Keegan – and an assistant. There was Ezra's son, Eli Banks, who seemed to be pleading with him; Eli's wife – Jimmy's mother – her youngest daughter, Rosie, who was weeping into her mother's apron; and a number of farm dogs who were unsure what to do and seemed to be torn between snarling, hackles raised, at the intruders and frisking in an inappropriate way around Eli's legs.

Everyone turned as Jessie entered, and relief registered on every face. Jimmy slid gratefully from the vanner's back and it snatched the rope from his hand and trotted fast past the whole crowd and into the stable, disappearing with a slither of hoofs into the darkness within.

Several people began speaking at once as Jessie freed her leg and slipped to the ground.

'Oh, Miss Jessie! Thank heaven you've come!'

'Mrs Compton! Perhaps you can explain to these people . . .'

'Miss Jessie, it's our dad, he won't let them take . . .'

'Miss Jessie, don't let them take our 'osses . . .'

She lifted her hands defensively, and the clamour died away, apart from the growling of a collie bitch who was stalking Brach, feeling that at least she knew what to do about an intruding dog. Eli stepped up, caught the bitch's collar, and said quietly, 'Miss Jessie, Dad's that upset about these gentlemen wanting to take our Boxer and Daisy and Duke, he's fair lost his mind. But, miss, what are we to do about th' harvest? It's not half in, and if they take three 'osses it only leaves us wi' Ginger, and he's just a young 'un, hardly broke. Miss, what are we to do?'

Keegan stepped closer, to get his word in. 'We're just doing our job, Mrs Compton. Can't you tell these people? It's government orders, and that's all there is to it.'

This angered Eli. 'Aye, that's all it is to you, but what about my harvest?'

'We all have to do our duty, Mr Banks,' Keegan began.

'Don't tell me about duty, young man. You'll be down quick enough to complain if there's no bread to feed your soldiers. The harvest comes first, everyone knaws that. Everyone who knaws the land,' he corrected, as if anyone else didn't count, 'knaws that.'

Jessie said, 'I know it's hard, but there really isn't anything we can do. These gentlemen have the right to take the horses.

The Government makes it so. They will pay you for them.'

'Payin's no good,' Eli said. 'Who's goin' to pull the reaper and the binder and the carts?'

'We'll send you another horse,' Keegan said. 'Or more probably a mule.'

'A mule!' Eli said disgustedly; but Jessie could see he knew there was no help for it. 'Aye, well, I suppose if it has to be, it has to be – but you'll still have to get past Grandad.'

'I'll go and talk to him,' Jessie said.

'Be careful, miss,' said Mrs Banks. 'He's that upset . . .'

Jessie had no fear of old Ezra, whom she had known most of her life. She handed Hotspur's rein to Jimmy, and walked across the yard to him. The shotgun wavered at her approach, and finally shifted aside, though his wary eyes kept watch over her shoulder for any other movement.

She stopped in front of him, and looked her deep sympathy. 'You know what I'm going to say,' she said.

'Aye,' he said. 'But *tha* knaws . . .'

'Yes. I know. They're going to come and take my horses soon, and I shall feel just like you. But it has to be. You have to let them go.'

Suddenly the old man's eyes filled with tears, and it was painful and terrible, as though a mountain had cried. 'Ma beautiful 'osses,' he said. 'Ma Boxer and Duke and Daisy. Ah bred 'em maself, tha knaws. Broke 'em and trained 'em wi' me own 'ands. They understand ivvry word Ah say. When Ah'm ploughin', Ah nivver put a hand to the rein, Ah just speak to 'em. Ah just tell 'em left or right, and they turn. Boxer an' Duke work together, an' they move like one 'oss, like twins. An' Daisy – our little Rosie used to play between her feet when she were a bairn and nivver took 'arm. Gentle as kittens, all three. Ah put ribbons in their manes when we go out to plough, just like ma dad did afore me. Eh, Miss Jessie, how can I part wi' 'em? They're like ma children to me. Them soldiers won't understand 'em. Someone might speak rough to 'em, or hit 'em, like, not knawing they'll go along for a word. They don't understand anything but kindness, don't my 'osses. It'd break their hearts to be hit.'

Jessie had nothing to say. Her own eyes were filled with

tears now. She laid a gentle hand on his arm. His lips trembled, and he lowered the gun, defeated.

'Tek 'em, then,' he said. 'Tek 'em.'

He stood aside, and waited, head bowed, as Jessie beckoned to Keegan and his man. The two entered the dark stable, and came out a little while later leading the three great Shire horses, their coats gleaming where they had been lovingly groomed that morning, their great gentle heads nodding with their steps.

Ezra did not look up as they passed him; but then he cried out, 'Stop!'

Keegan and his man halted warily. Ezra came across the yard, walking like an old man, though before he had always stridden like a countryman. He went to each horse in turn, stroked their noses, murmured to them, and they dipped their heads, pricking their ears softly to hear his words. He fumbled a small windfall apple out of his pocket for each, and the soft, prehensile lips brushed his palm as they took up the sweet present, trusting and trustworthy. Then he stepped back and nodded, his throat working, and the two men walked on, leading the horses away.

Jessie stood beside Ezra and watched him watching them. 'Ah put ribbons in their hair, like a girl's,' he said, so quietly she could only just catch the words. Then he looked at her. 'Ah'll nivver see 'em again, will Ah?' he said.

She did not answer. Her throat was too tight.

Brach, standing beside Jessie, nuzzled Ezra's hand, and he caressed her absently. Then he sighed, pulled himself up a little, and turned away. 'Better see what we can do wi' Ginger. One 'orse, an' all th' harvest to get in,' he grumbled, in something like his old manner.

They came for her own horses the next day. John Forrester came himself, in courtesy to her. They took the half-broken horses she had been preparing for the Army. They took the hunters, the polo ponies, the horses she had been schooling for customers, the two- and three-year-olds. They left her with the yearlings, the stallions, the brood mares, and the Bhutias, who at little more than thirteen hands were too small for army use. They did not take Hotspur and Compass Rose, for which she was grateful.

'You will be paid, of course,' Forrester said. 'Seventy-five pounds a head for the hunters and polo ponies. They'll be officers' chargers.'

'They're worth five times that,' she said. More, much more, to her personally.

'It can't be helped,' he said, though with sympathy.

'I know,' she said. 'It doesn't make it easier.'

As she saw him off the premises, he said, 'I'm sorry about that upset yesterday, at Woodhouse Farm. I'll see to it they're sent a fine big mule – the best we've got. They'll be surprised at how hard a mule can work, I promise you.'

She stayed at the gate a long time after he had gone, unwilling to go back into the yard in its new emptiness, to see so many half-doors with no head looking over, to face the grooms who would be standing around like people at a funeral, bereft, with not enough to do. She thought of old Ezra being presented with a mule. Well, he'd make the best of it, of course, as his sort did, and if it were not one of the bad-tempered kind he would probably even make a pet of it. Perhaps he would be putting ribbons in its mane for the harvest next year. But it would be hard to get in the harvest with only one horse – and that half trained – and a mule. Two animals to pull the reaper and binder – but what about carrying? And when it came to ploughing, how would they get all done with only one team?

It was then she had her idea. Bertie had given her the Bhutia mares when he sold up his stock at the Red House, not wanting them put on the open market. Bhutias were small, but they were very strong and hardy. In the Himalayas full-grown men rode them incredible distances in the harshest conditions, and they could carry loads as great as mules did. A couple of them were in foal, but for the rest – it was a shame and a waste just to have them running off, and she did not mean to be breeding from them while the war was on. All the Morland estate farmers would be parting with their heavy horses – why not let them have the Bhutias as replacements?

They would take a little convincing, she thought, that the mares were strong enough – but not a great deal: in Yorkshire parlance it was commonplace that a good little 'un was worth more than a good big 'un – and they would always be on a little 'un's side. And the mares were all hand reared and as gentle as lambs. It would not be difficult to harness-break them and teach them their new duties.

She turned back into the stable yard and called for her head man, eager to put her new project in hand. She would enjoy helping to break the little mountain horses. It would give her something to do, and she liked to be busy. It was something to take her mind off the empty stalls.

On Friday the 7th of August all the newspapers carried a report of the speech the Prime Minister, Asquith, had made to the Lower House to enthusiastic cheers.

'I do not think any nation ever entered into a great conflict – and this is one of the greatest that history will ever know – with a clearer conscience or stronger conviction that it is fighting not for aggression, not for the maintenance of its own selfish ends, but in defence of principles, the maintenance of which is vital to the civilisation of the world.'

Teddy read it out approvingly to the assembled family. 'I never thought much of the fellow, but there's no doubt he's voicing the feelings of the whole nation this time, and in just the right words. He goes on, "We have got a great duty to perform; we have got a great truth to fulfil." I like that. Yes, there's no doubt it is our duty to defend what's right and put Germany in its place.'

The papers carried something else that was more immediately interesting to Lennie Manning: a call to arms by Lord Kitchener. The striking panel took up a whole page in the journal he had got hold of, and was topped by the stirring words, in bold black type, 'Your King and Your Country Need You'. Well, it was not Lennie's country and the King was not his king, but he felt the heat of excitement rush through him all the same. His family had come originally from England – from Morland Place itself – and right was right whoever you were.

The appeal went on: 'An addition of 100,000 men to His Majesty's Regular Army is immediately necessary in the present grave national emergency.'

Grave national emergency, thought Lennie, and his English blood surged faster.

'Lord Kitchener is confident that this appeal will be at once responded to by all those who have the safety of the Empire at heart.'

Well, there you have it, thought Lennie. You don't have to be English by nationality to care about the safety of the Empire. He loved his own country, but he certainly had England's safety at heart. He read on. Terms were general service for a period of three years or until the war ended. Age of enlistment was between nineteen and thirty. The warm surge had become something like an intolerable itch. He could hardly sit still. He wanted to rush away at once and enlist, before the 100,000 total was reached, before the chance evaporated. He wanted to put on a uniform and carry a gun and march across France and shoot the dastardly Germans. He sighed and fidgeted without realising it, and Polly, beside him, said, 'What's the matter? You look as though you had a burr in your trousers.'

'Polly, don't be rude, dear,' Henrietta said automatically.

'They're calling for volunteers,' Lennie said. 'A hundred thousand.'

'Yes,' said Teddy. 'It's in this newspaper too. Things must be even more serious than we thought, if the regular army can't handle it.'

'I wish I could go,' Lennie blurted out.

'Every man in the kingdom will feel like that,' Teddy said approvingly, 'and it's to your credit that you do, even though this isn't your country.'

'But I feel it *is* my country, sir,' Lennie cried. 'My ancestors came from England. I'm a Morland by blood, and in my heart.'

'That's well said, my boy, and we appreciate it very much,' said Teddy, in a terminal sort of way, as though there were no question of its getting any further than feelings. Lennie said no more.

Polly's urgent, excited glance caught his eye and he gave a little sigh and a shake of the head. She responded to that by saying loudly, 'If every man in the kingdom feels like Lennie, why doesn't Robbie volunteer?'

Robbie, who was sitting with Ethel on the sofa where they had been talking in low voices, looked up in annoyance. 'If I were a young man like Lennie, I would.'

'But it says in the paper, age nineteen to thirty,' Polly said. 'You're not thirty yet.'

'I'm a married man,' Robbie said, 'with two children. It's unmarried men they want.'

'That's right,' Ethel agreed. 'Robbie couldn't go and leave us, especially as—' She stopped, blushing, remembering they hadn't announced her hopes yet.

'If you mean the new baby, you needn't mind – everybody knows,' Polly said.

Robbie reddened. 'How did you find out?'

'Polly, don't be pert,' Henrietta said, and was glad that Sawry came in at that moment to announce dinner.

The thought of that call for volunteers gnawed away at Lennie all through Saturday and Sunday. His only confidante was Polly, with whom he discussed it again on Sunday afternoon when they went riding together. She could not offer any more help than agreeing with him that it would be 'jolly exciting' to go and that it was 'jolly unfair' that he couldn't. For somewhere to go they rode over to the Cornleighs' house – Ethel's family home. Eileen Cornleigh was Polly's particular friend, the same age as her, and Eileen's younger sister Marguerite, known in the family as Dodo, was not always a contemptible companion now she had reached twelve. While Lennie was kind and patient with children, he had no wish to spend an afternoon with three schoolgirls, but there was every chance that Arthur and Peter would be at home, and at twenty and eighteen they were just the right age to have something interesting to say.

They were at home, and once the courtesies had been done, the three young men strolled down to the end of the orchard. It eased Lennie's soul to hear Arthur bemoaning the fact that he was only just eighteen and too young, and had been forbidden by his father even to think about volunteering for another year.

'But the war will be over by then,' Arthur complained. 'You'd think a chap's father would have the sense to realise that, and not try to stop a chap taking the only chance he may ever have in his life of fighting in a war! The trouble is,' he went on bitterly, 'that old people like Father and the mater are so jolly far gone that they don't remember what it's like to be young. I'm sure if I told the recruiting people I was nineteen they'd believe me. Ada says I look jolly old for my age.'

'Don't you have to show a certificate or something?' Lennie asked.

'I don't think so,' said Peter. 'I think they just take your word, as long as you look all right. When are you nineteen?'

'In January,' Lennie said. 'But I don't know if they'd let me in, not being English. They'd know I was American because of my accent.'

'Well, I'm all right, anyway,' said Peter. 'I've just got to ask my boss about breaking my articles, and I shall be off. The thought of going down to the office every morning and coming back from the office every evening for the next four solid years! I'm not going to turn down the chance of breaking away and looking for adventure.'

'And I suppose Father will clap you on the back and say well done,' said Arthur, 'just because you're two years older than me. It's not fair!'

The unfairness with which life and adults in general treated men of eighteen was a fertile subject, which lasted until it was time to go.

The next day, however, brought better news. Arthur Cornleigh rode over to Morland Place on his bicycle and could hardly stand still to give the polite greetings to Henrietta, Alice and his sister before dragging Lennie outside for a secret conference.

'Look here, Lennie, I heard something this morning that'll jolly well interest you,' he said, as they reached the privacy of the Long Walk. 'One of the mater's friends called on her this morning – Mrs Arkwright. Ghastly, prosy old bore, she is, so I didn't want to hang around and get caught, but I was half-way down the stairs when she arrived, so I had to hide on the landing. Anyway, she came in in a terrific state, complaining at the top of her voice as soon as Mother came out into the hall to meet her, so I couldn't help overhearing, and once I heard the first bit, I crept down and stood outside the drawing-room door for the rest. It seems her chauffeur Peter went off first thing this morning to the recruiting office in York and volunteered!'

'Lucky fellow,' said Lennie.

'Well, Ma Arkwright was in a terrible bate about it, saying how she couldn't do without him, and calling him ungrateful and thoughtless and selfish and I don't know what else. But the thing is this – Peter isn't English.'

'What?'

'No, he's Polish. He's been over here years and years, and you'd never know he wasn't English, except that he's got an accent, though hardly enough to notice, but he's definitely Polish, and they still took him. So what do you think about that?'

Before Lennie could answer, he caught sight of Polly coming across the drawbridge from the back door. Arthur turned to see what he was looking at, and said, 'Oh, Lord, here comes the infantry. Let's go somewhere else. She'd hardly follow us.'

'She would,' Lennie said. 'But Polly's all right. She's on our side.'

So they waited, and Polly hurried up to them and said, 'What is it? I saw you from the nursery window. Is it something exciting?' Lennie explained, and Polly said at once, 'Well, what are you waiting for? I was going to suggest to you this morning that instead of hanging around being miserable you went to the recruiting office to find out what the rules are. But now you know they take foreigners, you can go straight away and enlist.'

Lennie had had time to think, and he said, 'It isn't quite that simple. This Polish chap lives here. I suppose he's never going back to Poland. But I shall have to go back to America some time.'

'I don't see why they should care,' Polly said.

'Well, I don't know. They might. The USA is very funny about some things, especially nationality and being loyal to the flag and so on. What I'm going to do is send off a cable to my grandmother and see what she says.'

'She'll just say no,' said Polly. 'Grown-ups always do, whenever you want to do something interesting.'

'I'm not so sure,' said Lennie. 'Granny's not a bit stuffy. I think she'd be on my side.'

To Polly's approval, he wasted no more time but walked in to York straight away to send a cable from the central post office. On his way home he passed the recruiting office and saw a queue of young men outside. He longed to be one of them, and felt agonisingly that his chance was slipping past him, that he must grasp it *now* or lose it. He clenched his fists in frustration. If the British Army would take him, what did it matter what the USA thought? Surely they couldn't object to something so noble? And if they did, what could they do – tell him he could never come home again? Well, in that case, he would just stay here – or travel the world! He saw himself, a bronzed, narrow-eyed adventurer, at home in every land, taking lifts on goods trains, working his passage on steamers, tramping dusty roads in far-flung corners of the globe . . . He shook his head to dispel the attractive images. That was all beside the point. The point was that there was a war to be fought, an adventure to be had right here and now, and whatever the price, it would be worth paying. He swerved so abruptly he made an old lady tut-tut, and ran across the road to place himself self-consciously at the end of the queue, sure everyone must be looking at him. The man in front of him turned and smiled – well, it was more of a grin, really, an excited, complicit, friendly grin.

'I hope they take us,' he said. 'They say the medical exam's pretty stiff.'

'You look healthy enough,' Lennie said.

'Yes, but there's a minimum chest measurement, thirty-four inches, and I've never been very big in the chest,' the young man confided.

'Take a deep breath just before they measure you,' Lennie suggested.

'I will,' said the young man. 'I say, it's going to be jolly good fun if we do get in, isn't it?'

It took half an hour of shuffling before Lenny got inside, and was directed to a trestle table where a corporal with thinning hair sat with piles of papers in front of him. 'Name?' he said, pen poised.

'Lennox Mynott.'

The corporal looked up at that. 'You a Yank?' he asked.

'Yes,' Lennie said. 'Does it matter?'

The corporal looked perplexed. 'Tell you the truth, I dunno. Never had a Yank through me hands before.' He ruffled through his papers for a printed sheet, and shook his head. 'It don't say anything about Americans. I'd better check. Wait here.'

He got up and walked across to an officer standing at the end of the room, and after a brief conversation and a long look in Lennie's direction, they both went through a glass-topped door into another room. Shortly they returned with an important-looking, white-haired officer whom they followed up the hall. He stopped in front of Lennie and eyed him up and down keenly. 'Mynott?' he asked.

'Yes, sir,' Lennie said nervously.

'I'm Colonel Clavering. I understand you're an American citizen.'

'Yes, sir.'

'And you want to volunteer to serve in His Majesty's army?'

'Yes, sir.'

'Well, we'd be glad to have you,' said the colonel. 'You look like a bright, fit young man, just the sort of chap we want. But it's a serious matter from your point of view. You do know, don't you, that if an American citizen serves in a foreign army, he has to give up his American citizenship – or, rather, has it taken from him?'

So that was it. A torrent of thoughts tumbled through his head at that moment, about the United States, and home, and the flag, and all the blurred patchwork of yearnings that make up the sense of belonging to one country or another. But they had no solidity next to the shining knowledge that the colonel had said he'd be glad to have him. He was not going to admit that this was the first time he knew what the penalty was that he would have to pay. His mouth was dry, but he said firmly, 'Yes, sir.'

'You did know it?'

'Yes, sir.'

The colonel looked at him shrewdly. 'Now, my boy, would you care to take a little time to think it over? Come back tomorrow, if you like.'

'No, sir, thank you,' Lennie said, more sure with every word. 'I'd like to volunteer now.'

The colonel looked at him a moment longer, and then nodded. 'Very well. Carry on, Corporal.' And he walked away.

'Right then, *Mr* Mynott,' said the corporal, with heavy irony, 'let's be having you. Age?'

'Nineteen,' said Lennie, almost absently. He was in a daze. He was *in*! The corporal did not ask to see a birth certificate, and he had no fear of the medical examination – he was very fit and healthy and a good size for his age. He was in!

The processes followed in efficient order. In another room he was told to strip to trousers and socks, leaving everything else in a neat pile on the bench that ran round two sides. He lined up for his height to be measured – 'No worries for you, my lad. Five feet ten' – and was then directed to stand against the wall and read the letters on an optician's card twenty feet away. He passed into a tiny side room where the medical officer met him with a kindly smile and looked him over, sounded his chest, listened to his heart, made him stand on one foot and then the other to check for flat feet, and asked him about his medical history. Out and into the next cubby-hole, where a dentist sat him down, tilted his head back, and examined his teeth. 'We're allowed some leeway with teeth,' said the dental officer, 'but it looks to me as if you have all of yours. Excellent mouth. Wish we had more of 'em.'

'Thank you, sir,' said Lennie.

The dental officer pricked up his ears. 'American, eh? Well, perhaps that makes the difference. You should see some of the mouths I get presented with. Horrible!'

Finally he was told he had passed 'A1' and was sent to put his clothes back on and line up to take the oath. They went in groups of four into the office at the far end of the hall where Colonel Clavering received them, told them to raise their right hands, and administered the oath. One of Lennie's group was Parker, who had been in front of him in the queue outside. When it was done they each signed a form, and then the colonel shook them by the hand, said, 'Well done,' and passed them out for the last phase.

A cheerful, elderly corporal gathered them in with a grin of sympathy and said, 'Well, you've been and gone and done it now! You've took the King's shilling and you can't get out of it. Come along, my lucky lads, and we'll have the tailor measure you up for your uniform.'

'What happens now – er – Corporal?' Lennie asked, as they followed him down the hall.

The corporal gave him a ripe look. 'Now? You mean when we've finished with you? Well, you go home, of course.'

'Go home?' Lennie said, and one or two others looked dismayed.

'Ho, sneaked out to enlist, did you? Don't want to face your mums? Never mind, they can't get you out now – unless you're under age,' he added, with a look at Parker, the smallest of the group, who shrank back from the knowing eye, 'and even then I'd back the colonel to talk 'em out of it. Doing the right thing, ain't you? Wouldn't be patriotic to object, now, would it? Ah, don't worry. They might have a bit of a rant to start with, but they'll be proud as Punch of their brave lads. Get yourselves measured up and then go on home. You'll get a letter in a day or two telling you where to report.'

With the three companions he had sworn his oath in front of, Lennie passed through the tailor's hands, and out onto the street. York was going about its business as if nothing had happened. They looked at each other, thinking it would be a bit flat just to go home.

'My mum's going to kill me,' said Parker, gloomily.

'She'll be all right when she sees you in your uniform,' said Gort.

'Wish we had that right now,' said Summers. 'I thought we'd walk out in it, and everyone'd know we'd volunteered.'

'I know what,' said Gort. 'You know Bacon's, the photographer's? They've got a uniform you can borrow to get your picture took in. They pin it a bit if it don't fit. Why don't we go down there now and get ourselves done?'

'Good idea,' said Summers. 'And then let's go and have a beer, to celebrate.' He looked at Lennie, who hadn't spoken yet. 'You'll come, won't you? I mean, us four ought to be pals, like, now we've took the oath together.'

'Yes, I'll come,' said Lennie, smiling. 'You couldn't stop me!'

'Good on yer, Yank,' said Gort. Lennie fell in with them as they walked off to the photographer's, thinking that there would be a scene of some sort – good or bad, he wasn't sure yet – to be faced when he got back to Morland Place, but that for now he had achieved his goal and acquired four new friends – and a nickname. The daze he was in was luminous and gold-flushed. He was very happy.

CHAPTER FOUR

There was a great deal to be done, and for Bertie more than most, for he did not have the advantage of already knowing the regiment, its traditions and ways – or, indeed, any of the men. Rumour as to when they would be going overseas was rife and various, but there seemed no doubt it would be soon. Meanwhile Bertie had to take over C Company, the domain of the luckless Captain Cartwright, incorporate into it the reservists he was allocated, get to know it, and get it into embarkation order.

Medical inspection was the first thing, and some of the reservists had not kept themselves in soldierly shape. One was rejected, almost in tears, for not having sufficient teeth – no small matter, given the nature of army rations on active duty: a man who could not eat would not march. He was given barrack duties for the duration. Another had evidently embraced the soft life and had lost his figure: at almost twenty stone, he would not fit into any uniform in the quartermaster's stores, and was something of a hazard on the barrack square when making quick about-turns. He drilled in his civilian clothes, and would not be going overseas until exercise and army diet had fined him down.

Once fitted with uniform and boots, each man had to be issued with a rifle, which he then had to fire in so that the sights could be adjusted for his eyes and the rifle's individual peculiarities. Much of the rest of the time was taken up with parades, inspections, drilling and marching, to get the reservists fit and to bind them and the regulars into one unit. There was a huge amount of kit to distribute and inspect, and such mountains of stores to shift from place to place that fatigues could not be reserved to malefactors alone but had to be allocated on rotation to everyone.

Bertie had also to accustom his horses to their new life. Both were of a sensible age – Kestrel was seven and Nightshade eight – but neither had any army experience. All the horses going to France had to be dark-coated so they did not stand out against the background. In a field next to the barracks the one or two light-coloured animals in the regiment had their coats dyed by grooms wielding buckets and large brushes, which caused some fun and not a few kicks. Nightshade was a black, and Kestrel liver-chestnut, so they were saved the full ordeal, but Nightshade had a white race and one white sock behind, and Kestrel had a white face. Bertie was rather sad to see the latter disappear, for it had given Kestrel rather an endearing, clownlike expression. When they were finished, he went and petted them and gave them lump sugar from the officers' mess to soothe their humiliated feelings.

He had his own comfort to see to as well. On Cooper's advice he sent a wire to Maud asking her to order certain things for him. As well as one or two items he had discovered he lacked, he asked for more cigarettes and chocolate, preferably in tins. These were not for his own consumption but for trading purposes.

'Chocklit an' ciggies, sir, good as coin o' the realm,' Cooper said. 'Better in fact, 'cause once you're in a war zone, money don't count for much any more. But most people'll do anything for a fag or a munch o' choc.'

By Sunday the 9th of August most of the muddle had been sorted out, and the barracks had ceased to resemble an eastern bazaar. The various companies formed up for church parade in good order and immense good cheer at the prospect – according to the grapevine – of a real blow-out of roast beef and pud when it was over. Bertie was satisfied that he had made a start on learning the names and faces of the men under his command. He had got to know a little of his platoon lieutenants – Yerbury, Oxshott,

Buckingham and, pleasantly for him, Pennyfather – and the NCOs; and had settled back with very little difficulty into army routines.

At dinner that night Colonel Abernethy tinkled his fork against his glass, and when silence had fallen, he said, 'I am able to tell you now that the advance parties of the BEF crossed secretly to France yesterday, and that we shall be in the forefront of the main force – an honour that I know this regiment will live up to. We shall entrain tomorrow morning for Southampton, and it is expected that we will sail tomorrow evening for France. Jimmy Penkridge will give you all your orders separately after dinner.'

Bertie noticed a little stir out of the corner of his eye and, turning his head, saw one of the mess servants – usually so impassive and immobile – address an urgent remark to his neighbour, who quelled him with a fierce frown. It made the following question, from Athersuch, somewhat point-less: 'Will we be informing the men, sir?'

'Yes, certainly. Some of them may want to get off last letters home.'

But word would have gone round the barracks like wild-fire, long before any of them left the table, Bertie thought.

The colonel had a few more things to say about the depar-ture from barracks, and then as general conversation broke out, the second in command, Major Beavor, raised his voice to say, 'There is one more thing: Lord Kitchener's address.'

'Whitehall, ain't it?' Harcourt-Miller drawled.

Beavor continued: 'As you know, on the 5th of August Field Marshal Lord Kitchener succeeded Lord Haldane as Secretary of State for War – the first serving officer ever to hold the post, by the bye. His lordship has gone to consid-erable trouble to compose an inspirational personal address to the men, a copy to be distributed to every soldier of the Expeditionary Force on the eve of his going overseas. The NCOs will distribute them this evening, and it's only right that all officers should have one, too. Penkridge, if you'd be so kind?'

The adjutant got up and walked round the table, handing one to each officer.

Bertie read it. The first paragraph was about honour, courage, patience, discipline, the traditional standards of the British Army – in effect, not letting the side down. The second began with an exhortation to treat the French and Belgians with courtesy and consideration and to avoid looting or damaging property. It was the latter part of the second paragraph that took Bertie's attention – and, to judge by the murmurs about him, that of his brother officers.

Your duty cannot be done unless your health is sound. So keep constantly on your guard against any excesses. In this new experience you may find temptations both in wine and women. You must entirely resist both temptations, and, while treating all women with perfect courtesy, you should avoid all intimacy.

These fervent words were causing suppressed hilarity all round the table, and even Bertie had difficulty in suppressing a grin as he thought of some of the men in his company. Kitchener himself was a man who notoriously had no time for women, and the latter temptation he spoke of was probably a mystery to him.

Beside Bertie, Wetherall said quietly, 'Well, this'll give the men something to cheer 'em up on the eve of departure. Nothing like a hearty laugh for dispelling any apprehension they might have.'

Fenniman spoke up seriously, addressing Beavor with a perplexed frown on his brows: 'Sir, this part about avoiding intimacy. I'm afraid some of the men may not understand what it means. If they ask questions, should I direct them to you?'

Beavor flushed a little, and said testily, 'I'm sure you can answer any questions yourself.'

'Oh, no, sir, really,' said Fenniman. 'Outside my family I don't know any women intimately.'

'Shut up, Fen,' murmured Harcourt-Miller.

The colonel stared coldly down the table at Fenniman and said, 'I suggest we remember the respect due to rank, and the danger to discipline if it is not seen to be accorded.'

Fenniman bowed his head in acknowledgement and as general conversation broke out again said cheerfully, 'Well, that's one for me! The Old Man had me that time. But I doubt the men will feel similar restraint in commenting on the great and good.'

He was right. Kitchener's address, which was supposed to be folded up and carried by each man inside his paybook as a constant reminder, caused great hilarity in the ranks, and gave the last night in barracks an air of festivity. Some of Bertie's company turned it into a chant, which he guessed he would hear again when the men were on the march:

> *Treat all women with court-acy*
> *While avoiding inti-macy . . .*

The next morning the battalion marched out, passing through Sandridge village on its way to the railway station. Word had evidently got out that they were off to war, for the residents were out in force to cheer them on their way, waving flags, holding up babies, throwing flowers. Small children skipped alongside or marched in step, stray dogs and errand boys on bicycles skirled around, and one young woman darted up and kissed one of the soldiers before running back to the crowd, pink-cheeked and already in tears. Bertie guessed she had been 'walking out' with him.

Bertie was riding Nightshade, who skittered a little at all the noise and attention, flicking his ears back and forth and peeking about him. Looking for hounds, Bertie thought, soothing his neck. When would they hunt together again? Not this winter, whatever the men and most of the civilians thought. Kitchener had talked about three years, and Bertie respected his judgement – in that, if not in the matter of advice to Tommies about women and wine.

It was a long and tedious day of travel. The commandeered train was waiting for them with steam up, but getting everyone and the horses and stores aboard was a lengthy business, and then the journey was slow and frequently interrupted as the train had to wait for signals or was moved to a subsidiary line to allow another, more important, to pass it. The initial excitement of the men died away, and they settled down to a soldier's more usual game of waiting. Smoking, chatting, playing cards or snoozing with their caps over their eyes, they passed the hours comfortably enough.

At Southampton the process of embarkation was even longer, for though the men could be marched smartly enough up the gangplanks, loading the horses was a far more arduous business. It was heartbreaking, too, for anyone who cared about horses, to see their terror as they were swayed up one by one with a canvas sling under their bellies, legs dangling, eyes bulging with fear, then swung over and lowered by the crane into the dark pit of the hold. There they were close-tethered in tiny stalls, deep below the water-line where the movement of the waves would be felt least. Bertie went down between embarkation and sailing to check on his own two, and already the dark hold – lit only by safety lanterns – was stiflingly hot, and the air smelled so strongly of ammonia from the urine and dung, it made his eyes smart. There was a continual chorus of unhappy neighing and restless stamping, and Bertie was reminded of lost souls in torment. He only hoped it would be a short voyage and a calm crossing.

It was a hope only partly answered. They completed embarkation soon after four p.m., but the order to sail did not come through until nine thirty. During the hours of waiting Bertie went down often to check on the horses – so often that Fenniman screwed in his eyeglass to give him a stern look and say, 'Oh, Lord, Parke, can't you sit still for two minutes together? You're up and down so often you're making me feel seasick, and we're not even moving.'

Kestrel and Nightshade were bearing up better than some, though they were sweating heavily and looked extremely miserable. He talked to them and petted them, but there wasn't much else he could do for them, and he returned to the deck cabin he was sharing with his fellow officers for the evening meal. During embarkation rations were carried 'on the man', and by pooling the various picnic items each had brought with him, they made up a pretty good meal. It featured tinned *foie gras* and biscuits, hard-boiled eggs, cold chicken, fruit, and some Stilton, which Harcourt-Miller decreed in his usual drawl had better be eaten up before they all died of asphyxiation. He recalled the episode of the cheese in *Three Men in a Boat*, and the meal ended in cheerful laughter.

They sailed at last. Bertie went out on deck to look. The sky was flushed red in the west with the last of the sunset; the sea was the glassy dark blue of enamel, and the land outcrops were painted in soft strokes of dusty purple. His country! It was so majestic and beautiful he felt a great surge of love that squeezed his heart, and for a moment there were tears in his eyes. When would he see it again? Whatever was to come, it was worth it – this England of theirs – worth every pain and toil and drop of blood that might be demanded. He remembered his little son left behind, and said a prayer in his mind that if he did not come back the boy would grow up to love it as much and serve it as faithfully.

The crossing took six hours. After creeping along the coast to Dover, the ship, which Harcourt-Miller had christened the *Tuppenny Sick*, swung out towards Boulogne. The Channel was remarkably calm, according to its own lights, but even so the shorter, steeper waves sent one or two of the men staggering to the rails. There was enough pitch and roll to have the horses continually scrabbling for foothold, and Bertie's checks found them increasingly distressed. He gave them water, stroked their trembling necks, and wished, as the suffering do, for dawn.

In the early hours Bertie woke from a fitful doze to creep out of the cabin and go below again. On another trip he had seen the groom, Williams, checking on the horses, but this time, to his surprise, he found Cooper there, standing between Kestrel and Nightshade and talking to them. They seemed much more comfortable than before, and when he came closer he saw that each was wearing a sack over its back. The sack had been partly stuffed with straw, and the straw pushed to the two ends, so that, with the empty middle part lying over the saddle-patch, the stuffed parts formed a sort of wedge between the horse's flank and the side of the stall, cushioning it and helping to keep it steady.

'Did you do that, Cooper?' Bertie asked.

'Yessir. Learned it on the South Africa campaign. Lost I dunno how many 'orses on the ship going to the Cape – mind you, it was crossing the Bay o' Biscay done it. Always rough on the Bay o' Biscay – nothing like this 'ere. Shocking cruel to 'orses that was. But your two seems to be doin' all right, sir.' And he crooned to the horses, who flicked their ears at him and seemed to sigh and settle more happily. Kestrel had even half closed his eyes.

'You have a remarkable way with them,' Bertie said. 'I'm very grateful. But really, there's no need for you to do this.'

'Ah, I like 'orses, sir,' Cooper said simply. 'I seen you was worried about 'em, so I popped down. You don't need to stay now, sir. You go on up atop and get some shuteye, sir, and I'll stick with 'em for a bit.'

They were off the French coast at Boulogne in the darkness before dawn. Bertie was woken by the cessation of movement and engine noise, and crept out, shivering in the early chill, to the rail. He could see the lights of the port, and just discern the darker bulk of the land against the sky; could smell, too, the difference in the air, which had tangs of tar and fish and oil mixed with the salt. As he stood watching, the first greyness began to seep into the dark, diluting it towards morning. The stars disappeared; the loom of the land grew sharper-edged, the lines of buildings etched themselves around the lights he had been watching, which themselves faded back into the grey. France! Though he had spent years in Africa and India, he had never been to England's nearest neighbour. He thought of snails, garlic, can-can dancers, the Eiffel Tower, King Edward at Biarritz, French fashion houses, all the conventional images, but all he had before him was a harbour that could have been anywhere: cranes and dockyard buildings, a mass of vessels, and a low, amorphous grey foreshore.

This was all any of them were to see of France for many more hours, for the port was crowded with shipping, and the word went round that they were likely to have a long wait for a berth. Bertie did the rounds of his own company and found that the men did not seem to mind the delay. They were in high spirits at finding themselves so close to a foreign land, and jostled each other at the railings. For most of the regulars it was the first time they had been abroad, the first country other than their own they had ever seen, and they were thrilled by the whole experience. Veteran reservists might tell them improbable tales about their exotic adventures in India, Egypt or South Africa, but it did not damp their enthusiasm, or their conviction that France was to provide them with the experience of a lifetime.

The sun rose, the grey of sea and sky deepened slowly to blue, the grey of the land acquired browns and greens and yellows, and the sparkling of the gently heaving water added to the gaiety of the scene. There was enough to look at and talk about to keep the men amused for hours, and the constant rumours that they were about to move kept the excitement at buzzing pitch. The day broadened towards noon, and at last the latest rumour that a berth had become free proved to be correct, and the ship began to move. They docked at half past twelve, and now excitement was to the fore again as the men got their first sight of real French people. As well as the dock workers, sailors and Customs officials, policemen and military men, the quayside was crowded with well-wishers. The men lined the sides and shouted greetings, waved and were waved to. Few of the crowd below spoke more English than 'Tommee! Tommee!' and none of the soldiers spoke French, but goodwill needed no language – although one of Bertie's reservists, who had served in South Africa, shouted to the natives in Afrikaans, on the grounds that a foreign language was a foreign language and they were all much the same, weren't they?

The adjutant came to the deckhouse where Bertie and his fellow officers were tidying themselves and packing up their belongings.

'We're going to start disembarking in company order,' he said. 'The problem is that the horses can't be got off until all the men are ashore. A detachment from A Company will be told off to help the Transport Corps, but even so it's going to take hours to unload them. Obviously we can't have the entire battalion standing around the dockyard, so the colonel's order is for all officers to lead their companies and platoons on foot.'

'On foot!' Fenniman exclaimed in horror. 'How far is it to the camp?'

'About four miles, I understand,' said Penkridge, who seemed to Bertie to be enjoying himself. 'And all uphill,' he added. 'Quite a steep hill, from what I remember. I was here in the year two with my people, and I remember thinking then what a *very* steep hill it was.'

'Penkers, my boy, I won't be mocked,' Fenniman said. 'I haven't walked four miles since I was gazetted. Find me a motor-car, an omnibus – even a motor-cycle!'

'No go,' said Penkridge, smiling. 'The colonel's going to lead the whole battalion on his own two feet, so he's not likely to let you off.'

'Oh, my blessed corns!' Fenniman groaned, rolling his eyes.

Penkridge paused at the door to mention over his shoulder, 'It's jolly hot outside as well. Probably you haven't noticed it in here.' And he disappeared.

It was an experience Bertie never forgot. The old town of Boulogne was built up the side of a hill, a place of tall grey buildings and narrow cobbled streets rising steeply to the ancient walled citadel. It was a hot afternoon, with a hint of sultriness that the narrowness of the streets and the height of the buildings intensified. The men were in full kit – pack, rifle, valise, 120 rounds in the pouches, and iron rations – in all weighing around fifty pounds. Bertie was saved the weight of rifle and pack, but his uniform felt hot and scratchy in the stifling streets, and the great round cobbles were as difficult and uncomfortable for him to walk on in his riding boots as for the men in their hobnails.

But as they plodded and slipped, faces red and glistening with sweat, up the cruel hill, they were surrounded on every side by cheering, delighted crowds. The whole of the town must have turned out, for the pavements were crammed and spilling over so that there was barely passage through the middle for the marching men. People hung out of windows, shrieking and waving; hand-held tricolor flags fluttered everywhere; children rushed up to give the soldiers flowers and sweets; soft-eyed young women smiled, blushed, and blew kisses. They cried 'welcome' and 'Tommee' and 'souvenir'. Young women were the most vociferous about the latter. They offered tricolor ribbons and rosettes and begged souvenirs in exchange, and when the grinning men did not understand or could not comply, some girls snatched at their buttons or tore off their cap badges. It did not make for smart marching or good discipline, but the warmth of the welcome and the delight of the townspeople that their allies had arrived were so tangible they lifted the battalion. Afterwards Bertie's memories were a strange mixture of euphoria and discomfort: of the hardness of the cobbles, the sweat trickling down inside his shirt, the aching of his leg muscles, and of the multicoloured, beaming, swaying mass of people, the pink faces, wide-mouthed, the reaching hands, the hats waved above heads, the wildly agitated flags, all saying in a language that needed no translation, *We are so glad you are here!*

Beyond the old citadel there was another long – though happily less steep – hill before they reached the top and the camp, a square mile of heathland on which the tents and horse lines had already been set up by the advance parties. Other regiments were already there, having come in during the morning, and from this eminence it was possible to see more troop ships waiting outside the harbour for a berth. The men were lined up, roll call was taken, and then they were dismissed to settle in.

Bertie was hungry and tired, but there was a stream of questions to be answered and complaints to be dealt with before he could find Cooper, his tent and something to eat. The first thing the men wanted was beer, and the queue outside the beer tent sprang full grown into existence almost the moment dismiss was called. The queue collapsed in on itself when it was discovered that beer had to be paid for in French money, and re-formed outside the paymaster's tent. A further problem was encountered here: the army did not have an unlimited supply of small change, and as man after man proffered his scraped-together pennies and ha'pennies the paymaster lost patience and decreed that the lowest amount that could be exchanged was eightpence, which could be translated into a one-franc coin. With beer costing the equivalent of twopence a pint, a thirsty Tommy had to get together with three pals before he could change his money and buy the necessary. It was a good way of building friendships within the ranks, Bertie thought, as he left the details of settling in to the NCOs and retired at last to eat.

The camp was not yet fully equipped so there was no provision for hot food, and the men were preparing, not without grumbling, to follow the beer down with their iron rations of bully and biscuit. Bertie had the remains of the picnic food he had brought for the journey, which were hardly up to the demands being made on them; but Cooper appeared miraculously with a foot-long garlic sausage, a jar of olives and a bottle of wine to augment them.

'Good Lord! Where the devil did you get those?' Bertie cried.

'Swapped for 'em, sir, with a Frenchy,' said Cooper impassively. 'There's a 'ole crowd o' Frenchies come up the 'ill, 'angin' around outside the camp callin' out for soovy-neers. Well, mostly they're young women, sir, and we all know what they want, but there was one bloke there looked like a shopkeeper, so I 'as a chat with 'im—'

'How?' Bertie interrupted.

'Oh, I know a bit of the old polly-voo,' Cooper said mysteriously. 'Anyway, the upshot is, sir, I got these 'ere, he got his soovy-neer, everybody's 'appy.'

'What did you swap?' Bertie asked, hoping it wasn't a vital part of his equipment.

'A tin ashtray, sir. Out o' your billet back at the barracks. It's got the regimental crest on it, you see, sir.' He met Bertie's eye blandly. 'Brought it with me just in case, but I reckoned you could do without it after all, sir.'

A number of questions jumped to Bertie's lips but he let them die there. How on earth had Cooper known before they left that anything with the regimental crest on it was going to be in demand by the locals? Or was there an even more convoluted 'wangle' in the background? This was not the time to upset the equilibrium. 'I'm very grateful to you,' he said, thinking that with the last of the biscuits he had a reasonable meal here.

'I dunno what these 'ere is,' Cooper said, looking doubtfully at the olives, 'but the Frenchy threw 'em in fer nuthin'. However,' he cheered up, 'I do 'appen to know, sir, as Captain Fenniman 'as a 'ole tinned pheasant in his kit, and Captain Harcourt-Miller 'as a tin o' peaches.'

Bertie smiled. 'What an excellent idea, Cooper. In times of hardship we should all share and share alike, don't you think?'

'My sentiments exactly, sir.'

It was a beautiful evening, clear and warm, and as it faded into violet dusk and then to velvet night, some of the Tommies left the beer tents and in the dark slipped past the pickets onto the downs, there to further the entente by a frank exchange of views with the young females of Boulogne who were waiting for them. Shadows flitted between the shrubs, outcrops and gorse bushes, and murmured conversation and muffled laughter enlivened the midnight hour. Returning from the horse lines where he had checked one last time that Kestrel and Nightshade were recovering from their ordeal, Bertie heard the suppressed giggles coming out of the darkness, and reflected that Field Marshal Kitchener had never had much hope of making his last two exhortations stick.

It was on Thursday the 13th of August that the four squadrons that comprised the Royal Flying Corps contingent of the BEF set out for France. They flew from Swingate Downs, near Dover, to the applause of an admiring crowd, in the sixty-three airworthy machines that Sir David Henderson had been able to scrape together, mostly Bristol BE2s and Maurice Farman biplanes known as Shorthorns.

Jack had hoped to fly one of them, but it was not to be. He was still undergoing his basic training – an odd and solitary thing, underlining his unusual position. Other flyers in training were infantry or artillery subalterns who had asked or been chosen to be attached to the RFC. They knew how to be soldiers: now they had to learn how to fly. Jack, by contrast, knew how to fly: he had to learn to be a soldier and an officer.

His training was undertaken by an NCO who seemed rather bemused at the task he had been given and, though he did not say as much, his comments were often instinct with the words, 'Don't you even know *that*?' He had to teach Jack how to march, how to manoeuvre a squad, how to handle a Lee Enfield, how, when and whom to salute, how to put on his uniform, how kit ought to be stowed, how to conduct an inspection. Jack had to learn the hierarchy of the army, and all the arcane language that surrounded the business of being a soldier of any rank. He did a great deal of firing and bayonet practice, and proved to have a good eye for the former, and not much stomach for the latter.

The difficulty was that the NCO had other duties to perform as well as teaching Jack, and could not devote all his time to him. Jack fretted at the waste of time when he was left to his own devices, but his instructor told him he should use the time to 'get yourself fit', and when his other duties called would as likely as not send Jack off on a solitary cross-country run. Jack had not thought of himself as a soft, unfit civilian, but only a few days of his new regime proved the case, and he began to fine down, to harden, and to go to the mess at the end of the day both tired out and ravenous.

He was something of an object of curiosity there, for the other trainee officers were younger than him, and the solitary nature of his training gave them the idea he was learning something secret and highly important. They were friendly, but in a deferential way. His entry into the mess was usually greeted by a silence, after which conversation would resume softly on the eternally fascinating subject of 'shop', while he ate alone and listened without appearing to.

They talked about spinning and diving, stalling and banking, and all the perils of getting something wrong. They were learning on Longhorns – pusher biplanes of now antique appearance, so called because they had a forward elevator mounted on long, curved outriggers. Longhorns would leave the ground at around thirty-five miles an hour, and their top speed was around forty-six.

'It seems to me,' one fresh-faced young man, Collins, said, 'that it's a bit like walking the tightrope. You've only got ten miles an hour to play with. If you go too fast, something's bound to snap or break off; if you go too slowly, you stall, and end up nose-diving into the ground and breaking your neck.'

'Yes, and if you run the engine at full speed for too long, it'll overheat and you'll lose power,' said another, Phillips. 'I suppose flying must be as much an art as a science.'

'Rather more art than science, to my mind,' said Collins. 'It strikes me the scientists are just waiting for us to find things out by accident and then let them know what's possible. How steeply can you bank? Keep trying until you go into a spin and crash, then you'll know. How steeply can you dive? Keep trying until the strain pulls the wings off! They sit there in their cosy offices while we risk our lives . . .'

At this point a grin had spread over Jack's face, which could hardly be missed by the other young men. Collins broke off and eyed him rather stiffly. 'Have I said something funny, sir?'

'No, not at all. I beg your pardon,' Jack said quickly. He had been remembering his office – cramped and over-crowded with papers but still cosy enough in comparison with the heathland he had run over that afternoon. 'I was just thinking about something.'

Now that the ice had been broken, Phillips asked the thing that had been exercising them all. 'I say, sir, we never see you at flying instruction. If you're not here to learn to fly – I mean, dashed impertinent of me to ask, but we all wonder—'

A third young man, Impey, said, 'One of the instructors said you could fly already. Is that true, sir?'

'You shouldn't call me "sir",' said Jack. 'I'm not even a second lieutenant yet. In fact, I'm in a sort of limbo.'

'We don't know your name,' said Impey.

'It's Compton. Jack Compton.'

Collins's jaw dropped a little. 'Not Compton of Sopwiths? Not Jack Compton the test pilot? I've seen you fly at Hendon, sir.'

'I saw you at Brooklands last year,' said Phillips. 'But you're a designer, too, aren't you, sir? You designed the Howard Wright monoplane.'

They crowded round him now, eager with questions. When did he first 'go solo'? What was it like flying a Tabloid? Was a Howard Wright better than a Maurice Farman? Had he flown a Blériot, a Martynside, a BE2? Had he ever 'looped'? No wonder he didn't come to flying instruction. Probably he could teach the instructor a thing or two! But then, why was he here?

So Jack was obliged to tell them, afraid that they would laugh at him. But they didn't laugh. They were shocked and sympathetic. How ghastly to be such an accomplished flyer and yet have to learn all that military nonsense before he could be allowed to fly in France!

'We'll help you, sir,' said Collins – it seemed he was never going to get them out of the habit of calling him that, Jack thought. He supposed it was his age that was to blame. 'I mean, we know all that tosh back to front. If there's anything we can do to get you out there quickly . . .'

So they helped him, talking through the evenings about every aspect of army life that occurred to them, answering his questions and resolving his puzzles. In response, he told them about flying, gave them hints and rules, talked about the aeroplanes and engines he had worked on and hoped to work on.

When the RFC left for France without him on the 13th he was depressed, and his nightly telephone call to Helen was full of gloom and the supposition that he would be left here, forgotten, for ever. If he had learned one thing in his short acquaintance with the army it was that things were always being forgotten. 'If a thing doesn't have the right paperwork, it doesn't get done, no matter if everyone is looking straight at it. I bet someone's forgotten a piece of paper in my case, and I shall just moulder here, half in and half out of the army, until the war's over.'

'You've only been there a week,' Helen pointed out patiently, 'and you told me they said it might be two weeks.'

'Two weeks *or less*,' he corrected.

'Well, it still *is* less than two weeks. Darling, don't be glum. I'm sure they haven't forgotten you. They wouldn't go to all that trouble to recruit you and then forget you.'

'You don't know the army,' he said.

'Of course I do, you idiot. Daddy was an officer.'

He laughed, the tension dispersing. 'Oh, I do miss you,' he said. 'I wish I could see you.'

'I wish it too,' she said. 'It seems like months already.'

'I'll have to go now,' Jack said. 'Someone else is waiting to use the telephone. I'll call you tomorrow at the same time.'

The next day when his instructor had finished with him, instead of sending him on a long run or march, he looked rather more sympathetic than was his wont, and said, 'There's a Longhorn no-one's using just now, Mr Compton. Would you like to take it up for a spin? Keep your hand in, so to speak?'

Jack grinned, realising he was being comforted again, and said, 'I certainly would, Sergeant!'

'Right-oh, sir. I don't need to tell you to be careful and not to get lost, do I? The mechanics know you're coming.'

It was a warm, still day, a little muggy, but clear enough and with no threat of rain. Jack walked towards the sheds and felt his heart lifting at the prospect of going up, and realised how much he had been missing it without knowing. There was the Longhorn waiting like a docile cow outside her byre, with a couple of mechanics leaning against her wings. To a man used to more modern aeroplanes it looked antique, a forest of struts and spars covered with dingy white canvas, meshed about with an impenetrable tangle of wires, in the centre of which was the nacelle – a term borrowed from ballooning – where the pilot sat. To a layman it would not have been obvious which was the front and which the back, since the elevator sticking out at the front was balanced by a double set of stabilisers sticking out at the rear.

Jack put on his flying cap and nodded to the mechanics. He climbed through the labyrinth of wire and onto the nacelle.

'All right, sir? Switch off?'

'Switch off,' said Jack, and pulled his goggles down and adjusted them.

'Contact?'

'Contact,' said Jack. After a couple of swings the engine clattered into life. He felt the warm draught of it behind him, its unemphatic sound like a couple of alarm clocks ticking on the nursery mantelpiece, hardly seeming to have the strength to move the aeroplane and him, let alone get them off the ground. It was strange to have no propellor in front of him, only the forward elevator, like a tea-tray suspended above the ground. But he felt safe in this kindly, gentle beast from the past. He waved to the mechanics and they pulled the blocks away, and the Longhorn trundled forward over the rough turf, lurching a little, the draught from the propellor making the grass ripple below him. He adjusted the throttle, the alarm clocks ticked more insistently, the elderly beast broke into an ungainly canter, and then, light as thistledown, rose into the air. It was an action so easy, so natural, so without fuss or fanfare, that it was almost as though the earth had peeled itself away from underneath.

Gently they climbed, and Jack felt absolutely at one with the Longhorn, the blue sky and the warm day. The airfield resolved itself quickly into green field, brown wooden buildings, dark hedges, then sank backwards into a larger landscape of squares of green and harvest gold, of roads, houses, and clumps of trees like dyed cottonwool on a toy train's layout. Hills folded themselves down into clefts; little villages nestled around the spires of churches; tiny brown cows and tinier sheep grazed in squares of the patchwork. The air speed rose to forty-six, the engine ticked away reliably behind him, and the wind of their movement sang in the rigging wires, a high, thin, sweet song he heard with something other than his ear. His feet and hands moved the controls smoothly without his knowing, operating by instinct; he was utterly happy.

He thought of Helen and how much he loved her; he thought about the war – the romance of it, the mystery and uncertainty of it, the chivalric ordeal of it. He was going to do his duty, to fight for England and decency and honour, and to deserve Helen. And up here he had no apprehension. All he wanted now was to get going, to start on the adventure. He had always felt at home in the air: it was his element, and it could not hurt him.

He had only another day of frustration to endure. On the Saturday morning, the 15th, the commanding officer sent for him, and told him that he had been gazetted to the RFC, and should report to the tailor's shop immediately to have his insignia and wings sewn on to his uniform. 'And if there's any last-minute things you have to do, you'd better do 'em,' he said, smiling, 'because you've got orders for France. You leave tomorrow morning.'

'I'm flying out, sir?' said Jack, trying to sound sensible, though his heart was beating faster and his thoughts whirling.

'No, you'll be going by train and boat. They've got a couple of Tabloids in crates in the aircraft park at St Omer – I think you're going to be given one of them. Things are hotting up out there,' he added seriously, 'and experienced pilots like you are badly needed.'

His new-found friends in the mess were delighted for him, cheered, clapped him on the back, admired his uniform – especially the wings, which they were all working to acquire – and wished they were going too. Helen's congratulations, when he telephoned her, were a little more muted, but she said all the right things, and promised to take good care of Rug for him. After he'd hung up, he remembered that he had promised her a photograph of himself in uniform. He had to get special permission to go into town that afternoon, and he left the money and Helen's address with the photographer, and received his promise to post a print to her as soon as it was ready.

CHAPTER FIVE

Amerval, near Le Cateau, Sunday 16th August

My dear Jessie,

I wrote to you a little about our journey to Boulogne. We were not there long – perhaps a good thing, given the passion of the local young ladies for our Tommies. Soon we were bumped out of bed to make way for more battalions coming in from England. We were up at 4.30 on departure day, but something went wrong with the arrangements for breakfast, and nothing was forthcoming but some tins of jam! The men grumbled mightily, but tucked in anyway with spoons.

We paraded at 5.30 and marched off to the sidings, where we had our first sight of a French troop train: forty common-or-garden-variety cattle trucks! On the side of each wagon it said 'HOMMES 40, CHEVAUX 8'. We were in some suspense as to whether this meant '40 men or 8 horses' or '40 men *and* 8 horses' – an anxiety each man felt more acutely as he was joined on the straw inside by 39 companions! The men were dreadfully cramped, and there was some grumbling, but on the whole they took it like good sports, and managed to make a joke of it in Tommy fashion. When the good people of Boulogne waved us off, our men responded with choruses of 'moo-o-o' and 'baa-a-a'.

We officers were treated more gently, with a cou of elderly first-class carriages hitched on for our be

93

They lacked anything so civilised as a corridor, and I was glad it was summer, as our compartment had no glass in its windows. The journey was tediously slow. Because of the great length and weight of the train, it could not do more than ten miles an hour, and generally not so much. Still, the advantage was that one could get down and stretch one's legs, or answer the call of nature, and easily catch up with one's carriage further down the track.

There were innumerable stops, for no apparent reason – we began to think the train needed to catch its breath! Wherever we stopped, a knot of little boys instantly appeared from nowhere with their cries of 'Tommee!' and 'Souvenir!' and begging for cigarettes. The men had only their iron rations of bully and biscuit (thirsty eating in hot weather), but the stops at least allowed them to brew up – tea is their life blood. One of the men in B Company couldn't wait for a stop. He jumped down while the train was in motion, ran up to the front, filled his dixie with hot water from the engine, then waited by the track until his wagon came by and jumped back in. We officers did better, with a luncheon basket of hard-boiled eggs, cheese, garlic sausage and fresh bread. All 'thirsty food' again. We were tempted by the orchards we were passing, but though the trees were laden with fruit we didn't see any that was ripe.

We arrived at last at Le Cateau and dispersed into billets. The countryside around here is very pretty, but growing every day more full of Tommies. My company is billeted in a farm in a little village, the men in the barns and outbuildings, the horses in the orchard. We officers have palliasses in the farmhouse attic – a long, low, bare wooden space under the roof beams, which creaks at night like a ship at sea. One advantage of being first out to France is that we now have a breathing space while we wait for the rest of the BEF to assemble here. gives us a chance to knock the men into shape. The her has been glorious, and early-morning route marches are actually a pleasure, when the air is still fresh and the dew is on the grass.

The farms here are suffering because the men are away at the war and the crops are ready. For once HQ used its imagination and ordered our men to help with the harvest. So every day they work in the fields in the sunshine, stripped to their shirts or sometimes their skin. They seem to love it – if it were not for the uniforms you'd think it was one long Bank Holiday outing! The women make a tremendous fuss of them. They call them heroes, and bring them out the local cider by the bucketful at midday, and at night provide wonderful stews of fresh meat, redolent of herbs, and fresh bread. Afterwards the men sit around campfires under the stars and sing the strangely maudlin songs they seem to like best when they're happy. I'm sure the regulars who have no battle experience are being given entirely the wrong impression of war. Most of them have never had a holiday like it in their lives. Perhaps they are right to take what comes without thinking too much of the future. It is pleasure now – later it will be pain and hardship. The stoicism we expect of the men comes from the same source as their present thoughtless happiness.

But for me it is a very strange feeling, having set out to war, to be enjoying such an idyllic interlude. Our hostess, Madame Albert, and her family are very kind. They show great gratitude, not only for the help with harvesting but for the fact that we are here at all, ready to face Le Boche – which is to say Le Diable. I am enjoying superb home cooking (Madame's *lapin à la moutarde* is a poem), drinking hearty rustic wine, playing cards in the evening with our hosts and my officers, and sleeping far too well each night in my creaking ship of an attic. I think rather guiltily of the concern with which you sent me off to war, but at least I am able to wri' you this long letter. Later it will be a much more ha scribble.

The only thing that concerns me is that we ha

war news, even when we fetch a newspaper from the town and laboriously translate it. There is much patriotic verbiage, and reports of stirring victories in the east, but as to what's happening over here on the left wing not a word, which strikes us as both odd and ominous.

Write to me. The field postal service is excellent and I shall have anything you send within two days. I am slipping into a delicious drowse, like a drunken bee, and need to be kept in mind of what I am here to fight for.

Your loving cousin,

Bertie

The plan had always been for the BEF to take up position on the French left flank, to the west of General Lanrezac and his Fifth Army, there to guard the Belgian border while the French conducted the real war on the right flank. The French had always assumed the Germans would attack in strength on the Franco-German border through the disputed territories of Alsace and Lorraine, and that any German movement in Belgium would be merely a feint, intended to distract them and tempt them to move troops away from the real theatre of war.

However, it was clear to many, Bertie included, that the left flank was the weakest spot, and that if the Germans attacked there in force, they might win decisively and march on to Paris; or they might outflank the BEF to the west, which would leave them an open road to Calais and Boulogne. The consequences of either were too horrible to contemplate. The BEF was a fine, professional body, but it was very small, hardly more than a token force compared with the French and German armies. Bertie thought it would have been better to keep it back, perhaps around Amiens, to hold open the lines of communication. If in its present position it was outflanked, encircled and overwhelmed, there would be nothing to stop the German army taking Paris, launching an invasion of England from the Channel And, Bertie told himself, if he could think of that, so did the Kaiser.

The absence of any information on the whereabouts of the German army that had been massing on Belgium's border was deeply worrying. It was the only thing that detracted from the peace of those golden harvest days and warm, starry nights at the little farm in Amerval.

Jack arrived, after a long train, boat and train journey, at St Omer, in company with two other flyers. Deane and Culverhouse had entered the RFC in the conventional way, as officers transferring from the regular army. One was twenty, the other nineteen, and they had around thirty-five hours of solo flying time to their credit, mostly in Longhorns and Shorthorns. They had heard of Jack as a designer and competition flyer, and began their journey in awe of him. Close confinement together in conditions of heat and tedium wore that away, and soon they were chatting easily to him, telling him about their experiences, and trying to get the benefit of his expertise with eager questions. It was rather like being back at the training school. They were charming young fellows, Jack thought, probably the delight of their mothers and sisters, and bubbling with enthusiasm for their present and future position. From what he gathered they were pretty much going to win the war unaided, and were looking forward to celebrating Christmas in Potsdam.

Jack said he had other plans entirely.

They arrived at the station at five in the morning of Monday the 17th, and stepped out of the train into the cool of a grey, sunless dawn. Jack looked automatically up at the sky, and tested the wind. It was still, and there was a smell to the air that suggested rain was on its way. 'Not good flying weather,' he said. 'I hope it won't delay us.'

'Golly, yes,' said Deane. 'I want to get up to the fron' right away. I wonder if we'll fly up.'

'I hope so,' said Culverhouse. 'I didn't come all this ʋ to sit about on trains and transports. They didn't act ʲ say, but they more or less promised me a BE2 as so I got here.'

'You've only been up in one once,' Deane objec

'Oh, anyone can fly a BE2,' Culverhouse said airily. 'That's the point of them.'

The rest of the train's passengers had dispersed and the three of them were standing alone on the platform with their kitbags. There was evidently no-one to meet them, and after a moment Jack stopped a porter hurrying by and asked him where the RFC office was. He shrugged in the most Gallic way, slithered out from under Jack's restraining hand, and disappeared. A deep early-morning peace had descended; the grey town slept.

'There's a light on along there,' Jack said at last, since the other two seemed to be looking to him to lead them. It was one of the wooden station buildings at the far end of the platform, which might once have been a coal-ordering office, and to his relief when they went in at the door they found a British Army corporal behind a desk, a sight so normal and reassuring he felt he had come home. The corporal was snoozing. His head had slipped over at an uncomfortable angle, so Jack felt no compunction about rousing him.

'Wassat? Warra want?' the man mumbled, bemused by his sudden waking.

Jack thought it ought to have been obvious from their uniforms and their presence, but he said patiently, 'We're RFC officers. We've just arrived and we don't know where to go.'

The corporal sat up, rubbed his eyes, smacked his lips and stared at them. Jack repeated his question, and the corporal shook his head. 'Not 'ere, gents. Up in the town. But there won't be nobody there yet. Won't be nobody nowhere this time o' the morning.' He gave them a knowing look. 'You'd do best to go and get yerselves some grub while ʼer can. Take it from an old sojer, gents – whenever nobody ɔnʼt want you for nothing else, get some grub, and get ɟe shut-eye. You never know when you'll get the chance ʌ.'

told them where there would be a café open, and ʻo find the HQ office, and then followed his own ʌ opening a drawer of the desk and removing a paper package, which he unwrapped to reveal a large ham sandwich. The sight of it reminded the three pilots that they were hungry and thirsty. They thanked him and walked out into the silent town, and up the cobbled street to the little patch of yellow light that marked out the café from the closed and shuttered shops all around.

Inside it was steamy, smoky and smelled welcomingly of coffee. Railway workers in their dark blue cotton jackets and black caps were sitting at several of the battered metal tables drinking coffee, reading newspapers and smoking execrable French cigarettes that smelled like burning compost. The counter was a bar, with shelves of bottles behind it, *pression* taps along it, and a monstrous hissing coffee urn at the far end. It was presided over by a large woman, as fully coiffed and maquillaged as if she had been going out to dinner. There was no sign of food, but when Jack asked hesitantly if one might find here *quelque chose à manger,* she beamed and said, '*Bien sûr, bien sûr! Pour les pilotes anglais, tout ce que vous désirez.*'

Jack ordered coffee and omelettes, and when the three of them turned away from the bar to find a table, they found every eye on them, and every face beaming approval. The workers nodded to them as they took their seats and one or two addressed remarks that Jack did not understand but which fortunately did not seem to need response other than a smile.

'I say, it's a jolly good thing you speak the lingo,' said Deane, as they sat. He took out a cigarette case and offered it round. 'I learned it at school but I'm afraid it didn't stick. I can do the old "pen of my aunt" stuff, but somehow one can't imagine anywhere that'll come in useful.'

A moment later the café door opened and a pretty girl came in with half a dozen long loaves under her arm. Sh was greeted with a chorus of comment, jointly from ↑ woman behind the bar and several of the customers talking at once and gesturing towards Jack and his fr⸱ It was so rapid he could only pick out the words *anglais*'. The girl smiled at them, and blushed richl of the comments, which, accompanied by phlegr were evidently of a personal nature. She hurried through the door at the back of the salon, and emerged soon afterwards in an apron to put a basket of the fresh bread and a dish of butter in front of the Englishmen, while Madame came over with coffee in three huge cups that resembled chamberpots in thickness and colour, and were, Jack thought, not much smaller.

The omelettes came and were excellent: enormous, golden on the outside, crisp at the edges and delicately runny inside. They ate a great deal of the crusty new bread, drank second cups of the coffee, which, Culverhouse said, was 'strong enough to trot a mouse on', and then were on their way. The warmth of the farewell was such that Jack was afraid Madame would refuse to accept payment, but he was spared that embarrassment. She was French, after all, and business matters occupied a discrete pigeonhole in her mind.

Soon afterwards the three new friends were parted, for at the HQ office they were told by the transport officer – the only person available – that Deane and Culverhouse were to go up to Le Cateau by train, where there might or might not be aeroplanes for them, the officer could not say. To Jack he was rather more friendly, said they had been expecting him, and that a transport would be there in fifteen minutes or so to take him out to the airfield where the Tabloid scout had been unpacked and assembled and was waiting for him.

'You're to fly it up to Maubeuge. That's where all the aeroplanes and personnel are at present. You'll get your orders and billet when you get there.'

'How far is it?' Jack asked.

'Oh, Lord, I don't know,' said the transport officer, in a ⸺arassed way. 'Haven't you looked at the maps?'

'Only general maps, back in England. I didn't know until ⸺minute where I'd be sent.'

'⸺, very well. Wait here and I'll see what I can do.'

⸺ae and Culverhouse took the opportunity to say
'I suppose if everyone's at Maubeuge, we'll meet
⸺ Deane.

'I'm sure we will,' said Jack. 'I hope they have aeroplanes waiting for you.'

'So do I,' said Culverhouse, gloomily. 'If I thought I was going to spend the war in trains I should transfer back to the infantry.' They shook hands, took up their bags, and left to walk back to the station.

The transport officer came back at last with a map, which he spread on the table, and beckoned Jack to his side.

'Here we are, you see, at St Omer. And here's Maubeuge. It's quite easy, if you follow the road to Lille and then Valenciennes, and then it's a straight road to Maubeuge. Just be sure to follow the right road at Lille, or you'll end up in Brussels.'

'And when I get to Maubeuge?'

'Oh, I dare say you'll see the aeroplanes all right. I'm sure you can recognise an airfield better than me,' he said rather crossly.

A head poked itself round the door to say that the tender for the aerodrome was outside, and Jack picked up his kit and the map and said thank you and goodbye.

'I say, you're not taking that map, are you?' said the officer.

'I thought you were giving it to me,' said Jack. 'I shall certainly need it.'

'Oh, very well. But it's a damned nuisance. I'm not made of maps, you know.'

At the aerodrome they were much more friendly, and took him straight away to the Tabloid, which had been run out from the shed and was waiting for him. He felt a sense of coming home at the sight of the familiar neat, work-manlike shape of the aeroplane he had helped to design and develop, and had flown so many times in exhibitions and races. It almost seemed to smile at him.

'Don't need to tell you anything about her, do we, sir?' said the mechanic, with a grin. 'Want to look her over, make sure we put her together right?'

'I'm sure you did,' Jack said, but he looked the machine over carefully anyway, checked the log book, tested rigging, then climbed up to start the engine and warm up, listening to its satisfying growl. The last thing he flown was the Longhorn, and it was good to have the propellor in front of him again. When he was satisfied everything was running smoothly, he waved to the mechanics, who pulled away the blocks, and then he was rolling forward over the turf. The Tabloid took off like a bird, as if glad to be off. He circled the aerodrome to get his bearings, then circled the town once or twice until he felt confident he had located the road to Lille. It was very warm, there was hardly any wind, and the clouds were low and grey. He hoped they would not get any lower or greyer, and that their threat of rain would not be fulfilled.

He passed to the south of the great Forest of Clairmarais outside St Omer and picked up the road to Hazebrouck and Lille easily enough, following it but keeping to one side, flying over the fields. This part of France, on the border of Flanders, was a patchwork of little fields and hedges, and it all looked very peaceful. He saw harvesters working in the fields, a loaded farm cart drawn by two horses rocking down a narrow lane, a toy train puffing along a track with a tiny thread of smoke rising from its funnel, barges apparently immobile on a canal, they were moving so slowly. Roads were dark threads, country tracks pale ones, rivers a silvery glitter, reflecting the light. Another mass of trees to the south was the Forest of Nieppe, and shortly afterwards he crossed the River Lys, a bigger waterway, sinuously winding its way to Armentières. And then the mass of Lille was ahead of him. So far so good.

He flew to the south of Lille, knowing that his route after the city was to the south-east, hoping he would easily pick up the Valenciennes road. But there were all too many roads out of Lille, which was an industrial and commercial centre of some importance. Going by the compass he selected a road and followed it for a distance, until he felt it was making too much southing, and at a fork turned to follow he branch that bore a little more to the east. He passed er a town that he felt was much too small to be enciennes. He tried to remember the map. Were there r towns he should pass over? Now there was a canalised running parallel with the road. On the map there *was* a river running south-east out of Valenciennes but he didn't remember that it was canalised. Now the canal branched south and east, and he was pretty sure he was lost.

There was a town up ahead, a bigger town with a church spire in the centre and a wide river running north-east to south-west through it. He was not convinced that it was Valenciennes either. He would have to put down and ask directions. He passed to the north side of the town, looking for a suitable field, and found a small village just outside the town where there was a good flat pasture between what seemed to be the main road and a small cluster of farm buildings. He landed cautiously, keeping a good look out for drainage ditches, and bumped over the rough grass towards the grey stone walls of the nearest barn.

He had hardly stopped before two figures came running out from the farmyard towards him, an elderly man in working clothes and a rather more nimble young woman outstripping him despite her long skirts. He pulled off his flying cap and goggles and jumped down as the girl came panting up to him, and said, '*Bonjour, Mademoiselle. Quel est le nom de ce village, s'il vous plaît?*'

She laughed and said, 'You are English! I speak English. You are not hurt?'

'No, not hurt. Only lost.'

The old man reached them and demanded urgently, '*Qu'est-ce qu'il dit? Qu'est-ce qu'il dit?*'

She answered him in rapid French, addressing him as Grandpère, and turned to Jack again. 'He was afraid you might be German. He is very frightened that the Germans will come, but I tell him he is foolish, because the English are here. *Les anglais sont partout, Grandpère!* He wanted to hide when we saw you come down in our field.'

'Please tell him I mean no harm, only to ask directions,' said Jack, smiling what he hoped was a reassuring smile at the old man, who responded by waving his hands and breaking into rapid French in a cracked and, to Jack, unintelligible voice.

The girl addressed him sharply, and then said to Jack, 'This village is Cauroir, and the town there is Cambrai.'

'Cambrai!' said Jack. So he had come too far south. She nodded, looking at him hopefully, as if she had given him a gift of whose worth she was not sure. 'But what did you mean, that the English are everywhere?'

She waved a hand and said, 'Everywhere. *Dans tous les villages. Les soldats anglais logent partout. Le quartier générale de l'armée britannique est là-bas, à Le Cateau.*'

The name 'Le Cateau' alerted him to what *quartier générale* must mean. 'Headquarters. Of course. How far is it to Le Cateau?'

'Twenty kilometres only,' she said eagerly. 'Do you wish to go there?'

'I am on my way to Maubeuge to report,' Jack said.

'Maubeuge,' she said. 'It is perhaps forty kilometres beyond Le Cateau. A long way.'

'Not in an aeroplane,' Jack said, smiling, while the old man broke into '*Qu'est-ce qu'il dit?*' again. It would be less than an hour's flying.

The old man spoke again, and the girl said, 'Grand-pére says that there is bad rain coming and that you should shelter with us until it passes. We will give you dinner.'

Until that moment Jack had been concentrating so much on the terrestrial that he had not noticed the sky. Looking up now, startled, he realised that it had lowered and darkened to plum-purple, and the light in the distance had the strange silvery look to it that betokens heavy rain. A little cold wind had got up, ruffling the girl's hair and the back of his own neck. He gauged its strength and direction and calculated quickly that the rain would be here in ten minutes. If he took off now, he would be forced to land again very soon. And then he remembered the advice of the corporal in St Omer.

He smiled and said, with a bow to the old man, 'Thank you. You are very kind. *Vous êtes très gentil, Monsieur.*'

The old man gave a cackling laugh and waved his hands in what looked like delight, shooting rapid French at Jack and almost capering on the spot. Jack looked enquiringly at the girl. 'He says he will be the first in our village to have an *anglais* to stay – and a *pilote*, especially, is better than a Tommee. You make 'im very 'appy.'

The old man's name was Bécasse, his granddaughter was, perhaps inevitably, Marie. Jack gave his name, and Marie approved. '*Jacques*. It is like a French name. And *Comme-ton*, it is not too difficult. Some English surnames I cannot say.'

Inside the farmhouse it was very dark and almost chilly, because of the great thickness of the walls and the small-ness of the windows. The room into which he was led was, he guessed, both kitchen and sitting-room, a large, long chamber with a heavily beamed ceiling, stone floor and a massive fireplace at one end, in which a range was alight. The room smelled of unwashed bodies, dogs and, more attractively, of something meaty cooking.

'*Ici. Ici. Asseyez*,' old Bécasse said, pressing Jack down into a wooden chair at the long, scrubbed table, then hobbled off at top speed through a door at the other end, to return a little while later much more slowly, carefully bearing a full glass of beer. Jack sipped, smiled and thanked him, and the old man beamed again and, satisfied, sat down in the high-backed chair at the end of the table.

Soon Marie put down in front of Jack a large earthen-ware bowl full of something that smelled very savoury. She served herself and her grandfather, put bread and butter in the centre of the table, and sat down. Jack tasted. It was a stew of beans and onions, flavoured with garlic and herbs, in which chunks of meat had been cooked – he guessed – long and slowly, for the meat was tender and almost as soft as pâté, and its flavour had richly permeated the beans.

'It's delicious,' he said. 'What meat is it?'

There was a little duck, she said, a little pork, and some sausage. She put in whatever was to hand. Jack ate hungrily, his omelette of the morning now but a distant memory, and, seeing it was the custom of the house, mopped up every last drop of the delicious juices with hunks of bread. Meanwhile, outside, the rain had arrived, and it was almost as dark out there as it was in the kitchen. One of the small windows set deep in the thick wall was open, and through it came the sound of the rain hissing down, and the smell of wet greenness. Presently there came peals of thunder and the whiplash snap of lightning, slashing the dark with electric blue and leaving the tang of ozone on the air. The old man finished his last piece of bread, leaned back in his chair, unbuckled the enormous leather belt that seemed to hold him together in the middle, and lit a pipe, which, amazingly, smelled even worse than the cigarettes in the café. A large, old, very hairy dog crept in through the far door, plodded up to each of them in turn to smile a greeting, then ambled down to the fireplace to flop onto a rug before it, leaving behind a miasma so penetrating that Jack was glad of the pipe-smoke.

And in the atmosphere of ease, and of safety from the storm, Marie propped her elbows on the table and talked. Her father, her uncle and her brothers were all away at the war, she said, fighting the Boche. Her mother was dead many years, one sister was married and the other worked in a factory in Lille, so she had to do everything, look after Grandpère, keep house, mind the farm. Her cousin Henri, who lived in the village and was a shoemaker, helped out when he could, and there was Christophe, who had always worked for them and was an idiot so couldn't go to war; and Grandpère was still very fit, though he was not as strong as he used to be. They managed as best they could. Worst of all for her was that Pierre Picard had also gone to the war, who had been walking out with her for ten years. He was in the east, where the fighting was fiercest. She had last heard from him from Verdun. She was so afraid that something would happen to him, and then what would she do? She was so glad the English had come. Pierre and Papa had both been very worried about going to the war and leaving the farm with no man but Grandpère to guard it, in case the Boche came and overran it, but now that the *anglais* were here they would be safe, because everyone knew they were the best fighters in the world and the Boche would have no chance against them. So she was safe and the farm was safe, but, oh, what about Pierre? If he should be killed, what would her future be? She would never have a husband and a place of her own. Oh, these Germans were wicked, wicked people. She hoped Jack and the other *anglais* would kill every one of them!

106

The old man had fallen asleep, his pipe had gone out, and the rain had stopped. The background to the girl's soft rhythmic plaint was the steady dripping from the eaves outside, the distant, occasional grumbles of departing thunder, and the gentle snoring of the dog by the fire. It grew lighter, and now there was sunshine outside the window again, sharply contrasting with the dark inside wall, like a square of white painted on black. Presently there came the sound of a blackbird singing. How old was this building, he wondered. Five hundred years? Perhaps more. For five hundred years people had sheltered in it from storms like this, had listened to just such a blackbird afterwards, had scratched a living from the fertile but indifferent earth, leaving little of themselves behind but the simple continuance of habitation and cultivation. Three thousand Maries had cooked under that chimney, borne children in the dark bedrooms above, stared at the white square in the black wall and dreamed their dreams; three thousand Bécasses had snored in their chair after dinner, and lay sleeping through eternity in the graveyard in the village. There was nothing about this place except the fact that it was here, and always had been. He hoped the Germans would not come.

They both escorted him out through the dripping world to his aeroplane, where he got out his map and spread it between himself and the girl to find exactly where he was. She did not know how to read a map, so was of no use to him, but he found Cambrai and Cauroir easily enough. From there the road just beyond the hedge ran as straight as a die and the next place he would come to would be Le Cateau. Maubeuge then lay to the north-east, on the other side of the great Forest of Mormal. And as if the forest wasn't enough, there was the River Sambre which snaked up its eastern side and ran right into Maubeuge. Now he couldn't get lost.

He thanked his hosts, offered them money, which they refused, and enlisted the girl's help in starting up. The Tabloid caught, despite her soaking, like the good little thing she was, and with a final wave goodbye, he ran her up the field, turned round, and took off. The Tabloid shook the rain from her planes and wheels as if glad to be on her way again, and the wind of passage sang in her rigging, like a song of joy.

The sun was out again, and very hot, but visibility was not good. The tremendous rainfall was now being sucked up in the form of a haze almost thick enough to be called a fog. He had to fly very low to keep the road in sight.

As soon as he had gone a few kilometres he began to see soldiers, and it became obvious that Marie had spoken no more than the truth when she said they were everywhere. There were fields full of tents, of horse lines, of transport lines, soldiers in the villages, in the farms, groups of them walking along, lounging, helping farmers, making camp and doing fatigues. Almost everyone looked up as he flew by – aeroplanes were still a novelty to most people, and probably most of the Tommies had never seen one before in their lives. Some of them waved, and he waved back. But as he neared Le Cateau a danger presented itself.

He had been flying over the fields, to the north of and parallel with the road, but near the town there was a river valley that was full of mist, making the visibility even poorer. Afraid of missing the way, he altered course a little to fly directly over the road. Ahead of him a detachment of Tommies was marching towards Le Cateau, and as they heard his engine they looked back over their shoulders. Then suddenly a group of men at the rear halted, turned, and shouldered their rifles. For an instant he did not understand what it portended; then there was a prickle of fire sparks, the sound of musketry, and almost on the instant something whined past Jack's head like a giant hornet. He had been looking down at them – now he jerked his head back so violently he ricked his neck. They were firing at him! The bloody fools didn't know a British aeroplane when they saw one!

He felt something strike the fuselage; heard something else ricochet off one of his hard surfaces – he did not see what. Some officer down there must be giving them orders, for while the first men had fired in a haphazard, spur-of-the-moment way, evidently simply reacting to his sudden appearance, he could now see the men forming up to aim properly at him, ready to fire a full broadside. There was no way to communicate with them, to tell them who he was. He could only veer away as quickly as possible and climb, fulminating on the idiocy of an army that would fire on its own aeroplanes.

Because of the haze he could not fly high for very long, and soon had to reduce height again to see where he was. After that he stayed away from the roads as much as possible, kept an eye open for groups of armed men and tried not to fly directly over them. Once he hit the river he felt safer. The road ran parallel with it, but two to three kilometres away, and the river was fringed for most of its length with a shielding line of poplars.

Soon Maubeuge came up before him, indistinct in the sun-dazzled haze. Given that the RFC was supposed to be concentrated in the area, he hoped that he would be safe from being shot at, and came in a little lower to look for the airfield. He saw aeroplanes in several fields but there was no mistaking the main aerodrome, with its row of portable hangars, motor lorries and store tents. He passed over it once to check for any hazards, then came in and put down. A tributary of the Sambre ran round one side of the field, and the inevitable poplars threw long afternoon shadows, dusky mauve, across the glittering grass. Beyond the hangars and transport line the rosy-tiled roofs of a cluster of farm buildings caught the westering sun. He taxied up to the hangars, cut the engine, and in the following silence heard birdsong.

Two RFC mechanics came out of one of the hangars and ran across to him. One checked the number on the Tabloid's side with a notebook in his hand and said, 'Mr Compton, sir?'

Jack pulled off his cap and goggles and smiled in relief. 'You don't know how glad I am to find myself expected.'

'We was expecting you quite a bit since, sir. Thought you must have got lost.'

'I did. I got lost, I got rained out of the sky, and then I got shot at – by our own side.' Both men grinned broadly at this. 'Nearly took my damn' head off, the idiots. Missed me by this much. I felt something strike, but I don't know whether it did any damage.'

He and the mechanics looked over the Tabloid and soon found where she had been hit. There was a chip out of the varnish on one of the landing skids, and a small hole through the lower left side plane.

'You must've been flying low, sir,' said one of the mechanics.

'I had to, with that damned mist, to find my way,' Jack said.

The man sucked his teeth and shook his head. 'This'll have to be entered in the log, sir, this here damage. Brand new machine she was, when you left St Omer. I dunno if they're going to charge it to you, sir – take it out of your pay.'

Fortunately Jack realised just in time that he was being roasted, and he grinned, happy to feel the welcome it implied. They directed him to the squadron commander's office in the farmhouse, and as he entered, the major stood up and actually came round the desk to shake his hand, making the welcome complete.

'I'm Major Pettingill. Glad you made it, Compton, damn' glad,' he said. 'We can do with someone of your experience around here. Now, first things first, you'll want to settle in, have a wash and brush-up before dinner and so on. I'll get someone to take you to your billet, and show you where everything else is. We've a pretty nice mess here. After dinner I'll be holding a meeting to outline the situation, and if you've any questions you can put them then.'

The junior officers, Jack discovered, were billeted in a pair of small cottages on the other side of the little river, which they reached by means of a wooden footbridge. The senior officers were sleeping at the farmhouse, where the officers' mess was. Jack's room was small and spare, but clean, with freshly whitewashed walls and a bare wooden floor that smelled of wax. A high iron bedstead, a wooden kitchen chair and a row of pegs for clothes was all the furniture there was. It made Jack think of a monk's cell, a likeness increased by the rather beautiful wood and ivory crucifix on the wall over the bed, left presumably by the previous owner. The cottages did not boast anything so up-to-date as sanitation: the latrine and bath tents were behind, in what had been the garden.

He visited the latrine – the view was charming, over the pretty, tangled remains of a flower garden, and a low hedge full of birds, to lush green meadows and a golden stubble field, with the red roofs of a village nestling on the horizon. He had a wash in cold water – there was hot only in the morning – and blessed his fortune that he was not one of those benighted souls who had to shave twice a day. Then he passed a pleasant hour lying on his bed and writing a long letter to Helen.

On his way back to the farmhouse for dinner, Jack stopped in the middle of the bridge and looked down at the slow-running water. The evening sky had cleared, and it was warm without being oppressive. There was even a little breeze that moved the rushes in the river, making them bend and straighten as if they were at some task there, like women washing clothes. Down in the water a pair of coots swam busily, darting in and out of the reeds and the overhang of the bank, and disappeared below him under the bridge. The poplar leaves rustled and whispered, the light catching them making it look as though the trees were shivering all over. He saw that one or two of the leaves were turning yellow already.

The mess occupied the sitting-room and dining-room of the grand old farmhouse, which had been built on so generous a scale that the space was quite adequate. There was comfortable old furniture, a jar of cottage-garden flowers in the grate of the vast inglenook, the smell of furniture wax, and oil lamps lit to make the place seem welcoming. The first two people Jack saw were Deane and Culverhouse, standing with drinks in hand near the door and beaming in delighted welcome.

'The flight commander said you'd come in,' said Deane, wringing Jack's hand.

'We got sent here straight from Le Cateau, by tender,'

said Culverhouse. 'Beat you to it by hours. We've been here since luncheon.'

'Wondered what had happened to you,' Deane said with a grin. 'Barnes – down at the hangars – said you were shot at.'

'They've got aeroplanes for us here,' Culverhouse said, cutting in with the really important news. 'They're only Shorthorns, but at least we'll be flying. For a while there at St Omer I thought we'd be spending the war twiddling our thumbs.'

The flight commander came over to shake Jack's hand. 'Melville,' he said. 'Didn't see you when you got in. Glad you made it – I hear you got shot at. Awful problem. Come and have a drink. Damn' glad to have you. Comfortable all right over at the cottages? What'll you have? Squadron commander'll be giving us all a little talk after dinner, but it's time to relax first. Is that a letter for posting? Stick it in my pocket, I'll put it in the box for you when I go past later. Not at all. Now then – whisky, was it?'

With such a welcome, a glass in his hand and an interested party round him eager to hear the story of his day's adventure, Jack couldn't have felt more at home at Fairoaks or Morland Place. It wasn't, he thought warmly towards the bottom of his second whisky before dinner, such a bad old war after all.

CHAPTER SIX

The squadron commander's talk after dinner had been grave, informative and inspiring. The fact was that no-one knew where the German army was. On the eve of war there had been a large force massed on Belgium's borders. Where had they gone, and what had they been doing in the intervening fortnight? Fearful rumours were spreading, and army top brass feared that what the French believed to be a feint might be a more concerted attack. The BEF was exposed out here on the wing, and if they were outflanked and the Channel ports were taken, England herself would be in danger. On the other hand, the missing German army could be heading in a different direction altogether, and threatening quite another part of the line. No counter-action could be taken without intelligence. It was imperative to find the German army – and the RFC was the unit to do it.

Here, said Major Pettingill, was a chance to show the sceptics in the army's high command that the aeroplane was more than a glorified taxi-cab. This was a scouting job the cavalry could not undertake. Only the RFC had the range and speed for this most vital task. In their – the pilots – hands lay perhaps the future of the Corps and the safety of England!

Not a man went to bed but his blood was stirring with anticipation of the morrow. But, as Jack thought the next day, man proposes but God disposes. It was all very well for the Old Man to 'sic' them on to the job, but the infernal late-summer weather had other ideas. The storm that had grounded Jack the previous day was a taste of things to come. Each day the heat continued unabated, and brought great masses of black thundercloud boiling across the landscape to dump torrents of rain in such a short space of time that the farmyard was frequently ankle deep in running water. Then, just as suddenly, the clouds would roll away, leaving behind such a steaming landscape under the fierce sun that it was like being shut in a small kitchen with an over-enthusiastic kettle.

'Weather unsuitable for flying' and 'weather unsuitable for reconnaissance' were the official phrases sent up to HQ to describe these phenomena. The pilots, longing to get on with the job they had been primed to do, hanging around the base in a mixture of frustration and boredom, described the weather as 'bloody awful'.

'I knew it!' Culverhouse fulminated. 'I knew something was going to happen to stop me flying. I'm never going to get off the ground in this damn' war!'

Deane, though less emphatic, was just as upset, and flopped from one chair to another in the mess with the expression of a martyred Labrador. They were not alone. Everyone grumbled, smoked too much, read the few available magazines and books until they fell to pieces, and at intervals went to stare out of the window at the drumming rain or the white-gold, sun-flushed haze.

'I don't see why we can't at least *try*,' said Culverhouse. 'It'd be better than sitting around doing nothing.'

'Don't be an ass,' said one of the other pilots, Vaughan, looking up from a French school textbook he had found in his bedroom. 'It's dangerous. You'd get lost thirty seconds after leaving the ground. And if you kept on flying, you'd never find your way back.'

'That's not all,' said Captain Melville, as he came in. 'I've just heard that one of our chaps has been shot down.' There were cries of concern and enquiry. 'No, not by the Germans. A chap from another squadron over to the west of Maubeuge evidently felt the way you do, Culverhouse. He got permission to take a scout up, flew over a French unit and got peppered. They managed to do enough damage to bring him down, though fortunately he wasn't hurt.' He smiled sourly. 'Interesting that our first casualty of the war should be at the hands of our allies.'

'I suppose he appeared out of the mist and panicked 'em,' said Harmison.

'You see?' said Vaughan to Culverhouse. 'I told you it was dangerous.'

Jack shook his head. 'It doesn't matter whether you come out of the mist or not. Look at me, yesterday. Your arrival is always sudden to the fellows on the ground – you can see them from miles away, but they don't see you until you're right overhead. And remember, most of them have never seen an aeroplane before. It's a bit much to expect them to know whether you're friendly or not, just in that instant.'

'But our machines and the Germans' look completely different,' said Flint, indignantly. 'You can't mistake a Taube or an Eindecker for a BE2 or a Shorthorn.'

Melville smiled. 'My dear chap, Compton's right. The difference may be obvious to you and me, but the fellows on the ground just see a great bird shadow come over them, and react like a sparrow to a hawk.'

'I wish they did,' said Vaughan. 'A sparrow flies away. He doesn't shoot at the hawk.'

Everyone laughed. Melville said, 'You know perfectly well what I mean.'

'Well, it's about time they gave the infantry some lessons in aeroplane recognition,' Flint went on. 'Apart from the shape, there's the colour. The Bosch use a completely different dope from ours.'

There was a chorus of objection. 'Oh, rot, Freddie! If they can't tell a bloody great bird shape like a Taube from a snub-nosed Shorthorn, how are they going to tell grey from brown?'

'Perhaps we ought to have some kind of symbol,' Jack suggested. 'Painted on the underside of the wing – the Union Jack, perhaps.'

'That'd identify us to the German troops,' Harmison objected. 'And then *they*'d shoot at us.'

'Better to get shot at by one side than both,' Jack said.

'No, Jack my lad,' said Vaughan, 'better to get shot at by *neither*.' And everyone laughed again.

The conversation at least used up a little of the time that hung so heavily on their hands. Jack was better off than most for he could always go down to the sheds to potter about with the machines and talk engineering to anyone who was around. It not only occupied him, it endeared him to the mechanics, who were used to being ignored by the lordly flyers. And when the rain let up he was happy to go for a walk and explore the immediate countryside, even if it meant wet shoes.

And then there was no limit to the number of times he could reread Helen's letter, which had found him at Neuf-Mesnil that morning. Helen wrote an excellent letter, full of incident and the small detail so valuable to a man far from home and with nothing to do. Reading her words he could see Fairoaks clearly, homelike to him now, see the shrubbery, the garden, the Dachies, Mrs Ormerod pottering about cutting flowers and talking seamlessly about this and that, Mr Ormerod reading the newspaper with his spectacles slipping to the end of his nose, Molly thundering down the stairs on one of her breathlessly urgent missions.

Helen could make the most of a little material, but she had one out-of-the-way incident to describe.

I know you are not intimately acquainted with the village, but perhaps you remember the pork butcher's shop in the High Street, two doors down from the post office. At all events, you may take my word for it that there is a pork butcher's there, called Mannheim's. The Mannheims have been there for ever, everyone knows them, and they are very nice people, as honest as the day is long. This morning when Molly and I went into the village for one or two things there was a crowd standing around outside Mannheim's, blocking the pavement so that we could hardly get past. We thought it was just one of the rushes that happen these days, when everyone suddenly decides at once that there won't ever be any more butter or rice or tea or whatever, and they all try to buy it up at once. But then we heard what they were saying. They were abusing the Mannheims for being Germans, calling them dreadful names, and wanted to drag them out and – well, I leave it to your imagination. It was very ugly.

It was all the worse because the Mannheims are hardly German at all, really. *He* has lived here since he was four years old, and *she* is actually of French blood and was born in London. I got to the front of the crowd and tried to calm them down, reminded them that they knew these people, and told them they should be ashamed of themselves, but they wouldn't listen. Then someone threw a stone through the shop window and they all surged forward and started smashing the glass and grabbing the meat that was inside. I became worried about Molly, and told her to go and find the policeman. But she said, 'Hold them back as long as you can. I'll get the Mannheims out at the back,' and darted past me into the shop. She wasn't the least bit afraid – though I suppose my part was the worse! I stood in the doorway, shouting at people, but eventually they just pushed me back and surged into the shop. By then there was no sign of the Mannheims or Molly.

I must confess to some trepidation, but in fact no-one was trying to hurt me. They wanted the Mannheims – although there was another element, some rough-looking people I didn't know, whose desire was to loot the shop. They took everything and did a lot of damage, before Constable Jackson arrived and everyone ran away. When all was quiet again, I discovered what had become of Molly – about which I was in some anxiety, imagining how I was to explain things to Mother! She had got the Mannheims out of the back door and taken refuge with them in Henderson's, the drapers next door. Mrs Henderson hid them upstairs in the living quarters until the mob had gone. Molly was such a heroine! We begged Jackson and the Hendersons not to tell anyone, though, because if Mother heard about it she'd have a fit. But in any case the Hendersons didn't want it known they'd taken the Mannheims in, in case *they* were attacked, so the secret will remain between you, me and the protagonists.

The final word on this episode is that the Mannheims are going away to some relatives of Mrs Mannheim's in Hoxton and the shop is to be boarded up. Really, it's too dreadful! And no more Mannheim's sausages for us, which is a shame because they were quite the best. Constable Jackson said a lot of this sort of thing has been going on all over the country. People with German names are being attacked, and their shops looted, which is quite disgraceful. I dare say most of the victims are like our poor Mannheims, people who had lived in England so long they had assumed they were regarded as English too.

At the end of the letter she wrote the more tender and personal words.

I miss you quite dreadfully, every day, and long for the time when we can be properly together. I wish I had been able to be hard-hearted enough to deny Mother the grand wedding, and marry you at once, so that at least I would have that to remember. As it is I have to make do with your dear picture, which receives my kisses every night before I go to sleep. It seems an impertinence on the part of the Kaiser that he should interrupt my intimate life in this way for his surly purposes.

As a woman, I can't help thinking that war is an absurdity. The idea that men lining up and trying to kill each other can solve a dispute or make anything better is intrinsically ridiculous. And yet as an intellectual being, I have a part of me that thrills to the romance of it, the glory and honour and pride, the stretched sinews of it. It is, after all, the subject that has inspired the greatest literature throughout history (except perhaps for love).

Tonight, however, love is uppermost in my thoughts,

and I will end this long letter with it, with the outpouring across the miles that separate us of every tender thought and wish, in the hope that it can reach you and touch you in some way, that you may, however fleetingly, *feel* me close to you. I kiss this letter. Lay your lips where mine have touched and think of your Helen.

He waited for the privacy of his room to obey the last injunction, but it did not much comfort him. When the light was out and he lay in his bed staring at the flicker of starlight beyond the uncurtained window, he thought of her, her face, her hands, her lips, imagined holding her close to him, imagined everything else he longed to do with her. We should have got married, he thought. Christmas was so far away.

On the morning of Thursday the 20th of August, Jack was woken from a quiet sleep by the sound of a robin thrilling the air from the gutter above his window. The patch of sky he could see was high and clear, the faint blue of dawn. He jumped out of bed and went to look, throwing open the window so that he could lean out and snuff the air. It was clear and clean, cool and grassy, promising heat but without the oppressiveness that foretold thunder. There was not a cloud to be seen. The rising sun was gilding the fields. The poplars stood still, only their gold leaves flickering and quivering in the mysterious way they had, as if they lived half in another world where there was always a wind. He could smell the river, the flat brown breath of running water, and an unseen duck's sudden voice commented raucously on the absurdity of existence.

Jack stretched luxuriously, and felt the excitement go running through his blood at the thought that they would fly today. No doubt about it. No more 'unsuitable weather'. It was a beautiful, perfect day. They would fly, and they would find the German army, and everyone would know that aeroplanes had a vital part to play in war. There was only one more thing wanted, he thought, to make the morning perfect: bacon. He was ravenously hungry.

Wonderful, fragrant bacon, and fried eggs, and coffee in large quantities, and crusty bread and creamy butter, and perhaps some of the damson jam they had had yesterday, if that hog Harmison hadn't finished it all. And then they would go out and find the Bosch and save the day! Whistling, he went down the narrow stairs two at a time, and through the wet grass to the wash tent.

Everyone was in the same buoyant mood. After breakfast they gathered round to study the maps and be allocated their areas of search; then they were walking briskly across to the hangars, where the mechanics had already pushed and pulled the machines out onto the grass. One by one they taxied into position, turned into the wind and took off. Climbing up through the air, Jack felt his happiness was complete. It was so clear and the sky was so intensely blue it was as though the colour itself was the medium through which he moved, as effortlessly as a fish in water. Down below him the fields of Belgium unrolled like a painting of a patchwork quilt in shades of green and gold, decorated with little clusters of red dots, the roofs of farm buildings, and the woods like splatters of dark green where the painter had carelessly let his brush drip. Sometimes he saw birds below him, the straight, urgent flight of a lone pigeon, the lazy flap of a crow, or a scatter of starlings like tea-leaves tossed into the wind.

The Tabloid was so familiar to him that it was like a part of his own body. His eyes went from time to time to the instruments, but he had no awareness of this, any more than of his hands and feet minutely correcting the aeroplane's performance. The movements were so automatic that they bypassed his conscious brain, and he flew as effortlessly as a man walks a familiar road and is able to think of something else at the same time. At last he was doing what he had been brought here to do, what he had wanted to do ever since Colonel Morton had walked into the Fairoaks dining room and said they were at war. He flew, and looked for the Germans.

He passed over the town of Mons, surrounded by its sprawl of suburbs, the almost engulfed villages, pitheads and

120

slag heaps, factories and blast furnaces that went to make up what the Belgians called *le Borinage*, their version of the English Black Country. He crossed the east–west Canal du Centre, on which the massive black barges carried the coal and steel down to Condé, then flew on northwards over rolling farmland, with nothing bigger than villages to break the pattern of fields, no features of significance but the railway line that ran north-east towards Brussels, and the River Dender. All was peaceful, much as it must have looked – the railway excepted – when Napoleon was heading for his meeting with Fate at Waterloo. The Germans were not here; nor, to judge from the integrity of the countryside, had they been here. He saw the town of Alost over to his right, and banked gently into a right turn to head eastwards towards Brussels.

The sprawl of the city came into sight, with roads and railways running into it as though it were sucking them in, and the gleam of the canalised river running through the middle. He passed over on the north side still heading eastwards. Fifteen or twenty miles beyond Brussels was Louvain. There he was to turn south and fly back over Namur and Dinant to Maubeuge. Louvain came up, and he was about to make his turn when he saw something that made the hair lift on his scalp. To the east of the town, heading towards it, was a greyness, filling the road: a greyness that quivered with movement like a shivering snake, throwing the occasional spark of reflection back at the sun. As he stared, the head of the snake inched forward, gaining a little ground every moment as it quested towards Louvain and the short road to Brussels.

He circled lower. Now he could see little specks on the road between Louvain and Brussels – no snake these, but ants: individuals fleeing, displaced from their habitat as game is flushed out by beaters; or perhaps as small creatures flee in the path of an oncoming forest fire.

Lower again. It was the German army, no doubt about it. No French blue or British khaki, but sinister German grey, with the cohesion of a rigid discipline holding the mass together, pushing the snake's head forward inexorably. Still lower, and he could see the regular swing of the front rank's legs: it looked like one single leg, the width of the road, shoving out and drawing back like some piece of factory machinery of unknown purpose. He could see the officers on horseback to the side of the ranks, and a dot of a horseman cantering back to pass a message. There was a ripple of pink as the men turned their faces up to look at the aeroplane coming over. He must remember the fate of the airman shot down by the French. He did not want to be the second RFC casualty of the war. He swung away and climbed rapidly, spiralling up to gain enough height to see where the end of the column was. But the grey snake had no end. His stomach tried to fold in on itself. Part of his job, if he found the Germans, was to estimate their number. But how do you estimate an army that reaches to the horizon?

He must get back and report. He turned away, taking his bearing on Brussels, and heading south-west towards Mons. It was only then that he saw the other aeroplane, below him at a little distance and on the opposite heading. He knew it for a German by its colour, even before he recognised the shape of an Eindecker. It was the first enemy aeroplane he had seen, and evidently his opponent shared his interest and curiosity, for the pilot climbed to Jack's height as they approached. Then for what seemed like a long moment they were opposite each other. Jack saw a goggled face turned towards him. It was clean-shaven, but otherwise there was nothing to tell about it, from the little of it he could see between cap, goggles and collar. A Bosch, a Hun, he thought. The enemy. If they had been soldiers on the ground they would have tried to kill each other, but up here in the great blue there was nothing to be done about it – though it did occur to Jack that the other fellow had probably been on the same mission as himself, and that if it *were* possible, it would be his duty to stop him reporting back what he had found out about the British and French dispositions.

Wanting to keep the other in sight, he had instinctively begun to turn; and the German must have done the same, for they remained opposite each other, circling in the same direction. Jack grinned at the thought of what it must look like to an outsider, and raised a hand in acknowledgement to his opposite number.

The German raised a hand too. Jack thought he was merely waving back, until he saw that there was something black in it – a pistol of some kind. He saw the jerk of the recoil as the man fired – once, twice, three times. He did not hear the reports over the noise of his engine, and had no idea where the shots went. The chances of one moving airman hitting another with a pistol were so remote that he had not even flinched. He was not afraid, only surprised; but it had the effect of reminding him of his duty. He had essential information to impart, and he straightened out of the circle to the south-west, heading home. He did not accelerate at first, thinking that perhaps he could lure the German in the direction of his side's guns, but after pursuing for a few moments the Eindecker veered away and resumed its north-eastward course, as the pilot presumably remembered his own duty.

Here was the frustration, Jack thought. If only he had been armed in some way, he could perhaps have prevented the German pilot from getting his intelligence back. Flying automatically, he pondered this. Would it be possible to fire a Lewis from a scout? Perhaps. With a machine-gun's rate of fire and greater range you had a real chance of hitting another aeroplane. But perhaps the weight would be too much – not only the gun to consider but the ammunition too. Would it weigh as much as a man? The Tabloid, for instance, could not take off with a passenger. He did calculations in his head, hampered by his ignorance of the weight of armaments, as he flew as fast as he could push the Tabloid towards Mons and Maubeuge with his message of alarm. The Germans would reach Brussels within hours, and what hope was there that the Belgians could stop them? And beyond Brussels lay the open road to France.

The order had come at last to the troops around Le Cateau to move up. From Le Cateau to Mons was a march of about thirty miles. The British Army's full rate of marching was twenty miles a day, but it was rarely demanded, fifteen being more usual. Certainly, Bertie thought, in the present circumstances it would not be more than fifteen, and two days would be needed to cover the distance. He paraded his company in the early morning, in the field behind the farmhouse. The sun was just rising, and there was a little white mist over the damp grass, ankle deep in the lowest corner of the field where a few stolid brown cattle were lying down, chewing the cud and regarding the human activity with the mild surprise of their species.

The men, he was glad to see, were in good spirits, looking both rested and alert after their 'holiday' in the harvest fields. All were sun-browned – there were one or two burnt noses and ears – and all had benefited from the exertion of harvesting, together with the training he had fitted in in the mornings and evenings. All had enjoyed the delicious, hearty food and the novelty of being in a foreign land. Bertie had learned something about his officers, too. Yerbury was intelligent but quiet – perhaps a little too quiet with the men, who would instinctively take advantage if they could; Oxshott was stolid, an obeyer and purveyor of orders, without imagination, but a good, reliable officer; Buckingham was lazy, would always avoid exertion if he could and leave disagreeable tasks to others, had a plausible fund of excuses to cover his deficiencies, but was amusing and popular with the men. Pennyfather, Bertie thought, was the best of them, energetic, intelligent and loyal, and with a sense of humour that would endear him to those following him.

It remained to be seen, of course, how they would perform in battle – how any of them would perform. His eye scanned the ranks, picking out the faces of the veteran reservists from the inexperienced regulars. But they were all professional soldiers, and he was glad to be commanding them. They would not let him down.

'Well, men,' he said, 'the holiday is over. We're moving up today to what will be the front line. We will join forces with the French, on their left flank, and when we are all in position, we and our allies will advance together and kick the Germans right back to Germany.'

The men cheered, and he saw pleased anticipation on all faces at the thought of action. That was as it should be. As he watched them about-turn by sections and march out through the field gate onto the road, he thought of the orders and information he had received late last night. A German force was in Brussels – which had fallen without a fight – and was coming south and west on several roads. The BEF was to move up and take position along the Central Canal to the north of Mons. When they and the French were all in position they would advance to Soignies where they would make their stand. In two or three days at the most they would be in action.

But before that came the march. It was hard work. The sun rose on another bright, hot summer day, and the men sweated in their uniforms under the weight of full pack and rifle. To make things worse, the going underfoot was painful and treacherous. Through each village, and for a distance on either side, the road was paved with great cobblestones about eight inches square, roughly and unevenly laid. They dug into the instep, caught at toe and heel, and made the men's nailed boots slip, doubling the labour of putting one foot in front of another, making the legs and knees ache with the effort of keeping balance. There was no chance of getting into a rhythm and swinging along without thought: everyone had to keep his eyes on the ground to see what was coming next. The men cursed the French and their cobblestones bitterly. Where villages were close together, as was often the case, the cobbles of one would join up with the cobbles of the next and there was no respite.

The sun blazed down, and no-one spoke. It was too hot, and the effort to keep going was all anyone could manage. The men tucked their handkerchiefs under their cap brims so that they hung behind to protect their necks. The sweat dripped off their noses and eyelashes and soaked their uniforms. Where the road was not cobbled, their passage raised a white dust that stuck to their faces and damp clothing.

The custom was to march for fifty minutes and rest for ten in each hour, and when the halt was called the men simply flopped down at the side of the road, without the energy to remove their packs. Some managed to fall asleep in the brief pause, and had to be kicked awake when the time came to continue. In the heat and dust, thirst was a torment. The men carried water-bottles but Bertie knew well enough that the thoughtless would empty them at the first halt and have nothing for the rest of the day. He gave orders that they should only take two swallows at a halt, and told the NCOs to keep a sharp eye on them.

The reservists were having the hardest time, for despite his efforts to get them fit, they were not accustomed as the regulars were to sustained marching, and they had not had time to break in their new boots. The combination of stiff boots and cobblestones had them dropping out at the side of the road, their feet an agony of blisters. Knowing the importance of morale during a trial such as this, which did not have the compensatory excitement of action, he abandoned his horse from time to time and marched with the men, allowing the worst affected soldier to ride for a space.

As the burning eye of the sun rose up the sky, he moved almost in a dream, thirst bringing mental images of water, not just drinks of it, but rivers, ponds, lakes and canals: as his legs moved automatically, he drifted in a punt along a willow-fringed stream, gazing through the dappled shade at glimpses of sky, trailing a hand in the deliciously cold, flat-smelling water. Then a stumble would bring him back with cruel suddenness to the prickly, hot, thirsty reality.

Passing through the villages they were cheered by the populace, who ran out of their houses to line the way, to wave, to give the Tommies presents of apples or flowers. In one village, a buxom young woman ran alongside begging for souvenirs. On the generous bosom of her dress were the badges of half a dozen different units, sign of those who had passed along this road before them. In another, a woman gave Bertie a bottle of wine. He thought there wasn't a man in the company, himself included, who wouldn't have swapped any quantity of wine just then for a mug of water.

The heat was relentless, the sun blinding. It reflected off the whitewashed walls of cottages in waves of pure light.

They passed an *estaminet*, its green shutters closed against the noonday, its open door giving a glimpse of an interior cool with darkness, men sitting at tables with glasses before them. The young soldier nearest Bertie faltered a step at the sight, and he smacked his lips unconsciously at the thought of cold beer. Even the church they passed was a temptation, with its dim, echoing spaces promising relief. Bertie longed to go in, lie down on the stone floor and press his burning cheek to its coolness.

The sun went over the zenith, and a little cloud gathered and covered it from time to time, giving slight relief. The burn went out of the day, to be replaced by a stiflingness. Bertie took his horse back for a while and rode at the front, sending Pennyfather ahead to find out where they were and how far it was to the village where they were to halt for the night. Gommegnies was that day's halt; Pennyfather came back to say it was a mile and a half ahead, and that the battalion was to bivouac in the fields around a neighbouring hamlet.

Orders were that there were to be no fires that night and no lights shown. Fortunately it was a fine night, and very warm. His company found a good field next to a farmhouse, and an ancient farmer came out shyly to welcome them, to direct them to a wide stream on the other side of an orchard, and to beg them to help themselves to what apples remained on and under the trees. He invited the officers to eat and sleep in his house, but after such a day Bertie could not contemplate even that comparative luxury, when the men would be eating bully and biscuits washed down with water. Instead he asked the farmer if it would be possible to use his range to heat water so that the men could have tea. Hot tea made all the difference to a meal of iron rations.

The farmer continued to press hospitality on the officers, and Bertie accepted a gift of three bottles of wine and some cold sausage to add to their own rations, and a vast whole cheese, which he had cut up and sent round to the men. There was only a taste each among so many, but they enjoyed it out of all proportion to the amount, because it was unexpected. Splashing in the stream had raised their spirits again,

127

and cooled the feet of the worst-off; and they were all so dog-tired they had no difficulty in falling asleep on the hard ground.

Bertie, though just as tired, had more difficulty in dropping off. He could not get comfortable, and envied Yerbury's youthful bones as the young man snored happily at a little distance. He lay looking up at the sky, crusted with fat stars, listening to the small sounds around him – the steady scrunch of the horses grazing, making up for time lost during the day; the intermittent coughs, snorts and grunts of the sleeping men; the call of a nightjar; the occasional furtive rustle of something moving down the hedgerow. He did not think of the trials to come: he thought of home, of Maud and the boy, of Beaumont and his plans for his cattle herd. Then his mind drifted inevitably to the Red House, and Yorkshire – his heart's home; and he finally slipped into sleep with Jessie's bright image in his mind, and dreamed of riding with her over an endless landscape on tireless horses.

Morning came, and they turned out, rising cautiously to stiff legs and painful feet, comforted by more hot tea, readying themselves for another day of marching. The second day was a repeat of the first, varied only by a brief, sharp rainstorm around midday, which soaked and cooled them. The men turned their faces up into it and let the rain fall into their mouths; and afterwards, when the sun came out again, they steamed, smelling like wet dogs, until in an amazingly short time they were dry again. Those who had blisters were worse off today, and hobbled pitifully, crouched like old women over their pain. Bertie gave up his horse again and, though he had not ordered it, his lieutenants followed suit – Buckingham last and with obvious deep reluctance. They bivouacked again that night some miles short of Mons, and a supply lorry arrived to dump rations: tins of bully, but this time fresh bread instead of biscuit – a large loaf between four men – and an issue of cheese. There was no nearby farmhouse to provide hot water for tea, and everyone had to make do with water. During the evening some girls from a nearby mining village came to hang around on the other side of the hedge and call wistfully, 'Tommee! Tommee! *Promenade!* Cigarette!' Whether they wanted cigarettes or were offering them in exchange for a walk Bertie didn't know, but he posted pickets with firm orders not to let anyone past, in either direction.

And on the morning of Saturday the 22nd of August they marched into Mons. It was market day: Bertie wondered whether HQ had taken that into consideration when ordering the army to concentrate there. The Grande Place and all the streets that led off it were filled with stalls, gay with striped awnings, and busy, shopping citizens; the cafés and bars and *estaminets* all had their doors wide open, their cool interiors tempting. The air was filled with the smells of coffee and baking bread and the multiple odours of meat and fish. There were stalls multicoloured with heaps of fruit – apples, cherries, plums, greengages; stalls piled with golden onions, vast green cabbages the size of human heads, scrubbed turnips and bright orange carrots; stalls hung with the limp corpses of white ducks and brown rabbits, iridescent pigeons, and pink cuts of pork and mutton hung up on steel hooks.

Bertie's company arrived with eager faces and cries of interest and amusement, as the holiday feeling they had lost over the last two days returned. There was so much to look at and enjoy. A halt was called and they sat down on the cobbles around the edge of the square. Rations were supposed to be brought up to them here, but nothing appeared – perhaps the lorries were unable to get through the crowded streets. It didn't matter. The local townsfolk almost fought each other for the privilege of showering gifts on the welcome defenders. Hunks of fresh bread, lavishly buttered, garlic sausage hacked into lengths, wedges of cheese, any amount of fruit were brought forth. A restaurant sent out hot sausages, those strange pallid objects that appeared so alien to Tommies in the light of English 'bangers', but were surprisingly tasty, despite looking inside as if they were packed with gristle. Tobacconists sent out boxes of cigarettes and packs of chocolate. A barber offered free haircuts. It was impossible to keep the men together in such a crowd. Some were dragged into bars by enthusiastic locals and given coffee or beer. An aristocratic-looking lady invited one section into her house for tea and cakes; a schoolteacher seized the day and captured another group to exercise her English class's conversational skills.

And Bertie was besieged by citizens eager to tell him what they knew of the war, which was that the Germans were coming, the Germans were coming! Brussels had fallen, and fleeing Belgians had brought stories that the Bosch were heading this way. They were somewhere on the other side of the canal – ten miles away, twenty, thirty, five. He found their attitude remarkable. Despite the fact that all of them were convinced a German army was approaching, they would not allow that to distract them from the important business of the weekly market. The British Army was here. It would keep the Germans out of Mons.

He received more reliable information from a cavalry officer he met outside a café, drinking coffee and eating bread and cheese. The British cavalry had been in contact with German Uhlans, and the 4th Dragoon Guards had been in battle with them and driven them off in a magnificent charge. The French were already in action, having met the Germans around Namur, which was now besieged. And refugees spoke of Germans approaching from every direction, streaming down every road, reports that had been echoed by the RFC.

Bertie frowned. 'But if the Germans are engaging the French at Namur and on the border, *and* occupying Brussels, how can they have large numbers left over to be coming this way? Surely it must be an exaggeration?'

The officer shrugged. 'I don't know. Of course civilians always talk about an army when they see four men in uniform. And those airmen don't know anything about army matters. They wouldn't know a corps from a company. All the same, I have an uneasy feeling about it. And it's never any use trying to plan operations with allies. They're never where you want them to be, and they turn and run and leave you in the lurch. We're only about twenty miles from

Waterloo here, you know, and look how the Belgians let us down then.'

Bertie hadn't time to answer, for a messenger came up from the colonel with orders for Bertie to form his men up and march them through Mons and Nimy – one of the villages on the north side that the octopus of Mons had engulfed – and take up position on the south bank of the canal.

'Ah, well,' said Bertie to the officer, 'I suppose we shall soon know the truth of it.'

'Ours not to reason why,' the officer said, with a tight smile. 'Good luck, old chap.'

'The same to you,' said Bertie.

The night was very dark and, unlike previous nights, chilly. There had been a sudden rainstorm at ten o'clock, which had soaked everyone, and now uniforms were damp and everyone was shivering. There was a mist along the canal. The dank air smelled horribly of burnt wood and tar: the canal had been lined with empty barges, which might have given the Germans a means to cross, and since the water was too shallow to sink them, they had had to be set on fire. The engineers had mined the bridges, too, just in case. Tomorrow, when the French came up, the combined force would cross those bridges and confront the Germans somewhere around Soignies, but it was as well to be prepared so that, if the worst came to the worst, they could blow up the bridges and hold the Germans on the far bank.

The battalion had arrived in position with just time before dark to dig shallow trenches, enough to protect them from any skirmishing advance party. They were positioned on a stretch of scrubland and allotments between Nimy and the canal, and had settled down to make themselves as comfortable as they could. Rations came up: fresh bread again, and one tin of food between two men. The tins caused much loud comment, because they had no labels, and were so battered – and some so rusty – that Pennyfather said to Bertie he was sure they must be surplus from the South African war. But the men in their usual way made amusement out of the novelty of the situation, and seemed quite excited at hacking the tins open and comparing the contents. They were varied: stewing beef, bacon and beans, pilchards, herrings, Irish stew, even apple dumplings and custard. A brisk trade ensued as the men bargained with each other for swaps. When leftovers from the market-square feast had been added, everyone ended up with an adequate meal.

The night seemed long to Bertie, sleep hard to achieve in the damp chill, the darkness alive with sounds and movement, wheels and hoofs, the jingling of harness, the stamp of feet, and quiet orders as more and more of the BEF moved up into position. In the dark before dawn he bundled himself in his greatcoat and went for a walk to warm himself up. He walked the short distance into Nimy, where the battalion had its headquarters in a small house in the village street. As he approached it he saw Penkridge, the adjutant, standing on the doorstep smoking a cigarette.

'Hello, Parke. What's up?'

'Nothing. Just taking a walk to restore my circulation. You? Can't sleep?'

'Sleep!' said Penkridge, derisively. He offered Bertie a cigarette. 'No chance of that here tonight. I've just stepped out for five minutes for a fag to clear my head. We're pretty much for it tomorrow, you know. You won't have heard the latest, but the word is being sent down in the next half-hour, so there's no harm in my telling you now.'

'Telling me what?'

'French intelligence have sent a report about the Germans they've captured. Half of them aren't trained soldiers at all – just conscripts. Ploughboys in uniform. It's the Reserve Corps, which everyone's been assuming was being held back in Germany. You do see the significance of that?'

'I'm not sure,' said Bertie.

'If the reserve is here,' Penkridge explained, 'it means that the German advance through Belgium isn't just a feint, or a probe with a couple of divisions. It's a whole army on the move. The Bosch are throwing everything at us, even the reserve, hoping to take us by surprise and win a quick victory.

And there's worse news to come. General Lanrezac's Fifth Army is not going to attack with us tomorrow. He's in retreat. The French are already six or seven miles behind us, and the gap is widening all the time.'

'Good God! Then we must retire too. We'll be isolated here – cut off.'

'True enough,' Penkridge said gloomily. 'But we're not going to fall back. It seems that Lanrezac requested our chief to cover the left flank while the French retreat, so that the Germans can't encircle them. And Sir John French agreed. He's promised that we'll hold Mons for twenty-four hours, at our present position on the canal.'

'Just us?' said Bertie.

'Just us,' said Penkridge. He looked away down the street and said, as if indifferently, 'We'll be outnumbered two or three to one.'

They smoked in silence for a moment, and then Bertie said, 'Ah, well, we always fight best against the odds.'

'True.'

'And if their army is half made up of untrained yokels, their advantage is wiped out. Our force may be small, but it's the most professional army that's ever taken the field. I'd back them against anyone. Any one of my men is worth ten of theirs.'

Penkridge laughed. 'Parke, you're a gem. I shall tell the others what you said.'

'You're not succumbing to gloom and despondency in there, I hope?'

'Good Lord, no! Just frightful annoyance that the French have landed us in it,' said Penkridge.

Bertie thought of the cavalry officer saying that it was never any use planning anything with allies. 'We'll manage better without 'em,' he said. 'Well, I'd better get back to my men.'

Once it became official, by a message from the colonel, Bertie went round to each section in person with the news of the changed circumstances. He was pleased to see that the men took it in their stride. The thought of fighting without the French didn't bother them at all – probably half of them had never believed in the French anyway, since they had never seen them. Out of sight was out of mind. They had come here to fight the Hun, and by God they were going to do it! They seemed, if anything, stimulated by the certainty of a fight the next day, after so many delays since they left England. 'We'll give 'em socks, sir,' said one veteran, which seemed to sum up the general mood, along with the words of another man, a regular: 'All in a day's work, sir.'

Bertie didn't sleep again, his mind too busy with plans and contingencies. The pre-dawn blackness gave way to grey. The mist was heavy and cold over the canal and there was a thin, prickling drizzle – hardly more than a haar, but just as wetting. The men stirred and stretched, stood up and stamped about to get their blood moving, urinated and scratched their heads. Buckets of hot, sweet tea came up, and bread and cheese for breakfast, which they augmented with the last of the sausage, cake and fruit from the market. The sky took on a lemon tinge along the eastern horizon. Somewhere in Nimy a cockerel crowed, and as if in response some invisible ducks along the canal answered raucously.

Across on the other side of the canal, smoke began to rise from the chimneys of the workmen's cottages, and the faintest smell of frying bacon came to tease the cold, waiting soldiers. Beyond the cottages the ground rose gently to a crest decorated by a thin fir plantation, dark upright strokes half showing through the murk. Then the drizzle stopped, the sun pulled itself clear of the horizon, and a little colour began to return to the world, just a touch here and there in the greyness: a spark of ragwort growing in a crack on the bridge, the brown of a bulrush, the red of a curtain at a cottage window. The white mist on the canal slowly dissipated, leaving the silent water like black glass.

It was very still. The men waited, rifles at the ready, facing front, quiet and steady. Behind them, in Nimy, the church bell began rapidly tolling to call the villagers to six o'clock mass. A dog barked once or twice, sharply, and then stopped. And after a while there was a movement in the plantation on the crest of the slope before them, as if the trees were shifting in their places. Gradually the movement resolved itself into a detachment of German cavalry, grey against the early grey sky.

A little ripple of reaction ran along C Company, and they settled themselves more firmly, sighting up the road. The cavalry rode down the hill towards the canal. Bertie swallowed to be sure his voice wouldn't crack after such a long silence, and called out clearly through the quiet air, 'At five hundred yards, five rounds rapid—' He paused. The jingle and hoofbeats could be heard quite clearly now. He narrowed his eyes, judging the distance. '*Fire!*'

BOOK TWO

Struggle

But with the best and meanest Englishmen
I am one in crying, God save England, lest
We lose what never slaves and cattle blessed.
The ages made her that made us from dust:
She is all we know and live by, and we trust
She is good and must endure, loving her so:
And as we love ourselves we hate her foe.

Edward Thomas:
This Is No Case of Petty Right or Wrong

CHAPTER SEVEN

Though this was the first time in action for most of them, the men fired like machines, steadily and without flinching. The intense training and hours of musketry practice now paid off: every man was required to drill until he could fire fifteen rounds per minute. Now together they put up a solid wall of shot. The German cavalry was clearly not expecting such relentless fire, and the advance was soon called off. Bertie shouted, 'Cease firing!' as they rode away up the hill, giving the men a first welcome sight of fleeing German backs to cheer their day.

'They'll be back,' Bertie said. 'That was just their eyes.'

'Damn their eyes!' someone shouted, and everyone laughed.

The canal in front of Nimy had a bend to it, outwards towards the Germans. The main road bridge was roughly in the middle of the curve, with, to the right, two more road bridges and, to the left, another road bridge and the railway bridge. Bertie's battalion was holding the left centre of the curve, with the Royal Fusiliers on their left and the Middlesex on their right. Nimy lay behind them, beyond the strip of scrub in which they had scraped their shallow trenches, and the town allotments.

Bertie went along his line, checking for casualties. There was only one: Sutton had torn off a fingernail when grabbing for a spare clip. It was bleeding freely, but the man next to him was already winding his bandage round it, and Sutton was looking annoyed and shamefaced at the triviality of the wound as his companions teased him for being the first casualty of the war. Spirits were high, he was glad to see, and he was almost grateful to the Germans for providing this first easy test to warm them up.

At nine o'clock – efficiently, on the hour – the Germans began a barrage. As the first shell came whining overhead there were some startled looks, and the first crash of explosion was simultaneous with a human shriek, quickly cut off.

'Keep your heads down,' Bertie shouted. The German artillery was too far back for them to be able to respond – that was their own gunners' job. There was nothing to do but wait it out. But the trenches were too shallow to offer them reasonable shelter. Behind them, among the allotments, there were sheds, small buildings and stone walls.

He called to Pennyfather: 'Retire your men behind those buildings.' He looked round for his servant, Cooper. 'Cooper, double along to the other platoon officers and tell them to find the men shelter until the barrage stops.'

He didn't need to tell Cooper to keep low. He watched him, bent double, jinking like a rabbit along the trenches, dropping flat when a shell came over. The men were beginning to retire now. A shell exploded to his right, and a piece of shrapnel the size of a dinner plate went past him and spattered his cheek with soil and stones as it buried itself in the edge of the trench. He brushed the dirt from his face and, seeing that everyone near him was out and running, took his own leave. Behind a low, stone-built tool-shed he found shelter with Pennyfather and a score of men.

'Why don't our gunners fire?' Pennyfather grumbled softly. 'It's one thing to be shot at, another to be shot at without reply.'

'I don't know,' Bertie said. 'Perhaps they haven't reached us yet.' He checked on casualties again. Four men had been wounded by the shrapnel, one seriously. He scribbled a report in his notebook and sent Cooper off to the colonel with it. Then there was nothing to do but wait the barrage out. With time to think, Bertie reflected on the fact that no British gun had replied. He concluded that even if the artillery had reached Nimy, they would have no clear field of fire. The German position was in open countryside, but the British line ran through the town, and the tangle of suburbs, mines and factories that spread out from it along the south bank of the canal. The gunners' view would have been obscured by buildings, factory chimneys and pithead machinery. But though the men grumbled about 'having to do it all themselves', he was not worried about them. For one thing, the British infantryman always liked to have something to complain about; and for another, he could see they were not dispirited but indignant, which would make them fight all the harder when the time came.

It was not long coming. After an hour the barrage slackened, and with his field-glasses Bertie could see movement along the crest of the hill opposite. He ordered his men to return to the trenches and stand-to. The last shell exploded, leaving a ringing silence behind it; the water of the canal, which had boiled with shrapnel hits for the last hour steadied to a gentle agitation and then to stillness. And then the Germans came.

'Bloody 'ell, there's millions of 'em!' someone nearby muttered.

It was a dense, grey mass, coming down the slope towards them, such a mass that it was as if the earth itself had got up and was rolling down on them. Bertie had no way to calculate the numbers, but though not in millions, the Germans must outnumber them three to one, four to one, five. He looked along his line. The men were ready, eyes front, fixed on the advancing enemy; they were tense, excited, but they were not afraid.

'This is it, lads,' he called out quietly to those nearest him. 'Now we show them. At five hundred yards – rapid – *fire!*'

After that there was no time to think. The men fired at the advancing grey wall – changed the clip, fired, changed the clip, fired again. Fifteen rounds a minute. The ammunition carriers scuttled along the line. The officers exhorted, pointed out targets, directed the orderlies to casualties. The grey wall was firing back, and men were being hit, but grey men were falling too, lots of them. And their firing rate was

141

nothing like that of the British. After an unknown period of slaughter, the enemy fell back, and Bertie shouted, *'Cease firing.'* The men wiped the sweat from their faces and grinned at each other. Casualties were few and the Germans had been repulsed. Their spirits were high.

'Here they come again,' someone said, as the grey wall resumed its advance.

So the morning wore away, under the blazing sun, with wave after wave of enemy infantry advancing, recoiling, advancing again, while the British fired with machine-like rapidity and flung back every wave like a rock resisting a breaker. The Germans seemed to be concentrating their attack on the curve of the canal, pressing in on the two sides in the hope of making the line snap like a bent twig flexed between the hands. With the main road into Nimy – and thus into Mons – behind them, it was the most vulnerable and perhaps the most important point of the British front.

Bertie came to the conclusion that the men facing them must be the reserve, for their firing rate was very low. They fell in terrible numbers, like wheat to a scythe. But still they *were* firing back, and his own men were falling – not in great numbers yet, but the line was thinning.

Then he heard the familiar hornet-whine of a shot coming too close, jerked his head away from it, and felt the violent blow and burning pain of the second hornet as it hit his right upper arm. Instantly he lost all sensation in his arm and hand. His pistol dropped from his grasp and he sat down hurriedly to retrieve it with his left.

Cooper was there. 'You're hit, sir. Lemme help you. Back here, sir, and I'll 'ave a look at it.'

As he hurried for the shelter of a wall, he saw Pennyfather's face turned towards him, enquiring and concerned. He smiled, shook his head and made a gesture with his left hand – *nothing serious*. He hoped to God it wasn't, but he still could feel nothing with his right hand. Behind the wall he sat and fumbled left-handed with his buttons, but Cooper pushed his hand away with, 'Let me, sir. I'll be quicker.'

Bertie's left was trembling. It was from reaction rather

than fear, but he didn't want it seen anyway, and dropped his hand to his lap. His tunic sleeve was torn and bloody, and when Cooper eased it off, the shirt sleeve was torn and soaked too. Bertie craned his head round to look at the purple-lipped mouth that had opened up in his flesh and wished he was a private so that he could reel off a good strong string of curses. His arm was blazing agony from shoulder to elbow, and without sensation below. Why couldn't it be the other way round?

'Taken quite a chunk out of you, sir,' Cooper said judiciously. 'I dunno if the bone's broken. Maybe you ought to get back and see the MO, sir.'

Bertie mastered the trembling of his left hand and felt his arm on either side of the wound. It didn't feel as if it was broken, and the wound itself did not seem to go that deep. As Cooper had said, the shot had taken a bite out of the flesh and muscle. Now there was a burning in his right fingertips – the 'pins and needles' of returning sense. He rubbed his right hand with the left to aid the process. 'I don't think it's broken,' he said. 'Get my field bandage from my tunic and bind it up, will you? I'll do for now.'

Each man carried a bandage and a small bottle of iodine in his tunic. Cooper anointed the wound and began to bandage it. The lint blotted instantly red for the first few turns, then reddened more slowly. But the feeling had come back to Bertie's right fingers, and he could flex them, so the bone could not be broken. It must have been just the blow that had numbed him.

'There, sir, best as I can do it,' Cooper said, tying the knot. 'But mebbe you oughter see the MO, sir.'

'No need. Just help me on with my tunic,' Bertie said. He tried his pistol in his right hand, and everything seemed to be working, only in a blaze of pain. The gunfire, which his ears had filtered out for a few minutes, came back to him, a continuous crackling sound that somehow suggested great heat, as though it were the voice of a forest fire. 'Go to Lieutenant Pennyfather and tell him I'm all right. I'll follow you in two minutes.'

Cooper gave him one doubtful look and obeyed. Bertie

used his two minutes' respite to ease his flask out of his pocket and take a good mouthful of whisky, which dulled the pain a minim and, more importantly, cured the shakes. Then he got to his feet and went back to the action.

'Mr Yerbury – that section of the enemy away on your right, trying to get onto the road bridge – concentrate your fire on them.' He scribbled a note and handed it to Cooper. 'Take this back to HQ – sharp now.'

And still the Germans came on.

Jack had been flying since dawn, bringing back reports of the German movements. He and his fellow eyes in the sky were proving their worth now, for the cavalry could not have brought in the reports the RFC had, nor once the battle was joined provided the overview of the German attack that could be seen from an aeroplane. Again and again he landed, made his report, and took off again. Flying over the German lines he had been shot at several times, but no-one had managed to hit him. The British soldiers did not fire at him – they had too much on their hands.

The information he brought back was that the Germans were attacking along the canal from Obourg in the east to Bustiau in the west, but that the concentration of the attack was on the curve of the canal at Nimy, which was the weak point of the line. But in the early afternoon he and other flyers brought back the news that behind the battle and out of sight to those on the ground there was other movement. A large German force was moving west and south with the obvious intention of outflanking the Allies and crossing the canal at Baudour and Hautrage, well beyond the embattled British left wing.

From what he had seen and what he had heard when he made his reports, Jack could have explained to Bertie where the missing artillery was. There was no field of fire, as Bertie had guessed, from Mons and its suburbs; but, more importantly, with the French in retreat, it was necessary to provide a second line of defence for the British front line to fall back to when the Germans finally broke through. The artillery, and the fresh troops that had been coming up from Le

144

Cateau all day, were being assembled on a new front to the south of Mons on a line across Harmignies, Frameries and Pâturages. The troops now in battle along the canal were the spearhead whose job it was to hold the town for the promised twenty-four hours. Then they would fall back to the new, more easily defended line in open country, and when the time was right, and the whole of the BEF was assembled, it was from here that the attack on the enemy would be launched.

Now, with the new information about the German movement, the front had to be extended. Circling the area after a snatched luncheon of bread and cheese, Jack saw with satisfaction that a battery had been moved up to a field outside the village of Dour. He reflected as he flew back towards the front line that the gunners down there must be puzzled as to why they were facing north-westwards, when all the firing they must be able to hear was coming from the north-east.

There had been no luncheon of any sort for the men along the canal. The fighting was fierce and there was no time for anything but to keep reloading and firing. An artillery unit had managed to set up in the small patch of open ground to the west of the village of Nimy, but it was able to give little more than moral support against the massive German armoury. The Germans had brought up machine-guns, which had improved their rate of firing. On the British side there were only two machine-guns, both mounted on the railway bridge to the left where, high up against the sky, they made an attractive target. The Germans were also dropping shrapnel shells from the open country behind their line. Casualties had mounted. The men were in good spirits still and were holding on, but as Bertie wrote in a note he sent to the colonel in the middle of the afternoon, 'Without reinforcements it must be a matter of time only before the enemy breaks through.'

In the baking afternoon sun the men fired at the never-decreasing hordes, sweating so much their clothes stuck to them, while the dust raised by the shells stuck to their faces and irritated their eyes. Ammunition was brought up, and drinking water, and the wounded and dead were helped or carried away. Bertie heard via the grapevine that Captain Athersuch was dead and Harcourt-Miller seriously wounded; his own Lieutenant Oxshott was also dead, and his other three officers had been wounded, Buckingham twice. His own arm wound had settled to a grinding throb, which he could easily ignore, and he had received two minor shrapnel grazes, one to the leg and the other to the head. He had been lucky to get away with that one: the shrapnel had sliced through his cap but only scratched his scalp. He looked along as much of the line as he could see, and estimated that he had lost about one in ten of his men, dead or wounded. There were noticeable spaces between them now, but they fought on, and Bertie thought they could hold out for a few more hours yet. Until nightfall, if they had to. He only hoped they did not have to.

The hateful sun was declining, though the day seemed barely less stifling for that. On the left wing the British line was still holding out, though with heavy casualties; on the right the Germans had managed to cross the canal at Obourg and the British were slowly falling back towards Mons, fighting every inch of the way. In the centre, the situation was grave. The Germans were pressing harder than ever. One of the two machine-guns on the bridge had been knocked out, and though the second was still firing, the bridge was in danger. A runner found Bertie with a note from HQ. It was the order to retire – for which Bertie sent up a weary *thank God*. The battalion had trained, as had the whole army, in the art of strategic withdrawal, and he was not afraid that any of the steady, grimy-faced men under his command would panic or run. He became aware for a moment of the pain in his arm, but shook the consciousness of it away as he read on. 'One platoon of C Company will form the rearguard and cover the retreat.' It was an honour for his company to be chosen.

He scrambled over to where Pennyfather was crouched with his men, firing steadily, and said, 'We're pulling back.

Your platoon will be rearguard. As soon as I give the signal, get back as quickly as you can to the line of that wall and those sheds. We'll hold out there while the others get away.'

'We, sir?' Pennyfather said.

Bertie grinned. 'You don't think I'd let you have all the fun, do you?'

Almost before the word had been passed to the last members of his company, the rest of the battalion had already started falling back. Bertie gave the signal to retire. The first part had to be done quickly: there was a stretch of open ground to be covered, and far from letting up, the Germans increased their fire as they saw the soldiers who had held them up all day turning tail. The scarred earth across which they ran seemed to boil with bullets and shrapnel; the air whined and rattled with shot from the German machine-guns. The British machine-gun up on the bridge finally fell silent, as the last person manning it was either killed or taken prisoner, and as the Germans began to scramble across, there was nothing left to stop them but Bertie and his handful of men. They crouched behind the wall and fired steadily as the rest of the battalion streamed past them towards the shelter of Nimy's walls.

The soldier next to Bertie – Private Miller – was hit. Bertie was so close he felt the shock of the bullet's blow. Miller fell back without a cry, shot through the neck, writhed a moment, and was still. Bertie shoved his pistol into his belt, grabbed up Miller's rifle and put it to his shoulder, ignoring the fiery protest of his wound. A rifle had a better range than a pistol. Now the last few West Herts were going past them. To the rear of the group, some way behind them, an officer was supporting a wounded man. He wove towards Bertie's group, staggering under the weight of the casualty and the pounding of bullets that were making the dust spurt almost under his heels. It seemed impossible that he had not been hit when the ground was leaping up all around him under the impact of shot and shrapnel, but he kept coming. It was Fenniman, Bertie saw now, half carrying, half dragging one of his own lieutenants, his face a snarl of determination.

'Gawd, it's old Winderpane!' someone said, and then shouted, 'Go it, sir! Go it!'

'Winderpane' was what the men universally called Fenniman – the usual soubriquet of the monocled man.

Others took up the cry. 'You can make it, sir!'

'Don't let the buggers get you!'

There were Germans on the near bank of the canal now, spreading out along its line, uncertain about advancing against the steady fire of Bertie's platoon. He saw an officer scramble down from the bridge and wave his arm, evidently ordering the advance. Bertie did not need to point him out: Pennyfather stood up, coolly aimed and fired, then ducked below the wall again as the German officer folded up. Bertie fired and was greeted only with an empty click, looked about him, reached into Miller's pocket for spare clips, reloaded and resumed fire. At last Fenniman was close enough for two of the men to stand up, reach out for the wounded lieutenant and manhandle him over the wall. Fenniman himself dived over inelegantly but effectively.

'Well done, sir!' one of the men said.

'Good work, old man,' Bertie said, as Fenniman wriggled round beside him and fired his pistol over the wall.

'Longest hundred yards I've ever run,' said Fenniman. 'Damned hot in this uniform. How's Buckley?'

'Out cold, sir,' said the private who was tending him. 'I think he's hurt bad, sir.'

Fenniman nodded. 'Took one in the chest,' was all he said, but he seemed upset.

'Everyone's back now, sir,' Pennyfather said.

'Yes,' said Bertie. 'We must retire. All right, Pennyfather, section by section. Fenniman, you'd better go with the first section, and see Buckley gets taken care of. Pennyfather, you go with the third section. I'll stay to last.'

Under the westering sun they played a deadly game of leapfrog, each section retiring behind the previous one, scrambling to some shelter, and firing to cover the next section's run. The Germans came on, but Bertie could see that the fighting had shaken them. They were reluctant to get to close quarters with the Tommies who had given them

148

such punishment all day. He could hear from time to time the officers exhorting them, and there were little rushes, which petered out when one of them fell. He was close enough to see one or two faces now, and they seemed very young, fair, reddened from the sun, somewhat bewildered, the faces of big, simple farm lads, who not long ago had been getting in the harvest from the fields and were probably wishing with all their hearts they could be back there. A glance at his own men showed the difference – the hardened faces, the narrowed eyes, the efficient and self-confident movements of professional, trained soldiers.

But there were so few of them now! On his last leapfrog only six men ran with him. The section's corporal was down, and one man wanted to go back for him, but Bertie yanked his arm and pulled him on. Dead or wounded, the corporal would be taken care of, and men who could still fire were needed elsewhere. The walls of the village were around them now, giving better cover, so that their game of leapfrog became less deadly; and the light was failing. It was a matter now of holding on until darkness released them.

The Germans brought a machine-gun across the canal and set it up to fire down Nimy's main street. Bertie and his men had been retiring steadily from one piece of cover to the next. They found the house that had been acting as Battalion HQ, but it was deserted, so there was nothing to be done but keep retiring towards the rendezvous, the village of Frameries a little way south of Mons. The machine-gun was making things difficult for them. If they allowed it to pin them down, they would either be killed or captured, and Bertie had no intention of accepting either fate.

The inhabitants of Nimy had already fled down the road into Mons, and the houses along the main street were all empty. They dodged from door to door, one of them covering the rest for the next dash. Now there was a long gap, the side wall of a small factory or workshop with no doors, before the next opening, an archway into a yard of some sort.

'We'll go together,' Bertie said. 'Keep close to the wall. *Now!*'

149

They spurted out of the doorway and ran. Dusk was coming on, which was in their favour, but they were seen, and the machine-gun spoke. One of the men, Willey, gave a shriek and staggered, and the man in front of him instinctively started to turn. 'Don't stop!' Bertie bellowed. He grabbed Willey's shoulder and shoved him forward. It was only a few yards now. A bullet smacked into the wall beside him and a shard of brick leaped out and cut his cheek. Willey's legs were buckling, but his momentum was enough for Bertie to keep him going those few more paces until the blessed archway opened to their right and they almost fell into the safety of a small enclosed yard. The machine-gun stuttered on a moment, then stopped. Were the Germans creeping from behind it, edging their way up the street? For the moment, Bertie had other things to think about.

For one, they were not alone in the yard. A white mule was standing there, oilcloth-covered packs across its back. It stared at them in mild astonishment, but made no effort to escape. Sprawled supine on the cobbles was the soldier who had presumably been leading it. Bertie could see he was dead: most of the top of his skull was missing. From his position, it looked as though the force of the shot had flung him through the archway – his feet were almost in the street and they had stumbled on him as they ran in – and the mule had presumably followed him in to escape the shooting.

Thorpe and Anderson had laid Willey down and were supporting his head. As Bertie crouched down with them, Willey's eyes met his, puzzled and vague with pain.

'How bad is it?' he asked.

'I dunno, sir,' said Thorpe. 'He got 'it in the back. There's a lot o' blood, sir.'

Bertie started to undo the buttons of Willey's tunic, and the man's hands fluttered towards them, whether to help him or stop him he couldn't tell. Then Willey gave a convulsive cough, and a gout of blood and tissue welled out of his mouth and spattered his chin and chest. The fluttering hands fell back, and the eyes glazed over.

Anderson, holding his head, felt the difference. 'He's gone, sir.'

'Yes,' said Bertie. 'Must have gone through the lung.'

Anderson laid the man's head down. 'Poor bugger,' he said.

Now there were five men with Bertie: Key, Anderson, Jones, Thorpe and Straw.

The machine-gun rattled again, sounding closer this time, and pieces broke off the brick edging of the arch in an explosion of red dust.

'They'll be moving up,' said Bertie. 'We can't stay here.'

'We can't go out there, sir,' Thorpe pointed out.

'No,' Bertie said, looking around. 'We'll have to go over the back wall.'

The men looked at it doubtfully. 'It's too 'igh, sir,' Thorpe said.

'We'll stand on the mule's back,' Bertie said. 'Which of you is the best at climbing?'

They looked at each other, and then Key, the youngest, half raised his hand. 'Me, sir, I reckon. I was a terrible one for climbing trees at home.'

'You'll go first then, and help the others. I'll come last. Let's see what's in the mule's packs first.'

'I hope it's grub,' Key muttered. None of them had eaten since breakfast.

'Thorpe, fire a few shots out down the street, in case they're coming, but don't stick your head out.'

Thorpe's shots were answered by the machine-gun. Bertie pulled out his pocket-knife and cut a corner of the pack covering. Underneath were boxes of ammunition. Must have been on his way up to the front line when an unlucky stray shot or piece of shrapnel had got him. But the ammunition was good news. They were all running short.

'Take as many clips as you can carry. Stuff them in your pockets and packs. We may not be out of the woods yet.'

The mule made no objection to taking up position by the wall, and with Bertie holding its head, Key climbed up, stood on top of the packs, and with an easy jump and scramble was on the top.

'What's on the other side?' Bertie asked.

'Gardens, sir, and fences. And more houses.'

That was good. He had been afraid it might be open space. 'Straw, you're next.'

Straw was the biggest and heaviest, and probably the least nimble. It took Key pulling and Anderson and Jones pushing to get him up, and the mule laid back its ears and shifted back and forth. Thorpe at the entry was still firing intermittently. When the machine-gun stopped for a moment he risked a quick look out, and called back over his shoulder, 'They're coming, sir. Up both sides o' the road.'

'Right, you two. Quickly.' Jones and Anderson were up in no time. 'Now, Thorpe. Run.'

Thorpe ran, slinging his rifle over his shoulder so hastily that the butt overswung and hit Bertie's ear. The mule shifted again, in alarm at the movement. Thorpe was up and over. Key and Anderson remained astride the wall, ready to help him. Bertie prayed that the mule would stand a little longer; that his wounded arm would be strong enough. The machine-gun had stopped again, and he heard a man's voice call something in German. It sounded horribly close. He let go of the mule's head, and speaking to it soothingly climbed up on its back. It began to walk forward. Bertie wobbled desperately. 'Whoa, whoa there, beauty,' he crooned, a little breathlessly. He had to give a little jump to get high enough, pushing off from the mule's back, and as he shoved down with his feet the animal tired of the game and trotted forward, out from under him. His outstretched fingers reached for the top of the wall, and though they hooked over it his grip would not have held. But Anderson and Key reached down and grabbed his wrists, and with his little momentum and the help of his toecaps scrabbling against the brick he was going up. His wounded arm screamed with pain but he managed to get his elbows over the wall.

Then Key said in a frightened gasp, 'Huns, sir! Right behind you!'

He heard their feet on the cobbles, heard them shout.

'Get down!' he blazed at the two men. 'Jump!'

A gun fired behind him, and Key and Anderson disappeared off the wall like ducks in a fairground rifle range.

Bertie did not know where the first bullet went. The second ricocheted off the wall beside him with a savage whine. A frightened man turning in at a yard where he expected to be shot at could not hope to do much better with his first two shots, but his third could hardly miss. Bertie hauled desperately with his elbows, swung his left leg up, got his knee over the wall. The third shot hit the brick next to his right leg, where his left had been the instant before. He swung his right leg up and rolled flat over the top, allowing himself to fall as a hail of shots passed over him, so close that he felt the wind of one in his hair.

Hands partly broke his fall, and he took Key down with him. They scrambled to their feet. 'You 'urt, sir?' Thorpe asked.

'No, they missed me. Come on, let's get going. This way.'

It was a row of gardens behind the houses in the parallel street, divided from each other by low fences or weedy hedges. They scrambled over cabbages and onions and the occasional flower patch and clambered over the fences. There were no sounds of pursuit. Bertie's wound had been woken into screaming protest by his exertions on the wall, and he could feel the flow of fresh blood from it, warm and then cold inside his sleeve. He hoped it would not bleed so much that he fainted. They would have to leave him behind and he'd be taken prisoner. He did not want to sit out the war in a prison camp.

At the end of the last garden was another wall, but not such a high one this time – no more than six feet; and there was a dustbin nearby to help them over. Bertie got up first to take a look. It was a narrow lane of mud and broken cobbles between the wall that flanked the gardens and the end walls of houses on the other side. To the right and opposite was the opening into an alley. There was no-one in sight. It was beginning to get dark, and a drizzle had started. The scene was one of grimy desolation. From behind and away to the east there were sporadic sounds of gunfire; from much further away to the west the occasional flat boom of heavy guns. The alley beckoned, offering safety and a route in the right direction. If they could keep to alleys and gardens they might get far enough in front of the Germans to get away.

'All right,' he said.

They went over the wall, one by one, waited pressed against its shadow until all were down, then ran across the lane to the alley. The going underfoot was greasy with the drizzling rain, and Straw slipped and fell flat, to be hauled to his feet by the two men nearest him without breaking their stride. They reached the alley and stopped, pressed back against the wall, panting, listening for pursuit. Bertie took a quick look out, and jerked his head back as he saw the German detachment passing the end of the lane, going down the parallel street that they had just fled.

The alley ran between the backs of two rows of workmen's cottages. At the end there was another lane, and beyond it a mess of small factories, workshops and yards flanking the railway that ran into Mons. They picked their way through the various yards, and on the other side found a muddy track that ran down through a small dripping archway under the railway – a pedestrian crossing of the line. On the other side of it, some way ahead, were lights: Mons and, presumably, the safety of numbers.

They ran across the brief stretch of open ground towards the railway arch, and a shout from away on their left was followed by a ragged brattle of rifle fire, which did not come near to hitting them – the German detachment, presumably, still moving parallel with them. But then there was another outburst, a proper volley this time, and from its direction it was being aimed at the Germans. They dashed through the arch, and on the far side looked up to their left, where a handful of khaki-clad soldiers had got themselves into a position behind the wall of the railway bridge that crossed the main road and were firing steadily at the approaching Germans.

There was an extraordinary feeling of relief at seeing some other British soldiers, even if their numbers were too small for it to make a great difference in the scheme of things; but in this case, their position was good enough to drive off the Germans. The enemy detachment retreated without another shot, and disappeared back into the shadows of the unlit street whence they'd come. Now with luck they could all get away into Mons where there must surely be plenty of British units still in the process of falling back.

Bertie and his men hurried forward to join their comrades – and then there was great joy as they recognised them.

'It's Mr Pennyfather, sir,' said Jones, in the lead.

So it was – Pennyfather and the remains of the section he had led from the allotments half a lifetime ago. He straightened up as Bertie approached, and the two men shook hands with probably equal relief.

'I can't tell you how glad I am to see you, sir,' Pennyfather said. 'We'd thought they must have got you. After that damned machine-gun started up . . .'

'Where's the rest of the platoon?'

'I don't know, sir. I haven't seen them. I suppose they must have gone on into Mons. I stayed back with this section in case you did manage to get through, and needed help.'

'I'm damned glad you did,' said Bertie.

'I was on the point of giving up,' Pennyfather admitted. 'Now it's getting dark, I thought we'd better move on, but then we saw the Germans, and then we saw you.'

Bertie glanced back down the street. 'We'd better get moving while we can. The rendezvous is at Frameries, which is about three miles south of Mons, so we've probably got about four miles to cover.'

'The going shouldn't be too bad,' Pennyfather said, 'now we can stick to the road without the Germans shooting at us. We should do it in an hour or so. Say an hour and a half.'

They formed the men up, and set off. 'I hope they've got some hot grub waiting for us,' Pennyfather said. 'The men haven't eaten all day.'

Mons was on the move. The entire population was in the process of fleeing, and it was easy to tell why: not only were the Germans behind them, in Nimy, but from here it was possible to hear quite clearly the boom of heavy artillery from away on the western flank, and to see the glow in the sky of burning buildings. The streets were crammed with people, all of them weighted down with possessions – suitcases, bulging bags, hastily wrapped parcels, bundles made of sheets and tablecloths into which precious possessions had been tumbled. A horse or donkey was worth its weight in gold. Handcarts were piled with furniture and possessions; even perambulators and wheelbarrows were pressed into service. People fled with their children and their old folk, their babes-in-arms, their dogs and their caged canaries, and they packed the roads from side to side, all heading south.

It was impossible in the situation to find one's military unit, to report, to rendezvous. All that could be done was to join the throng and shuffle in time with everyone else. Bertie saw soldiers everywhere, in small groups, in twos and threes, single men, and they were from every different unit that had been engaged with the enemy. He saw men from the Middlesex, from the Royal Fusiliers; he saw Royal Scots and Gordons. He didn't know where his own colonel was, let alone the rest of his company. He hadn't seen Cooper for hours, he had no idea where his horses or his kit might be, and could only hope they had been removed from the path of the Germans by the transport section. As they forced their way slowly through the main square, it was all he could do to keep his small unit together. He had eleven men, a corporal and a lieutenant, and was anxious that his command did not shrink yet further.

Once they were out of the main square, the press of people eased somewhat as there were more streets to take them, but the going was still painfully slow. It was dark now, and the drizzle continued, making the cobbles as slippery as ice underfoot, and there were unseen tramlines, gutters and potholes to add to the hazards. They were all hungry, but even more than that they were thirsty after the long hot day of strain and effort, sun, dust and gunsmoke. And more than either, they were worn out. They slithered and stumbled and cursed, their eyes sore and gritty, their heads aching, their limbs leaden.

Outside Mons it was a horrible terrain, a mess of grimy mining villages, the meanest sort of cottages, pitheads, slag heaps, factory chimneys, every surface coated with coal dust, nothing of nature but a few stunted trees and straggling hedges clinging to existence in the inhospitable environment man had made. In the villages there were lights on in buildings, just enough to see the way by; on the short stretches of road in between it was dark, and there was the added hazard of going off the road and into a ditch. Over to the west, where the heavy gunfire continued, the sky was lurid orange with the smoky flames from burning villages. There were fleeing Belgians on every road, and at every junction the flows collided, making additional confusion. It was impossible to march. Bertie kept his men together, and they proceeded at a staggering walk. Other stray soldiers had joined them now, glad of the company and of an officer to take decisions for them, and he had twenty in his squad.

And at last here was Frameries, as dismal a village as any, a thing of low cottages crouched among slag heaps. But there were two officers standing by the road, ready to direct soldiers to the appropriate rendezvous point.

'West Herts? Keep on going, through the village. There's a line of trenches on the far side, and about half a mile further on, on the left, is the field where you'll be bivouacking. There'll be someone posted there to put you right.'

'Thank you,' said Bertie. 'I've got some men with me who got separated from other regiments.'

'Odds and sods over there,' the officer said cheerfully. 'Plenty of those around tonight.'

Bertie's squad stumbled on, sleep-walking now. There was considerable activity along the line of trenches – men digging, stringing wire, sentries everywhere – and Bertie recognised the badges of regiments who had not been in the fighting on the canal.

'Those must be the troops who were still coming up from Le Cateau,' said Pennyfather, walking beside him. 'Pity they missed the scrap. We could have done with them.'

'Poor devils, they don't look in much better shape than us,' Bertie said. 'I suppose they've been marching all day and digging all night.'

And then at last there was a field gate with a West Herts sentry, and they turned in, every man straightening a little as his heart lifted with the momentary feeling of coming home. It was after eleven, and they had not rested since they stood-to at dawn.

The colonel came forward to shake Bertie's hand, and said, 'Damned glad to see you. Thought we'd lost you. We bivouac here for the night. Settle your men, and then you can come and report. Transport section hasn't found us yet. We were promised a hot meal tonight, but that hasn't arrived either.'

It was just an empty field, but the men were so dead weary they wanted nothing more than to slump down, take the weight off their legs, light a cigarette. Some didn't even manage to stay awake long enough for that, but fell asleep on the instant, heads cradled on their arms on the wet grass. Others propped each other up while they smoked and swapped tales with those from other platoons. They were almost too tired to complain about the lack of rations. Without their packs, the rearguard men did not even have the remains of their iron rations to eat. HQ staff donated a dozen hard-boiled eggs, which they had been saving for breakfast, and the eleven men and the corporal had one apiece – Bertie and Pennyfather went without. There was a stream behind the hedge at the bottom of the field and they were all able to have a drink and refill their water-bottles.

Having overseen these dispositions, Bertie dragged himself to the corner where Battalion HQ was now represented by an oil lamp, a camp stool and a flimsy folding table where the adjutant wrote the reports and listed the casualties. The first person he saw was Fenniman, looking worn but still smoking his cigarette with an air.

'How's Buckley?' was Bertie's first question.

'Didn't make it,' said Fenniman. 'When we got him to the shelter of the village street he was dead, so we had to leave him.'

'Rotten luck,' Bertie said. 'Yours was a magnificent effort.'

'Oh, rot,' said Fenniman. 'You'd have done the same. Hot

work, wasn't it?' And they smiled at each other with the comradeship of battle.

Bertie made his report to the colonel, gave the names of the men he had brought back to Penkridge, enquired about who was missing. The loss was terrible. Of the officers, Captain Athersuch was dead, Harcourt-Miller wounded and left behind at a Red Cross station. Four lieutenants, including his own Oxshott and Fenniman's Buckley were dead, and Buckingham had fallen in the retreat, it was not known whether dead or wounded. And the battalion had lost over three hundred and fifty men, dead, wounded or missing – a hundred of them from Bertie's own company, which, forming the rearguard, had suffered the most. Cooper was one of those missing, but Bertie bet silently that he was alive somewhere, merely separated in the dark and confusion. He didn't believe any mere German could kill Cooper. The colonel hoped that quite a number of the missing were stragglers and would come in during the night or the next day.

'From all reports it seems as though the Germans have stopped their advance for the night. Probably as much in need of a rest as our fellows. So there's a good chance the stragglers may get through. I hope so. We shall need every hand tomorrow. We make our new stand on this line – you saw the trenches?'

'Yes, sir,' said Bertie.

'It was a damn' good show today,' said the colonel, eyeing Bertie as if to gauge his thoughts. 'We held off the whole German Army – gave 'em a bloody nose. Now the rest of the Expeditionary Force has come up, we'll settle with them tomorrow, once for all.'

'Yes, sir,' said Bertie again, and tried to sound enthusiastic about it. He was swaying with weariness, his arm was throbbing like a rotten tooth, the wound in his leg had stiffened up, and his heart was full of the fallen, the men and officers he had known and begun to grow fond of.

But at that moment there came the welcome interruption of a lorry arriving, at last bringing rations. There was hot stew, bread and tea. They had to wake some of the men to give them their dinner, and it was strange eating at near midnight, but the hot food and drink was what everyone needed desperately after their long exertions. Afterwards they wrapped themselves in their coats and lay down to sleep like the dead under a clear and starry sky.

Even as they slept, the situation was changing. At midnight Sir John French received the news that General Lanrezac's Fifth Army, on the British right, was falling back in order to keep in contact with the Fourth Army, on *their* right, who were being forced back in fierce fighting with the Germans. By morning they would be a day's march to the rear of the BEF, and drawing further away all the time. The new front line, which the weary soldiers were only just finishing digging, would be hopelessly isolated, and vulnerable to outflanking on both sides. Alone, the British could not hold the position. There was no alternative but to retire, to move south towards Le Cateau, to try to catch up with the French and find some other place for them all to make a stand.

CHAPTER EIGHT

Left to themselves, the battle-weary battalion might have slept all day. Bertie was woken at around four thirty, in the grey of morning twilight, by an aeroplane buzzing overhead, but he was asleep again almost on the instant. He was woken again at six thirty by the sound of artillery, and tried to get up in a hurry, only to find various parts of his body would not obey him. The arm on which he had been cradling his head had gone to sleep, and there was no feeling in his left thigh where it had been in contact with the unforgiving earth. Apart from that he was cold and stiff all over, and he had an abominable crick in his neck. He rolled over and managed to sit up, rubbing various parts of himself, feeling the grittiness of his eyes and the sour taste in his mouth, and listened for the distance and direction of the guns. To the north-west, as they were last night, but surely closer now. Sometimes he thought he could feel the vibration of them in the earth.

A figure appeared beside him – Brevet, one of the men he had brought in last night. 'Tea, sir,' he said, proffering a tin cup. 'Compliments of Captain Fenniman, sir. 'E 'ad a twist of it in 'is pocket. It's a bit weak 'cos it's bin round all the officers. And no milk, sir,' he added regretfully. 'There 'asn't been no rations yet. I hope they gets 'ere before we 'as to stand-to.'

'Thank you, Brevet,' Bertie said, accepting the cup of warm, slightly coloured water with more gratitude than it would normally have elicited.

161

'Mr Pennyfather, sir, 'e says I'm to act as your orderly, temporary-like, until Cooper catches up with us, if that's all right with you.' Bertie was interested to note that Pennyfather and Brevet evidently didn't believe Cooper could be dead, either.

'Yes – thank you.'

Brevet eyed him judiciously. 'If you was to give me your jacket, sir, I could see what I could do with it. Lawson, sir, 'e's got a needle and thread with 'im. I could cobble it together for you, sir.'

'Transport's not found us, then?'

'No, sir.' Brevet had to help him out of it, for the blood had stiffened and glued arm, shirt and coat sleeve together in one mass. 'You ought to 'ave that looked at, sir.'

Bertie shook his head. 'It's not hurting much now, and I don't want anyone poking and prodding it.' Besides, he remembered an old army doctor in Pretoria saying that the best thing for a wound was to bleed freely, then be left undisturbed, bound in its own blood. Dried blood, the doctor had said, was the best protection from infection.

'Can't say as I blame you, sir,' Brevet said, and went away. Bertie hauled himself to his feet and went to find himself a hedge, then to the stream to wash his hands and face as best he could, working round the cut on his cheek so as not to open it again. The guns were definitely closer. He could see the surface of the water tremble with the percussion. He rubbed his chin, wishing he could shave – one felt so under par when one hadn't shaved – but until their transport got through he had no kit.

When he got back to the field, Brevet met him with his coat, which looked much better. He had washed most of the blood out of it, and the rent, far from being cobbled together, had been neatly patched. 'There, sir. It'll do for now, anyway.'

'That's very good, Brevet. Really, I wasn't expecting anything as good as that.'

'I was a tailor, sir, before I joined the army,' Brevet said, with a pleased look. 'I cut a bit off the inside of one of your pockets for the patch.'

'Excellent man. Thank you very much indeed.' A particularly heavy boom shook the earth under their feet, and their eyes met.

'Gettin' closer, sir.'

'Yes.'

'It'll be a hot one today.'

He might have meant the weather, for the sky was pale and clear, promising another fine day. Bertie didn't think so. But Brevet grinned when he said it, as though the prospect far from daunted him.

Just then the colonel's orderly ran up and requested his presence in the corner of the field. Bertie joined the other officers there, to receive the news that they were not to fight in the new line of trenches after all, but were to retire towards Bavai.

'The French have retired and we are out of touch with them, and we can't hold this line alone. The Germans are advancing from the north and north-west. Our artillery have already engaged them, and will hold them back as long as possible. The Ox and Bucks, who were not in action yesterday, will hold these trenches and cover our retreat. There is no time to lose. We have to make all haste, but our retreat above all must be orderly. This is a strategic withdrawal and I don't want anyone to be able to say the battalion ran away. We will parade the men at once, take roll call, then form up on the road in column of four and march off smartly – smartly, gentlemen, in the best tradition of the West Herts.'

Fenniman said, 'The men's breakfast, sir?'

Abernethy shook his head. 'We can't wait for the ration lorry, even supposing it is coming. There is a little biscuit that we brought from Headquarters yesterday – possibly, with our diminished numbers, enough for one per man – but we must keep it in case nothing is forthcoming during the day. The men had a good meal last night, and they may be much hungrier later.'

'How far is Bavai, sir?' asked Yerbury.

'About twelve miles. An easy day's march.'

'And when we get there, sir?' asked Fenniman. 'Will that be the new line?'

Abernethy looked away. 'I have no orders about that. My instructions are only that we retire to Bavai. Very well, gentlemen. With all speed, if you please.'

By the time the men had paraded and the roll had been taken, there was no doubt that the Germans were much closer. Shells had started to fall on the village of Frameries itself. The ground shook with the explosions, the air was full of dust from collapsing buildings, and with dark smoke from fires the shells had started. The inhabitants of the village had poured out onto the streets and were now desperately fleeing, dragging with them anything they had been able to gather up in their panic. They shouted to each other, screamed the names of relatives they had momentarily lost, waved their arms in violent imprecation against the Germans. Children howled, dogs barked, and women shrieked at every new explosion. In the midst of all this confusion, and with shells blasting close behind them, the West Herts men formed up calmly, the iron discipline of the army proving its worth now, steadying them when they might otherwise have felt part of the confusion. Breakfastless, unshaven, weary from the previous day's battle, many of them wounded, they sloped arms and marched off as if they were on the parade ground back home at Sandridge.

Bertie, despite the fact that, horseless, he was going to have to march with them, and that his injured left leg had stiffened up, was filled with pride and a sort of fierce love for his men that said, *The Germans can't match that. Let 'em come – we'll beat them anywhere, any time.*

A twelve-mile march would have been relatively easy in normal circumstances, and even tired as they were, the men could have covered the distance in reasonable time. But the roads were not clear, and before long it was all they could do to keep together. Marching, keeping up any sort of rhythm, was impossible. The stream of refugees slowed the general pace to their own, a sort of shambling walk, interrupted by many and lengthy halts. Usually it was not possible to see what the hold-up was. Some incident further down the road halted everyone in a chain reaction that ran back for miles, and by the time the place of the incident was reached there was no sign of what it had been.

The refugees stumbled along miserably, holding children by the hand and dogs by the lead, carrying bundles and suitcases, pushing carts and perambulators loaded with their belongings. Some had donkey carts, pony traps, or farm wagons pulled by teams of beautiful blond Belgian horses. They creaked and rumbled at farm-track pace, holding up the progress of the battalions of infantry all trying to retire south, so that the speed of the whole unwieldy mass was little more than a mile an hour. Mixed into the turgid flow were gun-carriages, ammunition wagons, supply lorries, and the odd officer's motor-car and despatch motor-cycle: sweating, red-faced NCOs had to try to get the crowds to shuffle to the side of the road to let them past.

The dust raised by so many feet and wheels hung in the air in a permanent cloud, coating sweaty faces, making the men cough. Their boots slipped on the hated cobbles. The sun shone down from a perfect sky and there was no shade on the route, so that their noses and ears began to burn all over again. The villages they passed through were all deserted now, the houses shuttered and empty, the inhabitants presumably somewhere in the column, refugees like the rest.

One of the mysterious halts came when the West Herts were passing through one of the villages, and they came to a standstill in the main street. As they stood waiting for the movement to resume, the upstairs shutters on one of the houses were thrown open and an old woman leaned out, looking dishevelled and wild-eyed, and began to shake her fist at the soldiers, pouring out a torrent of what was evidently abuse. She had few teeth and in any case spoke in such an extremely local accent that Bertie could not understand her, until she exhausted her vocabulary and fell into a repetition of '*Perfides! Lâches! Perfides! Perfides!*'

'What's up wiv her, silly old bitch?' one of the men muttered.

Brevet, who was beside Bertie, said, 'What's that she's saying, sir, *perfides*? Is that like the same as *perfidious*?'

'Pretty much,' Bertie admitted.

Brevet was indignant. 'Well, she's got a damn' cheek. What does she think, that we're running away?'

'We weren't beat,' said one of the others, and there was a mutter of agreement.

'The Bosch never got past us.'

'We give as good as we got, *and* better. We slaughtered 'em.'

'Right, and they outnumbered us three to one.'

'Blimey, she should be chucking us bokays.'

'They were all chucking flowers at us on our way up to Mons.'

There was a very different mood among the natives now, and no wonder, given that they were having to flee their homes. But Bertie could see that the men weren't downhearted. They knew they had done well, and though they did not like retreating, they felt this was only a temporary setback.

Brevet spoke up for all of them. 'That is right, sir, what they say, isn't it, that this is just a ruse? We're luring the Germans into a trap, aren't we, sir? And when we've got far enough back we'll turn round and give 'em 'ell.'

'That's right,' Bertie said. 'We need to get into a position where the French can attack them on the flank while we attack full front.'

The men looked pleased at that. 'We'll give 'em socks, sir!'

'We certainly will,' said Bertie.

The old woman was silent now, staring down at them with mad red eyes, her toothless jaws mumbling as though she were chewing bread. Bread! Oh, don't think about food, he told himself.

Thorpe waved his arms to attract the old woman's attention, and shouted at her, 'Oy, Missus! We're not running away, you daft ha'porth! We're gonna turn around in a bit and fight the Bosch. Comprendy? Fightee Boschee. Beat the f—ers. Muchee killee. All right?'

His explanation was accompanied with complicated hand gestures describing these actions, which, perhaps understandably, did nothing to placate the old woman. She stared a moment, then started up her tirade again, shaking both fists at Thorpe and almost choking herself on her rage. Finally she threw a china soap dish at him – with considerable accuracy, so that he had to put up his hand to protect his face. The other men were almost helpless with laughter, which added to Thorpe's embarrassment and the old woman's indignation. It was fortunate that they started moving again just then, or Bertie feared she might have come out into the street and started pummelling him.

It was well after dark when they reached Bavai. The town was at the junction of the east–west road from Maubeuge to Valenciennes and the north–south road from Mons to Le Cateau; but many other roads fed into it like the spokes of a wheel, and on most of them refugees and British troops were pouring in. It took time to filter through the packed, narrow streets and find the field on the south side where the battalion was directed to bivouac. A cornfield, this time, already harvested, so providing stubble for their night's rest instead of wet grass – not much of an exchange, Bertie thought. But there was good news awaiting them. Their horses and transport had found them at last, and a ration lorry had delivered a hot meal of stew, bread, cheese and tea, along with a breakfast ration of biscuit and hard-boiled eggs, so whatever happened tomorrow they would not have to face it on an empty stomach.

And there was a further treat – a bag of mail. With their bellies full, there was nothing the men could have wanted more. The lucky recipients were much envied, and each man reading a letter by the light of a pocket torch was surrounded by a little group of well-wishers who seemed to be bathing in the reflected warmth of words from home.

Bertie had a letter from Jessie.

Maystone Villa. 20th August 1914
My dear Bertie
I received your letter of the 16th and was delighted you had time to write in so much detail. Your French

'holiday' sounds idyllic – apart from the breakfast of jam! We have no news of the war here – the newspapers carry nothing but the official communiquet (can't spell it!) which says something like 'the BEF has reached its new position' and leaves the rest to imagination. But your letter allows me to imagine *un*-horrid things so I am content. We are all very excited here about the war. It seems to give an edge to everything, and one wakes up in the morning with the feeling that the ordinary, humdrum life of before is flown away, and that one is a part of great and stirring events. Everyone is anxious to be doing something 'useful'. I am lucky because my Red Cross classes count in my favour, and I am taking the First Aid and Home Nursing tests next week, which will give me certificates to prove my worth. Mrs Wycherley, who is doing them with me, says it is not possible to fail the tests so perhaps the worth is in question!

Apart from first aid I am busy with the horses, the more so as two of my lads have volunteered. There is a perfect craze for volunteering now, everyone is doing it. Military bands march about the towns and stir people up, and posters and advertisements in the newspapers do the rest. We are not behindhand in our family. First to go was Lennie Manning, who slipped away one day and signed up without telling anyone. It caused a perfect furoary (can't spell that either) because it seems American citizens aren't allowed to enlist in foreign armies on pain of losing their citizenship (very serious). Lennie's father sent a cable demanding he withdraw (and as he's a few months under age Uncle Teddy said it could be arranged) but Lennie refused and begged Uncle T not to make him. Of course we were all so proud of him for doing it we were on his side, especially Polly who has a crush on him, now worse than ever. Then a cable came from his grandmother saying, 'Attaboy', which is American for 'jolly good show', so Lennie kept his uniform (in which he looks rather splendid but *very* young) and marched off to camp.

Next we heard from Jack that he was specially asked to join the Royal Flying Corps as they needed experienced flyers. He had to do army basic training as he's never been in uniform but we heard from Helen that he has gone out to France now, so perhaps you'll meet up with him. I hope so. I like to think of my two dearest relatives together. It's sad for Helen because they had to put the wedding off but she says he is bound to get leave around Christmas and they will do it then. We are very proud of him as you may believe, and Helen sent me a copy of his photograph in uniform and he looks *very* handsome.

And then Frank surprised us all very much by telephoning to say he had volunteered for the Rifles! Of course, when he was a boy he always wanted to be a soldier, but since he has grown up he has been so dedicated to study and mathematics and so on that one didn't imagine him doing anything so physical. He telephoned me after Morland Place and I asked him about his research. He said it was important but not as important as saving the world from the Germans, and that he could go back to his work when there was peace to work in. Doesn't that sound heroic? I didn't see him in his uniform but I bet he looked like a hero. I must end this long letter as my hand is aching and there are horses to attend to. I think about you every day, and imagine what you are doing, and pray you safe.

Ever your loving cousin,
Jessie

With the pleasure of this letter warming his blood, and reunited with his kit, Bertie took the opportunity of shaving and putting on a clean shirt, and felt a great deal better, though his wounds were hurting and his feet were sore from marching. But tomorrow he would have Kestrel to carry him, which was a cheering thought. He raided his special stores for a bottle of port with which he regaled the other officers, repaying Fenniman's tea of the morning. The night was quiet, with no sound of artillery, and he was gratefully preparing to turn in, with the help this time of a blanket to roll himself in, when the colonel called all the officers to a meeting. 'New orders,' he said. 'We are to retire further tomorrow, to Le Cateau.'

Someone groaned softly, and the colonel looked round sharply, trying to guess who it was.

'It's a march of eighteen or nineteen miles,' he resumed, 'so we must start before dawn if we are to get ahead before the refugees take to the road. This will be the last retreat, gentlemen, and you can tell the men so in the morning. At Le Cateau we will make a stand along a line between Le Cateau and Cambrai. The 4th Division has arrived at the railhead there, and I am assured the French will be on our right.'

'Where are the Germans, sir?' Bertie asked.

'Those we engaged at Mons are following us but it seems are not pressing the attack tonight. Perhaps they are as tired as we are,' he added, with a grim smile. 'However, they will certainly do so in the morning, which is another reason for an early start. We will fight them, gentlemen, but it will be on a ground of our choosing, not theirs, and with our allies beside us. Any more questions?'

There was silence. 'Very well. We'll parade the men at four and march off at four thirty. Now, as to the route . . .' He spread out the map and they gathered round him.

When Bertie returned to his own company there was not a man awake. Beside him Pennyfather said quietly, 'We'll have our work cut out, waking them at four o'clock.'

Yerbury replied, 'The question is, who's going to wake us to wake them? I don't feel as though I've slept for years.'

'At least it's a fine night,' Bertie said. 'Better turn in while you can, and pray the Germans don't decide to attack us while we sleep.'

Jack was in the air as soon as there was enough light to take off. The sky was clear and it promised to be another hot day. He and his fellow flyers had had an exhausting day yesterday, and were anticipating another today, but their spirits were high, for they had unquestionably proved their worth, and no-one in the BEF command could now believe that there could ever again be an army without its air service.

The previous day – Monday the 24th – had been particularly trying since the RFC had had to move its headquarters from Maubeuge. Jack had said goodbye to his little monk's cell that morning, and for the rest of the day had great difficulty in finding anyone to make his reports to. The fleet of motor-transport that represented his home unit was now inextricably mixed with the rest of the military and refugee traffic, and spotting it was difficult enough, while landing anywhere close enough to make a report was near impossible. Added to the problem of flying low and hopping over hedges looking for somewhere to put down, was the hazard of being let fly at by Tommies, who were so bored and irritated by the slow and frustrating tramp south that the chance of taking pot shots was a welcome diversion.

Today as he took to the sky, pale with morning and decorated with innocent pink clouds like babies' blankets, he was more concerned with being shot at by the Germans. They had halted for the night north of Bavai, and when he passed over them for the first time they did not seem to be stirring. This was very well for the British Army, but a little puzzling, for the German forces were enormous, and spread over a wide front on a line from Maubeuge to Valenciennes. Perhaps the Germans were expecting the British to stand and fight there. He flew over the German front, keeping high enough, now he had found them, for their shots to pose him no danger, and headed further west.

The day before he had seen an enormous German force, a whole corps, he thought, far out to the west – too far away to be of immediate danger to the BEF – and moving steadily south-westward. His job was to report, not interpret, but it seemed plain enough that they were trying to avoid a battle and outflank the British to get to the Channel ports. Now, however, when he located the great grey snake that covered ten miles of road, he found that it had turned south, and was heading steadily towards a point south of Valenciennes. He thought he understood. If the Germans believed the British were going to make a stand along the line of Bavai, it made sense for them not to attack yet. They had only to wait, and this other German force would close round Bavai from the rear, trapping the British between the two of them for a complete slaughter.

It was hard to wake the men, who had been asleep only a few hours and needed more than a brief rest on the hard earth to restore them. The dew was heavy on their coats and blankets, and in the shadow of the trees and hedges it was chilly enough to make them shiver as they climbed stiffly to their feet, and to make their breath steam as they drank their tea and ate their biscuit and hard-boiled eggs. Wounds had stiffened, feet were swollen, and despite the colonel's orders it took time to get the men moving. The sun was up, its long rays turning the dew on the hedges to a sheet of glimmering gold, by the time they started out on the road. Bertie mounted Kestrel gratefully, but looking along the line of his men and seeing how many were hobbling even before they began, he thought with a sigh that he would not be in the saddle for long.

They did not make much distance before the road filled up again with refugees. As the sun shook off its autumnal languor and began to beat down, they found themselves in a repeat of the previous day, as if they were trapped in a recurring dream: heat, dust, slow, shuffling pace, sunburn, thirst, dry throats and blistered feet. Today, however, as the morning wore on, the tedium was enlivened by German aeroplanes, flying parallel with them and from time to time swooping low over the column before wheeling away, presumably to make their reports. Their activities terrified the civilians, who screamed, covered their heads and not infrequently fell to the ground or tried to get into a ditch, causing more delays in the slow march; but the Tommies were delighted at having something to do and someone to shoot at, and blazed away with a will at any airman who came near.

It was not possible, however, to stop the aeroplanes taking back their intelligence to the German command, and as th morning wore on it was obvious that the enemy was pursuit. From his vantage-point on horseback, Bertie saw the distant moving shapes of their own cavalry, keeping pace with the infantry columns and guarding their flanks, and sometimes heard the sharp rattles of gunfire as they engaged the German cavalry and drove them off. When they reached Le Quesnoy at around noon, the West Herts were almost trapped by a more serious threat. The walled fortress town was just ahead when a mass of German cavalry and horse artillery appeared from the west and bore down on them. The civilians screamed, and tried to break into a run. Bertie looked around. There was little cover, not enough for all the refugees, unless he and his men could hold off the attack long enough for them to reach the town.

He wheeled his horse and shouted to his company, 'Take up position along the hedge. Mr Yerbury – that way. Mr Pennyfather, over there.' The men had begun to move almost before he spoke, seeing the threat as clearly as he did. In front of him on the road he could see Fenniman directing his men to similar positions, and Spendlove, the lieutenant in acting command of B Company, intelligently following suit. Behind him D Company was dithering, its acting commander not as quick thinking. Bertie put his heels to Kestrel's flanks and rode down on them. 'Mr Crittal! Get your men into position along the hedge. Open fire when you have the range.'

For the civilians it was the first time they had actually seen a German, though their talk had been full of them for weeks past, and their nightmares for the last few days. Bertie wheeled Kestrel on the spot, trying to gauge their reaction. They were screaming in fear, but as the soldiers separated themselves from the column there was room for them to run, and that was what they wanted to do. There was no point in giving them orders. Better to rely on their instinct for self-preservation, which would hurry them towards the safety of Le Quesnoy's ramparts.

His own men were behaving in exemplary fashion. This was what they had dreamed of all through the last day and a half – a chance to get back at the Germans. They crouched behind the hedge, rifles loaded and ready, waiting steadily for the order to fire. The German cavalry were coming on; the horse artillery had halted and swung round to set up their guns. Hedges would not protect them against artillery. He must hope they could beat off the cavalry and run for the town before the guns were ready and had their range. He must hope the civilians got away quickly enough to give them a clear run for the gates.

Fenniman's company opened fire. The slight curve in the road gave him the advantage. Bertie yelled, 'Rapid fire!' and his company and Spendlove's opened fire at the same instant. He didn't hear Crittal's command through the noise, but D Company joined in a moment later. There was no trace of tiredness now in the men. They fired like machines, and the German cavalry were checked, swinging round as they had at Nimy in the face of this broadside. But they had only to keep the British occupied until the artillery was ready to fire. They came again, and were repulsed. Bertie looked back towards the town. The refugees were fleeing in good order, though the road was littered with the possessions they had dropped. The way was more or less open. He wheeled Kestrel and galloped up to Fenniman.

'I suggest we fall back by companies,' he said, over the rattle of rifle-fire. 'We can't stand up to artillery.'

'Just so,' said Fenniman. 'Will you pass the word to Mr Crittal? You'll be quicker on horseback than a runner.'

Bertie nodded and galloped back. D Company were reluctant to leave off shooting, but the German cavalry did the job. They jumped the hedge further back down the road and were now approaching along it. Crittal ordered one platoon across the road, and they fired steadily as the others scrambled away behind them, backing along the road until Bertie ordered Yerbury's men to take over. Now in the more confined space of the road the Germans were firing their carbines. Men were being hit. Further up the road half a dozen horsemen broke through and laid about them with their swords until they were driven back. Bertie's men had reached B Company now, while D Company had nearly reached the gates to take up what would be the last position. But the artillery were almost ready. Any minute now the deadly hail of shrapnel would be shredding the hedge like paper and tearing into them. Would any of them survive?

And then, suddenly, came deliverance. Someone was firing down from the town's ramparts – the rapid fire of a British detachment – and the German cavalry reeled about, disconcerted, men falling from the saddle in this sudden and unexpected attack. The West Herts cheered and redoubled their efforts. And then from around the north side of the walled town came British cavalry, charging down on the guns, which were of course facing the wrong way to defend themselves against this attack.

The German cavalry turned and fled, and Bertie and Fenniman took the opportunity of calling their men off and getting away into the citadel, carrying the wounded and leaving the dead.

The town was very small, the streets narrow and crowded, and the fleeing civilians were milling about, crying, trembling, wailing to heaven for deliverance and asking what was going to happen next. Forcing his way into the main square Bertie was relieved to see the colonel, who had gone ahead some time before with the headquarters staff but had presumably hurried back when he heard the firing.

'Fourth Dragoon Guards,' he said, anticipating Bertie's first question. 'Thank God for the cavalry!'

'Amen to that, sir.'

Abernethy looked around. 'We can't stay here. We'll be trapped. The Germans are everywhere, coming down from the Valenciennes direction. We must retire before they surround us. Jimmy, where's that map?' Penkridge passed it over. 'We'll follow this road, through Ghissignies, however you pronounce that – damned jaw-breaker of a language! If necessary we can turn and fight in any of these villages.' He stabbed a finger on them rather than pronounce them. 'The Engineers have been working all day, digging trenches and knocking out loopholes in the villages all along the route. But our main business is to get back in one piece to Le Cateau. If we can keep ahead of the Germans, all the better.' He glanced sharply at Bertie's arm. 'Are you wounded?'

Bertie looked down. His sleeve was freshly soaked in

blood. What a good thing, he thought grimly, that he hadn't changed his tunic as well as his shirt. 'It's one I took at Mons, sir. Must have opened up again.'

'Well, you can get it seen to in Le Cateau. We'll have all the facilities there – proper billets, stores, medical treatment. Ah, there's Fenniman. Pass the word to him, will you, and get going right away? Penkridge, go and tell Spendlove and Crittal. Parke – how many did we lose, do you know?'

'About twenty, I think, sir. Mostly from D Company. They took the brunt of it. I lost one dead and two wounded.'

'Damnit!' said the colonel.

The hot day ground on, the afternoon growing more sultry and humid as thunder began to mutter around the horizons. Jack could see that the German army, having been taken by surprise by the British retirement from Bavai, was making up for lost time. A large force of infantry and a train of motor-lorries were following the British down the same roads, and since they did not have to struggle with refugees blocking the way, they were making good speed. They were not far behind now. Their cavalry, travelling faster across country, had been harrying the flanks and being driven off by the British cavalry all day.

A violent storm was gathering, and by half past four Jack was wondering how much longer he could fly. The black clouds had closed up like heavy curtains drawn together over the whole sky, the temperature had dropped, and the smell of lightning was in the air. He had been observing the movement of the German cavalry as it came down from the north-west towards Solesmes. Solesmes was another cross-roads town like Bavai, but even more difficult to traverse: although there were five roads in on the north side, because of the River Selle there was only one main road out on the south side. As he flew over it for what he meant to be his last pass, he saw that there was serious trouble down there. The one road south had been closed in order to allow the French cavalry to cross from the right flank to the left where they had been ordered to take up a new position. Because of this, the town had become like a purse-string bag int which grain was being poured. The columns of British infantry and refugees were pressing in from several directions but there was no way for them to get out. Jack flew lower and saw how every street in the small town was crammed with people, and movement had all but ceased. Wagons and limbers, forced into unsuitable alleys, had got jammed, making the problem worse. And the Germans were approaching from the north and north-west.

Between them and the choked town with its trapped infantry were two battalions of a rearguard, fresh soldiers sent up from the 4th Division, which had arrived in Le Cateau that morning. They were dug in to some of the Royal Engineers' trenches, and if necessary from there could give a good account of themselves. But if the Germans found out that the British were stuck in Solesmes like a cork in a bottle and that only two battalions stood between them and a rout, they would roll over the rearguard at any cost. And even as he thought it, he saw a German aeroplane approaching from the north-west.

If only there was a way that he could shoot him down! He had his pistol out and loaded, but the chances of a hit, as he already knew, were minute. Still, he had to try. He turned towards it. The German came on for a little while, but then veered away and began to lose height. At first Jack was surprised at this, for in his experience they liked to climb when they felt themselves threatened. His opponent kept his distance but circled Jack, losing height gradually and drawing Jack in pursuit in wide spiral loops towards the north-west. At the sound of the first shot, Jack realised what the German pilot was doing. He was luring Jack over the lines of his own men, and trying to bring him down within range. It was a risky strategy, Jack thought, for the Germans below were just as likely to shoot either of them. But for now it seemed to be working, as it was Jack who was the target. He looked down and saw a grey mass of infantry, all with their rifles up and pointing at him. He swallowed in sudden fear and banked hard as the first volley sounded like an elongated crack of thunder. He felt the impact of shots on the body, saw holes appear in the wings, and felt one whistle past him, through the floor and up past his ear, having missed vital parts of his body by a miracle. He pushed the throttle forward and began to climb as fast as he could, turning to try to keep the German in sight. But he was flying away now, beating his retreat towards Valenciennes; and when Jack discovered he could hardly see the men on the ground any more, he realised why. The black storm was gathering pretty much right over Solesmes, and it was likely to break at any time.

Jack had to get down. He could not fly in the kind of downpour that was threatening; but he ought also to get back to Le Cateau and report what he had seen, in case no-one else had. He wheeled away, gaining height. It was too murky to see his way properly by landmarks, but he knew the compass direction of Le Cateau, and laid a course by that. Behind him there was a violent crack of lightning, like the sound of a giant stick being snapped, and he saw the purple reflection of it in the glass of his instruments. The air smelled like a brine barrel. He checked his compass again and saw to his horror that the needle was swinging wildly. He tapped it, and it performed a complete circle, then yawed back and forth like a frightened horse. The electricity of the storm must be affecting it. There was no chance now of his getting back to Le Cateau. He must land somewhere – anywhere – before the downfall started, and take shelter.

The first heavy drops, large as pennies and almost as hard, smacked down on him as he put the nose down and headed for the gloomy earth, then levelled out just above tree height to look for a suitable field. He caught a glimpse up ahead of him of what looked like a town, and he wondered if he had found Le Cateau after all. But there was no time to find out. The rain started in earnest, and he had to go in for a landing. He landed almost blind as the skies opened like a cataract. He bumped wildly over rough grass, and only just managed to stop as the wall of a building came towards him out of the unnatural twilight and the silvery curtain of the rain.

He climbed out and ran towards the wall for what shelter

it might provide, hoping against hope that he had been flying south-ish and not north-ish, or he might soon find himself a prisoner-of-war. On reaching the wall he flattened himself against it while the rain came down in cold torrents. The building had no eaves on this side. Was it worth the risk of capture to seek shelter inside? Surely he couldn't have been going north – couldn't have been that far off course. And then someone appeared, someone with a coat over their head, beckoning – a small someone – a woman. Not a German soldier. Through the tearing rain and the rumbling peals of thunder he just heard a voice shouting, '*Vite! Vite!*'

Oh, well, he thought. Here goes. He went towards the figure, and followed it round the corner of the wall, across what seemed to be a farmyard, and in at an open door. In the grateful shelter he shook the rain from his hair and wiped it from his eyes, and then the little figure ahead of him turned and removed the coat from over her head. A slow grin of amazement curved his lips as she stared in surprise and pleasure.

'*Monsieur Jacques! Vous voici!*'

Old man Bécasse cackled from the twilight of the long kitchen Jack remembered so well, and rattled off a high, cracked sentence.

'He says that he knew it was you all along when he heard the aeroplane come down. He says meetings like ours always come in threes, and that there will be another after this.'

Jack shook his head in wonder and pleasure. Of all the places to have ended up! So that had been Cambrai up ahead, and he was back in Cauroir.

'I am very happy to see you again,' he said, addressing them equally.

Marie stepped close, looking up at him through the gloom. 'You are not hurt? Is your aeroplane broken?'

'No,' he said. 'I had to put down because of the storm. But I cannot stay long. I must go as soon as I can. I have important information I must deliver.'

Marie glanced at the window. 'It will be over in half an hour, perhaps, but then it will be dark, and you cannot fly in the dark, I think?'

It was true, dammit, Jack thought. 'Is there a telephone in the village?' he asked.

'No,' said Marie. 'Perhaps in Cambrai – at the *mairie*, or the *commissariat de police* or at *la gare*. Surely there will be one at the railway station.' She looked again at the window. 'But you cannot go now, in this. You would not find your way. Stay a little. I will make you coffee. Are you hungry? I can cook something for you.'

She and the old man were looking at him with eagerness, and he would not break their hearts. It was true: he could not find his way in this downpour. When it stopped, perhaps there would still be light enough to fly. He pulled off his flying cap and began to shrug out of his jacket. 'I would very much like some coffee,' he said.

Bertie's battalion missed the bottleneck at Solesmes. The road they were on ran parallel but to the south of it, and they plodded on in the stifling afternoon without seeing any more Germans. They had not seen a rations lorry either, though they knew one must have been this way, for as well as the Belgian belongings discarded by the side of the road they saw empty ration boxes, which had been dumped for their benefit but emptied by others before them. Bertie was walking again, having given up Kestrel to one of his two men wounded at Le Quesnoy. The other had been so badly hurt he had had to be left behind.

When the downpour began there was nothing to do but go on shuffling through it. At least it made a change – and many of the men lifted their faces into it and drank the rain as best they could, their water-bottles long since empty. The rain fell in a torrent for about half an hour; but when the violence of the storm abated, the unnatural darkness hardly lifted. In the normal way of things, dusk was coming on, and there were low clouds from horizon to horizon, from which a steady rain continued to fall.

'Looks as though it's set in for the night,' Bertie said, falling in beside Pennyfather at the head of the company.

'At least it'll be raining on the Germans too, sir,' he said.

'Why is it I don't find that much comfort?' Bertie said.

'I hope we get decent billets at Le Cateau,' said Pennyfather. 'The men really need a night's sleep under cover.'

But before they reached the town, a cyclist from Division HQ brought them new orders. They were to bivouac on the far side of Le Cateau, in a field beside the railway station, where a ration dump would be waiting for them. In the morning there would, after all, be no stand. The retreat was to continue towards St Quentin, and the West Herts were to make their way to Réumont where they would form the rearguard.

The rain had eased to a steady drizzle as, cold, wet and tired, the battalion plodded into Le Cateau. Here they found scenes of confusion that made the flight from Mons look like a military manoeuvre by comparison. The townsfolk had been thrown into a panic by the sound of the guns to the north, and stories brought in of the British Army in retreat. The violent rainstorm had kept them indoors, but once it had passed they began to leave their houses, taking with them their belongings and their livestock. The streets had already been crowded with soldiers and army wagons trying to pass through the town in both directions, and the sudden influx of refugees, pushing carts, leading cattle, driving sheep, pigs and geese, jammed the traffic into a seething mass of insanity. Soldiers shouted and swore, cattle tried to stampede in pitiful fear, sheep bleated, horses screamed, small creatures got crushed underfoot, cart wheels locked together, teetering piles of household goods, insecurely tied, collapsed to the cobbles and added their hazard. And the more stuck they became, the more hysterical the refugees grew, and the more they struggled to get away, lashing out at anyone within range in their desperation.

It took the battalion more than two hours to fight its way through, and in the process transport was lost again. A scuffle broke out between some of B Company and a section of French reservists trying to pass in the other direction. Bertie had to force his way through and sort it out, as Spendlove had been separated from his men in the crush.

It was nearly ten o'clock by the time they reached their

destination, but for a wonder the rations were there, and the men were able to make an adequate, if dull, meal of bully and biscuits, washed down by most welcome tea. Stragglers – including Spendlove – kept joining them for an hour, and transport finally caught up after eleven, at which point the officers' luncheon basket made its very welcome addition to their comfort. Then they all found what shelter they could and, rolled in blankets or greatcoats, lay down to get some sleep. This was not, Bertie reflected, as he shifted uncomfortably on the hard ground, the war he had expected; but then he supposed one should not expect war to follow any pattern. It was a kind of madness, after all. He fell asleep suddenly, with no drifting, too tired even to dream.

It took some time for Jack to extricate himself from the warm embrace of the Bécasse house, walk the mile and a half into Cambrai, then find the railway station and persuade the station master to let him use the telephone. When he got through to his headquarters to deliver his news, they already knew it. He was relieved to be told that the Germans had not attacked at Solesmes, but had fallen back when the violence of the rainstorm hit them. Still, though the weather had obviously played its part, Jack felt he had been of some use in driving away the German aeroplane.

'You'd better stay where you are for tonight,' Flight Commander Melville said. 'Can't fly in the dark and you sound as if you're comfortable enough. But for God's sake get back here as soon as you can tomorrow. We've no idea what's going on but we shall need you. Is your machine all right?'

'As far as I can tell, sir.' It had been flying all right before he landed.

'Well, thank God for that. That idiot Freddie Flint got his Avro peppered today, damn' near killed himself and left us a machine short. Start as soon as you can see to take off tomorrow and come straight here for orders.'

'Yes, sir,' said Jack.

CHAPTER NINE

Sir John French's intention was indeed to retire still further. He wanted to fight, but not here, at Le Cateau. The BEF was a shadow of what it had been when it arrived in France, and even then it had been little more than a token force. It had acquitted itself magnificently, but the reports of German numbers were increasingly worrying. The BEF was so heavily outnumbered, it was a miracle that so many had been snatched away from under German noses, but they were exhausted with the effort. If they were to make a stand, what was needed was some large natural barrier, like a river, which could be easily defended by his handful of men until the promised reinforcements arrived from England. He needed to retire behind some big river, like the Oise, perhaps – or the Somme.

Orders were sent out at around eleven p.m. for the army to start moving out at seven the next morning, and for General Allenby's cavalry to cover the retreat by occupying the ridge before Solesmes. But in the middle of the night news came that the Germans already held that ridge; also that the Guards had been heavily engaged at Landrecies on the right wing. The enemy were much closer than had been realised. The only possibility was for the army to move immediately, and slip away in the darkness.

But General Smith-Dorrien, in command of the Second Corps, knew that most of his men were in no fit state to march now, having only just reached their bivouacs. And if they tried to march away – or, rather, limp away – early in the morning, the Germans would soon catch up with them and cut them down.

In his view there was no choice but to stand and fight. Messages flew back and forth between him and Sir John French, the latter urging that every effort should be made to continue the retreat, according to his plan, in the hope of catching up with the French. But at six in the morning, with the argument not yet settled, the quiet was shaken with the thud and boom of German artillery opening fire away on the right flank, which the Guards were holding, and it was clear that the decision had been made for them. There was no choice now for the BEF but to make a stand where they were, at Le Cateau.

The railway ran through the Selle River valley to the south-east of Le Cateau. In the grey of dawn the West Herts were astir to no more unnerving sounds than the steady murmur of the river and the calling of a few hardy birds. It was painful to get moving, cold and stiff as everyone was, short of sleep, sore of foot. Tea was brewed up, to wash down the dull breakfast of biscuit. The men washed and shaved as best they could in river water, and formed up to move off. It had at least stopped raining, and there was a mist over the valley, shot through with the first light of the rising sun. It was rather beautiful, Bertie thought, and imagined how it would be to set off for a morning's fishing at home. But the men were still in stoically good humour, more sleepy than downcast, and it was obvious that the honour of being chosen as rearguard weighed with them. He heard comments along the lines of 'couldn't trust no-one else with it' and 'they 'ad to 'ave the best for that job'.

They marched out onto the road, and as they left the shelter of the station yard's walls they came under fire. It was such a shock that for a moment everyone stood still, wondering where it could have come from. They were not supposed to be vulnerable here on the south-eastern side of the town – but evidently some Germans had worked their way round during the night.

'Take cover!' Bertie shouted. Everywhere, all the way up

the road, the battalion was dashing for garden walls, yards and side alleys. He was off his horse, flinging the reins to his groom, and ran with the men, pulling out his pistol as he did. It was Uhlans, mounted Germans, which perhaps accounted for the speed of their appearance. The steady crackle of rifle fire began as the men found positions and fired back. Bertie took a couple of shots and looked around. His company had been last in the column, and at the top of the road to his left he could see that the Uhlans were working their way round through the railway yard with the intention of attacking from that side, creating a pincer movement.

They needed a roadblock if they were to cover themselves.

'Mr Yerbury! Take a section and get those transport wagons across the road. Fill in with anything you can find to make a roadblock. I'll cover you. Corporal, take your men up that side of the road. You men, follow me.'

The corporal led his men along the road, keeping close to the wall. Bertie's group had to dash across the road to get to the cover of the railway yard's fence. 'Now!' he shouted, and ran. A crackle of fire followed them, thudding into the ground all around them, and he felt something whiz past his cheek, but they made it untouched. He could hear the sound of horses on the other side of the fence, and made a gesture to the men behind him for silence. They were crouching, tensed for action, watching him with hard, steady eyes, and he felt a surge of affection for them. Quickly they crept up the line of the fence to where a railway building marked the junction with the cross-street, the other section mirroring their action on the opposite side of the road. Then suddenly half a dozen Uhlans burst into sight in the gap ahead, and all three groups opened fire at once. The shelter of wall and fence was not much, but it was better than nothing, which was what the Uhlans had – and they had not expected Bertie's men to be so close. As the hail of fire burst round them they faltered, the horses whirled, and such shots as they got off went wild. In a moment they turned and clattered back the way they had come.

But now the men behind the fence knew where they were. Bertie heard them shouting. They would ride through the yard and reinforce their companions, and the next time they appeared from the cross-street there would be more of them. He looked back. The wagons were nearly in place. The corporal was disposing his men in a series of doorways that would give them cover. Bertie reached the railway building and tried the nearest door. It was locked.

'Let me, sir,' said Colleymore, a big man with huge shoulders – he had boxed for the battalion. A couple of massive thuds from him and the door burst open with a splintery sound and a clang as the metal keeper, broken away from the jamb, fell to the floor. The door gave only onto bare wooden stairs ahead. From the strong smell of horses the building had been a stable block, and this must have been the entrance to the grooms' accommodation above. At the top of the stairs there was a narrow corridor giving onto a series of small rooms, poorly furnished, with windows looking down onto a yard. The corridor windows faced the street. Bertie could hear the corporal's section firing. They rushed to the windows and knocked them out, just in time to open up on the enemy and relieve their comrades down below. The Uhlans retreated again, but from the end window it was just possible to see down the cross-street, where more of them were massing. The next attack would be a heavy one.

He leaned out of the window and called down to the corporal: 'Get back behind the barricade now. They're coming in force next time. We'll cover you.'

The corporal signalled acknowledgement, and Bertie watched the men peel away and run back down the road, keeping close to the wall, 'leapfrogging' each other to keep a field of fire. The Uhlans came when they were just a few yards from the barricade.

Bertie's men opened fire. 'Make your shots tell,' he called to them. They were working steadily, aiming and firing. From up here they had a good field of fire, and they were pretty well protected at first. He saw several Germans fall from the saddle, others turn away wounded. But there were so many of them that fire began to be returned. He could hear bullets hitting the wooden walls outside, saw them splintering the window frames. He had to jerk his head back from the window as shots came through; and as the Uhlans moved into the main street, the fire became heavier and he knew they were in danger of being overwhelmed. The next thing was that the Uhlans would come up the stairs.

There was a horrid smack of a sound and a cry, and Edwards fell away from his window. He went down flat on his back, his heels drummed a moment on the floor, and then he was still, a bloody hole where his face had been.

They must get out. Bertie went into the nearest bedroom and opened the window. The yard was too far below to drop without hurting themselves. He looked round, then grabbed the mattress from the bed, staggered with it to the window and shoved it out. Enough to break the fall? Well, perhaps. It would have to be. He went back, grabbed Edwards's rifle, and said, 'Right, men, time to go. Through that window in there. There's a mattress below – try to land on it. I'll go last. Go now!'

He took Edwards's place and kept firing steadily through the window as the men went past him one by one. As the last one left, someone appeared at the top of the stairs. Grey! A German. He looked nervous as he well might, and Bertie shot him full in the chest before he could aim his weapon. He fell backwards. Bertie hoped he would block the stairs for those behind him, and took the chance to leap across the passage and through the bedroom to the window. He scrambled out without looking, using his feet and knees to let himself down to the full length of his arms before he dropped. At least, that was what he meant to do, but his wounded arm would not take the strain, and he fell awkwardly, not knowing if the mattress was beneath him. As he fell he heard someone fire from behind him across the yard, and a face at the window above jerked back violently. Bertie hit the ground, one foot on the mattress, hands grabbing him to break his fall. His ankle twisted under him with a sharp pain, but at least he didn't break his leg.

It was Colleymore who held him. 'All right, sir?'

'Yes,' Bertie said. 'That way. Quick!'

There was a sound of breaking glass above, as the Uhlans knocked out the windows to make loopholes. They ran towards the gate across the yard. The first touch of Bertie's foot to the ground caused agony in his ankle, and he nearly fell, but Colleymore was there and steadied him, his big hand gripping Bertie's elbow and taking half his weight. They were the last two. They flung themselves through the gate as shots screamed down from above, and their companions crouched to return fire from the gateway.

Now they were in an alley, and there was no need to tell anyone what to do. They ran as fast as they could, Bertie half running, half hopping, knowing it would take the Uhlans time to get back down the stairs and round to the alley from the street. They would not risk jumping out of the window after them. The alley ended in another at right angles, and they could hear firing from the left. As they emerged into the cross-alley they almost got shot by their own people: they had come out on the British side of the road barricade.

'Mr Yerbury, we must retire,' Bertie said, limping out into the street. 'The enemy will be coming the way we just did, along this alley.'

'Yes, sir,' said Yerbury. 'The rest of the company is already falling back.' His face was dirty and one hand was bleeding. There were dead men behind the barricade, Bertie saw. 'Are you hurt, sir?'

'Twisted my blasted ankle,' Bertie said. 'Had to jump from a window. We lost Edwards.'

And Colleymore was wounded. He had been shot from behind in the last scramble across the yard. The bullet had lodged in the mass of muscle at the back of his left shoulder. In a less powerful man it would have gone right through and smashed the bone. 'I'm all right, sir,' he said. 'Can't hardly feel it yet, but I can't hold my rifle any more.'

'You saved my bacon,' Bertie said. 'Thank you.'

The Germans didn't pursue down the alley, perhaps not liking the idea of being a target in that narrow space. Bertie's company retired in sections, covering each other, and by the time the barricade was breached they were back with the rest of the battalion, which then made a slow and steady withdrawal out of the town, fighting all the way. At last the Uhlans gave up and turned back, and the battalion marched off along the river valley. Now that they were away from their own battle, they could hear the noise of heavy artillery above them on the high ground, and wondered what was going on. Bertie supposed it was their own artillery covering the retreat; but it suggested – along with the attack on them down here – that the Germans were a lot closer than expected.

They turned away from the river and onto the track that led up the hill towards Réumont, a village on the main road from Le Cateau to St Quentin. The noise of artillery fire was getting louder all the time. The men looked at each other with silent questions. When they reached the village, a staff officer met them. Bertie saw him talking to the colonel, with surprise on both sides, and then there followed a series of directional gestures, nods and salutes. The head of the column moved off again, and the colonel rode slowly back down the line, stopping to address each officer as he passed. The news was passed from man to man more quickly than the colonel relayed it, and by the time Abernethy reached him, Bertie already knew the substance of it. Orders should have come to them in the night but had not found them, which, given the confusion in Le Cateau, was not surprising. The retreat had been cancelled. They were going to fight the Germans on this ground. The artillery had been engaged since six this morning. The West Herts were to take up position on a hill on the right of the Argylls.

The men raised a cheer when they heard that the retreating was over and they were going to have a proper battle at last. Bertie heard their excited chatter and saw their grinning faces, and wondered for just a moment how many of them would still be alive at sunset. Then he shook the thought away. It was a soldier's task to shoot and be shot at. They had had a taste of it this morning – but that had been mere skirmishing. This was to be the real thing.

* * *

On Saturday the 29th, Jessie and Ned were driving home from a dinner party at the Enderbys', of Skelton Grange. The talk, of course, had all been about the war, and though Jessie was a female and therefore supposed to listen with humility and awe to the menfolk expounding on the subject, she couldn't help thinking that an awful lot of what had been said was twaddle.

The trouble was that there was nothing in the newspapers. They printed only what the War Office told them, and the War Office told them as little as possible. Official communiqués, made up of a single sentence such as 'The BEF has been in touch with the enemy near the Belgian Frontier' (which Jessie thought sounded as though they were sending each other postcards), left everything to be imagined.

In the absence of more detail, men such as Ralph Enderby, their host of the evening, were free to make it up out of the whole cloth. When Bertie had been fighting in South Africa, Jessie had followed every stage of the war, read every despatch, followed the campaign on maps, and felt that she knew as much about warfare as the next civilian. She had had to 'sit on her tongue', as her mother put it, when Enderby loftily explained what the BEF was up to and what Sir John French ought to do next.

The rest of the talk had been a verbal contest as to who was doing most for the war effort. Mrs Ffoulkes (who, Jessie had heard, had added the extra *f* to her husband's name as a condition of marrying him) had been in York that day collecting for the War Hardship Fund. She had stood on corners and walked about the streets *all day* and approached people *herself*, and as a consequence had collected a *great deal* of money. 'Approaching strangers and asking for money is very foreign to me, I assure you. It is not what I was brought up to. But one must exert oneself for the war.'

Mrs Peckitt had said rather feebly that she had knitted five pairs of khaki socks, and was contemptuously overridden by Mrs Aycliffe, who said that she had sent away one of her housemaids in the interests of economy. Mrs Enderby topped that triumphantly by saying that she meant to give up tennis for the duration of the war. Jessie, puzzled.

190

was foolish enough to ask why, upon which Mrs Enderby gave her a crushing look and pronounced, 'We must all make sacrifices.'

Mrs Aycliffe, who was very close to Mrs Enderby, flew to her defence by asking Jessie with killing sweetness what *she* was doing for the war effort. Jessie would have liked to say something subtle and cutting, but she had been brought up to be polite – and also not to boast – so she merely smiled and shook her head, and it was left to Mrs Wilbey, who had known the Morlands for years, to come to her defence. 'Mrs Morland is breeding horses for the army, aren't you, my dear?'

Mrs Aycliffe was not to be bought off by that. She wasn't sure that an indelicate word like 'breeding' ought to have been mentioned in polite company, but in any case it was self-evidently something that horses could get on with by themselves, and was hardly likely to occupy much of Jessie Morland's time. 'I meant, what was Mrs Morland doing *personally*,' she said.

Mrs Beale, sensing an 'atmosphere' interposed in her most comfortable voice, 'My gardener has been put into a terrible taking because of an article in the *Daily Mail* saying that every garden should be dug up and planted with cabbages and onions and so forth. He came to me almost in tears, poor old fellow, begging me not to dig up the lawn because of the years of hard work he's put in on it, cutting and rolling and weeding it to make it perfect.'

Mrs Wilbey said, 'Mine was just the same, only it was his chrysanthemums. Why are all gardeners so devoted to chrysanthemums? Nasty, drab flowers, I always think.'

'I had great difficulty in calming McGregor down,' Mrs Beale went on. 'He's very deaf, in any case, and I do find shouting wears one out in a very short time. But I persuaded him in the end that Harry would never stand for a vegetable patch outside the French windows. He does so love to look out at the lawn – don't you, my dear?'

'Eh?' said Mr Beale, from down and across the table. 'I beg your pardon, my dear, I didn't catch what you said.'

'No matter, my dear,' Mrs Beale smiled, knowing that

the danger had been averted, for Mrs Wilbey had picked up the ball again and was describing the wearisome properties of a very deaf old aunt she had had to sit with when she was a girl.

The men had been discussing the suggestion that was going around, that gentlemen with estates should instruct their keepers not to feed the pheasants, thus releasing valuable grain for the army's use.

Mr Wilbey didn't agree. 'They've taken our horses, dammit, so there'll be no hunting. They have to leave us shooting. The war effort is all very well, but a gentleman must have some pursuits.'

Enderby, the only one among them who could claim to have anything like an estate, said, 'I'm not sure it would do any harm not to feed the pheasants. I dare say they can find enough to eat on their own – after all, they must have managed when they were wild birds. And it might even improve the sport. They'd be stronger, quicker and more cunning. Our birds last year were so fat they could hardly get off the ground.'

'But I expect they tasted the better for it,' Ned suggested.

Enderby looked superior. 'One doesn't shoot birds for the pot, but for the sport.'

Ned felt it was time to strike back. 'My uncle at Morland Place says there'd be no point in shooting pheasants except for the eating. He says you get far more sport from pigeons.' There was no harm in reminding Enderby that Morland Place was ten times the size of his estate, and the Morlands had owned it since time immemorial.

Wilbey sighed. 'I haven't been out after a pigeon since I was a boy.'

'We may all be reduced to shooting pigeons before long,' Enderby said. 'My keeper's threatening to volunteer. He says they need men who can handle guns, and that he'd be sure to be made a corporal right off.'

'I'm sure he's right,' said Beale. 'One must applaud them, of course, for volunteering, but it does make things dashed awkward at home. My man's volunteered, and it's taken me years to train him to clean my boots the way I like 'em.

Now I have to give 'em to the housemaid to clean, and she *will* grip 'em by the heel!' And he shuddered at the memory.

The conversation turned to volunteering, and male and female guests were drawn into it together. Everyone had someone's name to contribute. Ned and Jessie had lost the chauffeur, Purvis, who was a reservist, while the head housemaid, Martha, had left to go home and help her mother and father because her two brothers had joined up. Jessie could have wished it had been anyone but Martha, who was sensible and quick and knew the work. Of course, Jessie also had two brothers in uniform – to say nothing of Cousin Bertie and even Lennie Manning – which gave her the edge over everyone else until John Peckitt electrified the company by saying quietly that he was going to join up himself. 'Mary and I have discussed it, and we've decided that since we don't have any children, it's my duty to go.'

There was a silence, at the end of which Enderby said, 'I'm afraid all the decent regiments are full up now. The fellows who got in at the beginning were the lucky ones. I dare say there'll be more openings later, but of course one couldn't be expected to serve with just *anyone*.'

Mrs Enderby rushed to his conversational side. 'Peter Firmstone volunteered last week and he's been sent to something quite dreadful – I forget what it was, but the Sussex or Essex or something of the sort.'

'Suffolk,' Enderby said. 'He won't know a soul. And he won't find that his brother officers are *gentlemen*, in the accepted meaning of the word.'

'My cousin Bertie was sent to a regiment he didn't know,' Jessie said. 'He said it was his duty to go where he was needed.'

Mrs Ffoulkes said, 'Yes, but he was a professional soldier, wasn't he? So you wouldn't expect him to be particular.'

This was going too far even for Mrs Enderby, and she retrieved matters by standing up, gathering the female company with her eye, and saying, 'Shall we retire, ladies? I'm sure the gentlemen are eager for their port and cigars.'

Now, some hours later, as Ned was driving them home, he and Jessie were both silent in thought. After a while, Ned said, 'I wish Purvis hadn't gone. The motor isn't running quite right, and *I* don't know what to do about it. I can drive it, but I don't understand what goes on under the bonnet.'

'It seems all right to me,' Jessie said vaguely, not really listening.

'It's using far too much oil, and it's making a strange noise.' He sighed. 'I suppose I shall have to find a mechanic to come and look at it.'

She roused herself. 'Ask Uncle Teddy's Simmons.'

'I don't think Simmons really knows a great deal about anything but his own motor.'

'Well, an engine is an engine, surely. I expect it's something very simple – Purvis has only been gone a week, after all. Probably some nut needs tightening, or something like that. Simmons will spot it in a moment.'

'Perhaps you're right. I'll ask him – but, really, I don't like trusting anyone but Purvis with it.' He paused, and then said, 'I've been thinking of getting rid of the Avro, anyway, and getting something smaller.'

Jessie was surprised. 'Why? Because something's gone wrong?'

'Oh, it's not that – but with Purvis gone, you'll have to drive yourself, and the Avro's really too big for you.'

'I can handle it perfectly well,' Jessie said, nettled.

'I know you can, but you shouldn't have to. It's not suitable for a woman. It's too heavy for you. A smaller motor would be much better – a little "car" you can run about in.'

Jessie foresaw an argument over this, but decided against having it now. She said, 'If you get a smaller motor, people will think your business isn't doing well.'

She thought he would laugh at that, knowing how foolish she thought that kind of thing – the competition for status, the judging of people by their possessions. But he only said, 'Mmm,' in a vague way, and was obviously thinking about something else, so she let it go.

They didn't talk any more until they were alone in their bedroom. Jessie had dismissed Tomlinson and was sitting before the dressing-table glass brushing out her hair. Brach had done her usual frantic dance of greeting, as if they had been parted for the best part of a year, and was now lying down with her forelegs across Jessie's feet and her head on her forelegs, effectively nailing Jessie to the floor so that she couldn't get away. Every now and then Brach would roll up her eyes towards Jessie's face and heave an enormous sigh of melancholy content.

Ned was in the dressing-room, undergoing the attentions of his man Daltry. When he came into the bedroom in his brown silk dressing-gown with the white spots, he had a glass in each hand.

'I thought you might like a nightcap,' he said.

'Mm, yes, thank you,' she said. He placed the whisky in front of her and retired with his brandy to an armchair where he could watch her. He liked seeing her brush her hair out – hidden all day long in its practical coils, nets and pins, it seemed the stuff of magic when it tumbled free down her back at night. The stuff of fairy-tales. *Rapunzel*, he thought, or – what was that story about the goose girl who bewitched that poor fellow by brushing her hair?

She saw him watching her, and it gave her a strange, tingling feeling, as though he were touching her. Sometimes in bed he would run his fingers lightly down her spine as a prelude to love, and it made her shiver in just that way. She arched her back a little as she brushed, letting her head lean backwards so that her hair hung lower than ever, and she drew the brush through it slowly, knowing he was watching every stroke. Their bed-life together was the best thing in their marriage, she always thought. Whatever else they disagreed about, that was always good. And of late – since the war began, really – it had been better than ever. Perhaps it was because of the war – the excitement she felt that she had described to Bertie in her letter. Perhaps Ned felt it too, and that was the way he showed it. He worked longer hours at the mill, and came home tired out and not in much of a mood for conversation; but when they were in bed and the light was out he came alive, and loved her with a passion that reminded her thrillingly of the first days of their marriage.

She loved it when they made love together. She loved the sensations it aroused in her body, but she also loved the feeling of power it gave her. In the final moments he would be helpless in the grip of his passion, helpless in his desire for her and his need of her. She knew that in the rest of her life the ultimate power was with him, that he had control over her in many small ways. He was a kind husband, but still the fact was that she could not always do exactly what she wanted. He could allow and forbid things to her, and the world believed that that was right and good. So she revelled in the one area – no, in those few tiny moments – when he was as helpless as a grounded bird. When he cried out and shuddered in her arms, she knew she had him, possessed him, in a way that he never had her.

She sipped her whisky. One of the ways in which he was a kind husband was in allowing her to drink spirits – though only when there was no third person to see it. She smiled to herself at the thought. If he believed the servants didn't know it was her who accounted for the lowering of the level in the whisky decanter – given that he only drank brandy and that someone in the kitchen had to wash two glasses – he was a fool. But then his attitude to the servants was different from hers. He both thought more about them and ignored them more than she did. To her it seemed as natural as breathing to be served, and she never thought twice about it; on the other hand, she was always aware that the servants were individuals, with the same wishes, fears, weaknesses and dislikes as anyone else. Ned tended to see them as a homogeneous body, like a rank of soldiers, and while he worried about what they might do and think, he did not differentiate between them.

Thinking of soldiers brought her back to her musings in the motor on the way home, and she said, 'Did you hear what Mrs Enderby said about Peter Firmstone volunteering?' Firmstone had been one of her constant suitors in her dancing days, before she married Ned.

'Mm,' said Ned.

'That's all three of "my" young men,' she said. 'Frank Winbolt and George Ayliffe, and now Peter. Arthur

Cornleigh's gone, and Peter Cornleigh's desperate to go, Polly says, but he's only eighteen. And John, the footman at Morland Place, asked Uncle Teddy yesterday if he could go.'

'Hm,' said Ned.

'And then tonight at the Enderbys', I was so surprised when John Peckitt said he was going. You could see Ralph Enderby didn't like it at all. After all, he hasn't got any children either. Not that I can see it matters particularly. I mean, men don't look after children. Well, look at Robbie. Actually, Ethel doesn't look after the children, either – Emma does all that, and the nurserymaids.'

Ned put down his brandy glass. 'Is all this leading somewhere?' he asked. The smile with which he had been watching her brush her hair had disappeared.

Without realising it, she frowned in response. 'Where do you think it should lead?'

'Is that what's been on your mind all the way home? I thought there was something going on inside that head of yours.'

'You needn't say "that head of yours" as if it was something peculiar. Everyone has a head, you know – and I'll bet everyone was thinking the same thing at dinner.'

'Oh, and what thing is that?'

'You know very well.'

'No, do enlighten me,' Ned said, his lips tightening.

She put down the hairbrush and turned to face him, dragging her feet out from under Brach, who looked up reproachfully. 'Why pretend you don't know what I'm talking about?' she said, exasperated. 'When John Peckitt said what he said, I looked at you—'

'Yes, I know you did. I thought it was very obliging of you.'

She was wrong-footed. 'What do you mean?'

'You looked at me so that everyone in the room was able to read your mind,' he said. 'It couldn't have been more clear if you had written it out on a poster and held it up for everyone to read: "John Peckitt has volunteered, so why haven't you?"'

'I'm sure no-one saw me look at you. And I'm sure everyone was thinking the same thing anyway, without any help from me.'

'Really? So everyone was thinking, Ned Morland is a coward, were they?'

Jessie flushed, but stuck to her guns. 'I never said you were a coward. But my brothers joined up right away. Well, Jack was asked for,' she said, 'but I'm sure he would have volunteered anyway.'

'And I know very well what you think of Robbie for not going. You despise him.'

'I don't!'

'How painful it must be for you to have a husband you despise,' Ned said quietly.

'I don't despise you. I never said I did – nor Robbie, either. I just can't understand why you don't go. I'd go like a shot if I were a man. And you don't even have the reason that Robbie has.'

Ned moved his head a little, as though she had slapped his cheek. 'Ah! Thank you for reminding me I have no children,' he said.

She was silent, disconcerted to have come to this point. It was a subject she was usually at pains not to bring up between them, equivocal as she was about having children. But, she thought, anger restoring her, he has no right to take it all to himself like that, as if he were the only one affected. He doesn't know about my doubts. For all he knows, I'm as unhappy as he is about it. In fact, he ought to think I'm *more* unhappy than him. *I*'m the one who had the miscarriage.

In the silence, Brach whined, sensing the atmosphere, and Jessie bent down to stroke her head consolingly, which allowed her to hide her face.

Ned said, 'I'm sorry, Jess. That wasn't fair.'

Just for a savage moment she hated him, *hated* him. Why did he apologise, having just told her off for being in the wrong? Why didn't he stand his ground and fight fair? Now he had made her wrong twice, while making himself noble and magnanimous for apologising when he wasn't to blame.

Now she was supposed to soften and gush and cry *No, no, it was all my fault!* and fall into his arms for forgiving kisses. He was – he was *managing* her, as if she were a child in a tantrum. He would not do her the honest courtesy of fighting her foot to foot as if she were an equal.

She straightened up, hot with anger, ready for battle; but at the sight of his face everything ebbed away, leaving a sort of hopelessness. He was anxious and unhappy. He had not done what he did consciously, and if she accused him of it he would be genuinely surprised. The effect was just the same, of course, but because he wasn't aware of his own processes, it was not something she could struggle against. He did not want to quarrel, that was all. He would employ any means, fair or unfair, not to quarrel with her. It frustrated her unbearably, but there was nothing she could do about it. In that he would never change.

She said, 'I'm tired. I don't want to talk any more. I'm going to bed.'

He said nothing, only sat finishing his brandy and not looking at her as she completed her toilette, put Brach outside the door, took off her dressing-gown and got into bed. She felt sore with the unresolved argument, with his apology, with the knowledge that he probably now thought he had hurt her feelings over the baby business. When she was lying on her side he got up and took off his dressing-gown, turned out the lights and got into bed. She lay rigidly, listening to him breathing. Then he put his hand on her shoulder. 'Jess, I wasn't going to tell you yet, but I've been meaning all along to volunteer.'

She said nothing, though her attention strained into the darkness. What was this? Was he giving in again? Pretending he agreed with her?

'You probably remember that talk we had with Bertie a few weeks ago, when he said that chaps like me, public-school men, would be specially wanted because there was a shortage of officers.'

He seemed to want an answer, and she said stiffly, '*I* remember. I thought *you*'d forgotten.'

'God, no!' he said, and the simple vehemence convinced

her in that instant that he was telling the absolute truth. 'I've been thinking about it ever since. I was dreading the war starting because of it – I hoped that maybe it wouldn't come after all – but once it did, I knew what I had to do. I've been working since then to get the business into a shape where I could leave it.'

So that was why he had been working such long hours! She felt a rush of shame that she had misjudged him, and renewed anger that he had misled her. 'Why on earth didn't you tell me?' she asked stiffly.

'I didn't want to upset you. I thought it was better you thought I wasn't going until I had to.' She was about to retort when he went on, 'And – I wanted to wait until it actually happened. I wanted to surprise you.'

His voice was shy and boyish. She turned over to face him, and studied what she could see of his face in the little moonlight coming through the curtains. He really had wanted to surprise her, to see how proud and pleased she was when he gave her this gift – his doing the right thing, being brave, going to war. Now all her other feelings were washed away by a rueful tenderness. Men were so big and strong and had all the power, and yet could be as foolish as little boys, and as weak and needy. 'You wanted to surprise me,' she repeated.

He smiled hesitantly. 'I know you think the world of Bertie, and admire him, too. I wanted to see you look at me like that.'

'Oh, Ned,' she said helplessly.

'You do believe me?' he asked anxiously.

'Of course I do,' she said.

'I almost told you in the motor tonight – when I was talking of getting a smaller one. If I'm going away we won't need a big one, and you'll be better off with a little car you can dash about in. But I could tell you weren't really listening. The moment passed and I went back to the old plan of not telling you until I actually did it. But then, just now, what you said – well, I can't bear you to think I'm a coward.'

'I don't think that,' she said sadly.

'I don't *want* to go to war, it's true,' he went on, 'but it's not because I'm afraid. I don't want to go because it means leaving you. But I know it's my duty – and I think you know that too, don't you?'

'Yes.'

'We've got to smash the Hun once for all. Those stories in the newspapers—'

'Yes,' said Jessie. She had read so many of them, stories of the terrible things the Germans were doing in Belgium, bayoneting unarmed civilians, shooting hostages in cold blood, dashing babies' heads against walls, rapes, crucifixions – even acts of cannibalism. The *frightfulness* – that seemed to be the word – of the Bosch knew no bounds. They were inhuman fiends.

'It's going to need all of us who can go,' Ned said. 'Even Robbie might have to go eventually.'

She moved restlessly at this attempt at humour. It reminded her he believed she thought Rob a coward. She didn't, really – she just didn't understand why he didn't *want* to go, as she would have if she'd been a man.

'When will you go?' she asked.

'Soon,' he said. 'It will take me a little while longer to sort things out at the mill, and – and to do other things. A week or two, perhaps. And then I'll go and volunteer.'

'What "other things"?' she asked.

'Oh, legal things,' he said, unwillingly.

'*What* things?' she insisted.

'Things – in case I don't come back.' He said it not with melodrama, not with heroics, but with embarrassment at having to mention it.

Her heart melted. 'Oh, Ned,' she said, and put her arms round his neck, and gave her lips up to his.

They kissed long; then he drew back to say, 'I said I hoped it would never happen, but it was only because I don't want to leave you. Oh, Jess, I don't want to leave you.'

Through her thin nightdress she felt his arousal, and his hands on her neck and back were hot. Her body responded, the quick flame leaping up in her, and she pressed against him. Their mouths met again, and the terrible and tender longing in her loins yearned towards him. He was stroking her head, kissing her lips, eyes, brow, ready to please her, to take his time from her. But she wanted him *now* – no butterfly touches, no sentiment, but right now, the whole thing. 'Come into me,' she begged in a whisper. 'Do it *now!*'

She felt him shudder with excitement at the words, and pulled him across her, and then he was inside her and they were locked together. She thrust against him, wanting more and more of him, feeling as though she were opening up inside and pulling him in like a vortex. He gripped her head by the hair and groaned as though it was an agony for him, and they thrust madly together, panting almost in desperation. 'Oh, Jess, I love you, I love you!' he cried out in pain as the moment came. She made no sound – she never did – but her body convulsed against his and he felt the single violent indrawn breath at the moment of accomplishment, as though her soul gasped.

When his breathing slowed, he withdrew from her – that was an agony too – and rolled onto his back, and she came nudging after, turned into his arms, and they were instantly asleep.

In the early hours they both woke, and made love again, but slowly this time, almost drowsily, making it last. He lay awake after that, while she slept again, thinking how wonderful it was, and how lucky he was to have her for a wife, the woman he loved – and a woman for whom these things were as good as they were for him. It was not a subject gentlemen ever talked about, of course, but he remembered at school he had heard other boys saying that nice females *didn't like it*, and that if you wanted 'fun' you had to go to other sorts of women. He had always hated the idea (and hated the language even more) but he supposed there might be some sort of truth in it. He was so glad and grateful that God had seen fit to give him Jessie, who could take pleasure as well as give it. Whether it was rare or not, it was very precious to him.

It began to get light, and he fell asleep with the pleasant thought that tomorrow (today!) was Sunday so he didn't have to get up early.

* * *

They were at peace together the next day, drifting in a haze of fulfilled passion over a late and leisurely breakfast, talking of what they should do for the rest of the day (a walk by the river? A long ride? A picnic somewhere?) when the atmosphere was rudely shattered by the arrival of Mr Cornleigh. He was red-faced, breathless, agitated almost beyond speech.

'I had to come and show you this. You won't have seen it. A special edition of *The Times*. By God, we've all been humbugged by the War Office! They've clamped down from the beginning. Nothing but the official line – Press Bureau – censorship – reasons of morale. But now the truth is out. Read it, just read it! Look at this! And this! We never knew what was going on.'

The whole special edition was filled with reports and photographs, telling in unsparing detail the true story of what had been happening in France. It was all there, the hasty march to Mons, the desperate battle on the canal, the retreat, and then, on the Wednesday previously, the terrible battle of Le Cateau: the British troops, hopelessly outnumbered, had fought almost to a standstill for six hours, before at two o'clock the order came for a general retirement. Some units had not received, or had been unable to act on, the order, and continued to fight until most of them were dead and the rest were overcome and taken prisoner. Losses throughout the BEF were enormous, terrible. The survivors were now limping southwards, ragged, exhausted, a broken remnant of an army, pursued by the Germans who outnumbered them now more than ever.

Ned and Jessie read in silence, shocked by the violence of comparison between this and what they had been fondly imagining before, when they had been lulled by the bland and cheerful tone of what the War Office had allowed to be printed. Jessie read words like 'enormous losses', and 'battalions reduced to half their original size' and 'all but two officers lost', and her numbed mind cried out only *Bertie!* and *Jack!*. She had heard nothing, nothing since the happy, harvesting days of Bertie's letter, nothing of Jack since Helen had telephoned to say he was safe at Maubeuge and in a very friendly mess. Where were they now? Were they hurt? Were they dead? And, above all, when would she know?

Ned looked up from the newspaper and met Mr Cornleigh's eyes. 'Well, there's no doubt about it now. Every able man must volunteer.'

'Aye, you're right,' said Mr Cornleigh. He tapped the page with a finger. 'The editor says so, here – see? "Need for reinforcements is desperate." Anyone who's been hanging back, he says, must come forward now.'

Ned nodded. 'My plans are well in hand. I'll be gone in a few days.'

'Aye, I know you will. Good lad,' said Mr Cornleigh. 'And my boy Arthur—' He swallowed. 'I wouldn't let him go because he's not nineteen. He wanted to lie about his age, said all the lads are doing it. Well, I've told his mother this morning I'll not stop him any longer. She cried a bit – you know how women are – but she's as proud as Punch, really. And our Peter's going, as soon as he's got free of his articles. By God, it makes you proud to have lads like that,' he concluded, and then disconcerted Jessie very much by putting his hands over his face and weeping.

CHAPTER TEN

At Le Cateau, the fighting was bloody and bitter. The Germans kept on coming – so many of them, so many! There were long, exhausting artillery bombardments, and when those stopped for a moment the enemy infantry would advance, firing as they came. It was not the rifle fire, however, that caused the casualties. The Germans, firing from the hip, were inaccurate, and the British, firing from position and at a far greater rate, mowed them down. No, it was the shells and the shrapnel that caused devastation in the British ranks. Still they kept on fighting, repulsing yet another infantry advance, enduring another bombardment. But there were so many of the enemy, Bertie thought, that there could be only one ending. The BEF could hold them up, but sooner or later they must retire or be overwhelmed.

But there was little time for thinking of anything but the immediate situation. Half deafened by the roar of artillery, eyes burning from the smoke, throat sore from shouting, sometimes half dazed by the percussion of a shell landing too close for comfort, Bertie had his own men to command and take care of. It was clear – in so far as anything was clear in that terrain of fields and hedges and walls, barns and farm buildings, hillocks and gullies and copses – that the Germans were trying to outflank them on the left. Again and again they had to change position, scrambling away a little more to the south to avoid finding themselves with the enemy behind as well as in front. It was Bertie's business to watch for that, to direct his men and find new positions for them. And at every move there were fewer of them.

He saw them die. Big Colleymore, whose muscles had made nothing of tossing a corn stook up onto a farm cart, had flung out his arms and thrown back his head like an opera singer when a shot had taken him in the chest. Brevet, the tailor, who had mended Bertie's coat so neatly, had his head taken off by a whirling piece of shrapnel. Thorpe, Jones and Anderson all disappeared at once in the blast of a single shell, and there was nothing left of them afterwards but some rags and shiny strings of flesh hanging on the singed hedges. Quiet, efficient Lieutenant Yerbury died shortly after both his legs were blown off, in a last pump of torn arteries. And he had lost Pennyfather in one of the moves – he didn't know whether dead, wounded or missing. The wounded who could, limped or crawled away to find a dressing station and were seen no more. The badly wounded had to lie until the orderlies could get to them, and some died as they waited; others were left behind in the scrambling to new positions. Bertie felt particularly bad about them. He imagined how they must feel as they saw their own side deserting them. Too much imagination was not good for a soldier. Would the Germans take care of them? Well, eventually, perhaps. They must have troubles of their own.

The uncaring sun strolled over the zenith and began to decline, throwing shadows from a different side, and still the Germans came. Bertie had no idea where he was now. At one point he had seen firing from the walls of Le Cateau itself, so he knew the Germans had taken it. He fancied the village away to his left might be Clary, which would mean that he was to the rear of Bertry, where General Smith-Dorrien had had his headquarters that morning. He hoped the general had moved in time.

The ground in front of him in all directions was littered with the savage remains of the battle – dead men, dead horses, shattered gun limbers, overturned guns, all amid a vile debris of flesh and cloth and metal shards, splintered wood, smashed trees, churned earth. There was so much of everything out there that it could not go on much longer.

He wondered what the time was. His watch had been a casualty, broken by shrapnel, though perhaps saving him from a wound in its last moments. He squinted at the sky. Two o'clock, three o'clock? There was a tearing boom as another artillery barrage began. He and his remaining men crouched a little lower. The Germans were firing over them, turning the ground behind them into a boiling inferno. Well, if the order to retire came now it would never get through to them, Bertie thought. The shell fire was so intense, it must betoken an all-out attack, perhaps a last effort to dislodge them. He risked a quick look. Yes, they were massing there at the bottom of the slope, dense formations of them, more than he had seen all day – which was something to say!

'They'll be coming on when this barrage finishes, men,' he shouted. 'Get ready.'

He saw the faces nearest him turn towards him, and shouted again, reinforcing his words with gestures. He saw them pass the word along the line. Exhausted though they must be, they were as steady as in the first battle, those heroes who were left. If not ordered to retire, they would die where they were, shooting to the last moment. No surrender for the West Herts. It was not in their history, and never would be.

The shelling stopped, leaving a silence that pulsed and rang in the ears with its memory. Bertie looked again. Still massing, only about a hundred yards away; not coming yet, but preparing. There must be more shell fire to come. He couldn't count them, they were so many. This was to be the end, then. He and his men would die here, in this place whose name he didn't even know. He thought briefly of Maud and little Richard, and of Jessie, and there was time for just an instant of sorrow that he would never see them again – just an instant – before his soldier's mind took over to calculate whether his men were as well positioned as they could be, how he would concentrate them as the numbers thinned, where they would fire the last shots from. He began to move along the line towards the place he thought they would make their last stand, by a knotty blackthorn bush.

There had been an elm tree here earlier, but it had been shot away above the line of the hedge some time ago.

Then there was a sound of hoofs behind him, and someone shouting his name. He turned, and saw a young Headquarters galloper, whose horse was so frightened he could hardly control it. Bertie had to put up a hand and grab the creature's head to stop it, or the messenger would have been borne straight past to the horizon.

'Captain Parke, sir. Orders from Headquarters, sir, the West Herts is to retire,' the boy panted. He was hardly more than a boy, his cheeks still rosy and smooth where he had not yet had to shave very often.

'Whose orders?' Bertie asked sharply. It was as well to be careful in such a situation.

'General Fergusson, sir. He gave the order for general retirement at two o'clock, sir, but we couldn't get through the barrage, sir.'

'What time is it now?'

'Three o'clock, sir. Will you take your men out, sir? I can't find any other officers. The West Herts and the Argylls are the last, sir.'

'Very well. Tell General Fergusson I will retire at once. Get on, now, and find the Argylls.'

He turned the horse and pointed in the right direction, and silently wished the boy luck of his task. The Argylls were still to their left but at a distance and on open ground, fighting from shallow trenches. For a moment he watched the boy galloping away, then turned and went further up the slope to get a better overall view. There was an over-turned ammunition wagon there – or what was left of it since the last barrage – and he climbed onto one of the shafts to look down the West Herts line. There wasn't much of it left. He could see perhaps a hundred, but there must be more hidden from him at this point. No other officers? Well, perhaps the boy hadn't looked too closely. Nothing for it but to take the message himself while the let-up lasted.

His own company first. 'C Company! We've had the order to retire. I shall take the message to the other companies myself. We'll go last. We'll leave in the best West Herts tradition – an orderly retreat. I know I don't need to tell you that.'

'Sir!' shouted one of the men. 'Why should we retire now, sir, just when they're coming on? We can beat 'em, sir.'

Bertie felt a rush of pride and love. They had been fighting since dawn, one way and another, but they had no thought of defeat or surrender. They were surely the best soldiers who had ever lived. 'We will beat them,' he said, 'but not on this ground. We have orders from Headquarters to retire, and so we will. There'll be another day.'

He went back along the line to take the news to the other companies. At D Company he found the sergeant commanding: Crittal was dead. B Company had lost Spendlove, and the transport lieutenant, Fassner, had taken charge. And at A Company he learned that Fenniman had been wounded early in the day and taken to the dressing station at Réumont. Wetherall, the quartermaster, was commanding, and told him that both the colonel and the adjutant were missing, he believed wounded, and that he himself had sent Fassner to B Company when their last lieutenant had fallen.

'I think you should take over command of the battalion *pro tem*,' Wetherall said. 'You've got combat experience, I haven't.'

'We all have after today,' Bertie said. 'Get your men away now. I've told the others the order in which to follow. I'll take C Company out myself, last.'

'Rendezvous?'

'I'm not absolutely sure where we are now, so it's hard to say. Just get your men back to the main road to St Quentin and we'll meet there.'

Before he got back to his own men, the shelling started again, and he had to crouch, and make his return in short dashes. There was no chance for the West Herts to march out in formation. It was every man for himself, across the hot ground to their rear. But he could see that, though they were running and dodging, they were not panicking. Away to the left, the Germans were sweeping the Argylls' trenches with machine-guns. Poor devils: with machine-guns in front and shell fire behind, they had little chance of retiring. He wondered if the rosy-faced boy had made it, whether he had delivered his message, had turned back or been killed.

A pause in the shelling, and suddenly from the German lines he heard, faint but clear, the astonishing sound of a bugle playing the British 'cease fire'. The men's heads went up as they heard it, too, and they looked at one another in surprise. Then one of the Germans in the front line stood up, waving his arms. Bertie stared, puzzled. Surely they weren't surrendering? Then, across the distance between them, he heard the man shouting: 'Hey, Tommee! Why don't you give up? Why don't you surrender?'

Another stood up and another. They waved and capered. 'Give up, Tommee!'

'You haf no chance! Surrender, Tommee! Save your life!'

'Not bloody likely!' someone shouted back. There was the crack of a rifle, and one of the waving Germans keeled over.

'That's a hit!' someone said, as they did on the shooting range at Sandridge, and there was laughter. The rest of the Germans hastily lay down again.

But it was time to go. 'C Company, we shall retire,' said Bertie.

And the shelling began again.

The 4th Division on the left wing, and the French cavalry on their left flank, were the last to retire. Together with a few scattered units whom the order never reached, they were enough to keep the Germans at bay while the rest of the army slipped away. There was no chance through the shelling for the West Herts to come out in a body. When Bertie reached the road he had only a dozen men with him. There he found Wetherall, who said, 'I've been standing here sending the men on. No place to rendezvous – and, as you see, everyone's going in the same direction. We'll have to sort the mess out later.'

'Quite right,' said Bertie. 'You go on. I'll wait for the last stragglers. They're nearly all through now.'

The main road from Le Cateau to St Quentin was an

old Roman road, straight as a die, but narrow, too narrow to cope with the amount of traffic now trying to use it. The exhausted men, who had been fighting all day, poured down onto it, where they struggled for space with guns and horses, wagons and ambulances. They overflowed the road and trudged along through the fields on either side of it, through standing and half-cut corn, through stubble, through field crops, through farmyards – hard going even for fresh troops, heartbreaking for these. Some fell and simply couldn't get up, and were left to sleep with their faces cradled in the furrows between rows of turnips and flax. Men so tired they could hardly move their feet helped wounded companions along.

The battalions were hopelessly mixed up, and there seemed to be hardly any officers left, but the men didn't need orders. The straight line of the road was their guide, and everyone was going the same way. St Quentin lay ahead and the Germans were somewhere behind; that was all they needed to know. Now that they were retiring, they must not stop or the Germans would catch up with them, and there would be a rout. No-one knew exactly where the enemy was, so they stumbled along as fast as they could, and in grim silence, saving their breath for the effort.

Progress was agonisingly slow. It began to drizzle, and then night came on. With the clouds covering the sky it was pitch dark, and men stumbled over unseen objects, too tired even to curse. Some fell into ditches and couldn't get out. Sometimes they stubbed their toes on boxes of rations, dumped at the side of the road by the Army Service Corps, which had retreated ahead of them, but with the steady press of men behind them they couldn't stop to pick them up. And the darkness to their right was enlivened from time to time with the crackle of rifle-fire and the occasional flash of an explosion as scattered units still fought their way out from German clutches.

Bertie walked with the rest. He had not seen his horse since they got to position in Réumont. The groom would have had to retire away from the shelling and there had never been an opportunity since for them to reunite. It occurred to him, with grim humour, that there had been hardly any point in his bringing horses to France – he had been on foot far more than in the saddle. His handful of men kept close to him, evidently finding comfort in having his authority nearby.

They had been plodding for some indeterminable time when the rain stopped at last. Then Bertie noticed that the night was definitely grey, rather than black, around him. He could see the man shuffling along in front of him, rather than just perceive the bulk of him. Never had a dawn been more welcome. He straightened his shoulders and looked at the sky, watching greedily for every little sign: a yellowish stain to the grey in the east; then a clear, watery strip of lemon, darkening to slate blue above as the clouds cleared away overhead; then a gleam, a tiny seed of fire where the sun was coming up behind the eastern cloudbank. Then the upper edge of the cloud, straight as a tabletop, caught alight, and slowly, majestically, the golden disc raised itself into view.

It was going to be hot again. As the sun rose, the chilled men began to warm a little, their uniforms to steam. At Estrées two staff officers – who looked the most exhausted of all, their faces grey, their eyes red-rimmed, their voices cracking – directed the flow, trying to separate the infantry from the horse and wheeled traffic, turning the former onto the shorter road to St Quentin. Bertie watched his handful of men through the turn, then fell in beside the rear marker. It was Underwood, a scrawny man with, at the best of times, an odd, uncomfortable-looking gait. At Sandridge he had been the despair of the RSM because his march did not look like everyone else's – but he was valued as the crack shot of the regiment. Now he was hobbling agonisingly. 'How are the feet, Underwood?' Bertie asked.

Underwood turned up mournful eyes. 'Me boots is full o' blood, sir. They never liked me, these 'ere boots, and now I don't them, neither.'

Bertie searched for some comfort for him. 'Never mind, look, there's the river up ahead. That's the river that runs through St Quentin.'

'Is it, sir?'

'Only three or four more miles. We'll be able to rest in St Quentin, and there'll be food.'

From a village over to his left, Bertie heard a church clock striking, and counted – eight o'clock. The town was in sight now, the morning sun glinting off its windows. Up ahead there was a cottage beside the road, and under a large tree in front of it a trestle table had been set up. As they drew nearer, Bertie could see two young girls in charge of two tall white enamel jugs, from which they were pouring something into tin cups for the soldiers. A stout woman in an apron came out of the cottage with two more jugs, which she exchanged for the emptied ones. Even before they reached the table they could smell that it was coffee.

'Gawd, sir,' Underwood said, and it was eloquence itself.

The girls smiled shyly as they poured and handed over the cups. Bertie's tongue and throat yearned for it. He sipped to test the heat, and then shot the whole cupful deliciously down his throat. It was strong and black, and both eased his thirst and quieted his anxious stomach.

'*Merci, Mesdemoiselles*,' he said, handing the cup back. They looked at each other and giggled.

One small cup of coffee was not much, but it was enough to put new hope into the men – that and the kindness behind it. It got them over the last mile to the town. Staff officers now began to appear at the sides of the road, directing people to rendezvous, trying to sort them by division and brigade, at least, if not yet by battalion.

'When you get to your collection point there'll be food for you, and you'll be able to find your own unit. Then when you've rested you'll be able to cover the last few miles to the Somme.'

'What's that, sir, the Somme?' one of Bertie's men asked.

'It's a river,' the staff officer said. 'We'll cross it at Ham and make it our new line. It'll be easy to hold while we rest and recuperate, and wait for reinforcements. Don't worry, this will be the last retirement. The next time we're on the move it'll be the Germans that do the retreating.'

A ragged cheer met his words. They shuffled wearily into

St Quentin, and through the town to the rendezvous on the south side.

There was food, as promised, and water, and the men, having eaten and quenched their thirst, fell asleep where they sat, heads cushioned on the earth, on their gunstocks, on each other. It was hard to rouse them when the time came. But it was another twelve miles to Ham, and the Germans must be somewhere close behind. It was after one o'clock – Bertie had borrowed a watch from one of the corporals – as the battalion lined up for roll call.

There were two hundred and four of them, and three officers.

After the shocking revelations of the 30th of August, censorship was reimposed on war news, but the one lapse had had its effect. The cheerful exhilaration of the first weeks of the war changed to a furious determination. The Germans must be beaten at all costs. They *would* be beaten, by God! The second great wave of volunteering began. The recruitment office in New Scotland Yard had so many volunteers in the first two days after the news broke that a second office had to be opened in Trafalgar Square.

Anti-German propaganda filled the centre pages of every newspaper, and readers were reminded of how the Hun had sacked Belgian towns, massacred their inmates, burnt the famous library at Louvain because its citizens would not surrender, marched civilians in front of them towards guns as a sort of 'human shield'. Hatred of all Germans surged up again. Windows of shops with German names were smashed, businesses with German names shunned. Ten thousand German men living in Britain were interned, though for lack of facilities many more were left at liberty or encouraged to return to Germany. Those not interned had to register as aliens at the nearest police station, and report if they changed their address, on pain of imprisonment.

Such was the antipathy that senseless stories appearing in the press were believed wholeheartedly: a German barber in north London had vowed that if an Englishman came into his shop to be shaved he would cut his throat; a German watchmaker in Soho was using his skills and tools to make bombs; a German pork butcher in Woking was putting poison into the sausages he sold English customers. So great was the appetite for such tales that the *Daily Mail*, which had never allowed truth to get in the way of a good story, saw its circulation rise to over a million in the first weeks of the war.

Everything German was now rejected. The German mineral water Apollinaris, so favoured by restaurants that the common term for gin-and-water was gin-and-polly, was banished in favour of Perrier, which advertised itself as 'The Table Water of the Allies'. German bands, which had been immensely popular before the war, disappeared, and it was now said that marching about the streets playing their 'oompah music' had only been the excuse to cover their spying activities. The grocery family, Messrs Lipton, had to take out a full-page advertisement in the main newspapers denying they were of German origin after their business rivals, J. Lyons, asserted they were. Ladies carrying pet Dachshunds were abused in the streets, and breeders of German shepherd dogs hurriedly claimed they were really Alsatian. Steinway pianos had their names blacked out, and music by German and Austrian composers was struck from concert programmes. Eau-de-Cologne could only be sold as eau-de-toilette, an outbreak of German measles in Liverpool was described as the Belgian Flush, and anyone with a German-sounding name changed it if they could.

Jessie did not have long to wait in anguish after that terrible Sunday. Thanks to the excellence of the postal service set up for the men in France, she received a letter from Bertie on the morning of Wednesday the 2nd of September, and opened it with hands that shook so much it was a while before she could read the opening words.

Saturday 29th August. Near Soissons.
My dear Jessie,
This is the first time I have had a moment's leisure to write. I hope the news back home of our brave doings

have kept you all cheerful. We have been in action twice, at Mons on the 23rd and at Le Cateau on the 26th, and both times our men fought like tigers and punished the Germans severely, despite being outnumbered. We are now retiring to find a better position from which to launch the final attack and drive the enemy back to Berlin. Since Le Cateau we have been retiring with the Germans hot on our tail, which has meant hard marching. We try to keep going through the night, just snatching a few hour's sleep in a field by the road, so as to keep ahead of the Germans, who never advance after dark. Night marching is at least cooler – by day it is scorchingly hot, as bad as South Africa!

Getting enough to eat has been difficult. The RSC lorries dump food by the side of the road for us, but the units at the head of the column take most of it, and sometimes the Germans are so close behind we can't stop to pick it up. Morale is high, but there is no doubt the past week has taken its toll on us physically. The men were on their last legs when we arrived here last night, so imagine our relief when we were told we were to have a day of rest today as the French are engaging the Germans on our right. We all slept like the dead for the rest of the night and late into the morning, when we woke to a breakfast of tea and bacon and real bread. I can't tell you what it means to have hot food again! The men slept again after that until late afternoon when there was a rush for the stream to get clean before dinner – we hadn't washed in a week! A delicious veal stew was followed by cheese and, astonishingly, cake, sent up by a grateful confectioner from Soissons who I suppose hopes we will keep the Germans out of his town!

After a long sleep and hot food we felt like new men. My company is now sitting round a campfire singing 'Hold Your Hand Out, You Naughty Boy', their favourite marching song. When we entered Boulogne (it seems a lifetime ago) the townsfolk thought it was our national anthem and stood to attention! The rest day has also given stragglers a chance to catch up, including – thank God! – my groom with my horses. They got separated from me at Le Cateau and were 'borrowed' by a major in the Ox and Bucks, who was most reluctant to hand them over to a mere captain, even if he was the rightful owner! I am also relieved that two of our officers have reappeared, and twenty of our men, including my servant Cooper who has been missing since Mons. He has some hair-raising stories to tell about narrow escapes, some of which may even be true! I must close this letter now as the bag is about to go off and if I miss this chance I don't know when there will be another. Don't worry if you don't hear from me for some time. Assure Aunt Hen and everyone I am well.

I think of you often.

Bertie

The letter had come by the second post after Ned had gone to work. Jessie could not help crying a little with relief, before telephoning Ned to tell him that Bertie was safe, then riding over to Morland Place to share the letter with her mother and family. Henrietta didn't cry, but she looked as though a weight had been taken off her shoulders. 'Now if only we can hear from Jack!' she said. 'I suppose if everyone's retreating he won't have a chance to write either.'

'Probably not. But the RFC haven't been in the fighting, anyway, so I'm sure he must be all right,' Jessie said. On this second reading she couldn't help remembering the reports in the newspaper about 'terrible losses', battalions reduced to half their strength, and the ragged remnants of the army, many of them wounded, limping desperately away from the pursuing Germans. Had the accounts been exaggerated, or was Bertie concealing the worst from her? If the latter, what was he concealing about himself? But he was alive, at all events, and well enough to hold a pen and write a long letter.

When she had finished a second reading, all Henrietta said was, 'So he has only just got his horses back. It must have been hard for him to walk all that way. Bertie never did like to walk, even as a boy.'

Henrietta was glad to have one thing less to worry about. She was struggling with the chicken-pox. It said in the newspapers that there had been a lot of such outbreaks of minor infections all over the country, caused, it was thought, by the sudden influx of soldiers from far and wide, coming together in crowded cities. Certainly it had got into the house with one of the housemaids after she had spent her day off with her fiancé, who had enlisted. Betty swore that her Harold didn't have the illness, but it soon emerged that it was all round the barracks, rife among the volunteers and territorials who had taken over the empty spaces left by the regulars gone to France. Betty didn't have it badly, but two other maids had caught it, and in a house like Morland Place such things could spread all too easily. Henrietta had been obliged to set up the day nursery as an isolation ward, and to do most of the nursing herself. She and Teddy had both had it in childhood and so were immune.

Teddy was out on the estate when Jessie came, so Henrietta left a message for him downstairs. He came up to see her when he got in and read Bertie's letter. 'Well, that is good news! And from what he says here things aren't half as bad as they were painted in the newspapers,' he said. 'I suppose it's the usual press hysteria. As soon as they hear the word "retreat" they assume it's a rout, and panic. They don't understand that sometimes you have to change position. You see Bertie has no doubt that they will beat the Bosch.'

He went away cheerfully, and Henrietta went back to the sick-room, pondering that the war had seemed to have a bracing effect on her brother. Ever since it was declared, he seemed to have looked forward to each day with much more spirit.

He had been depressed and withdrawn after the *Titanic* episode, and though he had recovered to an extent, for more than two years he had avoided company and hardly left the estate. Cruel, false accusations had been levelled at him:

they said he had forced women and children aside to get himself into a lifeboat. His name had been linked with that of his friend Bruce Ismay, and both had been reviled. Teddy never talked about it or referred to it in any way, but he had suffered deeply because of it ever since. He never gave or accepted invitations, except among family members, and never went into York, where he might see looks of hatred and contempt.

So it was a happy surprise to Henrietta when he said at breakfast on Thursday the 3rd of September that he was going in to Makepeace's, his drapery and haberdashery store in York. 'All this German hatred, you know,' he said, waving his hand at the paper. 'It says here a shop had its windows broken last night because it had Mechlin lace in the window display. I must make sure there isn't anything in Makepeace's that looks or sounds German. And one of the seamstresses has a German name – a Miss Muller, I think it is. I must see that she's all right.'

'You're going into York yourself?' Henrietta said, hardly able to believe it.

'I think I must, my dear,' he said. 'It could be a delicate business. Why? Is there something I can get for you?'

'Oh, yes, please! More calamine lotion – half a dozen bottles. And if you could pass a message to the doctor to make up more of the fever drink—'

'You can telephone for that.'

'Oh, yes. I keep forgetting we have it. I wonder if I should have him visit. I think Elsie is coming down with it now. I knew she would, the wretch. She never can do things when everyone else does them, and there's such a lot of washing to do.'

Alice spoke up in her faint, faded voice. 'Sweetlove can do the delicate things. She does mine so beautifully.'

'You don't think she'd mind giving a hand?'

'I'm sure not,' said Alice, profligate with the sensibilities of a highly trained and paid lady's maid. 'After all, it is an emergency. And we must all pull together now there's a war on.'

'So, just the calomel,' Teddy said, trying to get back to the point.

'Calamine, dear,' Henrietta corrected.

'Same thing, isn't it? Oh, all right, calamine, then. Anything else? Anything for you, my love?'

'Oh, yes,' said Alice. 'As you're going to Makepeace's, you might match some thread for me, if I give you what I have left.'

Teddy looked worried. 'Match thread? But I won't do it right.'

Alice smiled. 'Give it to Mrs Ordshawe in the haberdashery department. She'll know.'

'Right you are. Ethel, my dear?'

'Nothing, thank you. Robbie gets anything I want every day,' Ethel reminded him, with faint pride. Robbie was a very attentive husband, and thought pregnancy required constant presents and little luxuries.

Now Teddy turned to Polly, who was fairly bursting for her turn. 'Oh, Daddy, take me with you! Oh, please! I haven't been in to York for ages and I'm so *bored*!'

'How can you be bored at Morland Place?' Teddy asked, with simple disbelief.

'You'll be back at school next week,' Henrietta warned. 'Better make the most of your freedom while you can.'

'Oh, I *will*, Aunty, but can't I make use of it in York instead of here?'

Teddy said, 'Of course you can come, love, but I don't think it will be very interesting for you. I shall be at the shop quite a while, and then I might call in at the workshop, and perhaps at the mill afterwards, but only if there's time.'

'I don't mind,' Polly said. 'I like the shop, and I like just looking out of the window. There's always so many people going past, you never know who you might see. And York is full of soldiers just now.'

'She thinks she might see Lennie,' Ethel remarked to her toast-and-marmalade.

'Lennie won't be there,' said Henrietta. 'He's gone to camp.'

'Well, you just never know, really,' Polly said, with huge dignity. She was at the age when any change was welcome, and putting on 'town' clothes and a hat and gloves (Alice was particular about her appearance in public) and riding into York in the motor-car was inducement enough. Besides, Makepeace's had a wonderful lift with an attendant in smart uniform who treated her like a queen; and Daddy had named a colour of ribbon after her – 'Polly Blue'. She loved seeing it printed on the card, so official-looking.

But the lift-man had gone, called up as a reservist, and the lift was being run now by a very undersized boy hardly older than her. The shop was not at all busy, and Teddy feared there had been an upsurge of the hatred against him that had emptied it for months after the *Titanic* business.

But Mrs Lowe, the manageress of the ladies' side, said that it was just the war. 'People have so much else to think about at the moment, they aren't wanting new clothes and furnishings. And, of course, there's all this talk about economy and making do and no extravagance or needless spending. I've got hardly any work on hand. Frankly, sir,' she lowered her voice worriedly, 'we ought to lay off a couple of the women, because there just isn't the sewing to do. There's the Inglethorpe wedding – fortunately that's not been cancelled, like so many, in favour of a register office – but the work for that's nearly finished, and there are only two other gowns in the order book. Of course, things might pick up at any time,' she added, with professional, if unconvincing optimism. 'And Mr Buckley in the gentlemen's has done very well in leather gloves and attaché cases – officers, I suppose, going away.'

In the office, Miss Muller from Millinery was interviewed. She was a black-clad pipe-cleaner of a woman whose native accent had been overlaid with tortured shop-assistant's refinement. Her iron-grey hair was rigidly disciplined into a tight bun behind, and she had permanently red eyes, which made her look as though she had been crying – it upset Teddy at first, thinking the persecution had already begun. But she said she had not had any trouble, and seemed a little surprised at the suggestion. 'May customers are kaynd enough to ask for me by name, sir, and to say they do not layke to be served by anyone else.'

Nevertheless, Teddy mused as he looked at her, she had not a naturally warm and lovable appearance. Devotion to her skills could wear thin. He suggested she allowed herself to be presented in future as Miss Miller. Customers who already knew her well would understand. Miss Miller bowed her head once, sharply, in acknowledgement, and he thought, though he did not say so, that she could well dispense with the gesture, which brought to mind a Germanic click of booted heels.

With Mrs Lowe at his side he went carefully through every department, looking for anything that might cause offence. Their own Mechlin lace he ordered to be sold as Brussels lace – 'Anything "Brussels" should go down well,' he said – and they conferred long and hard about the Chantilly: would customers think that was German? To be on the safe side, it should be relabelled French. Vienna crape had better be Belgian crape – oh, and he must remember to speak to Mr Buckley about the Homburg hats.

Colours of ribbon and fabrics had to be adjusted. There was Brunswick, for instance, and Saxe Blue – and Cobalt. People might mistake that for Coburg, especially when it rested next to Saxe. Reinhart had to go, and Danube and Meissen – who would have thought there were so many German-sounding names of colours? What about Taupe? Ah, but would people know that? Better be on the safe side. Likewise Ecru – and Siena. Foreign was foreign to most people.

While they were thus engaged, he was addressed by a soft, female voice saying, 'Why, isn't it Mr Morland?'

He straightened abruptly and turned, reddening a little in anticipation of what might be coming. A smart young woman in a preposterous hat (Teddy took hasty mental notes for Alice) was smiling at him. She extended her hand. 'Mary Dyke,' she said. 'Mary Micklethwaite that was.'

Now he remembered her. The Micklethwaites were very old friends of the Morlands, who had remained constant through the troubles. She had married Jack Dyke, the banker's son. He bowed over the proffered hand and said, 'Of course, of course. Forgive me. How do you do?'

'I don't wonder you didn't know me. You haven't seen me since I was in pigtails. But I had my wedding gown from you – from here, I should say. I saw your motor-car and your little girl downstairs and wondered if you might be here. What a pleasure to see you out and about again, if you don't mind my saying so.'

He smiled nervously, not knowing quite how to respond. 'Well, it's the war, you know,' he said vaguely – which was the truth, even if it didn't sound as though it made sense.

But she seemed to accept it. 'Yes, I know. We're all so busy now, aren't we? I can't imagine how we managed to pass our days before! For instance,' she added, with a dimple, 'I'm collecting for the Fund for the Relief of Soldiers' Families. It's a very worthy cause. Our heroes in France often leave behind considerable hardship for those at home. Army pay doesn't go far.'

'Oh, indeed, indeed,' Teddy said hastily, reaching for his notecase.

'Why, thank you,' Mrs Dyke said, with a charming smile. 'Goodness! That's most generous! Thank you so much. Just let me make a note of it.' She took a small black book out of her bag, wrote in it neatly, then put away the money and the book. She looked at him a moment consideringly, as a pretty bird might gaze at a tasty worm. Teddy was so enjoying this little piece of human interaction he didn't mind at all being the potential meal.

Mrs Dyke laid a gloved hand delicately on his forearm and turned away with him a trifle. Mrs Lowe had stepped back discreetly the moment she addressed him, but Mrs Dyke, for all her youth, had a short way with shop assistants.

'You've been so generous, dear Mr Morland, I wonder if I might make another request of you.'

'Oh, certainly, certainly,' Teddy said, reaching for his notecase again.

She laughed prettily. 'No, it isn't that this time. Let me explain. My brother Sidney volunteered, but when he went to be fitted for his uniform, there was just one poor old creature there, labouring away on a sewing-machine making the alterations, and the work was plainly far too much for her, so he won't get his uniform for a week or more. He's so disappointed, and of course so is Mother, and all of us, because we so long to see him in it. Now, it occurred to me,' she looked around, 'that it isn't very busy here, and I suppose people aren't ordering new clothes, because of the war effort. So I imagine that your seamstresses are quite idle at the moment.'

'So I'm told,' Teddy said. 'If I understand you, you think I should – let's say – *volunteer* my sewing women to help out with the uniforms?'

'And the machines,' she added quickly.

'Why, yes, of course I can do that,' Teddy said, happy that there was something so directly useful he could do. He loved to be useful, and to please people, and it was a long time since he had dared hope he might please the denizens of York. Also it would mean he wouldn't have to turn off the seamstresses, something he never liked doing to loyal employees. 'I can have one of my motors from the warehouse take the machines round, and the sewing-women can do their usual hours there.'

'What an excellent man you are!' Mrs Dyke said. 'Mother will be so delighted I've seen you here. I'm sure she would send her compliments if she knew.'

'Mine to her, if you please,' said Teddy. 'It has been a long time since I saw any of my old friends.'

'Oh, the war will change everything,' Mary Dyke said, and took her leave of him.

Down below, Polly had overcome her prejudices and got talking to the lift boy. Once he knew she was the owner's daughter, he had become so struck with awe she had had to work pleasantly hard to get him to talk to her at all; but now, while still gazing at her as if she were royalty, he was telling her all about his home and ambitions. When her father appeared she said, 'Oh, Daddy, this is Horace Ames, and he's longing to join up. He went to volunteer straight away, but they wouldn't take him because he's too young.'

'Well done, good show,' said Teddy, and found a sixpence for him, gathering Polly in the same gesture and ushering her towards the door. 'We've lots to do now, no time to waste,' he said, and told her about Mrs Dyke's suggestion.

Polly was thrilled with the idea. 'Oh, Daddy, how super! I was worried that you wouldn't be able to do anything, because of course you're too old to go and fight, I do see that,' she said sympathetically. 'But now you'll be really helping at last. Oh, I do wish I could do something.'

'You're only fourteen, my lamb. No-one expects it,' he said. He saw that that didn't satisfy her, and added, 'I tell you what, I'll teach you to shoot – how would that be? Then if the Germans do invade you can shoot them from the barbican walls, as well as pouring boiling oil on them.'

'Oh, yes, please! Oh, thank you, Daddy! But I'll pour the oil first, and then shoot them,' Polly decided after some thought, 'because they jolly well deserve to suffer, the Horrid Huns!'

CHAPTER ELEVEN

Polly was disappointed that her father made her stay in the motor-car while he went to the recruiting office, saying it wasn't suitable for her to go inside, as men might be taking their clothes off. But when he went down to the warehouse and workshop in Skeldergate she had a fascinating half-hour, while Teddy made his arrangements, poking around among the wonderful bales of material and boxes of fastenings and reels of thread, and watching the women cutting out and working away at their whirring machines.

Then they got back in the motor-car and drove over to Ned's mill in Layerthorpe. Ned received them with great pleasure in his office. It was rather grand, for the previous owner, Alice's first husband, had had it done out in oak panelling with a dark red Turkey carpet on the floor. Ned sent for coffee for them, and when it came it was accompanied by a plate of the very best selected biscuits, which kept Polly interested for a while, as it was past time for lunch by Morland Place nursery standards. Business people like Ned didn't ever have luncheon, as she knew very well, so she was particularly glad he had provided biscuits when he might very easily not have thought of it.

Ned was delighted to see his father out and about, and listened with interest to his account of what he had been doing that morning, and how glad he was to have found a way to help. Ned told Teddy about his own plan to volunteer as soon as he had the business on a good footing to be left. Teddy asked what that entailed, and the conversation then became technical and Polly lost interest and stared out of the window.

The two men were still deep in conversation when a knock came at the door and Ned's secretary came in. He stopped abruptly, and said, 'Oh, I'm sorry, sir. I didn't know you were engaged.'

'What is it, Fisher?'

'Three of the clerks wanted to see you, sir, in their luncheon period, but I can tell them to come back later.'

'It's a personal matter, then, is it?' Ned asked.

'I believe so, sir. I believe it's something about enlisting.'

Teddy's ears pricked up at that. 'Do see them now,' he urged Ned. 'Good intentions ought to be encouraged. Don't mind me – I'd be interested to hear what they have to say.'

'Very well, Fisher. I'll see them,' said Ned, and to his father added with a smile, 'Better to see them on their time than mine, I suppose.'

Fisher showed them in. 'Hirst, Brown and Iles, sir.'

They were all young – though grown-up to Polly, being around nineteen and twenty years old – and one of them, Brown, was quite good-looking. They were all dressed in clerkly suits with waistcoats, and had their hair brushed back and firmly held down with oil, as clerks did, but Brown had a nice curly mouth, and warm brown eyes that jumped instantly to Polly, which recommended him to her. She always liked people to notice her first.

Brown, it seemed, was the spokesman, for he said, 'We're sorry to disturb you, sir. We didn't know you had visitors.'

'It's quite all right, Brown. My father and sister were interested to hear what you had to say.'

'Well, sir, it's about this idea the Earl of Derby was talking about in Liverpool on Friday – last Friday, sir, the twenty-eighth. I don't know if you read about it? There was a piece in the *Yorkshire Evening Post* – about the "Pals" battalions, sir?'

Teddy answered first. 'Oh, yes, I did see something about that. That was General Rawlinson's idea, wasn't it, to help recruitment – where people could join up and serve with their friends?'

'That's right, sir,' said Brown. 'He said that if people from the same street, or the same office, or even the same sports club or society, were to volunteer together, they would be put into the same unit so that they could be sure of serving with people they knew.'

'Yes, I understand,' said Ned. 'Lord Derby was suggesting the city of Liverpool raised a whole battalion that way.'

'That's right, sir,' said Brown, and he turned to Iles, who was holding a newspaper, took it from him, and offered it to Ned, folded open to the letters page. 'Well, sir, there was this piece in the *Mercury* yesterday. Perhaps you'd be so kind as to read it, sir.'

Ned took it, and Teddy stationed himself behind his son's shoulder so that they could read it together.

Sir, Regarding the Earl of Derby's scheme, is there no influential citizen of York who will come forward and call for a 'pals' battalion for this district? There is a vast and, as yet, untapped recruiting ground in the middle-class population engaged in commercial pursuits. Young men from the factories, warehouses and offices of the city, who desire to go to the front, hesitate about enlisting lest they should be sent to a regiment in which they will not find kindred spirits. These young men, who spend their leisure in cricket or on football fields, playing golf or lawn tennis, hiking or bicycling, are as fit and active as any labourer, but with the additional advantage of a greater intelligence and education. A York commercial battalion would yield fine fighting material, and the discipline of the playing-fields will have formed a firm basis for the discipline of the ranks. Will nobody come forward and organise this?

'By Jove,' Teddy said, 'that is an idea, isn't it?'

Ned looked up at the three clerks, 'What is your interest in this? What is it you've come to see me about?'

'Well, sir,' said Brown, 'we thought a business battalion would be just the ticket for us. We've been talking for days about enlisting, sir—'

'Only we weren't quite sure about it, you see,' Iles interrupted, 'thinking that we'd get split up and find ourselves side by side with – well – people we didn't like.'

'Like it says there, sir,' said Hirst. 'Not kindred spirits. We know most of the volunteers so far have been labourers and farm workers and coal miners and the like, and we didn't fancy the idea of having to serve the whole war with chaps we didn't know and had nothing in common with.'

'But if we could serve with our chums, sir – fellows we know from work, or play cricket with, well, that'd be a quite different thing,' Iles completed.

'It would indeed,' said Ned, thoughtfully. He hadn't pondered the subject much, feeling only that he had to go, but obviously it would be much more pleasant to be in with one's own sort, from one's own home town. 'What is it you want me to do?'

'Well, sir,' Brown said shyly, 'there is talk, sir, that you mean to go yourself—'

'The dickens there is,' Ned muttered. How on earth had that got round? He didn't think he'd told a soul.

'And, well, we thought perhaps you'd be the one to step forward, as it says in the newspaper, and propose it,' said Brown. 'There's the three of us want to go, and some chaps in the warehouse, and a couple of the engineers – I don't know how many more from here. But then there'll be friends of ours from other offices, who'll want to go if they know we are, and the fellows in the cricket team—'

'And I belong to a choir, sir,' said Hirst, 'and I bet they'd all join – all the unmarried ones, anyway – if there was such a thing.'

Ned held up his hands to quell their enthusiasm. 'I think it's a fine idea,' he said, 'but I hardly think I'm an "influential citizen" in the way the letter means – and I simply don't have time at the moment, with the mill to run. I'm here from seven in the morning until seven at night as it is. An idea like this would need someone to devote himself to it the whole time.'

'Someone like me?' Teddy said.

Polly clasped her hands together. 'Oh, yes, Daddy! Oh, do, do! It would be so splendid.'

The three clerks turned their eyes on him. 'Would you, sir? Would you really?'

'I think it's a first-rate idea,' said Teddy, 'and I'd be proud to be associated with it. I'm sure there are plenty of young businessmen in and around York who feel just as you do. The first thing, I suppose, is to get the mayor and corporation involved.'

Ned looked at Teddy too, and his eyes held an urgent message. 'Father,' he said warningly.

Teddy looked at him, and his mood sagged a little. He was forgetting – he had been *persona non grata* in York for the past two years. Was he the man to get such a scheme going forward? Would anyone listen to him? Would not his involvement rather kill the idea? And would he not be exposing himself to the risk of terrible snubs and hurt?

Polly looked from her father to her brother and back, and understood what worried them. It was outrageous, and made her very angry, that her father should have to think like that. The Morlands were the oldest family in York. Her grandfather had practically built the railway with his own hands, to say nothing of the slum clearances. And her father had been on any number of committees, had done so much good for the city, given so much money to various causes – and yet because of some horrible lies and untrue stories in the newspapers, he was to be prevented from doing this wonderful thing.

An idea came to her. 'If you had someone to suggest it *with* you, Daddy? Some military person, perhaps. Ned, what about your friend Colonel Wycherley? He knows everyone.'

'That's a good thought,' Ned said; and then, 'Oh, but he's already gone to France. Let me think. Wait, of course – I'm sure Mrs Wycherley could suggest someone from among their acquaintance.' He looked across at the clerks. 'Leave it with me. I will let you know as soon as anything has been done.'

'Thank you, sir,' they said, and filed out.

Left alone, father and son looked at each other.

'Are you sure you want to do this?' Ned asked.

Teddy met his eyes. 'I can't let my feelings stand in the way of something that ought to be done. We all have our duty.'

Polly said, 'Perhaps it will be all right, Daddy. It was only silly people who didn't like you, and I expect they'll have forgotten by now.'

'You may well be right,' Ned said, and to Teddy, 'I just don't want you to be hurt.'

'The important thing is to get the idea forward,' said Teddy, 'whatever has to be done to achieve it.'

'And you'll join it, won't you, Ned?' Polly said urgently.

'Of course,' he smiled. 'I'll be the first to put my name down.'

Mrs Wycherley also thought the idea excellent and, after a brief pause for thought, said, 'I know absolutely the right man. You must speak to dear old Colonel Bassett. He's an absolute darling, but he has tremendous presence and there's not a soul in the world could say no to him if he's set his mind on something. He's retired now, and of course he's been aching for something to do ever since the war started. He hates to be inactive. It would be just the thing for him. He'd take hold like a bulldog and not let go until the thing was up and running.'

'He sounds perfect,' said Ned.

'But why doesn't your father want to put his idea forward himself?' she asked. Ned hesitated, and she went on, 'You're not thinking – he isn't thinking about that old business? Oh, my dear, that's surely all forgotten now.'

'I'm not sure,' Ned said. 'Unhappily, some people like to hold grudges, and they're always the ones with long memories.'

'There may be one or two like that,' Mrs Wycherley acknowledged, 'but I think it will be very few. The war has given even the most narrow-minded something new to think about. And, if I may speak frankly, being involved with – being seen as the author of – a scheme like this would be the very thing to get your father back into the swing of things. He *ought* to be at the centre of our civic life, and there would be so much goodwill involved in something so patriotic that I'm sure this could be the way to establish him there.'

'Perhaps you're right. I know he's longing to be fully involved with the scheme. I could see his disappointment at the idea of having to take a back seat.'

'Well, let me speak to my dear old Hound – that's what the men used to call Colonel Bassett, you know, in a very affectionate way – and we'll see. I'll ring you again as soon as I've spoken to him.'

Colonel 'Hound' Bassett did not waste time. As soon as he had grasped the nature of Mrs Wycherley's suggestion, he asked her to arrange a meeting between him, Ned and Teddy that evening at her house.

He proved to be both a delightful and a formidable figure. He was a big man, broad in the shoulders, with brushed-back white hair, bushy white eyebrows, and a thick white moustache above a mouth full of humour. He had evidently been extremely handsome in his youth, and still had that air about him of expecting to be liked and obeyed, which was so valuable to an officer. His face was brown and firm, his eyes in their nests of wrinkles shrewd and kindly. He obviously held Mrs Wycherley in great affection, which she cordially returned.

'By Jove, this is just the thing! Don't know why I didn't think of it myself,' he said, when he had shaken hands all round. 'Must have been half asleep. Damned grateful to you, Mr Morland, for coming up with it, and for bringing me in on it.'

'We're hoping you can give us an idea of how to go about it,' Teddy said.

'I suppose the first thing is to throw out a lure to the city,' said Mrs Wycherley. 'Do you think they'd bite, Hound, dear?'

'Oh, bound to!' he said cheerfully. 'Did you know Leeds city is doing the same thing? Yes, my housekeeper told me when I mentioned this to her. Her son works in Leeds and told her about it. So York won't want to be behindhand. What Leeds can do, York must do better. You know the old rivalry.'

'So what must our first move be?' Teddy asked.

Bassett smiled. 'I've already taken it. Hope you don't mind – I assumed you'd want action quickly, being a businessman yourself.'

Mrs Wycherley laughed. 'That's my Hound – hot on the scent! What have you done?'

'I spoke to the mayor by telephone. There's a regular meeting tomorrow – first Friday of the month – and I asked his permission for you and me, Mr Morland, to attend it in order to put an important proposal about York's war effort. He agreed at once. The war effort is dear to everyone's heart. So we're to meet the mayor and aldermen at ten tomorrow morning at the council chambers.'

Teddy paled a little. 'I'm to meet them? I thought perhaps – I supposed you would make the first approach.'

Bassett shook his head, but there was a hint of sympathy in his eyes that suggested he knew of Teddy's troubles. 'No time, I'm afraid, for testing the water. We must jump straight in. No time to waste.'

'I'm sure the colonel's right, Father,' Ned said, with a look that meant *everything will be all right.*

Teddy could not allow himself to be seen to lack backbone. 'Of course, of course. Shall I pick you up in my motorcar, Colonel?'

'Thank you, that will be most convenient. The other thing I have done,' Bassett went on, 'is to send a telegraph to Lord Kitchener asking his permission to raise a commercial battalion for the city.'

'You went direct to Kitchener?' Mrs Wycherley marvelled.

'Oh, I just know him. Met him in South Africa. Best to go to the top if you can. Now if I know the War Office, I'll have a reply to that by tomorrow morning, and we can go to the city council with it in our hands as ammunition.'

'Do you think you'll need ammunition?' Ned asked. 'Didn't you say they would take the lure, sir?'

'Quite, quite, but they will have to think about it – there

will be expense involved – and we must have every means possible at our command to make their deliberations short.'

Teddy went to the Council Chambers the next morning with some trepidation, still unsure of what his reception would be. If there were any hostility towards him, he decided, he must back out of the scheme at once, rather than jeopardise it. But the colonel was serenely confident, and it was a comfort to have him at his side.

They were led to the chamber by a clerk, who eyed them curiously, thinking perhaps that they made an odd couple, the colonel in his Territorials uniform, Teddy in his usual frock coat and top hat. In the magisterially dark chamber Teddy found it difficult to gauge the temperature from the austere expressions on the aldermen's faces. It was the sort of chamber in which everyone was naturally grave. But Hound was undaunted, gave a preliminary few words saying that he endorsed heartily what Mr Morland was about to say, then handed over to Teddy.

Teddy cleared his throat, and explained briefly what the idea was and how it had come about. Out of the corner of his eye he thought he could see some hostile looks, and one man was shaking his head. He concentrated on the mayor's face, and found it receptive. The mayor was in the clothing business himself, so perhaps had a brotherly feeling for him. When he had finished, Bassett spoke again, saying that he endorsed everything Mr Morland had said, and was offering his own services in organising the affair. And he concluded by saying with an air of innocence that he understood a similar scheme was already in train in Leeds.

It was masterly. When Teddy dared to glance at the hostile ones, he saw they had been completely distracted by the notion that Leeds might be getting ahead of them.

'I really think that anything Leeds can do we can certainly manage a great deal better,' said one.

'Quite so,' said the mayor. 'And the thing is good in itself. I've heard a lot about these so-called "Pals" units. It should certainly aid the recruitment drive if the men know they will serve with people of their own sort. York ought to have a battalion. It is not only our duty to do everything we can for the war effort, but I believe it will add very much to the prestige of the city to raise a superior body of this sort.'

The head-shaker cleared his throat as a preliminary to a statement. Teddy now saw it was Alderman Cherry, and his heart sank in anticipation: Cherry had been one of Teddy's most bitter critics.

'I wonder, Lord Mayor, how much credit it *will* do the city, when it is known that the scheme is associated with someone of Mr Morland's unsavoury reputation.' He looked at Teddy with dislike. 'I wonder, sir, that you have the effrontery to put yourself forward in this way among decent folk.'

Teddy felt the blood rush to his face. He saw that two of those sitting nearest Cherry were his acolytes and willing to be persuaded by him.

But the mayor spoke up. 'Now, now, Mr Cherry—'

'*Alderman* Cherry, if you please. We must do all properly. And if you think, Lord Mayor, that Mr Morland's actions have qualified him to—'

'Alderman Cherry, I am very well aware that Mr Morland comes from a distinguished local family, and that he has done a great deal for the city of York. His actions have qualified him to receive our respect and courtesy, not to say gratitude.'

'Gratitude!' Cherry was fortunately rendered speechless by indignation.

One of his acolytes spoke up, a small, dark, bespectacled man called Wicksteed, who had the air of an overworked clerk. 'We all read the newspapers, Lord Mayor, about that dreadful incident concerning that ship, whose name I need not mention.'

'Perhaps we did,' said the mayor robustly, 'but do we always believe that everything printed in newspapers is the unvarnished truth?' Teddy could see that this struck t[ ] doubters. 'Any of us – I repeat, *any* of us – could f[ ] ourselves the victim of an unjustified smear of that so[ ] an unregulated press. For my own part, I prefer alv[ ] judge any man of my acquaintance by what I know[ ] If his behaviour has always been generous, bene[ ] public-spirited, it will take more than a tissue[ ] by a newspaper only to increase its sales, to make me believe otherwise of him.'

'Hear, hear,' said one of the aldermen at the other end of the table, and there was a general, if hesitant, murmur of agreement. Alderman Cherry did not look convinced, but his acolytes were looking towards the mayor as novices towards an inspirational father abbot.

Colonel Bassett said, with an air of overworked patience, 'I wonder, Lord Mayor, if we can return to the point in hand?'

'This *is* the point,' Alderman Cherry insisted. 'This is very much the point, sir. Mr Morland's reputation—'

'Now then, Tom,' said Alderman Bickersteth at the far end, leaning forward so he could see him, 'nobody believes those wicked stories any more. I think it's too bad of you, bringing them up and embarrassing Mr Morland, when he's come here with a very sensible and patriotic suggestion – which is what we all ought to be talking about now, to my mind, and not a lot of spiteful taradiddles from years ago. There is a war on, you know.'

The waverers nodded at this, and seemed relieved that the unpleasantness was going away. They liked to be led, but they preferred to be led in the direction of harmony, if at all possible.

'Thank you, Alderman Bickersteth,' said the mayor. 'I couldn't have put it better myself. There *is* a war on, and the people of York are entitled to ask what we, their representatives, are doing about it.'

'We shouldn't forget there's a state of national emergency,' said Mr Wicksteed.

'And Leeds has got two days' start of us already,' said Mr Brotherton urgently.

Colonel Bassett smiled behind his moustache and said, 'anticipation of your approval, I took the liberty of taking first step, so that no time should be wasted. I telegraphed d Kitchener asking his permission to raise a battalion, ve his reply here.'

sed the telegram to the mayor, who read it out. chener and the Army Council thank you, Mr

Morland and the City of York for your patriotic offer to raise a new battalion, which offer is gratefully accepted."'

'There!' said Mr Bickersteth, with satisfaction, feeling that the names Lord Kitchener himself had joined together, no man should put asunder. 'Now, what have you to say to that, Tom?'

Everyone looked at Alderman Cherry, who, though as red as his name, felt he could not stand out against the whole board, and might as well put a good face on it. 'I merely did my duty in pointing out what *might* be said by certain persons in certain circumstances. However, I am happy to be overruled. I hope I am as patriotic as the next man, and when the country is in great peril, we must all work together for the greater good.'

'Thank you, Alderman Cherry. I'm sure the country will be grateful to you,' said the mayor, sweetly. 'What I propose now is to nominate a committee to administer the details of the scheme, the committee to meet this afternoon at two o'clock to make a start. The proposal will have to go to the full council for approval, but I believe we may anticipate that. And may I say on behalf of us all that we are most grateful to Mr Morland for raising the idea, and to Colonel Bassett for helping to bring it before us?'

The committee applauded, and though Teddy's life had held many triumphs, he felt then and afterwards that none had gratified him as much as this one, the moment of his rehabilitation.

The day of rest on the 29th of August had come in the nick of time, for the whole division – what remained of it – had been on the brink of collapse. After fighting all day at Le Cateau they had been marching south-east, skirmishing as they went, with little rest and very little to eat. The day were burningly hot and the nights beginning to be shar cold, and there always seemed to be a heavy shower of which soaked them through just before sundown, whe was no chance to get dry again. After seventy-two ' heroic exertion, the men were filthy, unshaven, h so exhausted they could hardly put one leg in ' other. Bertie had only got his men along at all by allowing them to abandon more of what little kit they still had. Judging by the litter of cook-pots, greatcoats, washbags and personal belongings that lined the road, other units were doing the same. When they reached the bivouac near Soissons, they carried little more than rifle, ammunition and entrenching tool.

But the restorative effect of a long sleep and a couple of hot meals was astonishing. Everyone took his turn to strip off and plunge into the stream that ran alongside the field, to wash the sweat and mud and blood from his body, the caked dust from his hair, to rinse his filthy socks and shirt. The sheer pleasure of getting at least a degree cleaner had them whistling and indulging in horseplay – men who, only hours before, had looked like barely animated corpses. The arrival of twenty of their missing companions and two of their officers put the seal on the day. The singing round the campfires that night was an expression of sheer high spirits.

It was true, as Bertie had said in his letter to Jessie, that morale remained high. The men had been close to physical collapse, but there had never been any question of despair. They were the best soldiers in the world and they knew it, and every one of them firmly believed that as soon as they had regrouped and found a position to the generals' liking, they would turn on the enemy and drive them back to Germany.

Bertie had found the going as hard as anyone, perhaps harder than most, for he was older, and the unyielding nature of the bare ground communicated itself to his bones in a way that prevented sleep even when he was exhausted. Besides, as the only one of the three surviving officers with campaign experience, he hardly dared to sleep even during those few snatched hours. His wounds ached, his stomach complained bitterly, his feet were a constant misery from unaccustomed walking. Yet perhaps the hardest thing of the discovery that the passing of years had made civilian at heart. The biggest difference between this South Africa experience was that now when he lay the chilly night, he thought longingly of home, of Maud and the boy, and of Beaumont and its lush green acres, his cattle and his plans for the future. During the day, and when they were marching, there was enough to occupy him to prevent other thoughts intruding, but in those unresting moments of silence his mind escaped his control and turned inexorably towards England. And though he tried not to, in the dead of night and the weakness of exhaustion he thought of Jessie. England and Jessie – those two things now seemed to symbolise all that he longed for and was impossibly out of reach. He felt his loneliness creeping into his soul, even as the cold of the damp earth crept into his bones.

But the day of rest restored him, too, and the greatest pleasure of the day – more even than that veal stew, in which heavenly little herbed dumplings floated – was the arrival of some of his missing men, his horses and, above all, the two officers, Fenniman and Pennyfather. The sight of the former, filthy, unshaven, hollow-cheeked, his uniform torn in several places and a dirty bandage round his left leg above the knee, gave Bertie an idea of what he himself must look like.

Fenniman grinned with delight, pumped his hand, almost embraced him in the joy of the reunion. 'Never thought I'd be so damned pleased to see a reservist,' he said. 'Thinking of naming my firstborn after you.'

He told how he had been carried to the dressing-station during the battle with a piece of shrapnel in his leg. 'They bandaged it up, and told me to rest for a while. They were planning to send me back to a field hospital to get the damned thing chopped out. Then when the retreat started and they brought up the ambulance and asked if I could walk out to it, I put foot to floor, found it would take my weight, so I thought I might as well get back to my company. Only by then, of course, my company was gone. I've be following in your wake ever since, trying to catch you

'So the shrapnel's still in there?' Bertie asked. He see from the drawn lines of Fenniman's face that been in pain.

Fenniman shook his head. 'Dug it out mys

penknife.' He produced the fragment from his pocket and jiggled it in his palm for them to see.

'Good God!' said Bertie.

'I say, sir!' said Pennyfather.

But Fenniman made light of it. 'Couldn't throw it away. Quite fond of it now. Thinking of naming my firstborn after it, in fact.'

Pennyfather was in better shape, unwounded, and Fenniman was outraged when it emerged he had ridden part of the way on a supply lorry. 'You've been swanning along with your own motor transport while I've had to walk the whole way? I have holes in my boots that go all the way up to my knees, you know!'

Pennyfather apologised. 'I assure you I feel it as deeply as the situation warrants, sir.'

'Impudent pup!' Fenniman laughed. 'So what happened to you?'

Pennyfather explained how he had been separated. At one of the moments when Bertie retired the company to a new position, he and half a dozen men had been isolated. Harried by shot across a stretch of open land, they had taken shelter behind a group of corn stooks. 'Little enough cover, as you can imagine, sir. The Germans were advancing on both sides and there was nowhere to run. It wouldn't be long before they overwhelmed us. When my men were down to two, I decided if we didn't surrender we'd all die.'

Bertie nodded sympathetically, imagining clearly enough Pennyfather's feeling of sick horror at the shame of it, and the prospect of mouldering in a prison for the rest of the war. He must have wondered in that instant when he would see that little birdlike wife and those two sturdy boys again.

'So I stood up and shouted, "Don't shoot!" and waved my gun in the air. There was a Hun officer just a few yards ay. When he looked at me, I just knew he was thinking ould be less trouble to shoot us than take us prisoner, thought we were for it. But the German nearest us — he must have been an NCO, because he was a much n, and he had enormous moustaches — he looked the officer and the officer nodded, so Old

Moustaches took our guns and gestured with his that we were to walk in front of him. Well, sir,' Pennyfather divided the honorific between them, 'we were crossing open ground towards where I thought you were, and I reckoned if the Bosch didn't shoot us we'd catch it from our own side. But you must have fallen back, because we reached the hedgerow all right, and then Old Moustaches told us to get down on the ground, and I heard him tell a private to watch us. I tried to take a look round every now and then, because there was so much shooting going on and I was desperate to know if our side was winning, but every time I lifted my head the private hit me on the back of it with his rifle butt. I started to get a bit dizzy with it. Then I heard Old Moustaches' voice again, talking to someone – it may have been the officer – and I heard them say "English" so I guessed they were discussing us. I supposed we were a nuisance to them, and when they stopped talking, I was bracing myself for a shot in the back of the head. But nothing happened. It went quiet, the gunfire was getting more distant, and after a while I tried lifting my head again. We were alone, and I could hear that the fighting was much further off. So I nudged Johnson and Parry and we got up and made a run for it.'

He condensed his story after that, only saying that as they were now behind the German line they had to be careful and creep from cover to cover. It wasn't until the following morning, after a night of starting at every sound, that they had got to the Roman Road, only to find it occupied by German troops, marching in pursuit of the British. 'So we just had to make our way across country,' said Pennyfather. 'Eventually we managed to find a short cut and get ahead of the Bosch, and then we had a piece of luck and got picked up by an ASC lorry. So all's well that ends well.'

Despite his light words, Bertie could imagine well eno the terrifying journey, probably encompassing e adventure to fill a novel. 'I'm glad to have you ba us,' he said warmly. Pennyfather grinned, and Bert how much he had missed this cheerful young much he had dreaded discovering that he was

'So, how many of us made it here?' was Fenniman's next question. He glanced round the field and said, 'I suppose the rest are scattered about somewhere?'

'No,' said Bertie. 'This is all that's left. With the men who came in this morning we number two hundred and sixteen, and five officers – us three, Wetherall and Fassner.'

Fenniman said nothing, but Bertie saw in his eyes that he had known the answer to his question already; he had just not wanted to acknowledge it.

The next day they had resumed the march. Nothing much had changed. It was still horribly hot during the day – burning by midday and increasingly humid through the afternoon. Their passage raised thick clouds of dust that stuck to their sweat. Their uniforms were ragged and for many of them their boots were falling apart. But the survivors of the West Herts were now fit men, and they were in good spirits. They often sang as they marched, took an interest in the scenery and villages they passed, chatted and laughed during the rest breaks. Food was the biggest problem. Supplies were still haphazard, but at least the fruit in the orchards they passed was now ripe, and they supplemented their bully and biscuit (when it arrived) with apples and pears. And many of the houses they passed had vines growing up them, heavy with grapes, which at least served to quench their thirst.

They knew the Germans were pursuing them, but they hardly ever saw them. Before their rest day they had fought skirmishes, but since resuming the march they had not fired a shot, though they had sometimes heard gunfire in the distance, and once seen the edges of what was evidently a cavalry battle of some importance. The men walked through France and never gave a thought to wider matters of strategy. Bertie gathered from scraps he gleaned from staff officers going up or down the line that they were heading for the Marne somewhere around Meaux, which was to the and more or less on a level with Paris. Once across the, with supplies and reinforcements reaching them from Paris, they would join up with the French other British corps and make their stand. The engineers would blow up the bridges after the Germans had crossed and they would be trapped between the Anglo-French line and the river, and overwhelmed.

That seemed impossibly far into the future to Bertie, who walked almost in a dream – his were the only two horses to have come through, and he insisted the injured Fenniman rode one, and himself shared the other with the other three officers. Gradually the countryside changed, and they entered the wealthy, fertile region of the Île de France. The population had fled or been evacuated, and they bivouacked now in empty farmhouses and barns, village halls and large villas: Bertie was at last able to get some sleep, with something better than a field to rest on. Now that the supplies had only to come from Paris they were more reliable, and everyone had enough to eat. Occasionally there was even variety – crusty French bread, cheese and garlic sausage, meat and onions to cook. Something of the holiday feeling of before Mons returned.

On the 2nd of September they came to the end of a long, high brick wall running parallel to the road, which Bertie had no difficulty in recognising as the surround of an estate. He was riding, for a change, on Kestrel, and in the hot afternoon sun he had almost been dozing with the relief of not having to walk. He wondered idly what rich man or nobleman owned the land within. Then Kestrel stumbled slightly, which brought him fully back to earth. He had been worried for a while that the horse was going lame – he seemed to be favouring a little. This sort of life was hard on horses, and neither of them was what he had been back in England. They were thin, and their coats were poor – spasmodic grazing was no substitute for regular corn and proper rest. He stroked Kestrel's neck and concentrated on his walk. Yes, there it was, the faint breath of a pause in the four-beat, the slightest hesitancy as the off-fore went down.

He pulled up and slipped to the ground. Kestrel turned his head slightly to touch Bertie with his muzzle, then sig' the sigh of a very weary horse. Bertie stroked him, bru the flies away from his eyes, then felt carefully down foreleg. Kestrel took the opportunity to rest his

Bertie's back while this was going on. He did not flinch from Bertie's hands, but there was definitely warmth in the fetlock.

Fenniman, at the head of the column, had looked back and seen what Bertie was doing and now called a halt. It was near enough to ten minutes before the hour. The men fell out and sat down on the green verges, pulled out cigarettes and lit up. Some flopped on their backs and fell into a doze. Fenniman rode back to Bertie and dismounted. 'Something wrong?'

'Probably a strain. He's not lame yet, but he will be. Rest is what he needs.'

'And rest is what he can't get, poor brute,' Fenniman said. He took out his cigarettes and offered one to Bertie.

'I can't just abandon him,' Bertie said unhappily. Kestrel thrust his head under Bertie's arm, cocked one hind leg and fell into a doze in that position. It kept the flies off his face.

Fenniman looked his sympathy. The alternative was stark. To change the subject he nodded towards the high wall and said, 'Looks like a big place. I wonder who owns it.' A thought came to him and he brightened. 'There might be one or two staff still there – they wouldn't leave a place like that completely empty. Perhaps you could turn the old boy out in one of their paddocks.'

'It's a thought,' Bertie said, looking brighter.

Wetherall had walked up to them now. 'Nearly time to halt for the night,' he said. 'I was wondering about this place.' He, too, nodded towards the wall. 'Must be pretty big. Enough space for us all to lie down under cover – hot water for tea and shaving, and perhaps one or two other things to add to the festivities.'

'We were just wondering who owns it,' said Bertie.

Wetherall raised his brows. 'I thought everyone knew that. 't's Baron de Montmain's place.'

'The banker?' Fenniman asked.

As in Château Montmain?' Bertie added. 'The claret?'

he same,' said Wetherall. 'He's got houses everywhere 's is his real home. He likes to be near Paris. Of course 't be there now, but there's bound to be a caretaker.

And stables,' he added, looking at the two thin horses, 'and feed.'

'We can leave requisition forms for anything we take,' Fenniman said, and rubbed his hands together. 'Think of the cellar the old boy must have!'

'I don't think the British Army is going to pay for first-growth clarets for its officers,' Bertie said.

'I wasn't thinking of it,' Fenniman said with dignity. 'I was assuming Montmain would donate a few bottles in a good cause. Good God, we are saving his country, after all!'

Bertie laughed. 'So we are. Well, let's go ahead and reconnoitre, then.'

There was a caretaker – an elderly, dignified man with a bald pate surrounded by shining silky white wisps like travellers' joy – who was looking after the house, helped by his wife and a grown-up son. The magnificent mansion – symmetrical, of red brick with long windows and a white stone balustrade hiding the pitch of the roof – was his pride and he was in terror of the Germans coming and destroying it. He was so relieved that the army at the gate was British that he welcomed them in with open arms. The men could sleep in the massive entrance hall and ballroom; his wife would prepare bedrooms for the officers; and the kitchens were at their disposal. And, yes, there were stables for the horses.

There were – magnificent ones, in the charge of two men, a father and son, both keen-eyed men in the prime of life. Bertie was surprised that men of fighting age were still here – and why were they here at all? – until it emerged that they were not French but Irish, part of the baron's racehorse stud team, and that they had been left to take care of the five racehorses it had not been possible to move before the war began.

Bertie handed over Kestrel and Nightshade, who look[ed] a little bemused at finding themselves in such elev[ated] company, and asked the grooms to give them a good [feed] and bed them down deep.

'Ah, sure an' we will,' said the elder man. 'You do[n't want] to worry about that, mister. We'll take proper c[are]

poor beggars. I'll wager they've not been off their poor ol'
legs in a week. A mash an' a good feed of oats, and Declan
an' me'll give 'em a good strapping, an' all.'

'Oh, there's no need to trouble,' Bertie protested, but he
was overruled.

'Can't have coats like that in his lordship's stable,' the
man said firmly. He ran a fingernail through Nightshade's
coat and tutted at the dirt he harvested. 'War is cruel hard
on harses, an' that's a fact.'

'It is. By the way,' Bertie went on, 'the chestnut has been
favouring a little.'

The man needed no prompting. 'Saw that as you led him
over,' he said. 'Off fore, isn't it?' He ran a hand down
Kestrel's leg, and the horse nudged him, sensing this was a
man he could trust. 'It's hot. Bit of a strain, mebbe. I'll put
some of his lordship's cold lotion on it, and bandage it up
tight, and we'll see.' He straightened up and stroked Kestrel's
neck with real feeling. 'It breaks me heart to see a nice harse
like this in such a state. War is the divil's business, an' no
mistake.'

So Bertie left his horses with relief, knowing that for one
night at least they would be treated like princes.

It wasn't far below princedom for any of them. The caretaker's son produced a number of empty palliasses and camp
beds – a little musty-smelling – from the cellar, so that in
the end about fifty of the men had beds, and the rest managed
very well with straw stuffed under a blanket or rug. For the
officers, there were bedrooms of magnificence – though
Bertie couldn't have cared less about the Venetian looking-
glasses, the Sèvres groups, the Savonnerie carpet, or the
Boucher over the door: his mouth watered just at the sight
of a bed with a mattress and proper sheets and blankets.

In the kitchen the caretaker's wife stared in amazement
the initial efforts of the battalion cook (a temporary
ointment, the real one having fallen at Le Cateau), then
d him briskly out of the way and took over the manage-
f the meal. She raided the store cupboards to supple-
rations and, with an endless supply of willing
do the beck-and-call part, provided a meal of

such deliciousness that it became part of regimental folk-lore. She seemed to enjoy the process very much, not least the ordering about of a dozen or more huge and hairy kitchenmaids; and found time to cook a special meal for the officers who, she protested with feudal vigour as she ushered them into a small dining-parlour, could not be expected to eat like the ordinary men. Fenniman's dearest hopes were realised when the caretaker produced from the baron's cellar half a dozen bottles of Château Montmain Grand Cru 1898, with the explanation that he was sure it was what Monsieur le Baron himself would have ordered for the heroes who had come to the rescue of *la belle* France. From his red face and shiny eyes it might have been concluded that his large sentiments were fuelled by alcohol, but Bertie decided the old fellow was merely drunk on the excitement of the occasion, after weeks of solitude in the silent house.

After dinner the men poured outside to enjoy the evening sunshine in the lovely grounds, and the caretaker's son followed them and invited them to use the baron's outdoor swimming-pool. The men needed no urging, and took it in turns to strip off and plunge into the water. By the time the last of them emerged, the previously bright water was the colour of tea and quite opaque.

In the house, meanwhile, the officers had been regaled with cigars, Cognac and coffee by the insistent generosity of the caretaker. Afterwards they took a stroll round some of the rooms. Fenniman looked at the paintings, Pennyfather discussed the architecture with Bertie, and Fassner examined the family photographs grouped here and there and worried a little about what the baron would really say if he should arrive back suddenly and find his stately home infested by dirty soldiers. Wetherall was in a quartermaster's heaven. He soon left the formal rooms and hurried about inspecting the bedrooms (there were sixty of them, the caretaker had said) and storerooms, his mind listing ar counting and cataloguing automatically, without need of r and paper (which, however, he could have told any of t without thinking, was available in quantity in a rooms).

When he found his colleagues again, standing at the open main door and watching some of the men having a kick-about with a football they had acquired from somewhere, he presented the fruits of his research. 'We can replace a lot of our kit here,' he said eagerly. 'There's just about everything we need. A blanket for everyone – sixty beds, three blankets to each, and a storeroom full of spares on the top floor. There's soap, boot polish, cooking-pots, spoons, towels. I've counted ten sets of shaving gear in different bedrooms – there may be more. Drawers full of socks, shirts, handkerchiefs. Boots. Sewing thread and needles. Matches. Writing-paper. Cigarettes – the old boy has got hundreds in boxes in a special room, along with the cigars.'

'Hold on a moment,' said Bertie. 'We can't just rob the baron in his absence.'

'Requisition forms,' said Wetherall, simply.

Fenniman agreed. 'The army'll pay. They're scrupulous about honouring requisition forms – it's a point of principle.'

'We haven't got any forms,' Fassner pointed out.

'It doesn't have to be a form,' Wetherall said impatiently. 'Any piece of paper, as long as it's properly signed by an officer, is acceptable in an emergency for the acquisition of necessities.'

So they got together a foraging party to gather the things they needed, Wetherall sat and listed each item punctiliously as it was presented, and Bertie and Fenniman undertook the task of persuading, in their imperfect French, the caretaker and his wife that the British Army was an honourable brotherhood and that the sheets of paper would be as good as gold.

In the morning, much refreshed and with considerably more equipment about them, together with extra food to add to the day's rations when they arrived, the men paraded on the baron's lush lawn, while Bertie went down to the stable with Fenniman (wearing a new pair of riding boots donated *in absentia* by one of the baron's sons) to collect the horses. hardly recognised them, they had been groomed so thoroughly. Their gleaming rumps were now distinguishable from

248

those of their stable companions only by their thinness, and they stood hock-deep in straw, pulling steadily from full hay-racks with an expression of blissful content.

The groom, Doyle, came to meet him. 'I've bad news for yez, mister. The chestnut's dead lame. It's a case of Monday-morning leg, d'ye see?'

Bertie did see. It was a condition that often afflicted plough and bus horses, where a day of rest on Sunday allowed the strain of the week's work to make itself known on Monday morning in the form of swelling and pain.

Bertie went into the box and examined Kestrel, who nuzzled him happily but briefly, not wanting to spare more than a moment from the sweet and abundant hay that had magically made its appearance in his life. The leg had swelled up like a bolster. There was evidently no moving him. Bertie's throat closed up with sadness, and he stroked the thin neck in farewell. 'If I leave him here, will you look after him?' he asked at last.

Doyle nodded. 'Sure, mister, o' course I will. He'll get the best o' treatment, never fear.' He glanced along at the next box, where Nightshade was also busy eating. 'T'other one's not lame, but he's not fit to go in my opinion. He's as thin as a plate rack. He'll be breaking down next thing, wit' the life you're leadin' him.'

Fenniman spoke up. 'You'd better leave him, too, Parke. Not fair on the poor old nag to drag him away, just when he's found paradise.'

Bertie looked at him, puzzled that Fenniman of all people should be suggesting horselessness when he was known to abhor walking. Then he saw the gleam in his companion's eye. 'You don't mean—?'

'But I do,' said Fenniman. Beyond Nightshade's box were the boxes of the baron's racehorses, where five blood horse were looking out over the half-doors with the morn interest of the well fed and well rested. 'Five horses, fi us,' Fenniman concluded simply.

As Doyle caught the significance of the words, an look came over his face. 'Now, hold on, mister! W minute, will yez—'

Fenniman gave him a smile of shattering sweetness. 'We'll leave you a requisition order, old chap. The army will pay the baron the appropriate amount of compensation.'

So when the West Herts moved out onto the road towards Meaux, its surviving officers were all riding for the first time since Mons; and if Fassner and Pennyfather had difficulty at first in controlling their mettlesome and excitable animals, it was a small price to pay for being the best-mounted officers in the British Army.

CHAPTER TWELVE

The Raising Committee, which met in the afternoon of September the 4th, included Alderman Bickersteth and Alderman Wicksteed, with a number of substantial men of business, the chairman of the chamber of commerce, the headmaster of a leading school, an Anglican and a non-conformist clergyman, representatives of the Minster and the railway, and two landowners. Between them they embodied most of the important influences in York. Perhaps in a spirit of mischief, the mayor nominated Teddy as chairman. Colonel Bassett was vice-chairman.

Through the hard work and influence of the committee, things were moved along quickly: everyone was conscious that Leeds had had a head start. A notice appeared in all the evening newspapers that very evening, which was to be repeated in the Saturday and Sunday press. It said:

BUSINESS MEN OF YORK
Your Country Needs You
SHOW YOUR PATRIOTISM
JOIN THE
YORK CITY BATTALION
Your friends are joining
WHY NOT YOU?

The four corners were tastefully decorated w Union Flags, and at the foot in smaller print we of the recruitment. Applicants were to b workers between the ages of nineteen and thirty-five, with ex-soldiers up to forty-five and ex-NCOs up to fifty. Colonel Bassett had explained that experienced NCOs would be very much needed and the hardest to find, so the net must be spread wider for them. Enlistment would be for three years or the duration of the war, and the rate of pay would be the same as for the regular army.

Thanks to a suggestion of Teddy's, Mr Stead the printer had been included in the committee, and he had seen to it that handbills and posters were ready to go out on Saturday. They were to be distributed and put up throughout the city. With the dispensation of the two clergymen on the committee, a further distribution was made on Sunday, catching people as they came out of church, and as they gathered about their various leisure activities, at clubs and cricket grounds, railway stations and steamer jetties.

The enrolment office was to open at 9 a.m. on Monday morning.

The financial question was soon settled, without having to go through the process of a public appeal for funds. Teddy was so glad he was being allowed to serve in this way that he had told the mayor he intended to provide the uniforms for the battalion out of his own pocket. He had the mills to make the cloth and the workers to cut out and make up, and in any case his factories were short of work because of the fall-off of demand. It made sense for him to do it, and it was his gift to the city.

This generosity was quickly matched by other members of the committee, who did not want to seem behindhand, even if, as they explained to their wives, they were not all ⸱ the same happy financial position as Mr Morland of ⸱rland Place. Mr Peckitt, of Peckitt's Boots and Shoes, ⸱d to provide the boots, and Mr Kitson, whose silver- ⸱and jewellery business made him almost as wealthy ⸱, quickly offered to pay for a brass cap badge for ⸱and a silver one for each officer. Other items of ⸱ered by a consortium of committee members, ⸱ offered to do all necessary printing for no charge. The War Office would, of course, provide all military hardware, stores, tents and transport.

The notices in the press, the bill and posters, all did their part; and the news coming from Leeds of the success of its scheme added a sense of urgency. At 9 a.m. on Monday the 7th of September there were already fifty men queuing outside the recruitment office. Business was brisk all day, as articled clerks, solicitors, schoolmasters, insurance officers, confectioners, warehousemen, engineers, tax collectors, brush and comb manufacturers, mill managers and university students turned up to volunteer. Many came in groups, wanting to serve together. During the evening the entire male membership of the Clifton Bicycle Touring Club enlisted *en masse*, and on the second evening the men of the Acomb Archery Society presented themselves together.

The list of names of those who had volunteered was published in the local newspapers each day, and the excitement and interest was such that everyone wanted to be associated with the endeavour in some way. York businessmen who were not on the committee vied with each other to pledge gifts to the battalion: a pouch of tobacco for each man from Mr Tibbett of Tibbett and Earle, the tobacconists; a tin of chocolate ditto from Messrs Rowntree; a bugle, presented by Mr Archibald Hewson of Hewson's Metal Works; a pipe for each man from Godson's, the pipe manufacturer, with the city's coat of arms on the bowl. Canthorpe's Optical Equipment Company offered four pairs of field-glasses for officers. The Clifton Ladies Patriotic War Committee were making a flag to fly over Battalion Headquarters, wherever that might turn out to be. Brown's teashop on the corner of Coney Street rushed out a special York Battalion Teacake ('the teacake of heroes') and offered one free, with a pot of tea, to everyone who enlisted. Mr Enderby, owner of the drapery shop in Stonegate, annoyed by the prominence of rivals Mr Morland and the mayor the scheme, decorated his whole front window with a g Union Jack as a background to a picture of Lord Kitc and a tasteful tableau consisting of an officer's cap, c swagger sticks, Sam Browne, water-bottle and rifle

By 9 p.m. when the office closed on the first day, over five hundred had volunteered. By mid-morning on Friday the 11th the battalion was declared filled, with 1200 names on the list: it was assumed that about a hundred of them would not pass the medical examination, leaving a battalion strength of about 1100. Its official name was to be 'The York (Service) Battalion, the Duke of Richmond's Regiment (The 3rd North Riding Regiment of Foot)', but it was to be known by everyone as the York Commercials. This was felt to be a much better title than that enjoyed by the battalion raised in the city of Leeds, which was known as the Leeds Pals. Leeds might have got in first, but York was determined to do it better in every way.

Ever since they had left Maubeuge, Jack and his fellow flyers had been living a gypsy life. He sometimes thought with wistful affection of his little cell-like room and the comfortable, red-roofed farmhouse by the poplar-fringed stream: it seemed to lie in a distant and golden age of history. As the BEF retreated, the RFC's task was to find the Germans and report back on their position, direction and number. They got into the air at first light, flew according to orders, searched until they spotted the Germans – so much was straightforward. Then came the hard part: they had to find their own unit in order to report back. As the ground staff retreated along with the army, it was rarely in the same place they had left in the morning.

All they could do was search for aircraft on the ground, the only sign of a makeshift airfield – there was rarely time to erect the portable hangars. Failing that, they looked for their own lorries on the move. They were all gaining valuable experience in handling the machines in adverse conditions. Even Deane and Culverhouse were now expert at landing in spaces and on surfaces their instructors would ot have deemed acceptable.

The comfortable life of the mess was now but a memory. e wrote to Helen:

leep where we can these days. You will be surprised rn that a barn is now somewhat of a luxury to

254

your beleaguered boy! More often we find ourselves sleeping in the back of the lorries. At worst, after putting down at risk to life and limb in some bumpy cow-pasture, we feed on cold bully beef and biscuit and bed down under a hedge. If you have any young cousins longing to join the Flying Corps for a life of romance and ease, disabuse them! At Senlis we did rather better, though, for there is a racecourse there and we were able to land and take off from the nice smooth oval of grass inside the track. It was a pleasure not to have to hop over a hedge as soon as the wheels left the ground. But the real luxury was that we billeted in the race-course hotel for the night, which not only meant proper beds with clean sheets but a bath and a shave, the first for a week. The sight of us before that was enough to frighten a maiden aunt into fits! But afterwards, looking more or less human, we had a hot meal, and then settled down in the hotel lounge for an hour or two with brandy from the bar and – oh, the wonder of it! – coffee. Freddie Flint said wistfully, 'So this is what a mess is like.'

Apart from the difficulty of finding the squadron again, having once left it, the worst annoyance was the continuing hazard of being shot at by all three armies. Following Jack's suggestion, the ground crews had put in a couple of hard nights' work painting Union flags on the underside of all the aircraft, but it had not been a complete success. Either the soldiers below were in too much of a panic to try to recog-nise the insignia, or, in the bright sunlight, they could not properly distinguish it. The Germans had tried the same thing on their aeroplanes, and it might be that from below the German black cross and the central blue cross of the Union flag looked much the same. At all events, one never knew when flying over the Allied armies whether one would be shot at or not. It taught the pilots quick reactions, and on most days they would come home with a hole or two and a tale of dodging manoeuvres undertaken. Culverhouse had limped home one day trailing smoke, his Shorthorn riddled with bullets, and had only just made it to the temporary airfield. But Vaughan was their current hero. A German unit had actually shot him down, and he had managed to land on the bald top of a hill without crashing. The Bosch were still toiling up the hill towards him, giving him the chance to set the aeroplane on fire and escape before they arrived, panting, on the scene. He had made his way on foot across country – in his own words, 'running before them like Reynard, hearing them giving tongue behind me all the while' – but managed to give them the slip, and had the good fortune to be picked up by a staff officer's motor-car, which meant he arrived home in style.

On the 2nd of September Jack woke in a bed for only the second time since leaving Maubeuge, and stared around him for a long moment, puzzled, unable to recall where he was. The early light was filtering in through long voile curtains, which hung motionless in the still air. It lit an enormous bow-fronted wardrobe, elaborately carved and painted white; beyond it, a dim corner contained an old-fashioned armchair upholstered in pink silk. Straight ahead was a Louis Quinze dressing-table with gilt corners and a vast looking-glass above it in a gilt frame, which reflected a ghostly ship of a bed, curved mahogany below and glimmering white voile sails above. The carpet was rose pink; the walls were pale green silk and supported a number of heavy dark portraits of antique women and dim landscapes. Outside, somewhere very close, a ring dove was cooing with maddening insistence.

He sat up, remembering. Last night he had located his squadron in the grounds of a largish country house near a village named – aptly, he thought – Messy. They had put down on a long lawn with an awkward cedar tree at one end, but it had been worth it for the quality of the billet. The house held only an old concierge, who had admitted them tremulously and, having understood that they were British and not *sales Boches*, had bid them make themselves comfortable. There had been tinned and dry stores in the kitchen larder to add to their own, so they had had a better meal than usual; then cold baths and, with water boiled on the kitchen stove, hot shaves. Afterwards Major Pettingill had divided up the bedrooms between them, and Jack had retired gratefully to this pink and white bower, which, to judge from the dresses inside the wardrobe, had belonged to the young lady of the house. After kissing Helen's photograph – always his last act before sleeping and his first on waking – he had fallen into a blissfully deep sleep, and dreamed he was at a ball with Helen, who for some reason was wearing a vast crinoline skirt that kept tripping him up.

When he got downstairs into the dining-room they had used last night as a mess, he found the French windows open onto a terrace on which Captain Melville, Major Pettingill and Harmison were deep in conversation with Peacock, one of the ground crew. They turned as Jack appeared, and Pettingill said, 'Ah, Compton, there you are. We seem to have a problem with your machine.'

'A problem?' Jack said.

'Did you get fired at yesterday?' Melville asked.

'I don't think so,' Jack said, frowning. 'No, wait – some fellow on a church tower tried to pot me as I went past, but I don't think he hit me.'

'Think again,' Harmison said.

Peacock cradled a piece of oily metal in his hands as if it were a fallen fledgling. 'It's knocked out the fuel pump, sir,' he said. 'Must have damaged the prop, and when I started her up just now it sheered right off, and the fin shot into the engine cowling and bust it.'

'Can you fix it?' Jack asked.

'No, sir,' said Peacock. 'Leastways, not without the parts. We've been on the move quite a while now, and I'm clean out of everything.'

'It's a damned nuisance,' Pettingill said, 'but it could have come at a worse time. At least we've got a decent billet here, and a half-way decent airfield. We're well placed and we can afford to stay here another night. And we're only forty or fifty kilometres from Paris.'

'Yes, sir?' Jack said, a little puzzled.

'Harmison knows Paris like the back of his hand,' Melville said. 'We don't ask why,' he added, with a grin.

'Better not,' Harmison replied, grinning back.

'So I propose,' said Pettingill, 'that you and Harmison motor into Paris today and pick up spares. Peacock will give you a list of what he needs. I don't like having to do without both of you, but you're the only officer who knows the inside of the engines, and Harmison's the only one who knows where to go. Have a spot of grub now and get on the road straight after breakfast. Take my motor. I don't need to tell you not to hang about any longer than you have to.'

'No, sir.'

When Harmison joined Jack after breakfast at the major's motor-car, Jack had a list of spares Peacock said he couldn't live without – and Harmison had a list of things the rest of the mess said they couldn't live without.

'It won't take long to get Peacock's bits and bobs. We'll find half an hour to do some shopping,' he said, when Jack queried it. 'Can't let a golden opportunity like this pass by.'

Jack slipped behind the wheel. 'I hope you really do know your way around Paris.'

'Practically born there, old dear. And there's a little restaurant in the Place Pigalle – only if there's time, of course,' he added hastily, to Jack's raised eyebrows. 'But they do things to a duck – well, if angels ate duck, they'd send out to Philipon's.'

It was the hottest day so far, a day of still, simmering heat that fell from a clear sky of baked blue onto a land that seemed held in a spell by it, it was so quiet and still and empty. They motored along, enjoying the comparative cool of the air rushing by, raising clouds of white dust by their passage. They saw no-one, neither soldier nor civilian. The only thing moving in the stunned, heat-rapt countryside was an aeroplane that droned over at a thousand feet not long after they'd left. Harmison squinted up into the white light and said, 'That's Bell's BE. Going out on patrol. Probably the old man told him to check up on us. Gives you a warm feeling to be so loved, whàt?' He lit cigarettes for them both, and they drove on in silence.

When they got close to Paris, the eerie emptiness gave way to more normal movement. Villages were shut tight against the noonday sun, as French villages always were, but there were people about, old women with shopping baskets, old men tending vegetable patches, dogs crossing the dusty road as slowly as if the world belonged to them. Cafés and bars were open, giving a glimpse of tables and glasses and black-trousered behinds on stools inside. There was traffic on the road – not much at first, but increasing as they approached the suburbs. And once they entered the urban streets, there was no way to tell there was a war on at all.

'It looks just as I remember it,' Harmison said. 'No sign of evacuation here.' They had to slow down now, with the weight of traffic and pedestrians crossing the road. 'Smells just as I remember it, too,' Harmison added. 'Turn right here. And left at the end.'

It was not as easy as Harmison had given Jack to expect to find the engineering parts. The war had emptied Paris of a lot of things. They went to one *atelier* after another, gleaned a few pieces here and a few there, were directed to a small engineering works on the Rue Caulaincourt, and thence to another near the Porte Clignancourt. There a foreman, fully seized of the importance of the request, promised to manufacture what Jack wanted right away. It would take an hour or two, no more.

'There,' said Harmison. 'I knew we'd have time for shopping. And by divine coincidence we're no distance at all from the Place Pigalle. If we don't go back tonight reeking of garlic, my name's not Harry Harmison.'

There seemed nothing else useful to be done, since they had to wait for the part, so Jack obediently drove back the way he had come, parked in the Rue Caulaincourt, did some hasty shopping for the mess, then followed Harmison's eager almost hopping steps to Philipon's. It had an undistinguished façade, and the door from the street opened onto a small, drab bar, which contained only two silent men in shabby suits sitting on stools drinking coffee.

'I think it's closed,' Jack said, half relieved, half sorry – for breakfast was but a memory, and he was hungry.

'No, no, you'll see,' said Harmison, and led the way through a door in the corner and down a short, narrow corridor. At the other end, it opened out into a scene that was the complete antithesis of the bar – a vast, high-ceilinged saloon with a great glass dome in the centre, and below dozens of tables crowded with people eating, drinking and talking. The air was steamy and smoky and smelled of garlic and other good things that made Jack's mouth water. Aged waiters in long white aprons were rushing between the tables with plates and dishes. The first two who passed ignored them and were not to be stayed by a hand or an excuse-me; but then a small man in a suit, with oiled black hair parted down the middle and a frivolously waxed moustache, rushed up to them, grasped Harmison's hand and burst into a torrent of evidently welcoming French.

In no time they were seated at a table, napkins spread, and the food was arriving, with voluble explanations from the *maître*, none of which Jack could follow. But Harmison was evidently known and well loved, which was all that mattered. Jack, feeling rather bemused at the sudden changes in his fortune, sat back, allowed his glass to be filled with red wine, and tried to make mental notes of the scene for Helen's sake. After onion soup, snails in garlic, and the promised duck, Harmison protested that they must be getting back and had no time for anything more, upon which the *maître* protested that they would break his heart. He shook their hands heartily, and sent them on their way with a tenderly wrapped wheel of cheese that was bulging out of its corsets in a way that Harmison said promised delight in either the best Brie or the worst women.

When they got back to the engineering works, their piece was not quite ready, so Jack felt a little easier in his conscience. But by the time they had received it, and filled the motor with petrol, the afternoon was well advanced.

'We won't get back before dark,' Jack said.

'Don't worry, we shan't get lost,' said Harmison. 'By golly, that was a day! I feel set up now for anything that comes. It does one good to let the dog off the leash now and then.'

'It's your turn to drive,' said Jack.

'Do you really want me to? I'm a frightful driver. Oh, all

right, then. But don't doze off, or I very likely shall as well. I need you to talk to me and keep me awake.'

Dusk came on, and it grew chilly. Then it grew quickly dark, in the melancholy way of autumn, and the two men hunched down in the motor, trying to get below the stream of air and wishing it was not an open car. When they turned off the main road towards Messy, it was completely dark, and with no lights on in houses to direct them they had to go very slowly and follow the white thread of the road as it loomed up in the headlights.

'You've gone past it,' Jack said. 'Those were the gates, back there.'

'Were they? Dash it. Now I'll have to find somewhere to turn.' He found a slightly wider piece of road just round the bend. 'Jump out, will you, old fellow, and make sure there isn't a ditch for me to back into?'

He made a tortuous turn, Jack got in, and they motored slowly back round the bend towards the house.

'That's odd,' Jack said. 'They've put a guard on the gate. But who—?'

At that instant both men realised that the man on guard was no airman but a soldier, and a soldier in German grey at that.

'Oh, my God,' Harmison breathed. 'It's Fritz.'

The guard straightened, stared; his jaw dropped.

'Drive on!' Jack cried. 'Put your foot down!'

The guard pulled himself together. '*Halt! Halt!*' he shouted. The rifle swung round into operative position. Jack felt the hair rise on his scalp. '*Halt oder ich schieze!*'

'Go on, go on!' he cried. Harmison had needed no urging. The motor jumped with the violence of his pressure on the pedal, and coughed. For a heart-stopping moment Jack thought the engine would cut out. But it lurched again and accelerated, the wheels spinning and throwing up a cloud of dust. They shot past the guard, and from this direction Jack had a glimpse through the gate of two German staff cars and several lorries. He heard the guard shouting. There was the explosion of the rifle going off, and Jack felt his spine cringe cold, waiting for the impact; but the shot went wild. A second pinged off the back of the motor. There were more voices behind now. He risked a glance back. More soldiers had come running out of the gate across the road. He saw the first one out kneel and take aim. But the motor was throwing up the usual cloud of dust, and it was dark. The ragged volley of shots that came next went past them, unseen and unheard. Harmison was cursing fluently as he gripped the steering-wheel and stared wildly ahead, trying to see where the road would go. If he left the road and crashed they would be for it. The rifle fire sounded once more, raggedly, behind them, but the Bosch were firing blind and pointlessly.

'Here's the turning!' Jack shouted. 'Go left! Left!'

It was upon them suddenly, the junction with the main road. Harmison snarled and wrenched the wheel round. The car slewed out and across the road, swinging, the wheels screaming, two of them leaving the ground. Harmison wrestled the steering-wheel, Jack gripped the side of the motor, not breathing, waiting for it to go over. But at the last moment it tipped back, ran itself up the bank opposite, and stalled.

In the sudden silence Jack could hear German voices shouting behind. 'Start her up! For God's sake – they'll be coming.'

It took two attempts – Jack thought his heart would stop when the engine didn't catch the first time. Then it caught, and roared uselessly as Harmison pressed the pedal without engaging the gears. Jack bit back another protest – it wouldn't help. The gears crashed, the abused car leaped forward, and they were off at last down the main road.

'Why this way?' Harmison gasped out, remembering at last to breathe.

'It's the road to Meaux. The army was heading for Meaux.'

Behind them a beam of light swung across the road. 'Oh, God, they're following us,' Jack said. 'They've got a motor out.'

Harmison was suddenly calm. 'They won't catch us,' he said, and pushed the pedal to the floor. Another ounce of speed was forthcoming. 'They'll be hampered by our dust.

And they won't dare chase us too far, in case they catch up with our army.'

Jack knew this was sense, and tried to believe it, but the fact that there were Germans chasing him, determined to kill him, got in the way. They were firing again – he could heard the ragged spatter of shots – but none came near. He looked behind, and the smear of the following headlights seemed further away. Yes, definitely falling back. Can't hear the engine any more. No more shots. And now they had gone.

'I think they've chucked,' he said.

Harmison grunted. 'I just hope we're not driving into more of them.'

'Thanks for that thought,' Jack said. 'I've only just got over the shock of being shot at.'

They drove on in silence for a while, and then Harmison said, 'I suppose the Bosch advanced more quickly than expected. I hope to God our fellows got away. I say, do you think we ought to have gone back and had a look? Maybe they were prisoners inside.'

'What use could we be, just the two of us?' Jack said. 'There must have been at least a company there, probably more. I saw lorries.'

'I suppose you're right.'

'Our chaps would have had warning. I'm sure they got away. Nobody's been caught that way yet, have they?'

'True.'

'But they won't have been able to get my Tabloid out,' Jack mourned. 'I hope they had time to burn it before they left.'

They drove on, under a great dark arch of sky, fat with stars.

'Never mind,' said Harmison, after a while. 'You might get something better. An Avro, maybe.'

'If we ever find our squadron again.' Then suddenly Jack started laughing, seeing the funny side. 'What'll they say when we tell 'em we were one minute away from dining in a German mess? We talked about Christmas dinner at Potsdam, but we never thought of that.'

Harmison laughed too. 'It's a funny old war at times.'
'It has its moments,' said Jack.

On the 5th of September the French army turned at last
on the Germans and fought a desperate battle along the
bank of the River Marne. The impulsive French General
Joffre had decided on the action so quickly that by the
time the communication of his intent reached British
Headquarters, the BEF had already started out on its day's
march southwards, further away from the area. They
would not be able to join their allies on the offensive until
the next day.

The French threw everything they had into the action,
and the Germans did likewise. It was do or die for both
sides. The West Herts spent the day plodding along dusty
lanes in a manner that had become so familiar to them they
had lost track of the days and felt almost as if they were in
a recurring dream. Their numbers had been stiffened by the
arrival, the day before, of reinforcements – 110 men fresh
out from England via Boulogne and Paris, together with two
sergeants and six officers, including a colonel and second
in command. Even with this addition, the battalion was at
skeleton strength, and the remnant was still poorly equipped,
but their experiences had hardened them to the point where
they looked on the reinforcements as untried boys. Riding
along the lines that day, Bertie heard bloodcurdling stories
of Mons, Le Cateau and various skirmishes being recounted
in painful detail to amazed and sometimes frankly disbe-
lieving colleagues. The reinforcements were comically easy
to pick out by their whole, clean uniforms and full packs,
and if at rest breaks they could 'swank' by pulling out chocolate and cigarettes they had brought from Blighty, the
veterans could respond by pitying them for the weight they
had to carry, and howl with derision and sometimes fury
when they complained of sore feet. But the reinforcements
had cheered the remnant, and often as they marched that
day, they sang, the veterans teaching the newcomers the new
songs they had invented since they had been in France. They
had discovered that the name of the German general who

had been pursuing them for the last week was von Kluck, which rhymed amusingly with their favourite epithet, while 'German Mausers' conveniently rhymed with 'trousers'. They had a new favourite marching song about him, a rousing ditty averring that they did not give a damn for him, and describing where they would kick him.

They had been marched off early that morning – before dawn, in fact – to get some miles in before the burning heat of the day exhausted them. So they reached bivouac early, and were just settling in to make themselves as comfortable as they could in a field when a staff motor-cyclist arrived with their orders for the next day. The news that they were to turn and fight at last picked up their spirits better than brandy, and there were rousing cheers, followed by a satisfied buzz of excitement as they professed to each other their longing to 'have a go at old Fritz'.

Bertie and the other officers gathered round the messenger for news of the day: it was the first they knew of the French attack. The fighting had been fierce, and at times it had been touch and go, but in the nick of time General Gallieni had answered General Maunoury's plea for reinforcements by sending out the entire garrison of Paris. There was no army transport left in the capital, so the general had commandeered every taxi-cab on the streets and the garrison was carried out to the battle by a fleet of drivers who had never had a more important fare. The Germans had been repulsed, and were now in full retreat, heading for the River Aisne.

On the morning of the 6th of September, the West Herts marched out, turning north-eastwards at last, directed to help the BEF plug a gap in the French line to Maunoury's right. It was only a few days since they had ambled along dusty lanes through a pastoral scene that had seen few changes in a thousand years; but it became immediately apparent that things were very different now. They were advancing across a ruined country. The smiling harvest fields and little, somnolent villages had been fought over by two armies. Houses and barns not built to withstand shelling had been reduced to rubble, or burnt out to a grim skeleton of a few charred beams and posts. The smell of burning hung over the land, and the smell of death. But the worst thing was the needless destruction. The Germans had burned the crops in the fields, slaughtered the farmyard animals and, from what the residents had to say, they had done it out of wantonness. Distraught old people – the young men were all away at the war – came out when they saw that it was the British passing their gates, desperate to tell their stories. Their haunted eyes wandered from face to face, seeking an authority whom they could ask for reparation, as they raised their complaint, like an ululation, in their reedy old voices.

Once when they stopped at a farm to see if they could refill their water-bottles, the old farmer took Bertie's arm in a fierce grip and begged him to come inside to see what the Bosch had done. They had been billeted on the farmhouse a few days earlier, and had got very drunk on looted brandy which they had brought with them. They had rampaged through the house, smashing the furniture and ripping up the bedding and the clothes in the wardrobes. They had broken most of the windows, and in the old-fashioned parlour they had chopped up the armchairs with the farmer's own axe, smashed all the ornaments and defecated, to roars of hilarity, on the carpet. Then they had gone outside, trampled the vegetable patch – the old man had seen them *dancing* on it, he said, with a quivering mouth – and bayoneted all the hens in the fowl-yard. And they had killed his dog, his good hound, who was so gentle he would catch straying chicks and bring them back to the hen unharmed in his mouth. One of the soldiers had shot him, just for barking at him, as a good dog should, trying to defend his home.

What should he do? the old man asked. They had no food now, no vegetables, no hens. They would starve. What should they do? Where could they go? Bertie had no answer for him. They refilled their water-bottles at the well, which miraculously had escaped German attentions, and moved on. Bertie looked back and saw the old man and his wife still standing at the gate watching helplessly for as long as they were in sight, and his heart ached for them.

The misery of the ruined land was matched by the misery of the weather, which had broken at last on the 9th, banishing the long, blistering summer in favour of a more normal autumn pattern of cold, rain and mist. It would have been enough to dishearten the men, but the 9th was the day they recrossed the Marne, and they were so glad to be advancing again, and to have the Germans on the run, nothing could damp their spirits. They were sure now that they would beat the Germans and be home by Christmas. Every evidence they saw of German frightfulness increased their determination, and they were cheered to see the signs along the road that the Hun was abandoning his kit and his spoil as he fled, much as they had been forced to do on the retreat from Mons. There were whole abandoned wagons full of plunder from towns, fine clothes, plate, pictures, ornaments, furniture. The Tommies remembered how they had been forbidden by HQ orders even to take food, that would spoil if it was left; and their hatred and contempt for the enemy increased.

One day they found a German lorry that had gone into a ditch, broken its axle and been abandoned with its load. When they investigated, they found it full of British food supplies – bully and biscuits, tinned Irish stew and beans and other vegetables. It was stuff that had been dumped by the road by the ASC for the BEF during their withdrawal, which they had been too pressed to pick up. They took what they could carry now, for supplies had again been problematical during the advance, and there was little to glean from the ruined houses they passed. The men stood in the road as the veils of cold autumn rain drifted across and drenched them, watching the food being passed down, and laughed with the pleasure of literally 'getting their own back'.

Bertie was most pleased of all when the back of the lorry proved to contain two sacks of oats. Baron de Montmain's racehorses had had a thin time of it since they had been requisitioned, with nothing but grass to eat, and a life of a sort of exertion and discomfort they were not used to. They were getting thin and miserable. Bertie's horse, which he had called Phoenix because he was a bright chestnut, looked as though he could not believe his eyes when Bertie gave him a feed of oats in his cap. Bertie had to coax him until he realised it actually was that fondly remembered delight. They carried away as many oats as they could, hung from the saddles in whatever kind of bag they could find. Men could endure hunger and hardship much better than horses.

They did not advance unchallenged, for the countryside was of a sort to offer plenty of cover – thick woods, rounded hills with concealed folds perfect for gun emplacement, high ground that commanded the road. The Germans were retreating, but they were not running yet, and the fighting was fierce, a series of short, hot skirmishes. The West Herts were battle-hardened now, steady under fire, better marksmen than the Germans and able to deliver more rapid fire, and they inflicted heavy losses on any units they met. They took casualties, too – and they were harder to bear now that the men had become a fighting unit, now they were so few and so close, and had so many memories to bind them.

From the packs of the German dead they took things to supplement their own kit. Clean socks were a great prize, as was a razor, a box of matches or a piece of soap. Often there was chocolate, sausage, a tin of meat – once a glorious tin of coffee, which Cooper instantly commandeered for 'his officer', though of course they all shared it. Bertie prized a pair of nail-scissors from one unexpectedly fastidious private; and several of his men were able to replace their worn-out boots. Bertie remembered his South Africa days – how by the end of the campaign it was impossible to tell the two sides apart, with everyone wearing a magpie garb gleaned from the dead.

They rarely saw other units of their own side, and information was hard to come by. The telegraph lines had been cut when they were all heading in the other direction, and had not been repaired; and the atrocious weather meant that the RFC could rarely get airborne and could see very little when they did. The army was advancing blind, with no idea where the main body of the enemy was, marching through the rain, through the closed-in countryside, fighting the

Germans where they found them in a series of private little wars.

And on the 12th of September, at the end of a day of ceaseless, torrential rain, the West Herts finally reached the River Aisne. They were all soaked to the skin, though they had been wet now for so many days they had almost ceased to notice it. The horses were rat-tailed with it, their coats dark, and they stood with their heads down and their ears out sideways, rain dripping from their forelocks and eyelashes and beading on the whiskers of their muzzles. The new colonel, Buckland, came riding back to speak to the company commanders individually. When he reached Bertie he said, 'It seems we're in a bit of a pickle. The bridges have been destroyed, and there's no fording the river – but cross it we must. You'd better come and have a look.'

Bertie joined the other captains, Fenniman and the two new men, Bithy and Fletcher, and they rode behind the colonel to the edge of a plateau. It was growing dark, with the normal shortness of an autumn afternoon closed in even further by the rain, but the light was just sufficient to see the problem. Down below them the Aisne plunged along, deep, wide and fast-running, impossible to ford. There was no cover on the near bank, and the further bank was steep and wooded.

'We don't know exactly where the Germans are,' said Buckland, 'but they're over there somewhere, and their guns will command the crossing. They have all the advantage of position. We will be extremely exposed. The only chance, I fancy, will be a night crossing, using whatever the engineers can put together.' He looked around them. 'I don't know yet what our orders will be, but I wanted to show you the situation before it got too dark. You'd better get back to your men now. If we have to bivouac in the open, we'll have a rather thin night of it. We may be sent back to one of the villages, in which case I'll do all I can to rustle up a hot meal.'

Bertie went back to his company. Cooper came to Phoenix's head – Bertie's groom had been a casualty and Cooper had taken over charge of his horse as well as his meagre belongings, seeming to find comfort in the former for the lack of the latter. 'Gettin' worse, sir,' he said, referring evidently to the weather. 'And no shelter anywhere. Any word as to what we're doin', sir?'

'Not yet,' Bertie said. 'We just have to wait.'

'Ah, well, we're gettin' good at that,' Cooper muttered. Bertie dismounted to rest his horse's back, and Pennyfather loomed up out of the murk, rain dripping steadily from the tip of his nose.

'We passed a barn a little way back,' he said. 'I wondered whether it would do for shelter.'

Before Bertie could answer, Cooper jumped in: 'If we don't take it, sir, one of the other companies'll bag it. Better get in first.'

'We have to wait here for orders,' Bertie said. 'It's almost dark, and I can't have people wandering about when we might be moving off at any moment.'

Cooper led Phoenix away to try to find the shelter of a tree for him, and Bertie and Pennyfather stood together in the teeming dusk, while the men sheltered as best they could and lit cigarettes, resigned both to the wet and the waiting by now. An hour passed, during which Cooper could be heard grumbling softly that they could just as well have waited in the barn as out in the open.

'Wind's getting up,' Pennyfather said, his first remark in half an hour; and at that moment a runner came up and summoned them both to the colonel.

They joined him in a huddle under a tree, and he said, 'Well, gentlemen, I've got our orders. It's going to take days to get the whole army across, but HQ wants to make a start tonight, send a brigade over, try to take the Germans by surprise, establish a foothold on the other side to keep them occupied tomorrow. The engineers are fixing up a temporary bridge they think will hold us. It should be ready by the time we get down there.'

Fenniman was the one who spoke. 'And who is to have the honour of testing this temporary bridge, sir?'

Short acquaintance had taught Bertie that Buckland did not have much of a sense of humour. He looked at Fenniman levelly for a moment, as if translating what he had said into a more familiar language. Then he said, 'I'm glad you think it's an honour, Mr Fenniman, because our battalion is to be the vanguard.'

'I guessed as much, sir,' Fenniman said sincerely. 'We've been honoured that way quite a lot since we reached Mons.'

Buckland let that pass without comment. He gave them their orders, and sent them back to their companies.

'You'll bait him once too often, Fen,' said Bertie.

'But he'll never notice,' Fenniman said. 'That's the beauty of it. He went to a grammar school – did you know? Shocking what the regiment has come to. Of course, the real reason they're sending us first is to test the bridge. They think that there are so few of us left, we won't be missed if we all fall in and drown.'

'Oh, well,' said Bertie, 'at least we can't get any wetter.'

CHAPTER THIRTEEN

Pennyfather was right – the wind was rising. By the time they had descended to the near bank, it was driving the rain viciously into the backs of their necks, and a noise they thought at first must be distant gunfire was thunder rumbling about the skies.

'Going to be worse before it's better,' said Pennyfather, riding beside Bertie.

'God help sailors on a night like this,' Bertie returned.

They passed through a small village, and saw longingly that there were lights at a couple of windows. They were wet, cold, tired and hungry, and never had shelter looked so appealing. Then they were on the flat ground, with the sound of the river just audible below the teeming of the rain and the buffeting of the wind. It was as black as Newgate knocker, and Bertie could imagine them all stumbling blindly into the torrent, but a pinprick of torchlight, waved in the agreed signal arc, guided them forward.

The holder of the torch proved to be an Engineer officer. Bertie got the impression of a large number of bodies moving around unseen in the dark, and heard the occasional shout and crash of activity somewhere nearby. He reflected that the Engineers must be having an even more 'thin time' of it than his own men.

'Are you the West Herts?' the officer asked, above a sudden howling gust of the wind.

'Yes. C Company. Captain Parke. My company is going first.'

'Shirling, Royal Engineers. Won't shake hands – I'm pretty filthy.' The man grinned, and jerked his head at the elements. 'Not as filthy as the weather. Be worse before it's better – you're well off going now. And at least it'll keep the Hun's head down. They won't be shooting at you tonight. Just as well – you'll have your hands full getting across the river.'

'You reassure me inexpressibly,' said Bertie. 'Is that the river?' He could see a gleam of reflected light ahead.

'No, that's the canal – runs parallel with the river. This road goes over both – or did. The bridge over the canal is still intact, but they've blown up the section over the river. The uprights were still sound, so we've knocked together a sort of suspension bridge – you'll see when we get there. Should take your weight.'

'Should?' Bertie queried.

'Nothing's certain in war,' said Shirling, and grinned again. He seemed to be deriving some amusement from C Company's plight.

'Shall we get on with it?' Bertie asked, with dignity.

Shouting orders was no good in this wind. He passed the word, then followed Shirling with the column following him, their new sergeant in the rear. The bridge came to an abrupt end in a tangle of stone and twisted metal, and another man with a torch was stationed there to stop anyone walking straight off the end. Once over the canal Bertie could hear the river – a deep, booming roar like a waterfall – and when the column had halted and he stepped to the parapet and looked down, he could see the glint of foam, reflecting what small amount of ambient light there was in this howling night.

Shirling tugged his arm and drew him away from the parapet. 'This is what we've rigged for you,' he shouted into Bertie's ear.

It was a footbridge of large wooden boxes – ammunition boxes, perhaps – strung together somehow and suspended from the uprights of the old bridge. It reminded Bertie of the swaying rope bridges he had sometimes seen in the Himalayas, crossing ravines. It would behave in much the same way as well, he thought. It was swinging now with

273

the pressure of the wind – not a great deal, but disconcertingly. There was no hand-rail – not even a rope. The wood of the first few boxes – all he could see – was dark with rain, probably slippery. And the river boiled about fifteen feet below.

'Just don't fall in,' Shirling shouted into his ear. 'You wouldn't last a minute in that lot.'

'What about the horses?' Bertie asked. They'd never keep their footing on that bridge.

'No go. I told your CO. But you'd never have got them up the slope opposite anyway. You'll have to wait for them until we've got something more permanent fixed up on one of the other bridges.'

So it was back to his own two feet again. He had no confidence that if he parted with Phoenix he'd ever see him again. A sudden whipcrack of lightning split the black sky with electric blue, and in the instant Bertie saw the whole scene: the flimsy-looking bridge swaying above the torrent of the river, the smashed end of the road bridge, the half-ruined uprights, the black, wooded further bank rising steeply beyond. And then, in the pulsating darkness that followed, the rain came down more heavily than ever, and all resistance went out of him. He wanted to laugh. This is *ridiculous*, he thought. Only in the army could such things be proposed with a straight face.

'All right,' he said aloud. 'We'd better start.'

'Take it slowly,' Shirling advised. 'I've a man on the far side with a torch to give you something to aim at. Good luck!'

'Thanks,' said Bertie, and turned away.

He had decided to go first, feeling that he could not ask his men to face something they had not seen him do. He called Pennyfather and the first six men, so that there were plenty to pass back the instructions; and told Pennyfather to cross in the middle of the company, and to tell the sergeant to come last.

Key and Straw were the nearest two. Key looked at the bridge and said, 'Bloody 'ell.'

Big Straw said anxiously, 'Will it take the weight, sir? Maybe I ought to go last.'

274

'It'll hold,' Bertie said firmly. 'The bridge will move under your feet a bit, but that's nothing to worry about. Go steadily: don't rush, but don't be too slow – there's a whole brigade to get across before daylight. I'll go first. Wait until the man in front of you is half-way across, otherwise your movements will throw him off balance. Pass all this back to the man behind you. Understood?'

'Understood, sir,' they said, and looked at him through the rain with an expression that reserved judgement until they'd seen him safe on the other side.

It was like a fit of madness, Bertie thought: mad orders and mad deeds to match the insanity of the storm; and since there was no making sense of it, he could only abandon himself to it. If his life was to end here, drowned in the Aisne, instead of by bullet or shrapnel in battle, or of old age in his bed, so be it. He couldn't worry or fear any more. He stepped onto the first box. It was not slippery after all – that was one thing to be thankful for – though the rain water ran off it visibly. The difficulty was in keeping one's balance against the swaying, and the up-and-down move-ment. The downward pressure of putting one's foot on a box raised the one before and the one behind; and the box underfoot rose sharply and disconcertingly as soon as one started to lift that foot. He concentrated on moving steadily, anticipating the underfoot leap, keeping his balance, bracing himself against the elements, the sudden buffets of wind. Emptying his mind of all other thought, he stepped from box to box, not allowing himself to look ahead to see how far he still had to go, in case it disheartened him.

Another flash of lightning was followed so immediately by a huge crash of thunder that it startled him out of his reverie, and he bit his tongue. The lightning had revealed he was about half-way across; and at that moment Key must have stepped onto the bridge, because the box under his foot gave a jerk and quivered sideways with a new move-ment. The combination was enough to unbalance him, and for a moment he teetered, waving his arms wildly, the glinting foam of the river fifteen feet below suddenly leaping into sharp focus in his mind. But he found his balance again and, sweating despite the cold rain, made himself move forward. The tiny guiding light was closer, and once he could see the loom of the man holding it the last part of the crossing seemed to go more quickly, and he was stepping off onto solid ground with such huge relief he wanted to sit down and put his head in his hands.

'All right, sir?' said the Engineer with the torch.

'All right,' said Bertie, and then, 'I'd sooner face shell fire than do that again.'

'Best we could do, sir, in the time,' said the Engineer, but he grinned too. Bertie imagined him running across the bridge with the insouciance of a tightrope-walker. All right for those who were used to it!

The crossing was desperately slow, and it was the early hours of the morning before even the battalion was across, and there was the rest of the brigade to come. Their orders were to climb to the top of the opposite bank and take up position along the hill. The Germans were up there some-where, and it was important to hold the high ground above the river to prevent German snipers picking off the army at its leisure while they crossed in daylight.

The climb up the bank was another part of the night-mare. The wind had dropped, but still it lashed the trees and made the wet leaves rattle, the saplings bend and groan. The slope was steep, the woods tangled with dense under-growth, and the sodden ground was soon one long mud slick. The weary men climbed slowly, slipping, falling, sliding, hauling themselves up by bushes, branches, runners of ivy. Towards dawn the storm had passed entirely, and the air was still, but it was dank, cold and miserable. The upper reaches of the wooded bank were hung with a wet, heavy fog; and when they came out onto clear ground and spread into position, they could see nothing. The Germans might be two yards or two miles away – no-one knew, and certainly no-one could see.

At last it began to get light – or, at least, less dark. Though there was foliage still on the trees, the evidence of autumn was in the yellow leaves plastered everywhere, where the wind had ripped them loose. Bertie eased his position a little, feeling the cold clamminess of the ground stiffening his muscles, and looked around. The mist was a chilly white wall reaching down to within an inch of the coarse, tussocky grass. He could see his own breath plume up to join it, a wraith of himself – how insubstantial he was against the great indifferent forces of nature! Behind him, only the trunks of the first few trees showed black, fraying into grey; everywhere was the sound of moisture dripping. It beaded every surface, droplets standing stiff and perfect on every fibre of his coat sleeve; the grass before his face shone dull silver with it.

It was very quiet, with that unnatural hush that fog and snow carry with them: no wind to rustle the leaves now, only the occasional hollow cough from some invisible companion, echoing strangely off the white wall. He expected no birdsong in such a dawn; but then from behind, somewhere in the woods, a crow yarked, and as if at that signal a robin began to sing from a tree just behind him – a hesitant strand of song, like a single filament of spider's web down which silver droplets ran. In all this madness, the constancy of a robin: it cheered him, warmed his cold blood. It had not yet changed key to its winter melancholy: it was still its summer song that threaded the air.

Some time after the bird had flown away, Buckland came along the line, checking and encouraging. 'There'll be a lot more of us in a few hours. The Engineers are working on another bridge, a railway bridge, which will be much easier to use, so our chaps will get across more quickly. We just have to stick it out here and make sure the Bosch don't get through.'

'Yes, sir,' said Bertie.

'Our horses would have been no use to us,' Buckland said next – by way of comfort, Bertie supposed.

'No, sir.'

'Fassner will see they're brought over as soon as the railway bridge is ready.'

'Yes, sir,' Bertie began to say; but at that moment the grey murk flashed orange, and there was a scream and a tremendous crash as a shell went over their heads and exploded in the trees behind. Both men fell flat without thought.

'Christ, that was close,' Buckland muttered, forgetting himself for an instant. 'How far would you say?'

'Where was it fired from? Two hundred yards, perhaps,' Bertie said.

'They're closer than we thought. I must get back,' said Buckland, scrambled to his feet and hurried away into the fog. Another shell screamed over and crashed, spattering twigs, leaves and earth against his back.

'Get ready, C Company,' Bertie called down his own line. 'Any minute now.' He looked at his watch. Almost seven o'clock. The Germans liked to be orderly – they would begin on the hour.

The mist erupted in flame and fury.

It was not the fault of the Royal Flying Corps that the BEF did not know how far away the Germans were. Jack and his companions had been doing their best, but the country through which the enemy had been retreating was, as Bertie had remarked, wooded and cleft and rich in cover. And then the rain had begun. They got airborne when they could, but there was almost nothing to see. With the veils of mist sweeping across the country, a glimpse of tree tops was the best to be hoped for; and the rain lashed into their faces so that they had to wipe their goggles every few moments with hands that were chilled and numb despite their leather gloves. It was hopeless. At times it was all they could do to fly to a new airfield so as to keep up with the army.

On the 12th Jack's squadron made the hop to a new airfield on the plateau above the Aisne, which they were sharing with another squadron. Because of the rain, the ground staff had arrived not long before them, and were still struggling to erect the temporary hangars against the rising wind. Jack taxied up in the Avro he had been given to replace his lost Tabloid.

He had been glad to know, when he and Harmison finally found the squadron again after their Paris adventure, that the old bus had indeed been burned before the

Germans could get hold of it. Major Pettingill had been given enough warning of the Germans' approach for everything to be packed up, and for the mechanics to strip a great deal of useful spares out of the Tabloid before setting fire to it and scrambling away in the lorries. There had been nothing they could do to warn Jack and Harmison, of course, and everyone was enormously relieved when they showed up the next morning, having spent the night with some Guards of the First Corps, who had given them hospitality before putting them on their way. Their story had lost nothing in the telling, and Harmison said afterwards that it had been useful to have the rehearsal with the Guards to polish up his performance. It was fortunate that the Avro, which had been expected for some time, arrived the day afterwards – though Deane, who had been waiting to take over the Tabloid was disappointed at having to stay with the Shorthorn.

Jack rolled up beside Harmison's BE, feeling the wind buffeting the machine from side to side – as though a giant were striking it with a pillow. One of the mechanics, Donner, ran up to push the chocks in and hold the wing as Jack climbed down. Already the storm was bad enough to make it necessary to shout to be heard.

'Going to be a bad one, sir,' said Donner.

Jack nodded. 'It's black as Hades over there – and the wind's getting up.'

'Yes, sir. We're having the dickens of a job getting the hangars up.'

'So I see. We'll have to get some lines over the machines if you can't manage it soon. Is everyone in?'

'All but Mr Culverhouse, sir – and that's him coming in now.'

Jack turned to watch as the Shorthorn came in low from the south. The machine was so light and flimsy and the wind so strong there were times he thought it must actually be going backwards. Lightning cracked behind him, and his heart was in his mouth as he watched the frail craft rocking from side to side as Culverhouse fought to keep it steady and get it down. There was every danger that a buffet of wind could flip it over onto its back. As soon as it touched down Jack ran with Donner to meet it, and took a wing while Donner took the other, to help keep it down as Culverhouse taxied it up to the line.

Culverhouse climbed down, and pulled off his rain-spattered goggles, revealing a whiter face than usual. 'Thanks,' he shouted. 'Thought I wasn't going to make it.'

'You cut it damn' fine,' Jack shouted back.

'Got lost. Couldn't see a thing in this rain.'

'It'll get worse any minute,' Jack said. He glanced behind at the ground staff, still struggling with the hangars. It seemed a hopeless task. He turned back to Donner to suggest they got all hands out onto the field to secure the machines, but Donner was looking in another direction.

'Here it comes,' he said.

Jack and Culverhouse looked too. The purple-black cloud had come up fast – faster than a running horse. Even as they looked it rolled over them, turning the day to an unnatural twilight. Lightning split the sky, simultaneously with a crack of thunder, and the rain came in a torrent, as if someone had turned on a tap.

And the wind leaped, almost knocking Jack off his feet. Culverhouse was just pulling off his flying cap, and it was snatched from his fingers and whipped away, instantly invisible. The men wrestling with the hangar suddenly found they had nothing to wrestle with. One of them fell down and two others reeled together and saved themselves by clinging to each other. The hangar was stripped from their fingers and flogged to shreds before the last guyline securing it yielded and the whole thing disappeared into the rapidly gathering dark.

Donner shouted something – Jack did not hear what – and at the same moment Culverhouse grabbed his arm in a grip that hurt. 'My Shorthorn!' he shouted. Jack turned his head in time to see the wind get under its nose in a huge buffet. They had walked a few yards away from it; now Culverhouse tried to run back, but it was lifted thirty feet into the air, blown as easily as a paper bag. Culverhouse made a wordless cry of despair, thrust backwards by the buffet, and the Shorthorn flipped over at the height of its rise and crashed down to earth on its back.

'Donner – the Avro!' Jack shouted. 'Culverhouse – help me!'

He ran – or rather staggered – forward against the pressure of the wind towards his precious new machine. Culverhouse seemed dazed, but after staring at the matchwood of his Shorthorn he shook himself into action. The Avro was already being jerked by the buffets of the wind, her nose turning a little with each blow. If she went round far enough the wind would get under her wing or tail and throw her over. Jack grabbed at the nearest wing-tip, while Donner struggled to the other side. Culverhouse came past him and got a handhold on the fuselage. The machine jerked and tugged under their hands. Out of the corner of his eye Jack could see more movement, men running to the other machines. Harmison's BE was making little jumpy movements as if it were having a fit.

Then the wind went round, so suddenly it was not like a natural phenomenon at all but a mad spite. Jack, braced against it, fell over, losing his grip on the wing. The Avro slewed round, shedding Culverhouse and Donner, and ran backwards into the BE, slewed again and, somehow locked together with the other machine, was blown rapidly backwards into the flapping canvas of a hangar that had been pegged down but not erected. And there the whole confused mass seemed to stabilise as the folds of wet canvas tangled the wheels and added weight.

A hand was on Jack's shoulder. It was Harmison, helping him up. They both staggered in a gust of wind, and Jack clutched his companion like a drowning man.

'No use!' Harmison yelled. 'Nothing to be done. Never get a rope on anything in this.'

Over Harmison's shoulder Jack saw another Shorthorn go flying backwards across the airfield ten feet up in the air. It turned over, catching a wingtip on the ground, then cartwheeled wing over wing until they both shattered and the gale threw the wreckage across the field with abandon. Two mechanics clutching the wingtips of a BE2 were dragged across the wet grass helplessly, as though they were on a skating-rink, until their grip failed and they fell flat, while the aeroplane performed three back-flips and finished up splintered, wheels in the air.

'Go inside!' Harmison shouted. 'Shelter!'

Jack nodded helplessly. Clinging like lovers they fought their way towards the farmhouse that was their present home. The darkness of night was coming up to reinforce that of the storm.

Inside the farmhouse Pettingill and Melville met them, grey-faced.

'Are you all right?' Melville asked.

'Yes, sir,' Jack answered for them. 'But the machines—'

'Yes,' said Pettingill, and there was nothing more to say.

The storm was fiercer up on the plateau than down below in the river valley, where Bertie spent the night crossing a bridge of boxes and struggling up a mud slide. In the first light of the morning of the 13th, the airfield was a sorry sight, strewn with wreckage. The BEs had been blown across the field like litter and half of them were on their backs. The Shorthorns were matchwood. Jack's Avro and Harmison's BE, locked together with a mass of canvas, had escaped serious damage; but the two squadrons had only ten aeroplanes between them that were in flying order that morning.

And as they stared miserably at the mess, the airmen heard the guns begin in the heavy mist across the river.

The York Commercial volunteers were required to present themselves for medical examination on Monday and Tuesday, the 14th and 15th of September, depending on the first letter of their surname. Ned went on the 15th, and came home to Jessie elated because he had been passed as 'A1'.

'What they're mostly rejected for is bad feet, or else bad teeth. They have to have at least four opposing molars in good condition, Dr Havergill told me, or they wouldn't be able to cope with army food. Oh, and of course there's the eye test – they have to be able to see well enough to shoot

a rifle. But it seems I had good scores in every department.'
He cocked an eye at Jessie, who had received all this information with, he felt, insufficient awe. It wasn't every day that a man was declared to be A1. 'Aren't you proud of me, Jess?'

'Oh – yes, of course I am,' said Jessie, rousing herself from her preoccupation. 'When do you go away?'

'I don't know yet. The Hound is out with one or two aides trying to find a suitable place for our camp. It will be a week or two, I imagine, before everything's ready for us. They'll have to get tents and equipment from the War Office, and an advance party will have to set everything up before the battalion can move in.'

'A week or two,' Jessie said. 'Well – that's good.' She lapsed again into thought, and Ned, disappointed, let it go.

Jessie had good reason for her preoccupation. She was fairly sure she was pregnant. She had missed her period in the middle of August. The next one had been due yesterday, on the 14th of September, but she didn't feel in the least as though it were about to happen. She felt *different*, although she could not really specify in what way. She didn't think Ned had noticed anything. It was normally the cessation of intercourse between them that marked the periods for him, and it was less easy to notice the absence of a negative than a positive, especially as, since the war began, he had been so busy. She was sure he would have mentioned it to her if he had noticed anything.

And now he was more involved than ever, and so excited and happy about going away with the battalion that she hesitated to tell him what she suspected. She didn't want to raise his hopes until she was sure – there had been false alarms before. Above all, she needed time on her own to discover all *she* felt about it. As the week progressed she became more sure that it was the real thing this time. The second missed period did not show up, and her breasts were tender. When the next week began she was seized, as she washed in the morning, with a feeling of dizziness and nausea. She wasn't actually sick, and it passed quite quickly, but she remembered the morning sickness from the last time, and it seemed to her the final confirmation.

She knew that as soon as she announced it, everyone would be delighted and happy, Ned would be excited, a great fuss would be made of her. But Ned was going away, with only brief periods of leave to come back to her until the war ended, which might be at Christmas but – she remembered Bertie's warnings – might not be for three years. Even at best, she would be without him for most of her pregnancy; at worst, perhaps until the child was toddling. He would not want to leave her. Would he perhaps try to get out of the battalion? She did not know if it was possible for someone to *un*-volunteer, but even if it were, she knew it would be regarded as a shameful thing to do. It would hurt his standing in society – and, worse, it would hurt his pride. She did not want to be the cause of that. It would be better, she thought, not to tell him until after he had gone away and was thoroughly involved in his training.

But then, what of her? She did not want to be alone with it. She was afraid that what had happened before might happen again. If she lost the baby, and he was not with her – oh, that would be hard indeed! And how would she manage her work when she was pregnant? She would have to give up riding – yes, completely this time. But would Ned allow her to drive herself in a delicate condition? Well, with Purvis gone, she would have to, that was all.

Another thought came to her: Daltry had volunteered as well, hoping that when Ned received a commission he could continue to be his servant. So the household would be left without a man, except for Gladding, the stableman-gardener, who was old and bad-tempered, lazy and self-serving – and much less use in an emergency, to her mind, than she was herself. When Daltry had wanted to volunteer, and Ned had said he did not like the idea of leaving her with only female servants, she had protested that she was quite capable of taking care of things, and he had agreed in the end that she was. But that was before he knew she was pregnant.

Mentally she squared her shoulders. There was a war on,

and everyone had to do their bit. She would *have* to manage, that was all. The country needed Ned in uniform – yes, and Daltry, too – and it was up to the women of England to make it easy for their men to go. And for that reason, she decided then and there, she would not tell Ned until she had to. She ought to be able to conceal it from him for another week or two, until he went away. She would make sure he could leave her with a light heart, and she would face what had to be faced without bothering him.

It turned out to be easier than she expected. Ned was not in noticing mood, with so much to do and think about; and apart from the morning sickness – she quickly learned how to retch silently – she felt extremely well and cheerful. It was harder to conceal the fact that she was not riding. Hotspur looked at her appealingly over the door of his box every morning, and she longed to be in the saddle, but she remembered the last time, and the terrible guilt that had haunted her when she slipped her child. So she borrowed her mother's phaeton and harnessed one of the Bhutias to it, and told anyone who asked that she was schooling it with a view to selling it as safe for a lady or child to drive. Gladding had to exercise Hotspur along with Compass Rose in the morning – and a great fuss he made about it – and turn them out in the paddock for the rest of the day.

She had to take her maid, Tomlinson, into the secret – if for no other reason than that it would be impossible to keep it from her. But Tomlinson had been with her a long time and was as deep as a well. She understood the reasoning perfectly, thought Jessie very brave and romantic, and promised to help her all she could. Tomlinson got Daltry to go through his jobs with her with a view to taking them over when the master was gone. There wouldn't be any entertaining, anyway, and a household without men always seemed to generate less work. Tomlinson would be housekeeper in all but name, and as far as possible spare her mistress the trouble of giving orders.

On the 25th of September Uncle Teddy visited in a state of excitement to say that the Hound and the Raising Committee had found the place for the training camp.

'It's up at Black Brow on the North York Moors, not too far from Grosmont. Miles of open land all around for training and marching about – couldn't be better.'

'Isn't that rather isolated?' Ned asked. 'What about supplies and so forth?'

'The regular railway runs as far as Grosmont, and from there to Black Brow there's a road and a light railway. There are quarries there, you see. The Black Brow Mining Company has given us the place. Digging will be suspended and the navvies will be moving out for the time being, so we can take over their camp.'

'When will it be ready?' Jessie asked.

'Oh, it won't be long at all,' Teddy said blithely. 'There are some good stout huts, which ought to house one company easily. The rest will have to live in tents until the rest of the huts are put up. You'll need to be under cover before the winter sets in.'

'Of course,' said Ned. 'It gets very cold up on the moors in winter.'

'It's a great piece of luck,' Teddy said, 'finding the place. There won't be too much to do after all. Water's already laid on, and the navvies have a fully-functioning canteen, and even a chapel. And there are a couple of bungalows, built for the quarry manager and the company owners, which will do for the officers. So it's really just a matter of getting the various stores from the War Office delivered, putting up the tents, and you'll be able to move in.'

In bed that night, Ned was particularly passionate, and afterwards he lay in silence, holding Jessie tightly. She waited for him to fall asleep, as he generally did after loving, but she could tell by his breathing that, despite his long day at work, he was wakeful. 'Are you afraid?' she asked at last.

'Afraid?' he said, and sounded surprised. 'No – no, not afraid. I don't know what I am,' he went on thoughtfully. 'Excited, of course. And—' There was a long pause. 'Apprehensive, I suppose. It will all be very strange to me. It reminds me of when I went off to Eton. I couldn't sleep the night before, wondering what it would be like and how I'd manage.'

'Well, I don't suppose the York Commercials will bully you and roast you in front of the fire,' Jessie said.

'No,' he said seriously. 'But this is a different sort of worry. I'm bound to be made an officer – Father says Hound has guaranteed it. I rather wish he hadn't asked, but of course he only did it for the best.'

'Don't you want to be an officer?'

'I don't know. I suppose I must do. I'd be very disappointed if I weren't chosen – it would seem like a reflection on me. I'd feel I'd let everyone down. But it's such a responsibility, having to take charge and give orders and so on.'

'You do that at the mill.'

'But it's different in the army, especially in battle. You don't have time to think things out and ask opinions and weigh it all up. And men's lives depend on you. I don't know if I'd be any good at it.'

'You won't be going into battle for a long time.'

'No, but I'll be an officer well before that, and I haven't the faintest idea what officers are supposed to do.'

'They'll give you training,' Jessie said, a little sleepily. She remembered for a moment how strong and capable Bertie had seemed that day when he came to say he'd been sent for. Perhaps some men were natural officers and some weren't. But Ned had never seemed to have any difficulty in taking charge – of his business, of her. She didn't say it out loud, however, because she was drifting down into sleep.

'I suppose they will,' Ned said. He lay holding his wife, listening to her breathing, and thinking about the parting to come. He didn't want to go: he didn't want to leave her. He wasn't afraid of war or death – his imagination didn't work that way – but he had a formless fear that if he once went away from her, he might never find his way back – or if he did, that what he came back to would be changed in some fundamental, undesirable way. He heard the clocks strike midnight before sheer weariness took him away into sleep.

The week went by quickly in preparation. Ned's luggage accumulated in the guest bedroom as Jessie, Tomlinson and Daltry between them laid out what was to be taken and packed a little each day. Brach found it a melancholy place. She went in there from time to time to sniff everything, and then would find Jessie or Ned and nudge their hands and roll her eyes in misery. One day when Tomlinson went to pack a freshly ironed nightshirt, she found an old and much-chewed bone lying on top of the last layer. She removed it thoughtfully, but didn't tell anyone. Fortunately it was so old and dry it had left no mark.

On the 30th of September an advance party of a hundred York Commercials under the control of the veteran sergeant-major and two sergeants went up to Black Brow with the stores to set up camp, and the order went out to the rest of the volunteers to present themselves at York station at eight thirty on Friday the 2nd of October. Despite her determination to be calm, Jessie was in tears that morning, and wondered if her condition had anything to do with it, for she was not usually a spouter. She was up at six thirty to have breakfast with Ned and be ready to go with him and Daltry to the station. He would have taken a taxi and saved her the trouble, but she said that she would not dream of missing it and that she wanted to see him off like a hero. Brach managed to slip out of the house and fling herself into the motor as soon as the door was opened, and had to be dragged out, with Ned ungluing one paw at a time while she looked up at him with the eyes of a martyr. He hurried her back to the house, and Tomlinson held on to her collar while she whistled her distress at the parting.

'I never realised she was so fond of me,' he said to Jessie, as he climbed into the driving seat. 'Silly dog, didn't you tell her I'll be back at Christmas?'

'I did,' said Jessie. 'She must have forgotten.'

There were such crowds at the station that it was difficult to find anywhere to park the motor, and they had to leave it at some distance and walk the rest. It was difficult to push through, and Ned worried fussily about Jessie being jostled, but when people knew it was a volunteer and his lady who were trying to get through they parted a way for them good-humouredly. Around the station the police had cleared a space in front of a low dais, where the mayor, the

Raising Committee, representatives of the Black Brow Quarry Company, and various York notables waited to congratulate the volunteers as they came through. The front of the station was decorated with flags, and a brass band was playing, the musicians crimson in the face in their efforts to be heard above the noise of the crowd.

Every minute an embarrassed-looking man would be expelled from the crowd into the open space like a pea being podded. Accompanied by proud fathers, tearful mothers and sisters, clinging sweethearts, they advanced to shake a great many civic hands before disappearing into the station, where Hound and his sergeants waited to direct them to this or that carriage. Each carried, in obedience to orders, a kitbag and a stout walking-stick; all were in civilian clothes and caps, for the uniforms were not yet ready.

Uncle Teddy was there to greet Ned and present him proudly to the entire row of the reception committee individually. 'My son,' he said. 'My son, Ned,' as though conferring a rare gift on the dignitaries. He had been accompanied to the station by Polly, who had insisted, like Jessie, that she would not miss it for worlds and was wearing her smartest sailor-dress and a straw hat with red, white and blue ribbons.

'Goodness, you look smart,' Jessie said to her, watching Ned and Daltry being taken down the line.

'You never know who you might meet,' Polly said. She examined Jessie's face. 'Have you been crying? Don't you want Ned to go? I'd be jolly proud if he were my husband.'

'Of course I'm proud,' Jessie said. 'You don't understand.'

'I bet I do,' said Polly. 'But I didn't make a fuss when Lennie went.'

Jessie was about to retort, then stopped herself and laughed. 'Well, you're just a lot braver than I am, I suppose.'

Polly didn't argue with this. 'I wish they had their uniforms. I bet Ned would look *splendid* in his. He will be an officer, won't he?' she asked anxiously.

'I'm sure he will,' Jessie said, and felt the tears rising again. She forced them down with an effort and said, 'Oh, look, they've finished and we're going in. Come on, or we'll get separated.'

Inside the station the noise of voices was a muted roar under the great arched roof, mingling with the panting of the railway engine. Ned and Daltry's names were ticked on a list and they were directed to a carriage towards the end of the train. They put their luggage aboard, then stood on the platform chatting a little awkwardly. Jessie was beginning to think it would have been better not to come, with her tearfulness, the beginnings of a headache, and the pressing need for a lavatory making conversation all but impossible. But Uncle Teddy had plenty to say about the camp and the organisation of the whole venture, and Polly chatted enough for everyone, though her eyes were everywhere but on her own people.

As the time of the train's departure neared, the crowd outside surged forward, broke through the police barrier and flooded into the station, making a solid sea of bodies that filled every inch of the platform. Ned looked round and said, 'I hope all the volunteers set off in good time. Any latecomers are going to miss the train. They'll never get through.'

Daltry said his polite goodbyes to the family and climbed up into the carriage to give his master privacy. Porters, bobbing on the tide like corks, were shouting for everyone to board. Ned grasped Jessie's cold hands and said, 'We must say goodbye, darling.'

Everyone else had probably said the same thing just at that moment, for there was a sudden heave of the crowd, and Jessie was thrust hard against Ned, who put his arms round her to stop her falling. Pressed against him, held in his strong arms, Jessie suddenly had a close and dear sense of his real presence, and knew how much she would miss him. Between them, pressed against him behind the barrier of her flesh, was their child, which he did not know about. She looked up into his handsome face, saw his eyes bright with tears, and was on the brink of telling him. But he bent his head and kissed her, his lips firm and warm, though his face was cold from the morning air, and any words of hers were stopped.

As he withdrew his mouth he whispered, 'I love you,

Jessie. I love you so much.' And then, too quickly, he released her and turned away, climbing up into the carriage. She saw him, with his back to them, dash a sleeve across his eyes.

'He didn't say goodbye to me!' Polly wailed. 'And I came specially to see him off.'

'Oh, hush,' Jessie said, distractedly.

'He didn't say goodbye to Daddy, either,' Polly said crossly. 'I call that jolly mean.'

'He said goodbye in his heart,' Jessie heard herself say.

'In his *heart*?' Polly queried derisively.

Jessie took her hand. 'He couldn't make himself heard in this noise, anyway.'

Either the words or the squeeze of the hand stilled Polly. Doors were slamming all up and down the train; and then the whistle blew, and a huge roar went up from the crowd, which made all the glass panels rattle. The train gave a great jerk and then the engine puffed forward. Faces crammed every carriage, heads and arms protruded from every open window. Ned appeared in the top half of the door to his carriage, craning over the head of the man who was there before him. He waved. Polly waved back, shrieking something Jessie couldn't hear. Jessie met his eyes, and held them as the train departed, exchanging a look as long as he was in sight. Only afterwards when they turned away and Uncle Teddy began forcing a way through the crowd for them, did she realise she had not said goodbye, nor that she loved him. She was feeling rather sick, her head ached, and she had a sense of oppression, as if, she thought, something bad had happened that she had not yet got to grips with. But that was probably just the pregnancy.

BOOK THREE

Determination

With BEF. June 10. Dear Wife,
(O Blast this pencil. 'Ere Bill, lend's a knife.)
I'm in the pink at present, dear.
I think the war will end this year.

Wilfred Owen: The Letter

CHAPTER FOURTEEN

The fighting that day – the 13th of September – on the ridge above the Aisne had been fierce and terrible. The Germans had machine-guns and artillery; the West Herts had only rifles. In the grey, soaking, misty dawn they had begun firing, and had beaten off wave after wave of advancing Germans, firing at a target when one presented itself, and when the mist came down more heavily, putting a curtain of shot into it that was enough to deter the enemy from advancing. They clung to their position on the crest of the slope above the river through a day in which the white fog never fully lifted, while below in the valley the Engineers laboured frantically to repair or construct bridges, as up and down the river the BEF crept and scrambled across.

They were not long alone, though it took the rest of the day to get the whole division across. In the early afternoon they were joined by another regiment, and the order came to advance. The mist had risen a little, enough to see some way ahead, though it hung like a nebulous and dripping pall a few feet above their heads. They were on farmland. They advanced first through a vast, flat turnip field, tripping over the swollen globes of the roots that protruded half out of the ground, brushing through the leaves that grew knee high and soaked their legs with the water caught in them. Then they were stumbling across bare plough, sinking into the furrows and gathering great clags of earth on their boots at every step. They were only half-way across when the enemy fire began again. They struggled desperately to run, their feet and legs weighed down by the sticky mud as though by some malevolent force. Bertie ran as in one of those dreams where one's legs will hardly move, while men fell on either side of him, men who were not just faces or names to him now but people whose characters and histories he knew, people he had relied on and suffered with. Sutton, a few yards from him, was cut almost in half by machine-gun fire, and his blood spattered on Bertie's hand and cheek, shockingly warm on his cold skin.

They reached a sunken lane running parallel with the crest and dived into it with relief. There were farm buildings over to the left and, judging by the firing, they were held by British troops. More orders came to move up and support them, but it was never possible against the weight of fire, and before nightfall the unit holding the farm buildings had fallen back to the sunken lane.

And there, in the event, they had stayed. As the days passed, they had seen the farm buildings shelled flat, creating an open no man's land between them and the Germans; and they had gradually dug themselves in as the whole of the BEF got across the river and formed a new front. Information came in slowly and in fragments – they heard about the damage to the RFC's aeroplanes, and knew how a few brave flyers in patched-up machines had managed to get airborne, despite the foul weather, to try to spot the German position. From what intelligence they brought back, it seemed that the enemy was well entrenched along the line of an ancient road called the Chemin des Dames and, far from fleeing, seemed set to defend the front where it was. Some British units had scored small successes here and there, enabling them to advance a little, and as a result the gap between the two lines varied along its length between two hundred and five hundred yards. The Germans outnumbered them heavily, but still they did not seem keen to attack, and the few advances they made were half-hearted and easily driven back by British rapid firing. After that first day, losses in Bertie's company were few.

By the end of a week, a routine had established itself. The men were gradually improving the trenches with the few tools that had survived the retreat and advance, and were passed up and down from company to company – even from regiment to regiment. With the repairing of more of the bridges, supplies began to come in and there was more food, and generally one hot meal a day, as well as the soldiers' lifeline, tea. Rations had been short at first. The terrible storm had delayed the ships bringing supplies and rein-forcements, which had been tossed about on the Bay of Biscay unable to make St Nazaire port, the new British supply base. It was typical of the average Tommy, Bertie thought, that his grumbles about the foul weather gave way to chuckles at the thought of the units trapped on board and seasick for two days. There was nothing cheered a soldier more than the suffering of his fellows. But then food began to come up; and, what was almost more welcome to the ragamuffin survivors of Mons, some new clothing – socks, shirts, caps. The West Herts were by now hardly recognis-able as soldiers, dressed as they were in whatever motley collection of clothes and rags they had been able to gather as they went along, with strips of cloth or sacking tied round their feet to hold the remnants of their boots together.

Bertie and his fellow officers were worse off in one respect. The army did not supply officers with their kit: they bought it themselves, with an allowance paid to them by the War Office, and the War Office was not going to change its methods now, even for officers in the thick of battle and long since separated from their belongings. When Cooper tried to brush the mud from Bertie's coat and his fingers went straight through the rotten material, he confessed himself at a loss. Up here on the plateau there was precious little room for 'wangling', especially as everyone else in the army was in the same position. The officers could only write home and beg their wives or parents to send out new kit for them, and hope that, now they seemed to be settled in one place again and a field post office was functioning, there was some chance they might receive the things before they were moved on again.

Before Bertie had sent off his request, he received a letter, long on its way, from Maud. In her elaborate prose – the lady's way of covering a great deal of paper without having much to say – she mentioned one or two committee things she was doing, and some dinners she and her father Richard had been to. She said little Richard was well and described how he had climbed onto a chair and taken down the nursery clock, which he had proceeded to disembowel, claiming when berated that he was 'mending it'. It was a letter full of nothing – and Bertie would have liked to know more about how things were going at Beaumont – but he read it a dozen times, trying to draw the essence of home from it. She ended by hoping he was well and was managing to keep his feet dry, which the senior Richard said was most important for a soldier. Bertie looked down at himself and laughed.

He hadn't told anyone at home about the wound in his arm. It was healing into an ugly, knotted scar, and there was a distinct hollow in the centre of it where he had lost some muscle. It pulled when he made certain movements, and it ached sometimes in the cold or the wet, but on the whole it did not bother him, and he knew he was lucky that it had healed so well. The advice of that old doctor in South Africa had been sound. And then he thought of all the men who had fallen, and knew he had been lucky, *tout court*.

On the 21st a second batch of reinforcements reached them, another eighty men, who brought the battalion's strength up to almost three hundred. They were received by the veterans with good-natured teasing because they were smart, clean-shaven, and had the full issue of kit stowed neatly in their packs.

'The war'll be over in no time, now you're here,' said Gayle, derisively. 'We'll stick you out in front and the Germans'll pass out at the sight of you.'

The newcomers were equally bemused by the sight of the sodden, bristling scarecrows the battalion had become, but kindly shared their riches with their companions.

The days began to fall into a pattern. After a few repulses, which cost them dearly in lives, the Germans seemed disinclined to attack *en masse*. They fell back on sniping, and the occasional burst of artillery. As they were a nation wedded to efficiency, the barrage always came at the same time of day, so the British soldiers knew when to take cover, and even facetiously set their watches by them. The West Herts settled down to sniping at the Hun by day, patrolling no man's land by night, and in between smoked, played cards, wrote home, and grumbled about the weather. One Sunday the colonel decided things were quiet enough to hold a church parade, and read the service out of his own Book of Common Prayer, which he had kept with him through every vicissitude. Fenniman complained to Bertie that he was too sensitive to be subjected to Buckland's dreadful mangling of Cranmer's sublime prose and ought to be let off church parade on compassionate grounds; but the men enjoyed it: it represented a taste of normality and home life. Buckland announced the hymns and Croner of C Company, who had a fine tenor voice, sang the first line before the men joined in, bellowing their favourite bits with fine disregard for Captain Fenniman's ear. The Germans were evidently having a church parade of their own, for across the short stretch of blasted ground between them, they could hear them singing – rather more decorously, and in three-part harmony. Evans, one of Bertie's men, was fiercely indignant when he recognised the tune and said the Huns had stolen it from the Welsh. He wanted to go straight across and teach them a lesson, and Bertie was amused to hear Pennyfather soothing him and explaining that '*Ein Feste Burg Ist Unser Gott*' had been a well-known hymn in Germany for decades.

But this quiet time was coming to an end. As the new front line settled down, it was noted by the commanders that the BEF was holding a section between two French armies, Maunoury's on the left and d'Esperey's on the right, and that it would make much more sense for it to be relieved by the French and to take up its former position on the left wing, in order to prevent the Germans outflanking the French, and to be on hand to protect the Channel ports.

So at the end of September Colonel Buckland called his officers together to tell them that they would be moving again.

'As you know, gentlemen, Antwerp is under siege, and if it falls – or I'm very much afraid that should be *when* it falls

– the two German army corps there will be released to march on Ostend, Dunkirk and then, ultimately, Calais. The BEF must take up a new position in that sector and drive them back. But it's vital that the Germans don't find out what we're doing. A mass exodus from the Aisne of British troops would alert them to our intentions, and they'd move too and reach the sea before us. So we'll be moving in small units, one by one as the French relieve us, and as far as possible under cover. The Germans have scouting aeroplanes as well as us, and we don't want them to spot us on the move. And we don't want them to notice extra train movements and draw their own conclusions, so we'll be going to different railheads, and none of them will be near to here.'

'How do we get to the railhead, sir?' Fenniman asked, more in hope than conviction.

'We'll march by night and lie up during the day in woodland,' said Buckland. 'Now, these are our orders . . .'

When the meeting ended Fenniman and Bertie walked away together. 'Marching again!' Fenniman said. 'I've pretty well painted France already with the blood from my feet. How far is this place the Old Man mentioned – this railhead of his?'

'Fifty miles, perhaps sixty,' Bertie said. 'It's going to be hard on the men. They're all very tired, and this spell of trench duty hasn't helped. They were keyed up to it before, and now they've relaxed.'

'Never mind about them,' Fenniman said. 'Think of me! That idiot Fassner should never have let the Lancers commandeer our horses down by the river.'

'I knew we'd never see them again,' said Bertie, 'but I don't suppose he had any choice. You can't expect a lieutenant to say no to a colonel. Well, perhaps they'll give us new ones for the move.'

Fenniman snorted. 'Parke, old fellow, you must be a religious man, because that's a pious hope if ever I heard one.'

Life at Morland Place had changed for the better, thanks to the York Commercials. Henrietta and Alice saw it in Teddy's improved spirits – the energy and cheerfulness with which he greeted each day, the interest he now showed in all his business. He thought nothing of taking the train over to Manchester in the morning to stir up the mill that was making the khaki cloth for the uniforms, and coming back in the afternoon to closet himself with his land agent, Pickering. He was a man reborn, brought out from under the shadow that the doomed ship had laid on him two years ago.

At Raising Committee meetings he was the driving force. Even the carping of Alderman Cherry could not dampen him. There would always be some who held to it that Teddy Morland was a wicked, callous man who had pushed women and children aside to save his own hide; there would be those who said his present benevolence was an attempt to buy his way back into society. But in the present climate they voiced their opinions carefully, and more waverers every day changed sides and began to shrug that one couldn't believe what one read in the newspapers. More important for Teddy than that York forgave him was that he began to forgive himself. He knew he had not done what they said he had – but he had survived when hundreds hadn't, and he had been ashamed of that. Well, here was a way to begin to pay back the debt, to make his life useful in the saving; and he began to let the nightmares go, and the recriminations die down in his soul. Henrietta had told him, on the one occasion they discussed it, that it had been God's will that he had survived, and that he should not baulk against it. Now as the shadows receded he allowed himself, just a little, to believe it.

It was not only Teddy who benefited from the new atmosphere. Robbie saw the change in the way he was greeted in the street and at his place of work. 'How is the battalion coming along?' they would ask, and he would bathe in the reflected glory of having an uncle and a cousin so closely involved. Now people remembered that the Morlands had always been a leading family in York, remembered their benevolence, their involvement in slum-clearance, in the railways. And, look, two sons of Morland Place had volunteered right away, as well as Mr Ned Morland and that American cousin of theirs! They were doing all they could for the war effort. They were good people.

Others remembered, with some wistfulness, the old days when Teddy Morland had exercised his lavish hospitality – the dinners, the balls, the shoots. Would those times ever come again? Of course, in the present emergency everyone was supposed to exercise restraint and economy. Still, if Mr Teddy Morland should think of issuing invitations to some more suitably modest wartime dinner-party, one would not want to be left off the guest list.

There had been a pent-up urge to be sociable, which Teddy's reclusiveness had stemmed quite as much as any odium directed against him, and his reappearance in public burst the dam. Morland Place was once more to be visited, and the curious and the genuinely friendly almost elbowed each other out of the way to be first across the drawbridge. The whole Morland Place household noticed the difference in traffic. Now there were people coming to the door all the time. Henrietta felt she could not begin a household task without having to break off to go down and receive some lady or other who had 'just dropped by to see how dear Mrs Compton was'. Gentlemen called on Teddy to discuss business, invite him to speak at meetings, propose putting him up for their club, ask his opinion of the latest news. Ladies in large hats came to beg for subscriptions to this worthy cause or that fund. Alice's friends from her Meynell days, Mrs Winnington and Mrs Spindlow, rediscovered her with relief, and she was besieged in the drawing room by those chattery ladies, who stayed for hours and could hardly be persuaded to leave. The servants were back and forth all day, answering the door, carrying refreshments, taking tele-phone messages.

Polly loved every minute of it, and needed no invitation to play her 'piece' to the ladies on the drawing-room piano, or hand round tea. Her only anxiety was that she did not have sufficient suitable outfits and that some of the visitors must have seen her in the same thing more than once. Alice sympathised – as no-one else in the house did – with this dilemma, and was very helpful with ribbons, sashes, artificial flowers, and advice on clever tricks for disguising a dress on its second and third outing. When Polly had to go back to school at last – it had been closed for a month because of the chicken-pox epidemic – she mourned over all the society she would miss.

Henrietta loved the liveliness of the house, for it reminded her of her childhood, when her parents had been the very hub and focus of York's world, but she found it exhausting. Her housekeeping took up a lot of her time, and she had been run almost off her feet by the chicken-pox outbreak. It seemed to be over now, and the sufferers were convalescing and off her hands, but she felt worn out with work, and with worry over Jack and Bertie, whose letters were not nearly frequent enough to calm her fears. And when Lennie, Ned and Frank finished their training and went overseas, it would be worse still. She wondered sometimes in a confused way whether she would have hours in the day enough for all the worrying she would have to do then.

Ethel came to her rescue, not by taking over her housework but by firmly denying her to visitors and passing them over to Alice. Alice never minded how many people she had to entertain in a day. She liked to dress nicely, sit in the drawing-room and be visited – or, equally, to go visiting and sit in someone else's drawing-room. She was not a lively woman, or a woman of much conversation, but she would listen happily to other people's chat, and prime them with gentle questions if they seemed to be running down. She would not have noticed that Henrietta did not feel the same, or have thought to rescue her from what to her was a pleasure; but Ethel saw the fatigue and exasperation in her mother-in-law's face, and quietly and efficiently solved the problem. Sawry, who loved his mistress, was more than willing to enter into the conspiracy, and thereafter Mrs Compton was only 'at home' to personal friends and family.

Teddy and Alice accepted several invitations before they felt it was essential to repay the hospitality with a dinner of their own. Henrietta entered into the plans with enthusiasm. Though most of the work of organising it would fall on her, she loved an occasion, and was happy to do it. As she told

Ethel, who tentatively wondered if it would not all be too much for her, she never minded hard work, only being bothered and interrupted.

Everyone had their part to play for the dinner. Henrietta decided the menu, ordered the food and organised everything; Ethel wrote out the invitations; Teddy paid the bills and spent a happy evening down in the cellar with Sawry; and Alice bought a new gown. The party was a great success. In deference to the war effort, Henrietta ordered simple dishes, but there was no use pretending, as she said to Ethel, that there was not plenty to eat at Morland Place; and Teddy could never bear paltriness when it came to wine. He was genial, Alice was her usual calm, sweetly smiling self, and there was a sufficient mix of people to ensure the conversation was lively and no-one was left out. Polly, who came home from school at weekends, was in the drawing-room to greet the company before dinner. She was deeply upset that she wouldn't be allowed actually to dine down until she was sixteen – an aeon away – but Jessie promised to come up and see her when the ladies withdrew and bring her a bit of the Nassau tart, her favourite, if there was any left.

Jessie felt strange being there without Ned. She had not really missed him since he went away – indeed, she had rather enjoyed the sensation of being on her own for the first time in her life, to do just as she pleased, servants permitting. She had enjoyed having the bed to herself, to stretch out in luxuriously. It had been delightful to get up and go to bed when she liked, to order what *she* wanted to eat at meals, to come and go without permission. During the day she had plenty of work with the horses to keep her busy, and if she wanted company there were the Cornleighs and Mrs Wycherley to visit – though the latter was very busy herself these days; and of course Morland Place was her constant resource. Ned had managed to telephone her once since he had left for camp, and she had been able to tell him cheerfully and positively that she was managing very well without him. Whether that was what he had wanted to hear she did not stop to wonder.

Determined this time to do things right and avoid self-reproach, she had been to see Dr Hasty, who had confirmed what she already knew, that she was pregnant, and told her that she was a healthy young woman and should have nothing to worry about. 'As long as you don't overdo things,' he warned. 'You must not think you can carry on just as before.'

'Oh, no, I understand that,' Jessie assured him hastily. 'I stopped riding as soon as I was sure.'

'Good,' said Hasty, 'as far that goes. But I should like to know you are not working too hard. In fact, I would recommend that you give up working altogether, except,' he added, seeing her expression, 'that I know you would not listen to any such recommendation. But please try to avoid any great exertion. Supervise, don't do things yourself. Don't go dashing about all over the countryside. Really, a gentle walk each day is all the exercise you ought to take. No tennis, and no dancing or gaiety of that sort in the evenings.'

'With my husband away, I shan't be tempted to anything like that.'

'Quite so, quite so,' said Hasty, and gave her a sympathetic look. 'Of course, with things as they are, a great many women are having to face pregnancy without their husband's support. But after the wonderful victories on the Marne we may all hope it will be over soon. Perhaps your husband may not have to go abroad at all.'

'I rather think he wants to,' Jessie said, with a smile.

Hasty did not respond to that. He was frowning thoughtfully, and said, 'You have the telephone, I believe? Good. Then you can call me at once if there is anything that worries you – not that I anticipate there will be anything untoward. As I said, you are a healthy young woman. But in view of your past experience, I should like you to lie down on your bed and rest for two hours every afternoon.'

He extracted a promise from her, so Jessie had to do it, though she thought to begin with that it would drive her mad. But after a day or two she found she really enjoyed it. Pregnancy did make her tired, and it was delightful to be *ordered* to rest, so that the responsibility was taken from her. Tomlinson thoroughly approved, and made her comfortable with pillows and light coverings, and brought her tea. And Jessie rediscovered the joys of reading, which she had rather lost the habit of since her schooldays. There was always so much to do out of doors; and at home – well, Ned was not a great reader, except for the newspaper, and it was impossible to read if the other person in the room preferred conversation.

But now, with her evenings to herself, and the two hours on her bed in the afternoon, the most inviting of the sedentary occupations was reading. She hated sewing, had nothing to sketch, didn't care to play the piano without company, and though she liked playing cards she found solitaire a bore. So she picked up a book, and within minutes was transported. She had read everything in the house in a couple of days. As her appetite grew she borrowed from Morland Place, revisiting childhood friends such as *Gulliver*, *Jane Eyre*, *Alice* and Tom the chimney sweep, and joined the subscription library on the corner of St Leonard's Place for more modern sustenance.

She had been quite content with her new routine; but today Ned's absence had suddenly struck her. Dressing for a dinner, driving over, being received, mingling in a drawing-room with other guests, all without Ned beside her, did feel definitely odd, in an unpleasant rather than an exciting way. She didn't relish going home alone afterwards, either. They had always discussed parties together as they undressed, and she would miss that; and sleeping alone suddenly seemed a chilly and lonely thing. For the first time she felt a pang of apprehension about her pregnancy, about going through it without Ned there to support her. Suppose the war did go on for years? She would have to endure childbirth without his nearby presence; there would be no proud father to receive the new baby into his arms; no Ned to discuss Baby's delights and little troubles with.

Well, as Hasty had said, a great many women were going to have to get used to doing things without a man beside them. At Morland Place she banished troubled thoughts and concentrated on enjoying the evening. It was wonderful to see Uncle Teddy again doing what he did best – being the genial host; and everyone was especially nice to her, as the wife of 'one of our gallant volunteers'. It amused her at first to see how it annoyed Robbie to hear all the praise heaped on Ned, but afterwards she felt sorry for him, because he obviously took it as a criticism of himself, which she was sure it was not.

Perhaps because of his sensitivities, Robbie chose that evening to announce to everyone his and Ethel's expectations. Jessie could see from Ethel's expression that she had not known he was going to, but she made the best of it, received congratulations blushing prettily, and clung to Robbie's arm like a frail little woman who depended utterly on her strong and capable husband's presence. It all went down very well, and Robbie beamed and looked more comfortable with himself. Jessie was glad she had decided to keep her own condition secret: not for anything would she want to eclipse Ethel and Rob's glory.

She sat at dinner with Lord Lambert's son: the Hon. Richard had been invited 'for' her, and at seventeen only just qualified for dinner, though his upbringing ensured he was not overwhelmed by it. She guessed it had been hard for Uncle Teddy to find someone, when so many must have volunteered. The Hon. Richard was desperate to volunteer himself, but was rather too well known in the district to lie about his age.

'I did think of going to London and volunteering there,' he confided to her. 'Some of the men in my year at school have done that. They simply said they were nineteen, and no-one asked any questions or bothered a bit. But somehow I don't quite like to do it, knowing the guv'nor wouldn't like it. I mean, he said he won't try to stop me volunteering when I'm old enough, which I suppose means he *would* stop me *now*. Wouldn't you think that's what it means?'

'I imagine so,' Jessie said obediently.

'The trouble is,' he went on, 'a lot of fellows are saying it will all be over by Christmas, and then I shall have missed my chance. What do you think? Do you think it will be over by Christmas?'

'No, I don't,' Jessie said, more to cheer him up than because she had a firm opinion.

He brightened. 'Well, that's good. Because it would be awful to miss the whole show, just because one wasn't quite old enough.' His talk was all of volunteering. He explained to her that he had given a lot of thought to which regiment to join and rather fancied the Sherwood Foresters, because his friend Shaw said they were a fine outfit and *he* was joining them, and it would be nice to serve with a friend. But on the other hand, the guv'nor had been in the 11th Hussars and might expect him to follow suit – and there were a lot of splendid chaps in the 11th. Also, his friend Worsley said it was a fool's game to go through a war on your own feet instead of on a horse. What did she think?

He chattered on and she nodded and smiled and agreed but stopped listening, allowing his voice to sink into the background stream of conversational noise, on which she drifted, observing the movements of the staff as they served and cleared, of the heads and bare shoulders and hands and mouths of the guests as they turned this way and that, talked, fed themselves, responded to their dinner partners. She watched the small by-play between her mother and Sawry, a nod here, a movement of the eyes there, controlling the whole event just as she, Jessie, might control a horse in harness, guiding it with delicate, imperceptible pressures. Her mother, she thought, was looking tired. When she answered someone and smiled, the smile looked strained; and she seemed more comfortable when both of her dinner partners were otherwise engaged and she could sit in silence. Having once noticed her, Jessie watched her on and off throughout the dinner, and saw that she didn't eat very much, only pecked at what was on her plate and then left most of it.

When the ladies withdrew, Jessie remembered her promise to Polly. She hung back a little, then turned away from the scented, twittering cloud of ladies to cross the hall and go through the green baize door to the kitchen passage. The servants were just about to sit down to their meal, but she had always been a favourite with Mrs Stark, who came to meet her at the kitchen door with a beaming smile. 'Eh, Miss Jessie, what a nice surprise! You've not been in ma kitchen for I don't know how long.'

'I don't mean to disturb you, when you must be ready for your supper.'

'Nay, it's a pleasure to see you, and looking so well. It must be strange for you without Mr Ned. Have you heard anything from him, might I ask? We were all so proud of him – and Mr Jack, in the Flying Corps. And Mr Frank – what a surprise that was, him joining the Rifles! My sister's husband's cousin has a lad in the Rifles, which is quite a coincidence, when you think of it.'

Jessie chatted to her for a few minutes but, aware that the rest of servants would not sit down for their supper until the cook was there, broke off to ask about the tart for Miss Polly.

Mrs Stark smiled. 'Aye, ma Nassau's a favourite o' hers. I put her a bit by, and I suppose she can have it now, seeing she's prac'ly grown up. I knaw Emma doosn't approve o' sticky things late at night for her children, but rightly speaking Miss Polly's not in the nursery n'more, is she? Just bide a minute, Miss Jessie, and I'll put it on a plate for you.'

When she brought the covered plate on a tray, Jessie asked on an impulse, 'I noticed my mother didn't eat very much tonight – and everything was quite delicious, I must say.'

Mrs Stark's smile clouded. 'Sawry told me she hardly ate more than a bird. She has us all worried.'

'Is she not well?' Jessie asked, with her heart in her mouth.

'She's tired out, that's what,' said Mrs Stark. 'She needs a holiday. Seven days a week she works, keeping this house running, and fifty-two weeks a year. There was all that trouble for the poor master, and the master's poor wife losing the baby, and who shoulders all the burdens? She's hardly set foot outside the house in two years. Even the kitchenmaid gets her day off every week, but when does the mistress?'

Jessie nodded, glad to hear there was no worse apprehension. 'I'll talk to her,' she said.

'I wish you would, Miss Jessie, and see if you can't

persuade her to take a holiday. Me and Sawry can manage things all right if she goes away. A bit o' sea air would set her up, to ma mind.'

Jessie slipped upstairs to the Red Room and delivered the tart to the eagerly waiting Polly, and assured her that the dinner party was *very* dull, and that the Hon. Richard Lambert was not as handsome as rumour had it, and spoke about nothing but the war. Then she went back down to the drawing-room. As she reached the bottom of the stairs, she had a dizzy spell, and had to grab the newel-post as the staircase hall whirled round her. The drawing-room door opened at that moment and her mother came out, probably looking for her. Henrietta saw in an instant what was wrong. She hurried over to put her arm round Jessie's waist, helped her into the dining-parlour and onto a chair. 'Put your head right down, that's right,' she instructed. 'No, don't try to talk for a moment.' A cool hand was laid across the back of Jessie's neck, and she suddenly felt the huge comfort of having her mother close by: it was a castle keep, it was a safe harbour, it was the lights of home on a dark winter evening. Nothing could ever replace 'mother' in a person's life.

The dizzy spell passed and she sat up slowly, testing whether she would be sick – but it seemed not. Her mother drew up another chair and sat facing her. Her eyes were bright and smiling in her pale face. 'Well, Mrs Ned Morland,' she said, 'and have you got something to tell me?'

'What do you mean?' Jessie said feebly.

'You know very well what I mean. My girl Jessie doesn't have fainting fits for nothing.'

'Well . . . ,' Jessie began, wondering if she could still avoid a direct answer.

But Henrietta took that for confirmation. 'I knew it!' she said. 'Somehow I knew it. I've been watching you all evening and there was just something about you. A mother's instinct, I suppose. Oh, Jessie, I'm so pleased! How far along are you?'

'About twelve weeks. It was at the beginning of August, I think. But, Mother—'

310

'And what did Ned say when you told him?'

'I haven't told him.'

'You haven't—' Henrietta stared.

'I haven't told anyone. And, Mother, I don't want anyone to know, not yet. Promise you won't tell anyone.'

'But *why* didn't you tell Ned?' Henrietta was perplexed. 'Twelve weeks? You must have known before he went away.'

'I didn't tell him *because* he was going away. I knew he wouldn't want to go if he knew about it, and that he'd worry and be miserable all the time. He was so pleased and excited about going to camp. I couldn't spoil that for him.'

'Oh, Jessie,' said Henrietta. She leaned over and laid her hand on her daughter's. 'It was a good, kind thing to do. But I still think you should have told him. It's his right to know.'

'But there's nothing he can *do* about it, away at camp, except to worry.'

'All the same—'

'All the same, I'm not going to tell him, not yet – and you must promise me you won't tell anyone, either. Because if you tell *anyone*, Uncle Teddy will find out, and I know he'll insist on telling Ned.'

'You can't keep it a secret for ever,' said Henrietta.

'Of course not, I know that. When he comes home on leave from camp, then I'll tell him. He's pretty well bound to come home around Christmas-time. That will be soon enough.'

Henrietta sighed. 'Very well, if you insist, I won't say anything. But it's very hard on me, you know,' she added, with a twinkle, 'not to be able to make a fuss of you.'

Jessie leaned forward and kissed her. 'When we're alone together, you can fuss as much as you want. I'm *glad* you guessed. Despite what I decided, I really wanted *someone* to be excited for me.'

A new idea dawned in Henrietta's eye. 'Darling, why don't you come and live here? It can't be nice for you, all alone in that house, and there's really no need for it. You could have your old room, and I could take care of you – without telling anyone, of course.'

'I wouldn't put you to the test,' Jessie laughed. 'It would be sheer cruelty. And Emma would guess in a second – she has a mystical sense about pregnancy. Besides, I like my house, and I'm enjoying having it to myself.'

'Perhaps just now – but that will wear off.'

'Well, if it does, I promise to let you know.' To forestall further argument, she changed the subject. 'As for taking care of me, I want to know why you aren't taking care of yourself. You aren't looking well, Mother, and you hardly ate a thing.'

'I had a large lunch,' Henrietta said smoothly. 'Alice's friends called so close to luncheon I could hardly avoid asking them to stay.'

Jessie was not convinced. 'You look pale.'

'I have a headache, that's all. It's nothing. Please don't fuss.'

Jessie smiled. 'All right – I won't if you won't.'

Henrietta pressed her hand. 'I'm so happy for you, Jessie! You will take care of yourself, won't you?'

'Don't worry, I don't want to risk any trouble this time. I've stopped riding and I rest every afternoon. I promise you, I shall treat myself like one of my own brood mares.'

'Then I shall have nothing to worry about,' Henrietta smiled.

Up at Black Brow, things were gradually getting organised. On their arrival on the first day, the York Commercials had been paraded and given an inspirational talk by Colonel 'Hound' Bassett, who reminded them that they were part of the Duke of Richmond's Regiment, a body with a proud record and reputation. 'I am sure,' he went on, sweeping them with his eyes, 'that I shall not need to urge you to uphold the best traditions of that fine regiment.'

The ground was uneven and Ned was standing on a ridge just a little higher than the rest. From this vantage-point he, too, could scan the whole group. It was a sea of tweed caps, arranged in fairly neat lines, below which were men in ordinary suits, most of them with a coat over their arm. It looked very odd to Ned, and nothing like an army. It was a bright day, but with a cold breeze that ruffled the leaves on the trees edging the field in which they stood, and bowled a succession of watery-looking clouds across a sky of thin autumn blue. The sound of the leaves and the strangeness of the sea of caps gave him a sudden, piercing sense of homesickness, though he had only been gone a few hours. He was in an alien place, and these were all strangers, who would test him and judge him without any requirement to like him. Talk of the honour of a regiment touched him only with foreboding. He felt very alone.

Bassett went on to urge all the men to practise punctuality, to get up the moment reveille sounded, which would be at five forty-five so that they would have plenty of time to prepare, and to be ready before the actual time of parade, which would be six thirty. He sweetened the injunction by promising that hot coffee would be served before parade. He introduced the sergeants, all veteran regulars in their fifties, and his second-in-command, Major Foster, a thin, scholarly-looking man who had been a Territorial officer. Then he called out the names of the sixteen men who would be the temporary subalterns, four to a company, and who would later be given commissions if all went well. He asked them to come out to the front of the parade so that the men could see them and learn their names. Ned was, as promised, one of them, and he stepped out to line up beside the others and be stared at. He felt awkward and apprehensive – the word 'temporary' had unnerved him – and tried not to meet anyone's eye. Each was given a light-coloured armband to wear, since none had uniforms.

Then a hearty lunch was dished up, and the afternoon was spent in sorting everyone into companies. The men who wanted to serve together were put into the same platoons, and there was a great deal of to-ing and fro-ing as old friends searched for each other, new friends pledged eternal allegiance, and unattached men were recognised by acquaintances and invited to join this or that group, or stood forlornly until despatched to a company. When the sorting was done, the sergeants asked for anyone who had any experience of drilling – for instance, in the Boy Scouts or the Boys' Brigade – to come forward to be temporary lance-corporals. Then all were shown where they would sleep, and were free for the rest of the day to fill their palliasses, unpack and settle in before supper at half past six.

By a drawing of lots, A Company were allocated the huts, and the rest separated into the neat rows of bell-tents, looking very white against the dark grass, which the advance party had erected. The subalterns were taken away by the colonel and the major and shown the officers' accommodation. There were four bungalows, simple, single-storey wooden buildings, each containing four rooms and a bathroom and lavatory. The rooms were small, but sound and dry, each with a tiny fireplace. By a misunderstanding, the Quarry Company had removed all the furniture, but the War Office had provided each with a camp cot.

The other building was a large, solid house, built for the Quarry Company's owners, which was to provide accommodation for the senior officers, and the officers' mess facilities. There was a large dining-room, the drawing-room was to be the officers' smoking-room, a small sitting-room was to be the colonel's office, and the morning-room was to act as the medical officer's room. They already had a medical officer, Captain Flowers, a regular from the Royal Army Medical Corps, sent to them by the War Office; and a volunteer acting quartermaster, Charles Hunter, who was a York JP and alderman and had served in the Engineers in his youth.

Ned was pleasantly surprised by the quality of the dinner that night in the officers' dining-room. The Quarry Company kept a permanent staff at the house, including an excellent cook, and had generously donated them to the battalion along with the site and the buildings. There was soup, fish, entrée, sweet and dessert, well cooked and plentiful. Ned found himself unaccountably hungry, perhaps because of all the fresh air and anxiety. Afterwards they retired to the smoking-room to get to know each other, while the Hound and Major Foster did the rounds like good hosts and tried to make everyone feel comfortable.

'Don't worry if it all seems a bit strange to begin with,'

Hound said, when he reached Ned. 'You'll soon get used to it.'

Ned smiled ruefully. 'Was it so obvious?'

'You look like a fellow bound for the hangman's noose,' said Hound. 'But I'll tell you a secret — everyone feels the same. You just don't know it because you can't read their faces yet.'

'I'm only afraid I shall let you down,' Ned confessed.

'Poppycock!' said Hound. 'I wouldn't have picked you if I had the slightest doubt. And between you and me,' he lowered his voice, 'I have you marked out for early promotion. You're the only chap here who went to Eton. The only other public-school fellow is Whittaker, over there, who was at Rugby.'

Later in the evening Whittaker came over and introduced himself. 'I understand you were at Eton? So Colonel Bassett said. Whittaker – Rugby and the House. Glad to meet you. Cigarette?'

Ned accepted and Whittaker lit them both.

'Bit of a rum set-up, don't you think?' he said. 'I was rather afraid it might come to this, considering the way it was undertaken. I'm sure these are all very decent, good-hearted fellows, but not one of them is a gentleman, as far as I can see.'

'I don't know how you tell,' Ned said. He did not like this line of conversation. He had been to Eton, but because of his birth he was not everyone's idea of a gentleman, and he was afraid that this man would soon find it out.

'My dear chap, you're too liberal,' said Whittaker. 'You only have to listen to their accents – so very Yorkshire! The doctor and Major Foster are very pleasant, but not quite gentlemen. And even the colonel – charming man, but he started out in the ranks, you know.'

'I didn't know,' said Ned.

'Oh, yes. Worked his way up to sergeant and then was offered a commission. Very worthy sort, but—' He shrugged. 'It may be up to you and me to keep up the standards, you know.'

Ned wasn't sure he did know. 'I wonder,' he said

315

cautiously, 'whether being a good officer depends on being a gentleman, in the sense you mean. Might there not be other qualities required?'

Whittaker raised his eyebrows. 'No doubt, no doubt. But when one is confined in a small community for perhaps three or four years, one may be forgiven for hoping to be among one's own sort. I must say I'm rather disappointed. It was the whole idea behind these "Pals" battalions, after all.'

'Well, the men are probably happy,' Ned said.

'Quite so. And when the War Office sends us down the senior officers, I suppose we may get some gentlemen. But that won't be for a month or more, so Bassett says. Until then, it's up to us.'

Ned had nothing to say to that. He looked down at Whittaker – he was several inches taller – and wondered what gave him such a good opinion of himself. He had a rather unfinished-looking, pinched face, a bony nose, thinning, fuzzy, sandy hair, and freckled hands. Perhaps he thought Ned looked like a gentleman because he was tall and (everyone said) good-looking. What would he think if he ever discovered that he was the illegitimate son of a housekeeper? Ned didn't think he liked Whittaker – and it was part of the strangeness of his new army life that he realised at the same time that he must find a way to get on with all his fellow officers, and therefore could never let him find it out.

It was very cold that night, with a searching, icy wind, and Ned found that the narrow cot, while comfortable in a Spartan way, did nothing to insulate him. He tossed and turned and shivered, and had to get up and put on a pullover and lay his greatcoat over the bed before he could get warm enough to go to sleep. He pitied Daltry and the other men in the tents – although they had been issued with three blankets each, while he had only two. Once he had stopped shivering, he lay and listened to the different sort of silence around him, and thought about Jessie. He imagined himself in bed, with her soft, sleep-hot body curled against him. It was a good thing, he told himself, that the cot was narrow, or he'd have felt the empty space beside him like a hollow tooth. He slept badly, and it was no hardship to get up in the morning at a quarter to six, when one of the servants brought him a cup of coffee and told him that there was only cold water to wash in.

The days passed, spent in Swedish exercising, to make them fitter and more supple, parade-ground drill, route marches, fieldcraft lessons, and rifle and bayonet training. They had as yet only twelve rifles, so most of the latter training was done with the men's walking-sticks. And out on the moors they dug trenches and learned how to construct cover for themselves. Men with special skills were allotted particular jobs: those with catering experience became cooks, anyone who had served behind a counter was allocated to quartermaster's stores, anyone with first-aid knowledge was attached to the MO. Tailors were put into the tailoring department – always busy patching up the men's clothes, which were not designed for this strenuous life. Two engineers were put in charge of improving the water supply and the latrines and laying on hot water to the subalterns' bathrooms; and a butcher was rather surprised to find himself made camp barber, but took to this new use of sharp implements with gusto.

By the end of October the huts were ready, and none too soon, for though the weather was still fine, it was bitterly cold at night, and due to get colder. The huts were strongly built and raised off the ground for insulation, and each housed a platoon, with a closed-off room at one end for the NCO, and a wood-burning stove at the other, which kept them wonderfully warm. The subalterns were provided with furniture – an iron bedstead, wooden chair and small table, wardrobe and chest-of-drawers. Ned stood a photograph of Jessie on the chest-of-drawers and laid out his writing-case on the table, and felt it was adequate.

Also at the end of October, the uniforms were delive̶ It was a great coup for the York Commercials, for the I Pals had no hope of getting uniforms for many wee Khaki cloth was in desperately short supply everyw̶ even in many of the regular regiments the volu̶ no uniforms, or had temporary ones of blue cloth. But Teddy had put his own mill to work and, by cajoling, demanding and paying overtime, had got enough cloth for his own seam-stresses to make up. The York Commercials were as excited by their new clothes as girls trying on party frocks, and when they were all kitted out, it made a difference not only to the way they looked but the way they felt and acted. Now that they looked like soldiers, they held their heads higher, swung their arms more smartly, marched in better time, and were proud to be part of the same unit, and a small cog in the mighty British Army.

Teddy was rewarded for his altruism, because the War Office placed an order with him for khaki cloth, which in the long term would recompense him amply for the setting-up costs.

Ned was beginning to get used to the new life, to learn the names of his platoon, and to understand the drills, orders and routines he had to initiate. He still felt a little uneasy in the officers' mess – although most of his fellow subal-terns were more likeable than Whittaker. But they all got on so easily with each other, as if they had known each other for years, while he felt, instinctively and of himself, like an outsider. It reminded him of when he had gone to Eton – he had joined late, and had found it difficult to make friends, and only through his prowess at games, especially cricket, had he found a niche there. He *knew* he was not like the other boys, because of his background, and being naturally rather solemn he could not laugh or jolly his way to acceptance. He did not understand their jokes, could not use their slang without self-consciousness, watched their schoolboy pleasures and pranks with a slightly mystified air, unable to join in. He had left at last liked by many, admired by some, but not intimate with anyone.

At home, with his family, he was able to relax and be ˌural; and at the mill he was required by his position to ˌand rather than be friendly; but he was inclined to be ˌh strangers. He quickly found the right tone to take men of his platoon, and they responded to the ˌe had built up over the years at the mill; but in the mess he remained apart. The other subalterns, seeing him hold back, but not disliking him, decided he was 'a quiet one' and left him alone. Whittaker at first was inclined to see him as an ally, but getting too little response from him transferred his attentions to the quartermaster, who if not a public-school man was at least a university man. So Ned spent most evenings reading a newspaper in a corner and listening wistfully to the cheery talk all around him; and at night he lay cold in his narrow bed and longed for Jessie and home.

CHAPTER FIFTEEN

Bertie stepped down, weary and dingy from yet another train onto yet another French railway platform. It had been a long journey – long in hours rather than distance. The train had crawled through the countryside, with interminable delays as it was shunted to one side to let another past, or simply stopped between stations for no apparent reason. He had lost all sense of time since they had left the Aisne on this cautious and clandestine creep across France. In the process they had left behind the pleasant autumn weather. Here, closer to the English Channel, the sky was pewter with threatened rain, and the cold was clammy.

'Where are we, please, sir?' asked one of the men, as he jumped down.

'St Omer,' said Bertie.

'Omer? Not close enough to 'ome for me,' he said, passing along to make room.

All the railheads had been busy, but this was the busiest. Everywhere Bertie looked there were men in uniform scurrying, marching or lounging about. Pennyfather jumped down beside him and said, 'What's all this antlike activity? Oh, yes, of course, it's Sir John French's new HQ.'

'How do you know that?' Bertie asked.

'I heard the CO talking about it when I went to get our luncheon from the basket. Any idea how long we'll be here?'

'None at all,' Bertie said. Out of the corner of his eye he could see Cooper deep in conversation, head to head with soldier in ASC uniform. From the way he was standing,

something was about to change hands at any moment. The town that accommodated General Headquarters would naturally provide large opportunities for wangling – if they stayed long enough. Evidently Cooper wasn't wasting any time. 'Get the men lined up, will you,' he said to Pennyfather, 'before they start wandering away?'

They were still shuffling into position when the colonel came along.

'We'll have to get the men off the platform, Parke,' Buckland said. 'There's another train coming in. Lead your company off, will you, and form them up out in the station yard?'

'Yes, sir. Is this our destination for today?'

Buckland looked annoyed, as he always did when asked a question he had no answer for. 'I haven't any information about that. When I know, you will know,' he said crossly, and disappeared into the station building.

Bertie nodded to Pennyfather and stood back, watching as his company passed out of the wicket gate and into the yard. Despite the long, and tedious journey with all its frustrations and delays, they were still cheerful, looked about them with interest at the new surroundings, and chatted and chaffed each other in their usual way.

As the last one passed him he turned for a word with Fenniman, who was next with A Company, but he had no more idea than Bertie what was to happen next.

'God, I hope they put us in billets!' Fenniman said. 'GHQ is here, so there'd be the chance of some decent grub. The General Staff never go without their little comforts, which tend to trickle down to the more menial levels – which is to say, us.'

'By the same token, if the town is crowded with staff, there aren't likely to be any billets free,' Bertie pointed out.

'Oh, take your ghastly logic away, you doomsayer,' Fenniman said, waving him off.

Bertie grinned and followed his disappearing company. At the wicket he came face to face with an officer in khaki, who stood aside to let him pass, then said in tones of astonishment, 'Bertie! I say, Bertie!'

Bertie raised his eyes from the tunic to the face, and a slow smile curved his lips. 'Well, bless my soul! Jack!' They shook hands heartily. 'What are you doing here?'

They both stepped to one side as the first rank of A Company reached the gate.

'Our headquarters is here,' said Jack. 'My squadron is out near Lens, but I've come in to pick up a new bus. We lost half our machines in that beastly storm on the Aisne.'

'So I heard. That was a filthy night. I spent it trying to cross the river, in the dark, on a bridge made of old boxes and frayed string.'

'Yes, we heard about the heroic crossings. Stories will be sung around campfires of your exploits in years to come,' Jack laughed.

'I'll settle for telling my son in person,' Bertie said.

'But you haven't said what you're doing here,' Jack went on. 'I suppose you're going up to the line.'

'That's where we're heading eventually, but we've been on the road for so long I sometimes doubt we'll ever get there. You said you're at Lens – what's it like up there?'

'Pretty quiet at the moment, just skirmishing with German cavalry scouts. The French have got the line up as far as Lens and the British are taking over from there north-wards as they arrive. And then the Belgians are holding it from Eepray to the sea.'

'From where?'

Jack spelled it. 'Y-p-r-e-s. God knows how it's meant to be pronounced, but the Tommies call it Eepray, so it's as well to follow suit, to be sure of being understood. There's fighting every day along the line, but what's worrying the powers that be is that Antwerp's a lost cause, and they don't know where the Germans who've been besieging it will go when it falls. If they head our way . . .' He shrugged.

Bertie knew what that shrug meant. 'But we've been outnumbered from the start,' he said, 'and we've still beaten them back every time.'

Jack nodded. 'It has been rather a tea party, hasn't it?'

'It seems to have suited you,' Bertie commented. 'You look flourishing.'

'You look as if you've rather been in the wars, if you'll pardon my saying so.'

Bertie laughed. 'That's tactful! I look like a scarecrow. I've sent home for more kit, but I keep being moved before it can find me.'

Jack had not only meant the uniform. Bertie looked older, thinner, almost gaunt in the face, and his eyes had the long stare of the soldier who has seen men die – too many men. All of them in his squadron knew about the casualty rate in the BEF. Their own lives were safe and outrageously comfortable by comparison.

'Talking of home,' Bertie went on, 'I don't suppose you've had any news, have you? I expect there's a letter following me about as well as my kit, but I haven't heard anything in weeks. How is everyone at Morland Place?'

'Oh, very well,' Jack said. 'Uncle Teddy's busy with this volunteer battalion he's helping to raise – have you heard about that?' Bertie shook his head. 'The York Commercials – what they call a Pals unit.'

'Ah! I've heard of them.'

'I had a letter from Jessie a couple of days ago. Bless her, she's such a good correspondent! It's quite a lark. Everyone in York loves Uncle Teddy again because of all he's done to raise and kit out the battalion. He's a changed man, and Morland Place is buzzing with visitors. Ned's joined it, and they're going to make him an officer. They're all in camp now, in some God-forsaken place up on the moors – bitterly cold, apparently.'

'Ned volunteered? I thought he might.'

'And Frank is training in Hounslow, and Lennie Manning – I'm not sure if you ever met him?'

'Yes, at Morland Place when I went to say goodbye.'

'Well, he was the first to volunteer, and he's in camp near Scarborough.'

Bertie was not interested in this. 'So is Jessie left all alone?'

Jack laughed. 'You talk as if she's a frail little butterfly, helpless without a man to guide her, instead of a hard-headed woman with her own business – not to mention

Morland Place just down the road if she does want help, which I can't imagine.'

At that moment Bertie saw Buckland emerge from the back of the station building into the yard. He looked round and caught Bertie's eye. 'I shall have to go,' he said. 'My CO.'

No more needed to be said. 'Of course,' said Jack. 'Look, are you staying here for any length of time?'

'I really don't know. We haven't had our orders yet.'

'Because I'm staying the night. They haven't finished putting my new bus together, so I have to collect her tomorrow morning and fly back. If you are staying in St Omer, we could have dinner and a good long talk.' He scribbled in his notebook and tore out the page. 'This is the address of my billet. Come along if you can, and we'll go out and celebrate. If I'm not there, I'll leave word where to find me.'

Bertie folded the page and slipped it into his tunic pocket. 'If at all possible, I'll be there. There's nothing I'd like better than a chinwag.'

'Good. And I know a decent little café where the food's cheap and the wine's cheaper. We can down a bottle or two.'

'It sounds too good to be true.' They clasped hands again. 'If I don't see you – take care of yourself,' said Jack.

'You too,' said Bertie. They looked at each other consideringly for a long second, aware that danger and death could not be guarded against; then Bertie turned away.

When he reached Buckland, the colonel said with interest, 'Was that one of those flying chaps you were talking to?'

'My cousin, sir,' Bertie said.

'Ah, good show. Did he have anything interesting to tell you about the situation?'

'Only that Antwerp was a lost cause.'

'Oh, well, we knew that.' Buckland seemed inclined to be peeved. 'These Flying Corps types talk about being the only chaps who can gather information, but when you ask them they never seem to know anything useful.'

Bertie wondered how many RFC flyers Buckland had ever spoken to, to come to this judgement, but he couldn't very well ask. Instead he waited in silence to see what he had been called over for.

'We'll be moving out shortly,' Buckland said at last. 'I'm afraid it's Shanks's mare from here. We're heading for Cassel – that's about twenty-five miles or so. We won't go far today, though. We'll bivouac in a field and march to Cassel tomorrow, and I'm told there's a good chance we'll be given transport from there to the line.'

So, no dinner with Jack, Bertie thought sadly. But he had hardly dared hope such delight was possible. At least he had a horse: Fassner had been wise enough to get a chitty for the racehorses that the cavalry had 'stolen' from them, and by a stroke of luck there had been a batch of replacement mounts newly arrived at Soissons railhead when they reached the town. By a mixture of wheedling and threats he had extracted horses for all of them. Bertie had got a nice young bay with long ears – always a sign of equine good temper, he believed. He had needed a horse, for they had not taken a train at Soissons, but walked all the way to Compiègne. As he had ridden along beside or in front of his men, he had often thought about Kestrel and Nightshade, and wondered what had happened to them. Probably another passing unit would have taken them by now. It was sure that he would never see them again. It was as well not to get too attached to horses in a war.

The battalion was all formed up in the railway yard and ready to move off when a staff runner came and took the colonel away. Bertie ordered his men 'at ease', and when the wait extended he let them sit down and light up. They waited – and waited. It began to grow dark. At last Buckland came back and said that there was a change of plan: instead of marching to Cassel they would be taking a train to Hazebrouck, where transport would be waiting for them to take them to the line. The train would be coming in almost immediately – they must go back inside the station and cross to the other platform to wait for it.

The train eventually came in just after midnight. The men climbed aboard, cold, grumpy and hungry, and Bertie followed them up, with no great confidence that there would be either transport or food waiting for them at the other end. As the train jerked and huffed its way out of the station he reflected that there would have been ample time for him to find Jack, have the most leisurely of dinners, and still stroll back in time for the train's departure. Instead he had spent the evening standing around doing nothing. Well, that was the army for you. But the thought of the food and the wine he had missed haunted him for days.

The town of Ypres sat on the edge of the coastal plain, about twenty-five miles inland, as the crow flew, roughly south-east of Dunkirk. All around was flat and marshy land, except that on the north and north-east a semi-circle of gently rising ground created a series of ridges, like the stands of an amphitheatre. Nowhere in that part of Belgium was very high, but simply by contrast the highest point, at the village of Passchendaele, commanded a view of the surrounding countryside. From there the ground descended again eastwards to the plain and the industrial heartland of Belgium, now under German occupation. Ypres had been a wool town of importance, like Bruges and Ghent, in mediaeval times, and it had a large cathedral and many fine buildings built by rich wool and cloth merchants; but it had slipped into a backwater of history, and nothing much had happened there for centuries, apart from the arrival of the railway.

It was, however, at the centre of the last and most important part of the Allies' line. If the Germans attacked there – if they got through – the Channel ports were lost. Quietly and piecemeal the British troops were moved into position: the 7th Division, newly arrived from England, the BEF cavalry, then the 2nd, 3rd and finally 1st Corps as they were released from the Aisne by the French. The Germans, having taken Antwerp, were thought to be somewhere around Ghent. The Allied plan was to push outwards from Ypres, occupy Roulers and Menin, and advance from there to attack the Germans and drive them back.

But on Monday the 19th of October, Jack and his colleagues of the RFC, scouting ahead, found the Germans just beyond Courtrai, no more than twenty miles from Ypres.

They were crossing the plain from Ghent on every available road, moving fast, and in huge numbers – endless grey files of soldiers and artillery – and they were all too plainly heading for Ypres.

They shelled ahead of them as they marched, and soon there was the familiar pattern of empty villages, burning farms, and civilians fleeing with all they could carry, retreating by desperate stages towards Ypres with the dread cry of 'The Germans are coming!' The British advance parties retired before the overwhelming forces coming down on them; the forward establishments of artillery and cavalry fell back towards a semi-circular line around Ypres, which had to be held at all costs. By the evening of the 20th of October the Germans had taken Passchendaele, only six miles from Ypres; but there the line held.

It held, as day followed day, by dint of desperate fighting. Casualties were heavy. The British, outnumbered by factors variously calculated but never less than four to one, held on by the skin of their teeth. The Engineers crept out in the brief respite during the night to dig trenches – hardly more than shallow ditches, which were all they could manage in the time and with the equipment available – and during the day the Germans would shell and batter them to pieces. But the line held.

There had, after all, been transport waiting for the West Herts at Hazebrouck: a fleet of London omnibuses. The very sight of them had cheered the tired, supperless men: so very red, they were, in the grey of dawn, so familiar, so much the essence of 'back home' and the normality they were fighting for. Chattering like children and waving to anyone they passed, they had been carried in singular style towards Ypres.

Now for three days past they had been fighting in the line at Langemarck, to the north of the town. The Germans had thrown wave after wave of infantry against them, and they had mown down the grey hordes with their rapid fire and shrapnel shells. Bertie reckoned they must have accounted for a couple of thousand Germans; the West Herts had lost thirty men. But the losses were sharply felt in such a close-knit band of brothers. Croner, who had led the singing at church parade in his fine tenor, would sing no more. He had been beside Bertie when a piece of shrapnel had sliced through his carotid artery. Bertie had tried for a futile second or two to stop the pumping blood with his hands, but Croner was dead, and the Germans were still coming. He had to leave him, and Croner's blood dried on his hands, then flaked off as the fighting went on. Benn had also died, shot through the head by sniper fire; Church had been shot through the lungs; and Evans and his bosom pal Parry had been blown to pieces by the same shell. They had been at school together and, duffers both, had joined up together in the hope of a better life than manual labour could otherwise offer. It was sure that wherever they were now, they were together still. There had been nothing left to bury.

Last night the word had come along the line from the colonel that they were to be relieved by the French the next morning, and would be going into reserve behind the line, where they could expect to have three days' rest. The news was inexpressibly cheering. The fighting had been hard, and the shelling never stopped, so there had been no sleep for anyone. The men were exhausted and unshaven, and looked forward simply to sleeping and eating. Those of more fevered imagination might hope for letters from home, and the truly delirious even dreamed of a wash and a shave.

The exchange took place in the hours of darkness before dawn, so as not to alert the enemy. The West Herts were the last, for their relief arrived late, and just as the French unit was coming into their trenches, the Germans attacked. There was nothing for it but to stay and fight alongside the French, squashed shoulder to shoulder in the inadequate shelter, until they had beaten off the attack and the line went quiet. In the greyness of first light, while the Germans were licking their wounds, Bertie was at last able to call his men away – minus 'Chalky' White, who paid with his life for that French tardiness. The survivors crawled silently out of the trenches and assembled with the rest of the battalion back at the village, out of sight of prying Hun field-glasses. There was not much left of the village now, after days of German shelling, but there were walls enough still standing to give cover as they lined up and marched off.

Red-eyed, bristle-chinned and with a sore throat from shouting and inhaling smoke, Bertie recovered his horse, whom he had named Prospero for no very clear reason. He hauled his weary body into the saddle, and they set off down the road to Wieltje. Dawn was coming in in muted shades of saffron and pearl, and a few heroic birds were putting up silver threads of song, a counterpoint to the guns grumbling away like distant thunder on the other side of the ridges above them. It was going to be another cold, grey day, and the men would only be going into bivouac in the fields, but they were used to that now, and had learned how to make themselves reasonably comfortable. Bertie could see that the prospect of the rest, and a hot meal tonight, was enough to cheer them, and give a little of a swing to their walk.

Delayed by the German attack, the West Herts were the last of the brigade to reach the designated place, a cross-roads on the Ypres to Menin road, known as the Halte, because there was an important tram stop there. In the fields round about they could see the men of other battalions already settled in, a few on fatigues, fetching water and digging latrines, but most of them asleep, though some still lingered over the remains of their bully-beef breakfast or smoked a last cigarette. A staff officer was waiting at the Halte to direct the West Herts to their bivouac and their officers to their billets – various houses along the Ypres road.

'That's a nice surprise,' Bertie remarked to Pennyfather. 'Sleeping under a roof again.'

'Perhaps we'll even get beds,' Pennyfather said.

'Don't set your hopes too high,' Bertie said. 'Still, it may be possible to coax hot water out of someone. How I long for a shave!'

'Me too,' said Pennyfather. 'More even than decent food, really – the effects last longer.'

Colonel Buckland and the second-in-command, Major Hampton, were sitting their horses at the crossroads, in conversation with the staff officer, while the men stood easing their weight from foot to foot like tired horses, waiting to be dismissed.

'What else will you do with your rest?' Pennyfather asked.

'Apart from sleep, you mean?'

'Obviously,' Pennyfather said. 'Sleep comes first, always.'

'Oh, write home, I suppose,' said Bertie.

'Anything else? What would you do if you had the choice of anything in the world?'

Bertie played the game, letting his mind roam over exotic improbabilities. It came to him quite suddenly. 'Do you know, I have the oddest yearning to play the piano. I can't think why, because I haven't had my fingers on the keys for years.' He thought. 'I suppose playing the piano is the antithesis of war – of everything we've been doing for the past three days.'

'It's not entirely out of the question,' Pennyfather said. 'There might be a piano in the billet.'

'The merest cottage upright would do,' Bertie said, 'if Cooper can find one anywhere that hasn't been shelled to splinters.'

'I'd back Cooper to find a piano if there's one within five miles,' said Pennyfather. 'If he does,' he added wistfully, 'I'd love to hear you play it. You're right – it's civilisation. The gentle face of life – like a woman picking flowers.'

'Well, if Cooper does come up trumps, you're welcome to come and listen – though I have to warn you I shall be out of practice. Do you play?'

'I used to, when I was a boy.'

'We'll play a duet together, then,' said Bertie. 'And to hell with the Germans!'

But even as he spoke he was watching a messenger on a motor-cycle weaving his way up the road from the Ypres direction, towards the little staff group at the crossroads, and he had a sinking feeling that another disappointment was on its way. There was a despatch produced, urgent consultation, a map spread out, fingers pointing directions – not towards Ypres. Then the colonel and the major split up, the major riding towards the rear of the column and the colonel coming forward. The men stirred and straightened as Buckland passed, turning their heads to follow his passage, wondering what was going to be thrown at them now.

He reached Bertie and checked his horse to say, 'Form your men up, Parke. I'm afraid we shan't be going into reserve today. The Germans have mounted another serious attack, on Racecourse Wood this time. They're in danger of breaking through. We're wanted urgently to stiffen the line. We shall be marching off directly.'

He rode on, to repeat the message to Captain Bithy of D Company and to take his place at the head of the battalion.

Pennyfather said, 'The men are going to be awfully fed up, sir. We've only just got here. Some of these other units must have been here most of the night.'

'I'm fed up myself,' Bertie said. 'But it can't be helped. Obviously we're in a greater state of readiness. We can move at once.'

Pennyfather knew that as well as he did. It was just for relief of his feelings that he had complained. The men complained too, in undertones, as they stood to attention, then left-turned and marched off. They'd had no breakfast. They'd been without sleep for three nights. They'd been fighting only a couple of hours ago. They were tired, hungry and disgruntled.

Bertie listened to them out of the corner of his mind; the central part of it was occupied with a piece of music that had come into his head, and was rippling through it like a stream through a wood, glinting and flashing in and out of the undergrowth. He couldn't quite remember all of it – the tune disappeared and reappeared several bars later. Chopin, he thought. His hands on the reins were trying to remember the fingering. He would find a piano if it killed him, and play that piece. It was something from back home, from earlier in his life. Not from the Red House – it was Morland Place he saw behind the rippling notes. Someone playing at Morland Place, and the sense of himself being young and vigorous, happy and hopeful, everything safe and warm and lovely, as home was. The music – the music . . .

He was drifting. His body sagged as, for a fraction of a second, he fell asleep in the saddle. He jerked himself upright, and with an effort shook away the thoughts of home, and made his mind take a grip on the present. Fenniman came clattering up beside him on the wall-eyed black he had acquired from Fassner. He had managed to get more information out of Hampton than Buckland would ever impart.

'The Bosch have broken the line at the north-east corner of Racecourse Wood – it's up that way, on the crest of the next rise. The Warwicks have managed to hold them just inside the wood, and a small force of Hussars are fighting dismounted with them, but it's touch and go. We've got to get there before they're overwhelmed, and drive the Germans back out of the wood.'

'Oh, is that all?' Bertie asked.

Fenniman grinned savagely, as far removed from his bored, drawling persona of 'Ole Winderpane' as it was possible to imagine. The prospect of action still seemed to stimulate him, even after three days in the line. 'Just what we need to give us an appetite for lunch,' he said.

'I've still got my appetite for breakfast, thank you.'

'Never mind,' Fenniman said. 'When all this is over, I want you to meet me in Town, at Simpson's, and we'll have the two biggest beefsteaks ever consumed by mortal man.'

'Heroic beefsteaks,' Bertie agreed, laughing.

'Beefsteaks as big as our heads,' Fenniman said. 'Though perhaps not as fat as the colonel's.' And he turned and cantered back to his company.

They heard the gunfire long before they reached the wood, and as they lined up across the open field below and to the south-west of it, there was a continuous but irregular brattle. Racecourse Wood was also known as Polygon Wood, because of a cavalry school in the centre of it that was shaped like a polygon. It was a coniferous wood of tall, straight Scotch pines, with dense undergrowth of bushes and brambles, and heather and fern along the rides. The sky, Bertie noticed, seemed to be lifting somewhat, as if the weather might be clearing at last. Certainly it was the first time he had seen any wood around Ypres without the tops of the trees being wreathed in mist or snagged in the cloud layer. The few drifting snippets of grey vapour that he could see in the tree tops now were gunsmoke.

Wounded soldiers were coming down out of the wood, crawling, staggering, limping, helping each other along. The fighting was too fierce for regular retrieval: there must be hundreds lying wounded in there, unable to move. As Bertie rode over to the colonel for orders, a Hussar captain came towards them. He was limping, his face was black with powder smoke, and his right arm hung useless and bloody. His left arm was round a wounded trooper, who sagged at the knees, his feet hardly moving, his arm looped over the captain's shoulder as he was half helped, half carried along.

'What's the situation in there?' Buckland asked him.

The captain licked his dry lips and evidently made an effort to assemble his thoughts. 'We're pushing them back,' he said. 'But the fighting's still heavy. And there's no line in there. Men fighting everywhere, in small units, scattered all over the place. Can't see what's going on. Can't see anything but what's in front of your face. No idea who's near you.' There was a long pause while he drew his breath and his scattered wits. 'Colonel, my man here was hit by one of our own. Sir, if you go in firing, it'll be murder.'

Bertie looked anxiously at Buckland who, he had learned, had not much imagination. But Buckland said, 'I understand. Thank you.' The captain nodded and staggered on with his burden. Buckland swept his eyes round his captains. 'Tell your men it's to be cold steel only. Cold steel.' The words seemed to inspire him, and a glitter came to his eyes. 'We'll go in at the run. And let's have a good, loud yell – let our chaps know we're coming, so they don't shoot at us. Give them heart, too.'

And it might just *dis*hearten the Germans, Bertie thought as he rode back to his company. He gave the order, and saw a grin go round the grey, bristly faces of his men. An old-fashioned charge with bayonets at least made a change from the sort of fighting of the last three days. It would relieve their feelings to stab a few Germans at close quarters.

Buckland was out in front of them now, his sword drawn. Bertie thought it was a shame there was no sunlight to flash off it, which would have been in the spirit of the heroic moment. He dismounted, handing Prospero to the groom, who led him away, and drew his own sword. A small ripple of excitement ran through his men. The signal came, and Bertie shouted, 'Now, let's have a big cheer, you men, and follow me. *Charge!*'

It wasn't a cheer, it was a great yell of fury and determination. Where the energy came from it was impossible to guess, but the exhausted men ran, surged into the wood like a tidal wave. The cheer was echoed by unmistakably British voices as the unseen and beleaguered troops took heart. They hacked and forced their way through the brambles and bushes, tripped over heather roots, giving tongue like hounds. Bertie found himself yelling, without even having known that he had begun. And then there were grey men in front of him. He yelled louder, and went in with his sword, stabbing and slashing. There was a surprised German face in front of him. He noted, with some part of his brain that was standing aside from the rest, that the German was hardly more than a boy – a fresh-faced youngster, clean-shaven, fair, with that fine haze of blood under the skin that goes with extreme youth. His uniform was clean and whole. Bertie ran him through, dragged the blade clear and slashed sideways at the naked neck of the next man. They were all youngsters.

Within a few paces he had lost touch with his men, save the few on either side of him. The trees broke them up into small groups; but he could hear them yelling and cursing as they fought their way forward through the wood. There were men in grey everywhere – hordes of Germans. They hacked and stabbed and parried, and the enemy went down. Bertie took a slash across his forearm from a German bayonet, badly aimed, before he killed its owner. A rifle shot hit Henderson, beside him, and he fell, disappearing into the bracken as though slipping underwater. Bertie did not see who had fired.

He found himself face to face with a German officer, and

the officer was no older than the men. A cadet from a military academy, he thought, thrown into this bloody command when he should still be studying and chasing the town girls. Bertie had time to notice the unsuccessful moustache he was trying to grow to give himself authority. The lad had run someone through with his sword, and was now struggling to pull it free from the body. As he tugged ineffectually, he saw Bertie coming, faltered for an instant, and then began fumbling to get his pistol out of its holster. Bertie cut him down, and he fell on top of his victim. The button of his holster was still done up: he had not loosened it before entering battle. A green boy, Bertie thought. He would never learn better now.

Now the Germans were coming to him. He was able to stand still and kill them as they appeared. There were a dozen of his men in his sight, and perhaps half a dozen more khaki soldiers he didn't recognise. Warwickshires, probably. He hadn't had a chance to look at their badges yet. With the enemy thick before him he yelled, 'To me! To me!' They cut and stabbed at the grey wall, and it crumbled before them.

Now they were on the move again. A soldier appeared at his side, saying, 'Sir, sir!' Bertie glanced. It was a young man with the badge of the Wiltshires – the battalion that had been holding the line here – his face dirty and blood-spattered. His cap was gone, his hair standing up in matted spikes, his eyes crazed. 'All gone, sir,' he said. 'They're all gone. Only me left.' He was holding his rifle trailing at his side. 'No more ammo. No more nothing. Only me.'

'Use your bayonet,' Bertie told him sharply, hoping to stiffen him. 'Stick with us. Now cheer – cheer!'

Obediently the soldier raised a cracked cheer, and seemingly braced by this, or by Bertie's presence, raised up his gun and advanced at Bertie's side.

They fought on. At one time they came out abruptly onto an open ride that ran through the wood, and at once were fired at. The Germans were mustered across the path further up the ride. Bertie and his following dodged back behind the trees and, without needing orders, the men took positions and fired from cover. Some of the Germans fell, and the rest scattered, leaping for the trees.

There were still bullets flying about, and one struck a tree-trunk just beside Bertie's head, chipping out a piece of bark that grazed his forehead just above the eyebrow. The blood ran warm and freely, and he had to keep shaking it out of his eye. German backs flitted through the trees ahead, ghosts vanquished by the cock-crow of British yells. He changed direction and his men came with him, chasing the grey shapes and cutting them down as they turned to make a stand. More of them were glimpsed further ahead. These did not run, but turned and fired. The young Wiltshire at Bertie's side stopped with a jerk. Bertie had heard the smack of the bullet that had hit him – not a loud sound, but grisly. He glanced sideways and saw the small, greyish hole, quite neat, in the boy's forehead. His eyes were open, and he sighed as though he were very tired as he lay down. Bertie's yell went up a note higher as he charged. He did not hear the bullets that flew on either side of him before he reached the group who had shot the boy and, with his companions, accounted for them.

He did not know how far they had come, but the trees seemed more thinly spread, and he could see more of his men. And here was Pennyfather, by God! His sword was red to the hilt, and there was blood down one side of his face from a deep scratch on his cheek.

'Where have you been?' Bertie asked hoarsely – his voice was almost gone.

'I was just there.' Pennyfather gestured sideways. 'I was with you all the way. I could hear you.' He grinned. 'Good hunting this!'

'You're wounded.'

'Nothing heroic. Just a damned old bramble spray.'

'Sir, sir!' It was one of the Warwicks he had gathered, gesturing away to the left. Shots sang out, and grey shapes massed solidly, barred and striped by tree-trunks.

'This way!' Bertie shouted. 'Have at them, lads! Tally-ho!'

Pennyfather at his elbow, he plunged forward, and they crashed through the undergrowth back into the depth of the wood, towards the enemy. Now they were hunting back over the same ground. There were men underfoot, dead men of both sides. Bertie hated to tread on the bodies, but sometimes it could not be helped. Once when his foot struck a body, it groaned. Pennyfather fell, and he thought for a heartbeat that he had been shot, but he had only stumbled, and was up again. The men were not cheering now, not because they were downhearted but because they were breathless and dry-throated.

An unknown time later, the trees were beginning to thin again, and daylight was showing between them – not sunlight, but bright enough by contrast. They were coming to the edge of the wood. He could see more men, on both sides of him – and a lot of different badges there were, now he had time to look. Reinforcements had been sent up as they had become available, a company here, a platoon there.

And here was a new danger: a hail of fire from the open fields beyond the wood's margin. He had heard it in the background without really noticing it in the heat of the battle. They had driven the Germans back out of the wood, but they had not gone away.

'Take cover – take position!' he shouted. Of the men with him, probably half were not from his battalion, but an officer is an officer. They obeyed, glad to have someone direct them. He got down and crept forward to the edge of the trees. There were German trenches only fifty yards away. When driven from the wood the enemy had retreated to them and hoped the British would come coursing out under their guns. Some had, that was plain – there were khaki bodies as well as grey in what was now no man's land. The Germans had machine-guns, too, letting fly a stinging hail of shot. Bertie wriggled back under cover and went along his line, checking his men were in position and still alert. As more soldiers came up he directed them to extend the line, in case of another German advance. There didn't seem to be many West Herts, and he saw no other West Herts officers, though he counted the badges of eleven different battalions.

Though the sky had lifted, with perhaps the promise of better weather to come, the short day of late October was failing, and it was growing dark. The Germans were making the most of what daylight was left with a vicious barrage of machine-gun fire and shrapnel. The British troops kept their heads down and fired back when there was a lull, or when a target presented itself.

The German guns were making orange flashes now in the gathering dusk. Colonel Buckland appeared, his white face freckled with blood like the throat of an orchid. Bertie went to meet him, feeling suddenly how tired he was, how his eyes burned, how his muscles ached, as if he had been beaten all over with sticks. His sword arm trembled when he tried to lift it.

'We're going to dig in here,' the colonel said. 'We have to keep the Germans where they are at all costs. The Worcesters and Warwicks have got machine-guns, and they're going to bring them up and place them along the line – that should help. Knowing the Hun, they'll probably attack before dawn. HQ are sending up the sappers to strengthen the line, and to relieve the Hussars.'

'When are we to be relieved, sir?' Bertie asked, out of a dream of fatigue.

'Not tonight,' said Buckland. 'There isn't anyone to relieve us. We'll just have to stick it out.'

'What are our losses?'

'Impossible to say. The battalion is so scattered and mixed up with others. We'll find out tomorrow, I dare say. I know we lost Captain Fletcher and Lieutenant Biles. I saw them fall.'

'Fenniman?'

'I don't know.' Buckland fell silent, and Bertie got the impression he was struggling to remember if there was anything else he had to say. He was as tired as any of them. He roused himself. 'Do your best. Tell the men they will be relieved as soon as it's possible; but we have a job to do here, and we will do it.'

'Yes, sir,' said Bertie. He thought of the young German soldiers, the boy officer: they must surely be reserve troops. The German command was evidently throwing everything into this attack, to try to break through to the Channel. But we are denying them, he thought. The line was desperately thin, but the Germans could not break it, and never would. Never would. Fight them! German faces flickered before him as he hacked and thrust, parried and cut. He jerked awake. He had fallen asleep for a fraction of a second, even as he stood to attention before his colonel. 'We'll hold them, sir,' he said, and Buckland nodded and turned away.

They stood-to through the hours of darkness. There was a different kind of comradeship in standing shoulder to shoulder with strangers, men from different regiments, all survivors together. Now and then they fired a burst or two of machine-gun bullets at the unseen Germans, in case they were thinking of creeping up in the dark. The sappers came up to join them in what big Straw, a countryman, called the 'rabbit scrapes' that were serving them for trenches. The sappers were awed at what they had seen in the wood as they worked their way through. Bertie heard one of them say, 'It were awful – bodies everywhere. Lyin' in heaps, some places.'

And one of his own men, Baugh, still had the energy to reply, 'German buggers lyin' in 'eaps, mebbe. You wouldn't find no 'eaps of West 'Erts, mate. We was the ones doin' the killin'.'

The Germans attacked, true to form, an hour before dawn, and were beaten off, with heavy loss on their side; and as day came they retreated to their trenches and settled in for a day of shelling and firing at the line along the edge of the wood. As the previous afternoon had promised, it was a fine day, the best since they had come north: mild, with a high, transparent sky and soft, hazy sunshine. The British soldiers blinked at the welcome sunshine, and endured the shelling as best they could. The dark pines stood at their backs like sentinels, the wood quiet now, except for the sound, heard in the lulls in firing, of the stretcher parties cracking and crashing through the undergrowth and fallen trees, looking for wounded and taking out the dead. The West Herts had gone beyond tiredness now into a dream-like state in which they repeated the necessary actions without thought and almost without effort. Food came up, and ammunition, and in the afternoon the welcome news that they would be relieved after dark and go behind the line to rest.

That night they staggered out of the wood like sleep-walkers, stumbling over the tussocky grass beyond, feeling every muscle and every wound, now that the terrible effort was over. Half a mile from the wood was the safe place where the horses were being held, but though Bertie was glad to see Prospero and hear his friendly knucker, he simply hadn't the energy to mount. His groom led the horse, with Fenniman's wall-eyed black. Fenniman was not among them, and Bertie was surprised at how much he minded that. It helped to ease the pain of loss to make himself walk against the protestation of his joints and muscles.

They had not much further to go, in any case. Another half-mile further on were the grounds of a country house where they were to bivouac – the officers were to have palliasses on the floor of the orangery. Before they collapsed into the longed-for sleep, they paraded for the roll to be taken. The West Herts had lost fifty-two men, and six officers. They were once again the size of a single company, less than a quarter of the strength in which they had left Sandridge.

Despite the noise of shelling coming from beyond the wood, they slept that night like the dead, and woke late to a fine day, and the prospect of cleaning themselves up a little in the ornamental lake in the château grounds.

A messenger arriving from HQ made many hearts sink, supposing that new orders were going to drag them away from their promised day of rest; but it turned out to be news of their wounded. Eight men and two officers had been taken out of the wood during the night and were now in hospital in Ypres, wounded but not fatally. The officers were Major Foster, and Captain Fenniman.

His mind much relieved, Bertie allowed himself to be shaved by Cooper (who had managed to wangle a small amount of hot water), then went with Pennyfather down to the lake to bathe. It was very pleasant to get into the water, to duck his dusty, filthy head under the surface, to rub away

the blood and dirt from his body. Pennyfather even had a
frail sliver of soap, which he generously shared. Bertie's
various cuts stung at first when the water touched them –
there were eight altogether on his forearms, seven on his
right, the sword-arm, and the deepest the bayonet slash on
his left, plus the shallow cut on his forehead from the tree-
bark. The bayonet wound could probably do with a couple
of stitches, but it was unlikely he would get them today.
Cooper must find him a bit of clean cloth and bind it tightly
to hold the edges together. If they were not sent back to
the line tomorrow, he'd ask Buckland to let him go back
and find an aid station.

After the first sharpness to his wounds, the water both
soothed and buoyed him, and he felt a delicious lightness
of mind easing his thoughts. To be wallowing in a lake
seemed a carefree and lovely thing, a thing from another
age, from a place where men did not kill each other in dark
woods, giving tongue like hounds.

Afterwards they dried off on the grass of the lake edge.
The sun was just warm enough now, in the middle of the
day, for a ten-minute exposure; and besides, towels were
hard to come by.

'What's that you're humming?' Pennyfather asked, as they
smoked and stared at the sky. Far away the guns rumbled
on inexorably, but they no longer noticed them, any more
than their own heartbeats.

'It's that piece of music I wanted to play – you know, if
there was a piano. It's a piece by Chopin, but I don't quite
remember where I know it from.'

Then suddenly he did remember, and he began to smile.
It was the piece Jessie used to play, her 'party-piece'. He
had last heard her perform it when she was about fourteen
and he was back on leave from South Africa. And very badly
she had played it, too, thumping through it impatiently
because she wanted to be doing something else – riding, in
all probability. She had not valued the accomplishments of
soft femininity in those days, always wanting to ride and
climb and run about like a boy. Bertie remembered that he
had played that piece, too, at much the same stage of his

boyhood. He knew it well. Now he had remembered properly what it was, he was sure his fingers would recall the notes.

'I wonder if there's a piano in the château,' he said. 'I know it's all shut up, but it might be possible – don't you think, Penny? – to find a key. You said you wanted to hear me play. Penny?'

Pennyfather didn't answer. He had fallen asleep.

CHAPTER SIXTEEN

Day after day the battle for Ypres ground on. After the Allied victories at the Marne, their counter-attack had shuddered to a halt at the Aisne as the Germans dug in in a superior position. From there, each side had crept east and north-east in the attempt to outflank the other, until now the line reached all the way to the Channel, and at the other end to the mountains of Alsace and the Swiss border. There was fighting all along it, but the most crucial point was Ypres. Here the fighting was the most bitter. Here the Germans had to win, and the Allies must not lose.

Flying every day over the lines to bring back vital information, Jack had an overview of the battle, and often it was impossible to believe that the Germans would not break through. The Allied line around Ypres was desperately thin. In places they were outnumbered ten to one by the grey hordes; they were short of artillery and machine-guns; yet the British infantry's rapid fire inflicted huge losses on the enemy every day. After an attack Jack would look down on fields strewn with German dead, as thick as leaves in autumn. Even when the enemy managed to push the Allied line back a little, they seemed reluctant to build on their success, afraid to advance. Their losses unnerved them. They had not, it seemed, the spirit to press their advantage against opponents so fiercely determined not to yield.

Time and again disaster would threaten, and be averted. The ragged remains of the BEF were moved about, a company here, a platoon there, hurried into position to plug a gap, stiffen a section of the line; moved on somewhere else when the danger passed and the Germans once again inexplicably fell back. Exhausted, filthy and short of ammunition, the British soldiers fought and marched and stood-to again, almost without rest or sleep. Their numbers were shrinking all the time. Jack knew that the battalions down below him had been reduced to a shadow of their former strength. The Royal Welch Fusiliers had all but ceased to exist, with fewer than a hundred left of the eleven hundred who had come out from England. Some battalions were down to a third of their strength; he had heard that the West Herts numbered less than a quarter.

Jack often thought about Bertie and wondered how he was – wondered even if he had survived at all. He wished they could have had that dinner in St Omer; he was haunted by the thought that it might have been their last chance to speak to each other. He sometimes felt guilty, in the evenings at their billet, safely out of shelling-range of the enemy (for the precious aeroplanes must be preserved at all costs). He thought about Bertie and his men standing-to all night, unsleeping, unshaven, clothes stiff with dirt. The RFC took risks enough during the day – they had all been shot at, and mechanical failure was a constant threat. They had lost Hoggard, who had gone out on patrol one day and simply not returned. They had no idea what had happened to him. He might have run out of fuel, had to land behind the enemy line and been captured. He might have got lost in murky weather, ended up over the Channel and gone down into the sea with engine failure; he might have been shot down, and ended his life as a flaming fireball plunging to earth. Such fates could happen to any of them, at any time.

But though they flew in conditions that at home would have been deemed 'not suitable', and at risk to their lives, they could not fly in the dark. In the evenings they had the comfort of a proper mess, food that, if basic, was at least hot and plentiful, companionship, conversation, cigarettes and even alcohol; and they slept at nights under cover, and undisturbed by enemy attack. When he wrote to Helen, he wondered when Bertie had last been able to receive a letter

344

from his wife. When he sat in the battered armchair in the farmhouse kitchen that served them for a mess, smoking a cigarette and listening to Flint and Vaughan arguing about cricket, he thought of Bertie crouched in a shallow trench listening to the shells screaming overhead – or, worse, lying already cold in one of the mass graves around Ypres.

Since the beginning of the battle, the tiny Belgian army had been gallantly holding the northernmost section of the line between Ypres and the sea, along the River Yser; and overflights had told Jack, as clearly as it must have been known to those down below, that they could not hold out indefinitely. Only the marshes and the numerous waterways delayed the German hordes. At the end of the month, the order came from the King of Belgium to open the various sluices and dams that kept the marshy land viable. Helped by the rain, which had returned after a short respite, the ditches filled and the fields flooded, the sea ran up the tide-diks, the Yser spread out over its banks and captured neighbouring streams and canals, and soon a shining expanse of water stretched from Nieuport on the coast inland as far as Dixmude. It formed a natural defence against the Germans, and the weary Belgians were released to help with the defence of Ypres itself.

But the benefit worked both ways. The German troops on the Yser were also freed, and on the following morning, flying his Bristol over Courtrai, Jack saw huge troop movements: thousands of German infantry and artillery from the northern section, marching in that now-familiar grey caterpillar along the road to Ypres. There were troop trains, too – five of them – creeping along. Never before had Jack longed so urgently for a bomb. Hague Convention or not, he would have had no hesitation in dropping it.

The attack came on the last day of the month along the Menin to Ypres road. Overflights revealed the Germans massing about a mile to the east of the British line, which was across the road at a village called Gheluvelt. The defence was a brigade of five battalions, which nevertheless numbered only about a thousand men. They were dug in as best they could manage in shallow trenches and rifle pits. Entrenching tools and shovels were hard to come by, and as even a garden trowel was a prize by now, trenches could never be deep enough to give proper protection.

The West Herts had been in the line at Racecourse Wood, and had been pulled out at nightfall to go into reserve. They came out of the wood into the field on the south side, and slumped down to sleep on the damp grass, which was what passed these days, Bertie thought, for a bivouac. The bayonet slash in his arm had opened up again, and the wound nagged at him. They had only had one day of rest in the country-house grounds before going back into the line that same night, and he had not had a chance to get it stitched or find a piano. They had lost Major Hampton yesterday to machine-gun fire, which had torn open his chest and almost severed his right arm. The colonel had seemed surprisingly upset by the loss, given that he had only known Hampton a few weeks – but then there were so few of them now, they had all grown closer. Now as they settled down to get what rest they could, Bertie instinctively sat down beside Pennyfather, as though there might be warmth to be drawn from him. They didn't talk – they were too tired even to smoke – except that Pennyfather remarked, 'The rain's stopped,' and Bertie grunted in reply.

It was very cold – though Bertie thought they probably felt it more because they were all damp right through – and soon a little breeze got up, which bowled away the clouds, leaving the sky clear under a fine, almost full moon. Bertie lay staring up at it, fascinated by its brightness, hard silver, and the faint yellowish halo around it. It was the first moon he had seen for – how long? He couldn't remember. Perhaps since those early days before Mons, the golden harvest days. He felt the brightness of the moon ought to convey something to him – some message he was not getting to grips with – but then he fell asleep.

He was woken by the crash of shell fire, and jerked up, staring round wildly. Ah, there, away down to the south-east – the sky lit up dark orange for an instant before each thump. The Germans were shelling the line at Gheluvelt, he thought – that was what the moonlight ought to have warned him of. But there was nothing for the West Herts to do about it. He tilted his watch to the moon – two hours until moonset, when presumably they would have to stop. He lay down again to sleep.

He woke to darkness and silence: the moon was down and the sky had clouded over again, and there was no light anywhere, not enough to be able to read the time on his watch. There was no smell of dawn yet – he guessed it was about four o'clock. Beside him Pennyfather had rolled on to his back and was snoring lightly. The cold and damp had crept so far into Bertie's bones he felt for a moment that he would never be able to stand up again. He tried moving his feet and couldn't feel them; but at least his arm had stopped hurting. He contemplated getting up and walking around to restore the circulation, but fell asleep again even as he thought about it.

When he woke the luminous underlight before dawn had seeped in, and he could see men around him stirring, some sitting up and searching for cigarettes. There was a fine, prickling drizzle – the sort the Scots call a haar, hardly more than a heavy mist, really, but unexpectedly soaking. He sat up, rolled over to his knees, then staggered to his feet and stamped clumsily around, suffering an agony of pins and needles as the feeling came back to them. He sneezed several times and fumbled out a wet handkerchief from his wet pocket to blow his wet nose.

'Bless you,' said Pennyfather, sleepily. 'I wonder which poor devils were taking the shelling last night.'

He creaked to his feet, his hair a draggled haystack. Before Bertie could answer, the murk to the south-east flashed yellow and the heavy flat 'wallop' of an artillery gun followed. 'The same poor devils who are taking it now,' he said.

'God, those Huns don't waste a minute, do they?' Pennyfather grumbled. 'Oh, thanks.' He accepted a cigarette from Bertie and they lit up, and stood staring through the half-light towards the invisible guns.

'Softening up the line,' Pennyfather said. 'There'll be an attack later, sure as eggs.'

Bertie only nodded. As the reserve, that was probably where they would be sent.

The bombardment went on, gathering weight and pace until it was a continuous pounding, far beyond thunder, an unremitting insanity of ear-battering explosion that made the ground tremble, even all the way back here, well out of range. They knew enough to know what those 'poor devils' down there would be suffering, as the village, their trenches, the very ground disintegrated, boiling into fragments all around them. Nothing to do but keep down and endure, wait for it to stop. No way to avoid death, if it was coming for you. Just lie still, pressed as close to the earth as possible, and die or live as the whirling fragments decided.

A supply lorry came bumping across the field, bringing breakfast to the damp and hungry West Herts, cold bacon and, surprisingly, bread instead of biscuit – a little stale, but still wonderful to a palate starved of variety. And it brought something more delightful still to Bertie: Fenniman was there, having 'cadged' the ride from Headquarters at Hooge Château, two miles back down the road, where he had been left by the transport that had brought him from Ypres. When he had reported himself to the colonel he came straight over to Bertie and Pennyfather, and all three grasped hands in silent joy at seeing each other again.

Cooper came up with hot tea for them, three mug handles in one hand, rough bacon sandwiches in the other. He was the only officer's servant to have survived, and had taken Bertie's friends under his wing. He grinned at Fenniman. 'Welcome back, sir.'

'Thank you, Cooper. It's good to see you in one piece.'

'Same to you, sir. Breakfuss, sir?'

'I've had some, thanks. Give mine to these officers.' He turned to Bertie and Pennyfather with a teasing smile. 'I had breakfast at the château. By invitation – sat down at the aides' table. Linen, silver, eggs and bacon, sausages, toast, coffee.'

'That's enough of that sort of talk, my lad,' Bertie said sternly. He sniffed ostentatiously. 'What *is* that smell?'

Pennyfather fell in with it. 'I think it's cleanliness, sir. I think Captain Fenniman may have washed recently. With soap.'

'By golly, you're right. Now I look at him, he's had a shave, too. Fen, you're a disgrace to the regiment – going against all our finest traditions of dirt, filth and muckiness.'

'Laugh, do,' Fenniman invited kindly. 'I am impervious. I slept in a bed last night.'

'Swine! By God, it's good to see you, though,' Bertie said. 'I thought we'd lost you in that damn' wood. What happened?'

'Head wound, as you see,' Fenniman said, touching the bandage wound round his forehead, above which his dark hair stood awkwardly. 'Nothing too desperate, took a few stitches, but I was concussed as well, so they took me in to the hospital and made me stay until I stopped seeing double and hearing bells.'

'Well, you've come back at the right time,' Bertie said. 'Judging by *that* lot, we'll be in action later today.'

Fenniman nodded, and sipped his tea. 'They've been fighting down there already. I brought a message for the colonel from HQ. "The enemy attacked at Gheluvelt at daybreak, but were repulsed with heavy losses." God knows what our losses were. But the line held, at any rate.'

'And now they're shelling again,' Pennyfather said. 'I've never heard a bombardment like it. It must be the worst ever.'

'I heard something interesting from one of the aides at the château,' Fenniman said. 'It seems our signallers intercepted a Hun message early this morning. The Kaiser himself is visiting the area. He's going to be at their headquarters here around mid-morning – that's about a mile beyond Gheluvelt. Naturally the local commanders will want to put on a show for him. I dare say the old lunatic is not best pleased that they haven't broken through and squashed us yet. So we can expect to have everything including the kitchen sink thrown at us today.'

'Ah, hence this mighty barrage,' said Bertie.

They looked at each other thoughtfully. With the Kaiser himself watching, the Bosch would be determined to break through. No officer could afford to fail under the very eyes of the dictator. Every reserve would be called up. The Menin road was the road to Ypres, and if it were taken, Ypres would fall and Calais would lie undefended.

'You really have come back at the right time,' Bertie said lightly, to cover the sudden thumping of his heart. 'We'll soon dirty that uniform for you again.'

At last, in the middle of the morning – perhaps when the Kaiser arrived at Headquarters – the shelling stopped and the Germans advanced. The deafened survivors in the battered remains of their trenches and rifle pits lifted their heads from the debris and began firing. It was the same old rapid fire that had decimated the Germans time and time again, and though they were heavily outnumbered they managed to hold off the enemy for an hour. But it could not last. The order went out to save the guns. The artillery teams flew back towards Ypres, turning to make a stand half a mile further on at Veldhoek, and the infantry began to fall back. The Germans took possession of what remained of Gheluvelt – shattered, pitted, strewn with debris, its church spire ablaze, black smoke rising from a dozen burning buildings – moved their guns up and began to shell the area beyond, the Menin road, the woods, fields and villages on either side of it.

As the retreating British scrambled back towards Veldhoek, one unit, the South Wales Borderers, had managed to hold its position in the grounds of Gheluvelt Château, which lay just to the north of the road beyond the village. The West Herts, up on the higher ground below Racecourse Wood, waiting to be called into action, could see huge numbers of German reinforcements marching up the slope from the east towards the Gheluvelt village. The Borderers were all that stood between them and the open Menin road, and they were now perilously isolated, in danger of being surrounded.

At Hooge Château, General Lomax sent out his orders to Colonel Buckland: advance at once to the relief of Colonel Leach and the South Wales Borderers at Gheluvelt Château.

Every man of the West Herts could see the urgency of the situation. They were the last reserve troops, the last thing left for the general to throw into the fight, to plug the gap that had opened up to Ypres, Calais and England.

They fell in and Colonel Buckland gave them their orders. It was proof of the gravity of the situation that he even added a hurried few words of encouragement: 'I know you will all do your duty, in the best tradition of the regiment. This may prove one day to be the most important battle of our history. "And gentlemen in England now abed may think themselves accursed they were not here." Look to your officers, and give your all. Think of your wives and mothers and sisters at home.'

The men raised a cheer at the last words, though Bertie had thought they looked a little bemused at the rest. Buckland, he thought, seemed almost dazed.

Fenniman evidently thought so too. '"Gentlemen in England now abed"?' he muttered, as he passed Bertie to take up his position. 'The Old Man's been at the cooking sherry.'

Bertie shook his head slightly at Fenniman, and took up his own position. The order was given and they started down the slope towards the burning spire of Gheluvelt, between which and them, hidden behind trees in low ground, was their objective. The colonel's words had been oddly chosen, as far as the men were concerned, but they resonated in Bertie's head. He kept thinking 'We happy few, we band of brothers.' So few they were now, that they were as close as brothers.

There was a sickening scream in the air. The ground in front of him burst upwards in a fountain of earth and stones, and lethal shards of shrapnel whined past his head. The German artillery down in Gheluvelt had spotted them. Now they were for it.

They were in an open field on a hillside. There was no cover, nowhere to hide, nowhere to run but forward, nothing to be done but advance into the lethal storm of shrapnel.

'Come on!' Bertie shouted, and led the way at a steady trot.

It was worse, much worse, than lying down under a barrage, for the odds of being hit were infinitely greater; yet in another way it was not so bad. Lying down under a barrage your blood was cold. You had time to think, listen for the next shell, wonder if it was for you, brace yourself for the explosion and the ripping pain, then suffer the slump of relief and the rewinding of tension before the next one – over and over in a tightening corkscrew of anticipation.

Now they were simply running for their lives. Blood coursed hot through their veins, kept their legs pumping, their lungs dragging in air. There was no room for anything but effort, to get down to the trees. Fear became fuel. Bertie felt light with it, almost hollow.

Men were falling on all sides. He saw big Straw, the country boy, go down, decapitated by a whirring dinner plate of shrapnel. His body fell forward and skidded along face down on the grass for a pace or two. But what did you say instead of 'face down' when someone had no face? Duck-footed Underwood tripped and went sprawling, but Smith beside him caught his arm and jerked him back upright without breaking stride. A second later Smith was hit in the chest and went over backwards, his arms flung wide to the sky.

How any of them survived was a mystery to Bertie. The air was thick with death like a swarm of hornets, but it missed him and went on missing. He felt a sharp, burning pain along one thigh, but his legs kept running so he guessed he had only been grazed. And then they were slithering and scrambling down the last bank to the trees that surrounded the château's grounds. The château sat in its parkland in a natural hollow, and they were out of range of the guns. As they paused to re-form, Bertie looked back, and saw the hillside scattered with khaki shapes, abandoned in death. They must have lost fifty or so. Well, he thought grimly, there were enough of them left to let the Germans feel their presence.

Fenniman scrambled up to Bertie. 'Hot work,' he said. His bandage was missing, and the lattice of stitches was exposed, crusted with black blood, marching up his forehead and into the shaved patch in his dark hair.

'Where's the colonel?' Bertie asked.

'Gone,' said Fenniman. 'Poor devil.'

'You're in charge, then.'

'I'm going to recce,' Fenniman said. 'Come with me.'

They crept forward through the trees, which fell away to an open stretch of parkland, dotted here and there with oaks and cedars, beyond which was the château, its windows heavily shuttered. They could hear sporadic gunfire from beyond it, and further off the boom of heavy guns as the German artillery pounded the Menin road.

'The Borderers are still fighting, then,' Fenniman said. There was no time to waste. 'Which way do you think?'

'Round to the right,' Bertie said.

'I agree. Silent until we get round the side, then yell like hell.'

'Right.'

They hurried back to the men and passed the orders along the line. Bertie ran his eye along the rank, and thought he had never seen such a villainous-looking crew, nor one to whom he would more willingly trust his life.

'Right, lads,' he said. 'Let's go get 'em. Sic, boys!'

The men grinned back at him, the elation of battle washing away their tiredness.

They ran silently and quickly across the open ground to the château, skirted its side, and broke out yelling into the battle that was going on on the parterre. The remains of the Borderers were grimly firing from the cover of low walls and stone urns, but the Germans were creeping up and threatening to outflank them. As the West Herts appeared, it was hard to say who was the more astonished, the Borderers or the Germans. The former turned white eyes and black faces towards them, the Germans reeled back in shock. The West Herts took them at a run, before they could recover enough to form up and fire. They bayoneted them, grappled with them hand to hand, shot them as they fled. Bertie emptied his pistol and then, running forward across the lawn, stooped to pick up the rifle lying beside one of the many fallen and used that.

A crazed-looking German came at him from the side,

almost stumbled into him. There was blood running down his face from a head wound – probably he was dazed and hardly knew what he was doing. Before Bertie could get the rifle up the man had grabbed him by the throat with both hands. He was a huge, powerful man, probably a farmer or labourer, and his hands were like hams. Bertie choked and gasped, lifted off his feet. Black spots began to surge before his eyes. He pulled out his empty pistol and battered at the man's head with the butt, but he did not even seem to feel it. Bertie felt himself failing, and knew a moment of despair. And then there was a smacking sound, and the German's glaring blue right eye opened wide and turned red and black. Something warm spattered Bertie's cheek, and the giant released him and toppled backwards like a tree.

As he retched for breath, Pennyfather appeared beside him, pistol in hand. He had shot the German through the eye across Bertie's shoulder. 'Glad you didn't miss,' Bertie gasped.

'A target that size?' Pennyfather said. 'Are you all right?'

Bertie nodded, looked around. The Germans were running, unnerved by the sudden appearance of the West Herts. 'After them,' said Bertie.

They drove the enemy out of the château grounds, back towards Gheluvelt. The West Herts hunted them like dogs going after rabbits, their blood lust roused by the advance through the shrapnel and the number of their friends they had seen fall.

Bertie directed his men to flush out pockets of Germans sheltering behind trees and in shrubbery, behind the kitchen-garden wall and the potting shed. When the last of these was dealt with, and he was calling his company back together, the colonel of the Borderers ran across to him.

'Leach,' he said, shaking Bertie's hand. 'Commanding officer. Thank God you've come.'

'Captain Parke, sir. Our colonel fell on the hillside. Captain Fenniman is the senior officer now.'

Fenniman joined them at that moment. The colonel shook his hand, too. 'You were just in time. Damned Bosch were outflanking us. Fenniman, is it? Not related to Algy Fenniman, by any chance?'

'My father, sir.'

'Good God! I was at the House with him. Splendid fellow. You look just like him. Now, look here,' he went on, 'we've got these devils on the run, and we've got to keep it that way.'

'Yes, sir,' said Fenniman. 'They've taken Gheluvelt and they're moving reinforcements in.'

'Right. We must stop them advancing if possible. There's a sunken road on the other side of those trees, between the château grounds and the village. We must drive the Germans to the other side of it. Have you got a machine-gun?'

'No, sir. We lost ours some time back.'

'Right, we'll use ours, set it up in the sunken road, and we can hold them there. It's an open field on the other side. They'll have no cover closer than the village. Once we've driven them back, we'll reform the line across the road, with your men on our right, and retake the village. Clear?'

'Yes, sir,' said Fenniman.

The colonel suddenly noticed the state of Fenniman's head. 'I say, are you all right?'

Fenniman grinned. 'Never better, sir.'

From the sunken road, with the aid of the machine-gun, they inflicted a slaughter on the Germans, carpeting the field with grey. Bertie went along his line, encouraging his men hoarsely – his throat was sore and swollen from the German giant's hands.

Baugh called to him: 'Sir! Sir!' He was kneeling by a body in grey. There had been a number of dead Germans in the lane when they took it over. 'This bugger's not dead, sir,' Baugh said. 'He keeps saying something.'

Bertie went to him. Not one of the blond giants, this, but a thin-faced, dark man. The front of his tunic was black with blood. His lips were moving, but Bertie could not make anything of it.

'I was using him as cover, sir,' Baugh said, in offended tones. 'I thought he was a goner.'

'*Bitte*,' the German whispered. '*Bitte*.'

'Bitter it bloody is, an' all,' said Baugh, and made a gesture of hitting him with his rifle butt. 'I'll give you bitter, mate.'

The German flinched, and his shaking fingers went to the top pocket of his tunic. He pulled something out and offered it to Baugh, and then, as Baugh began firing again, to Bertie. '*Bitte*,' he whispered.

Bertie took it. It was a photograph of a very slender woman in white shirt and dark skirt, with her hair plaited into a crown round her head, and her hands on the shoulders of two children, a girl and boy of about ten and six.

The German mumbled something else, and made a gesture with his hand, away. Help me, for the sake of my wife and children – was that it? Bertie handed the photograph back. 'I can't do anything for you,' he said brusquely. The man's face was chalk white and his lips were shaking with terror. 'We've all got wives and children,' Bertie said.

'Right, sir,' said Baugh approvingly. The German mumbled again, and Baugh kicked him, not hard but emphatically. 'Shut your mouth. I haven't got time for you.'

Just then there was an officer's whistle, and Bertie looked away to see Colonel Leach signalling that they should advance. It was the agreed plan. Bertie shouted to his company and they scrambled out of the sunken lane, leaving the German behind. Bertie often thought about him afterwards, wondering what had happened to him. Probably he had died – there was a lot of blood on his tunic. It was strange that he could never afterwards remember the man's face, but the faces of the woman and the children in the photograph remained with him.

By nightfall they had driven the Germans out of Gheluvelt, and the enemy had retired out of range to lick their many wounds. The troops who had retired had come back up the road and the line had re-formed and was steady. The artillery returned and set up in the fields to either side, from which position they shelled the enemy all night, in retaliation for the barrage they had inflicted that morning.

Towards dawn the West Herts were relieved and came out of the line to a field just behind the artillery where they could sleep for a few hours. The messenger who brought the order talked earnestly with Fenniman for some time, and when they were settled in the field, Fenniman sought out Bertie and told him what he had said. 'It seems a German shell landed on the Hooge Château this afternoon, and completely wiped out Headquarters. General Lomax was killed. General Munro badly wounded. Seven staff officers killed.'

'And Sir John French?'

'No, by a piece of luck he was out in his motor. But listen to this: apparently when French got the news about HQ being shelled, he thought it was the last straw. The roads were choked with wounded and guns going back, the troops were retiring, the Germans were shelling everything within reach, and there were no more reserves to send in. He thought we were done for, that the Menin road lay open and the Germans were about to sweep through to the Channel. He was just about to drive off and find General Foch to ask him for help – and a thin help that would have been! – when the news reached him that the Germans had been driven out of Gheluvelt and the line was steady again.' Fenniman grinned triumphantly. 'And you know who that was.'

'Us,' said Bertie, with a deep sense of satisfaction.

'That's right. We saved the day, Parke old man. We saved the day! Three cheers for jolly old us!'

'Us and the Borderers.'

'Bless 'em. We couldn't have done it without 'em,' he acknowledged. 'D'you know? I think this may be the best day of my life.'

'It's one to remember,' Bertie said.

Fenniman stepped closer and lowered his voice. 'Do you know what I keep thinking of?' he said, almost shamefacedly. 'The colonel. Poor old Buckland and his speech. "And gentlemen in England now abed." It wasn't such rot after all, was it? And he missed it. I'd like to take back all the unkind things I've ever said about him—'

Bertie was surprised. This was sentiment of a high order. 'You would?'

'I would,' said Fenniman, 'but unfortunately they were all true. Still, if I had a glass to raise, I'd raise it tonight to the Old Man, poor devil. He loved the regiment, even if he

357

was an ass, and he ought to have been here. I shouldn't have laughed at him.'

Bertie laid an arm across Fenniman's shoulders. 'I think you're suffering from shock, old chap.'

'Perhaps I am,' Fenniman admitted. His face suddenly drained of animation. 'Christ, I'm tired.'

'We all are.' Bertie gave an ironic smile. 'But cheer up, it will all be over by Christmas – don't you know that? I read it in the newspapers.'

'Of course. I'd forgotten for a moment. I'd give anything for a drink.'

'So would I,' said Bertie.

Like magic, Cooper appeared before him at that moment, and proffered a leather-and-silver hip flask. 'Sir? A little nip to keep out the cold, sir?'

Bertie took it, staring. 'Where on earth did you get this?'

'Compliments o' Kaiser Bill, sir,' Cooper said smartly. 'I took it orf one o' the Germans in the sunken lane. He didn't want it no more.'

Bertie opened the cap, sniffed at it, and shook the flask to gauge its contents.

'It ain't full, sir,' Cooper said shamelessly. 'I reckon the only way them bastards can make 'emselves put one foot in front of another is with Dutch courage.'

Bertie had no doubt who had had the rest, but who was he to complain?

'What is it?' Fenniman asked.

'Schnapps, I think,' said Bertie.

'Enough for two?'

'Three. Must keep a bit for Pennyfather. He saved my life today.'

'Everyone saved everyone's life today,' Fenniman pointed out.

'True. Anyway, a toast – you first,' said Bertie.

Fenniman lifted the flask, said, 'To Colonel Buckland,' and drank.

Bertie took it, and swallowed. The fire-water burned, then soothed his bruised throat. It was wonderful. He said, 'To all the dead today.'

Cooper nodded agreement, folding his hands together, as if in prayer. 'A-bloody-men to that, sir,' he said fervently. 'Excepting the Germans, o' course.'

The immediate crisis had been averted, but the battle was not over yet. The Germans withdrew, the Allies dug in, and the following day the shelling began again. It was the new tactic, to pound the Allies and Ypres into submission. The town was bombarded mercilessly. Those civilians who could leave fled, the rest took shelter in cellars. On the 3rd of November, the Notre Dame hospital was hit; on the 7th, in the evening, incendiary shells were mixed with shrapnel shells, and the ancient town burned. There was no manpower to put out the fires and, after the days of shelling, no reliable source of water.

At intervals the shelling would stop, and the Germans would attack the line. There was no rest for anyone. The fragile defences held, but at desperate cost. A dreary routine set in – huddle under the bombardment, stand-to, beat off the attack, sleep standing up for an hour or two, lie down again as the shelling resumed. The only variation day to day was the weather. After several days of mizzle, there came two or three of pouring rain, then a spell of chilly mist, then rain again. The shrunken battalions were moved about from place to place as need dictated, but one part of the line was much like another to the weary men. Each day was like a recurring nightmare, from which there was no escape into blessed wakefulness. There was a shortage of artillery shells, of draught horses, of clothing – most of all, of manpower. Word was that the only reinforcements that could be sent out from England were a few thousand Territorials, due some time later in November. None of the new battalions was ready.

Short of sleep, wet through, dressed in rags, the BEF endured. The only thing they still had was belief in themselves. They would not be beaten. Every time the Germans attacked, rapid rifle fire drove them back, with heavy losses; and every time, the enemy's spirit failed in the face of the BEF's determination. They were the best, the most professional soldiers ever to bear arms, and their pride sustained them. But the shelling went on day after day, and man by fallen man the defences grew thinner.

It was a frustrating time for the RFC, for the weather was always bad and often impossible for flying. They went up when they could, did what they could, reported back about the movement of the grey masses beyond the line, always so many of them – always, it seemed, more coming.

Around midnight on the 10th of November the shelling stopped, and the sudden silence woke Jack. On his palliasse in the barn, where the junior officers of his squadron now slept, he lay looking up at the darkness and listening. There was gentle breathing, the occasional rustle as someone turned over, a more furtive rustle further off as a rat scuttered through the straw. There was the sound of the wind teasing a shutter, clicking it irritably against its fastening, and the slight groaning of the barn's fabric as it flexed under the wind's pressure, the occasional sharp crack as a wall settled back. Most of all there was the steady patter of the rain on the barn roof, and the gurgle of it down the drainpipe somewhere behind his head. Wind and rain together – would they be able to get up?

He was wide awake now, and knew he would not be able to turn over and go back to sleep. To stop himself fretting about the weather, he turned his mind to Helen's last letter, which he had read so often that he had it now by heart.

From what you tell me [she had written] it seems unlikely you'll know in advance when you will have leave, or even if it will be at Christmas after all. Mother has resigned herself to a small wedding, but even that involves forward planning, and she now begins to doubt we will ever be married at all! This, I hasten to assure you, is not meant as an aspersion on your character or steadiness, but rather the resurgence of her disappointment in me. She 'always knew' that my hoydenish, unladylike ways would have me left on the shelf. Our present bone of contention is my flying lessons, which she regards with primitive suspicion. If only I would give them up, you would get leave and I would get married! I shan't give them up, of course. I am to take my ticket next week, and feel confident of passing. My instructor is a wonder, and fits me in between army and navy fellows (and privately tells me I am better than any of them – but I had the best early teacher!). By the way, I met your friend Tom Sopwith at Brooklands the other day, looking well and prosperous. His most exciting news (from a feminine point of view, I admit) is that he is to marry Lord Ruthven's daughter at the end of December. I have met her, and venture to say she is perfectly lovely, and that they deserve each other! We shall have an invitation to the wedding, if you happen to be home. I hope so much that you will be. Oh, my very dearest, I do miss you so much . . .

He drifted off into a reverie of Helen, home, marriage, and all that might entail. Some time later a peripheral sense told him that something had changed. Coming back from his thoughts, he listened again, but could not decide what it was. He was still staring up at the dark underside of the roof, and became aware that he was looking at something tiny and bright, the merest pinprick of light that was not quite steady, but dithered slightly. It was a star, he realised, seen through one of the gaps between the old, warped tiles of the roof. And then he knew what had changed. The rain had stopped. All he could hear now was the slow, irregular drip of water from wet surfaces. The wind had dropped too: the shutter was still, the wooden fabric of the barn had stopped moaning and slept at last. No wind, no rain, and a star in the sky – suitable weather! If only it held, they would be able to fly tomorrow – today, rather, for it must be towards dawn now.

He dozed a little, and crept shivering to the door of the barn as soon as the grey of first light eased the darkness. Outside the world was eerily still. Nothing stirred, and the bare trees stood quietly like people with their heads down, waiting. The grass was soaked, and a spider's web across the top of the door frame was fantastically beaded, as though it were made of strands of grey pearls. It was very cold, and his breath clouded up before him to join the mist at tree-top level.

Behind him a cross, blurred voice said, 'Shut that bloody door!'

He obeyed, and crept back to his blankets.

Bell, who had spoken, said, 'It's stopped raining. What's it like out there?'

'A bit misty. It might clear, though. We might have a good day.'

'Guns have stopped, too,' Bell discovered. 'What's old Fritz up to?'

'I hope we shall find out later,' said Jack.

After an early breakfast the flyers gathered by the hangars and stared at the sky and the trees, tested the wind with a wet finger, sought clues of smell and 'sixth sense' as to what the weather would do. The air was cold and damp. The mist had lifted somewhat but the cloud cover had returned and the sky was uniformly grey.

'There's hardly any wind,' said Vaughan.

'Not much lift in the air,' said Bell.

They pondered. The mechanics had already run out the first two machines, and they stood shivering, gummy-eyed, holding the wings, waiting in silence. Whatever happened, the decision would not be theirs. Culverhouse, his hands stuffed in his pockets, looked gloomy. Vaughan's Avro was out of commission and he had had to give up his Shorthorn to the more senior man, so he had nothing to fly anyway. Weather talk was academic to him, but he would not have been elsewhere. There was a tension in the air today, and they all felt it.

Then in the distance they heard the heavy boom of artillery.

Flint grunted. 'Fritz has woken up.' They all listened as the distant sounds built into a continuous rumbling, increasing in weight until Jack could feel, intermittently, the ground tremble under his feet. 'Going to be a bad one,' Flint went on. 'Poor devils.'

They all knew what it would be like up there at the front,

as the men lay flat, clinging to whatever scrap of cover they could find, and the fires of hell raged above and about them.

Major Pettingill came out of the farmhouse and walked towards them.

Vaughan spoke for all of them: 'Are we going up, sir?'

Pettingill cleared his throat. 'I've just had HQ on the telephone. There's an idea that the Bosch are planning something big today. You know it was pretty quiet yesterday, but—'

'It was the hush before the storm,' Flint supplied.

'Yes, quite. Well, we're getting the storm all right now,' Pettingill said. 'It's pretty hot out there.'

They nodded. They could hear how the barrage was building up.

'HQ want to know what's going on,' Pettingill said. 'Difficulty is –' he glanced at the sky '– the cloud base is pretty low. There won't be much to see above two thousand, perhaps even fifteen hundred.'

Jack spoke up: 'I think it's lifting, though, sir.'

And Vaughan: 'I believe we might find clear weather beyond the lines, sir. Anyway, we can always turn back if it gets too bad.'

Pettingill looked around them from face to face, his expression grave – almost regretful. 'It's important that we find out what the enemy is doing behind this barrage.'

And Jack felt a thrill of excitement run through him. They were going to go. The Old Man was letting them go.

CHAPTER SEVENTEEN

There really was not much lift. Jack struggled to get into the air before the hedge at the far end of the field, and had to fly straight on for some way to gain height before turning. He flew back over the squadron's farm at fifteen hundred. Looking down, he saw Deane's Shorthorn lumbering up the airfield like a well-mannered cow, and Bell's Avro just clearing the hedge. He crossed the hangars, the transport lines, the grey-brown shingle roof of the barn where he had slept last night and the red-roofed cluster of farm buildings. Above and ahead of him was Flint in another Bristol, the red, white and blue roundels bright on the underside of his wings. It was the latest solution to the problem of being shot at by one's own side, and seemed to be working fairly well. Not that many of the poor devils down there were likely to be looking upwards at the moment.

There was Ypres – what was left of it: a flattened ruin of blackened rafters, mounds of rubble, churches no more than hollow shells, large buildings split open like fruit cleaved with a knife. There was a massive hole, thirty or forty feet across, in the square in front of the cathedral where the tram lines had been ripped up and flung twenty yards into the next street. Nothing moved down there, no living thing, not a dog or a bird. With the first thump of the resumed barrage, those people still remaining in the city would have fled to their shelters below ground. Beyond Ypres, the new inland sea spread away, gleaming dully like pewter under the grey sky, merging at last with the misty horizon.

He climbed a little. The cloud base was around two thousand feet. It could have been worse. He could see the shelling now, the flashes of orange, the spurts of black and white where the shells struck. The noise was tremendous, and the air quivered with the concussion, making the aeroplane rock. He noted that for some reason the Germans were firing a large proportion of their shells at the area just behind the British line, between the front and Ypres. He puzzled over it for a moment or two. Perhaps the idea was to prevent reserves coming up to strengthen the defence. The Germans would – it was fervently hoped – have no way of knowing that there *were* no reserves. The rate of British fire would always lead them to believe they were opposed by a great many more men than were actually there.

Now the Menin road was below, and ahead was Gheluvelt, or what was left of it. The Germans had retaken it in the past ten days, and the British line was on the Ypres side of it. The Germans seemed to be concentrating a large part of their fire on this point of the line. The bombardment was so intense Jack found himself thinking that a dog couldn't live through it; though there were men down there in inadequate trenches doing just that. He wondered a moment about Bertie, then shook the thought away.

It was not hard to find the reason for the concentration at this point. Beyond Gheluvelt the road sloped downwards, and drawn up on the slope, out of sight of any British field-glasses on the ground, Jack could see a host of grey. He saw faces turn up as he flew over, and some rifles were aimed at him, but they had no chance of hitting him at this height. He made a rough estimation – anything between fifteen and twenty thousand of them, ready to advance as soon as the shelling had 'softened up' the front. HQ had been quite right to be suspicious. It was going to be a big push – perhaps *the* big push. Fifteen, perhaps eighteen thousand fresh troops, against the British line at Gheluvelt of around six thousand exhausted men.

He made a large turn – the Bristol was a very stable machine, designed to be easy for an inexperienced pilot to fly, but its very stability meant that it liked flying level best of all, and didn't turn quickly. He flew back over the line, where the ground down below seemed almost to dance under the hail of explosives. The wings rocked as a punch of air pounded upwards, and there was a hard metallic sound as he felt something strike his machine. He realised he had drifted rather lower than he had intended, and increased speed and began to climb, banking gently to turn again over the line and make another pass.

Now he had found the cloud base. Suddenly the view below him in all its tiny, colourful detail disappeared, and he was held in mute dimness. The invisible air became grey and visible, whipping past him in damp strands. His goggles were pricked with needle-point droplets. He levelled out, ready to descend below the cloud again, when his attention was drawn to the sound of the engine. The back of his mind listened to it all the time, telling him all was well; but now there was an irregularity and he focused sharply on it. There was a clicking sound, a scratchy, regular tick as if someone was tapping one blade of a revolving fan as it came round. He looked at the revolution counter, but it seemed steady. What *was* it? There was definitely something amiss up front. He climbed a little more, frowning as he listened. The noise was increasing, the regular tick becoming a clunk, and now he could feel it too as a hard vibration. Whatever it was that had hit him – a piece of shrapnel, or debris thrown upwards by a larger than usual explosion? – must have cracked a cylinder.

How bad was it? Would it get him home? Had he climbed enough to give himself gliding room if the engine should cut out altogether? There was so little lift in the air today, and he felt a cold sensation of anxiety in his stomach. The noise was growing worse at a frighteningly rapid pace. Now it was a hard knocking, now a clanging as something threatened to shake itself to pieces. He started to turn towards the compass heading for home, and suddenly there was a violent explosion, and pieces of metal flew past his head. A gout of black smoke leaped up from the engine, quickly followed by a flash. Now he could see flames, deeply orange in the grey murk, fluttering around the nose.

Fire was perhaps the most feared thing in flying. Aeroplanes were good gliders, and unless some vital part of the fuselage had broken away you had a good chance of putting down without too much damage. But to be trapped in a burning aeroplane, or engulfed by flames in the air, with no alternative but to jump out to your death, was the fate pilots feared most. Jack wasted no second on these thoughts. There was just one chance: a steep dive might put out the fire. The altimeter said he had climbed to three thousand. He flicked off the switch, closed the petrol cock, opened the throttle and pushed the stick forward. The scout whined in complaint as it dived, but after a breath-holding moment, the strategy worked: the fluttering flames disappeared. He had dropped a thousand feet. Now it remained to see if the engine would start again, and if the fire would reappear.

He flattened out and switched on. Thank God, the engine coughed into life, and there were no flames. But it clanged and rattled with the sound of something mortally wounded. It could not last long in this state, he thought. The whole aeroplane shook with the vibration, and the stick jerked about in his hands so that it was all he could do to hold onto it. If he did not put her down soon, she would shake to pieces, and if she did, he was doomed. His only chance to survive was to land as quickly as possible.

He began to descend. He did not dare to use more than half-throttle, and even so she coughed and missed and caught again, making his heart jump into his throat. In his mind he crooned to her, the invocation that Jessie had used in their childhood when spinning the dice for a game. 'Oh, dear little, nice little, kind little engine, do be good! Dear little, nice little, kind little . . .'

Suddenly the earth reappeared, first mistily, as if seen through a dirty window, and then clearing quickly into its colours of green and brown. The cloud base must have lowered since he entered it, for the altimeter said only eight hundred. The engine banged and laboured, and he knew he must put her down, but he did not know where he was. Below him was nothing but empty fields. Flyers always navigated by sight. He was on the right compass heading, but compasses were notoriously unreliable and, in any case, he did not know how far he had come. The bombardment had stopped, so he could not get any information that way. What worried him was that there were no shell holes in the ground below. Either he had flown a lot further than he had thought, or he was still on the German side of the line.

There was a loud bang, a desperate clanging noise, and the engine cut out. Any last hope he had of flying on until he saw something he recognised ended. He had no height to spare, and the damp, still air gave him no lift. He would be lucky now to get down in one piece. He leaned out and surveyed the landscape. A wood was up ahead which he had no chance of clearing. There was a ploughed field, a hedge, and then a green field, beyond which was another hedge and the whitish streak of a road.

He held her up across the plough, skipped the first hedge, and put her down on the grass. It would have been a tidy landing, except that there was a concealed drainage ditch running right through the centre of the field. The wheels hit the ditch and she flung herself head over heels, landing upside down and skidding along for a few yards on her wings, with a crackling snap of struts and wire. Jack was thrashed back and forth in his seat, and felt a savage, searing pain in his left ankle. There was a confusion of sight, sound and fear for the few terrible seconds until all movement ceased, and he was hanging upside down in the cockpit, secured by his safety-belt, with his leg screaming agony at him. Broken, he thought, as a sweat of pain ran into his eyes. What the hell was he going to do now?

He pulled off his goggles and dropped them, wiped his face with hands that trembled with reaction, and listened. In the silence left by the cessation of the engine's racket, he could hear no sound or movement nearby, just the damp stillness of a misty day without birdsong. Beyond it there was gunfire, but it was distant, and it seemed to be coming from the north.

The bombardment was the worst ever, such a pounding and battering that it was impossible to believe anything could survive it. And when it stopped, the eighteen thousand

Prussian Guards Jack had seen, the Kaiser's élite, advanced in a line across the Menin road. The stunned survivors of the barrage got up and started firing. Royal Fusiliers and Camerons were to either side of the road. In the centre, on the road itself, the front was held by Zouaves, begged from the French by General Haig, as a last resort, to stiffen the line at that most important point. The Zouaves had thought their last hour had come as the shells rained down, and when the barrage stopped and the Germans came marching up the slope in a solid wall of grey, the Zouaves broke and ran. The Germans poured through the gap, and the British on either side had to fall back to avoid being surrounded.

The West Herts under Captain Fenniman were in reserve. Yesterday they had been on the line on the far side of Racecourse Wood, but they had been pulled out after sunset and had spent the night in the valley behind Nun's Wood, a narrower copse of trees about a quarter of a mile further west. Behind them was Corps Headquarters, manned now with nothing but non-combatants, cooks and signallers and the transport section. Even the guns set up to defend Headquarters were unmanned, for the gunners, like the Engineers, had all been given rifles and sent into the line. If the Germans broke through, there was only the shrunken battalion of the West Herts to keep them from capturing the leadership.

They did not think of that as they waited through the two hours of bombardment for the big attack everyone knew was coming. They hardly thought of anything as they rested on the sodden grass, leaning against each other and dozing on and off. After ten days in the line since the last big push, there were just a hundred and fifty of them, and three officers – Fenniman, Pennyfather and Bertie. It was no longer sensible to divide them into companies or platoons. The generals called such remnants a 'half-battalion', and they fought as a single unit. They knew each other so well now, they hardly needed orders. Bertie sometimes thought it was like riding a favourite horse, which almost heard one's thoughts.

When the bombardment stopped, everyone stirred, and

Bertie told his men to take up position. They had to be alert now. But nothing happened for a long time. They could hear the sounds of war away on the other side of the woods, distant rifle fire and shouting, and then steady, heavy rifle fire somewhat closer, but they had no idea what was happening until a runner came bursting out of Nun's Wood, leaping across the rough grass towards them like a hare running for its life.

He was a Cameron, on his way to Headquarters, and the fact that he was coming across country and on foot instead of down the road told its tale.

'The Germans have broken through, sir,' he panted to Fenniman. 'We didnae see them, what wi' the smoke an' all, until they came up behind us, and then we realised they wiz nearly surroundin' us. So we had to get oot of oor trenches and get back to the wood, sir, Racecourse Wood. We're holdin' 'em off there, but there's thoosands of 'em broke aside an' they're comin' up to Nun's Wood. So Captain McNair sent me off.'

'Quite right. Good lad – go on now. Run!' said Fenniman. The boy drew in a huge breath and bounded away. 'They're coming this way,' Fenniman said to the company at large, 'but if they come through the wood, we'll be ready for them. You know what to do, men. At the first sight of those grey bastards – rapid fire!'

A cheer went up. 'Don't you worry, sir,' someone shouted. 'They won't get past us.'

The boy had not brought the message any too soon. They had hardly braced themselves for action when the first of the Germans came bursting out of Nun's Wood. They had evidently not expected to find anyone there, for they had their weapons at the hip, and when the West Herts fired they reeled back in shock. Rank after rank emerging from the trees were shot down before any of them had the presence of mind to fire back; but even then they could not match the rapid fire of the British troops. Goaded by their officers, whose orders could be heard clearly on the still air, the Germans advanced into the curtain of rifle fire, and paid the price.

'Keep it up, men!' Bertie yelled encouragement. 'Give 'em what for!'

Another ragged cheer went up from the West Herts as the advancing grey line faltered, stopped, then went into reverse. Steadily at first, then breaking into a panicky run, the enemy turned back for the woods.

'After them!' Fenniman shouted. 'West Herts – advance!'

There was no need to say more. The men were up, alight with the fire of battle, ready to pay back the days and nights of lying helpless under shell fire, running up the hill, jumping over the fallen, giving tongue like hounds. Bertie ran with his men, those who were left, as so often before – men he knew as well as his own family now: Baugh and Cole, 'Lofty' Small, Binns and Cooper, Swan, Lorne, 'Windy' Gayle, Jack Joseph, Billy Smith and 'Snoddy' Smith, Heaton and 'Bill' Harper. He yelled as he ran, though he did not know it. They plunged into the trees after the fleeing grey backs, shooting, bayoneting when they came close, driving them like game.

'It's a bleedin' rabbit 'unt!' Harper shouted gleefully.

The belt of trees was not deep, less than a quarter of a mile wide, and they soon flushed them out of the other side into the open. And there the West Herts, obedient to a word, stopped, stood and fired at the retreating hordes. There, too, were the Camerons and the 1st King's, in their positions along the edge of Racecourse Wood, to join in with the 'rabbit shoot'. There were more Germans coming up from Gheluvelt, and those in flight passed through them, were steadied and turned; but though they formed rank and tried to advance, they were out in the open, and thoroughly unnerved both by the flight of their own and by the constant, rapid and accurate fire. There were shallow trenches all along the edge of the wood, and the West Herts dropped into them as soon as the Germans began firing back. The trenches were only 'rabbit scrapes', as Straw used to call them, but the heaps of dead Germans acted like sandbags and gave extra cover.

Finally, as the light started to fail, the Germans lost heart entirely and to a great cheer from the British fell back and were soon in full retreat down the road past Gheluvelt. The day was saved, Bertie thought, with weary satisfaction.

Dusk set in, and the cold mist, which had been sinking lower all day, chilled the excitement out of them. In their shallow trenches, the men shifted, feeling the aches and pains of the day, and shivered. A runner came up with orders for the West Herts to take up position in the trenches to the right of the Menin road. The Royal Fusiliers had held them that morning, but after the barrage and the German advance, there were hardly any of them left. Fenniman formed up the men and they set off down the hill. At one point Bertie turned and looked back. From this angle the whole field was grey, a carpet of German dead. Tired as he was, the sight sickened him. The Prussian Guard, the cream of the Kaiser's troops, hardly a man of them under six feet tall, glorious on the parade ground as they marched to crashing, stirring music with the light flashing from their helmets – now they lay like dead herons, their grey plumage dull in the failing light. What was the sense of it? The British had won today, against overwhelming odds, but where would it end?

He turned his head away and walked on. Pennyfather was limping, having turned his ankle on a root in the wood. 'I hope they send us up some hot food tonight,' he said, and brought Bertie's thoughts back down to a manageable plane.

Jack managed to undo his safety-belt and, by bracing his back against his seat, did not fall straight down on his head; but his ankle was an agony and it was not possible to extricate himself from the cockpit in any very controlled way. He fell the last part and the jarring as he hit the ground made him black out with the pain.

He came to himself, staring at a section of low grey sky seen between the struts. His cooling engine had ceased ticking; the sound of gunfire was no nearer. He had no idea where he was, how far from any help. He could not walk – he doubted whether he could even drag himself very far. His one hope was the road he had seen beyond the boundary of this field. If he could manage to haul himself that far, someone would surely pass along it at some time. Experimentally he sat up and took hold of his leg with flinching fingers. Even touching it sent the pain to a new peak. Holding it as tightly as he could bring himself to, he tried to wriggle his way clear of the aeroplane, but the agony was so bad he began to black out again, and had to stop and lie back to keep the blood from leaving his head. There was cold sweat inside his clothing, and he shivered. With shaking hands he fumbled out a cigarette, lit it and sucked down the smoke greedily. It cleared his mind a little, but his thoughts were of no comfort to him. If he could not move himself even a few inches, he would never get to the road, and would have to lie here until someone spotted the aeroplane and came to investigate. With a major battle going on, that would certainly be hours, perhaps even days. He might very well die here of exposure. The clammy cold was already seeping into him, and it would be worse after dark. He had survived the crash, but ironically there was a good chance he would not survive the aftermath.

No, that was ridiculous! He was not going to die here in this feeble way. He drew again on his cigarette and tried to think of a plan. There was a flare in the cubby-hole behind the seat. If he sent that up someone might see and come to investigate. But he could not reach it lying here on the grass. If only he had thought to get it out before he released himself! Well, too late now. He must work out some way of being able to move. He would have somehow to splint his leg. What was to hand? There was his silk scarf, inside his flying jacket, that would do for a bandage. Wood? Well, there was enough of that in the Bristol, surely. Some of the struts had broken. Would he be able to wrench them off and snap them to a suitable size? Ah, yes, he told himself bitterly, but that depended on being able to move. He could not move until he had made a splint, and he could not make a splint without moving.

He was just working himself up to make another attempt at movement when he heard a shout, then several voices, and his heart jumped with relief that someone was coming. He screwed his head round and saw three men running towards him across the field, with more behind them, perhaps a dozen in all. But his joy was short-lived. They were not Belgian peasants, nor dressed in khaki. He must have come down on the wrong side of the line. They were Germans.

For a moment his thoughts whirled, seeking escape. He ought to set fire to the Bristol, so that it should not be a prize for them. He had his lighter, his engagement present from Helen, and there was petrol enough in the tank – but he could not move. The flutter of his thoughts sank down again. He could not do anything but wait, and surrender.

The first man had reached him, a good-looking young man in the uniform of the German Flying Corps. He dropped to one knee beside Jack, and there was nothing but concern in his face.

Jack did not speak German, but hoping for the best addressed him in halting French: '*Herr Leutnant, je suis officier anglais. Mon jambe est fracturé, et je veux me rendre.*'

The German smiled kindly, and said, 'Yes, we know you are English. We saw you come over. Poor fellow, does it hurt very much?'

His English was perfect, and he spoke with hardly an accent. The others were crowding in behind now, all looking down at him. There was no triumph, contempt or enmity in the expression of any of them. They seemed only anxious for him.

'It hurts abominably,' Jack confessed, feeling a flood of relief weakening him. Had he, against all the odds, fallen in with friends? 'I can't move at all.'

'We will have to get a—' His face went blank for a moment. 'I cannot think of the English word. *Un brancard.*'

'A stretcher,' Jack said.

'Yes, yes, a stretcher. Our base is just a mile away. Some of us will go back, and the rest will try to make you a little more comfortable.'

He stood up and addressed his colleagues in rapid German, and after a short discussion four of them ran back the way they had come. The others gathered round again,

374

and one of them crouched by Jack, pulled a flask out of his pocket and offered it.

'Vould you like to trink?' he asked, with a heavy accent. 'Mine English is not so goot as Altmann. I learn only *im Schule* but he has in Englant *gewohnt.*'

Jack accepted the flask gratefully and took a mouthful, which burned down his throat and warmed him. Shock and pain were making him feel very cold and shivery. 'Thank you. I don't speak German at all, I'm afraid.'

The first German, Altmann, saw him shiver and quickly took off his jacket and laid it over Jack. 'Can you tell us your name?'

'Compton. Thank you,' he said, for the jacket.

Altmann made a graceful gesture. 'We are all men of the air. Before the war I was at Oxford University, and had many friends there. I like very much England and the English. We are enemies now, but we need not hate each other.' He looked at his comrades and translated rapidly, and they nodded and agreed.

The man who had given him the drink leaned over and said, 'I am Hinkel. But vy vere you flying today? It vas not goot *vetter.* We did not go up.'

'Reconnaissance,' Jack said shortly. He was finding talking difficult now.

'We saw you pass and heard your engine noise,' said Altmann. 'What was it that made you come down?'

'Broken cylinder.'

Some of them went round to the front of the machine to inspect the damage, and a discussion broke out, with shakings of the head and sympathetic noises. Hinkel said, 'It could happen to anyone. It vas bad luck.'

Altmann said, 'You are in pain, I see. Better not talk now. They will be back soon with the stretcher, but it will hurt you when we move you, I think. Have some more schnapps.'

Jack had quite a lot more, and then Altmann lit another cigarette for him. He felt warmer, and rather drowsy, the pain in his leg a more distant jangle. The Germans left him be and chatted among themselves. They inspected his Bristol very closely, but there was nothing he could do about that.

There were no papers of any sort, but he saw them take his maps, and he tried feverishly to remember what, if anything, was marked on them that might help them.

At last the men came back with the stretcher. They were accompanied by an army surgeon, an elderly man with sparse hair and gold-rimmed pince-nez below a worried frown. Altmann translated for him as he said he would splint Jack's leg before they lifted him onto the stretcher. This operation hurt very much, as did the movement, and he fainted again, coming to to find himself being carried on the stretcher across the rough grass to the gate onto the road. Waiting there was a donkey-cart, across which they laid the stretcher, two of them supporting the ends of it to stop it slipping while others led the donkey forward slowly.

Out in the road the sound of gunfire seemed louder. Altmann had stationed himself at Jack's head, and Jack asked him now, 'Where is the front?'

Altmann gestured. 'That way. About ten kilometres.' Jack nodded wearily, and Altmann looked sympathetic. 'Almost you made it, old chap. It was very bad luck.'

The German squadron was quite comfortably settled in a large house in a village near Wervik. They put Jack to bed in a large room, furnished in the heavy, old-fashioned style of forty years back, and he immediately fell asleep from a combination of shock, pain and schnapps. When he woke it was dark outside, though a lamp was burning in the room. He lay quietly, thinking about what had happened, about the mixture of good and bad luck that had attended him. Bad luck to have been hit, good luck to have been able to put the machine down, bad luck to have broken his ankle, good luck to have been found so soon, and by airmen, of all people, who would be kind to him, bad luck that they were Germans. He thought of Hoggard, and imagined the talk back at his own squadron, as they realised he was missing. They would not know what had happened to him, either.

The door opened and Altmann came in, his fair head bare, his face ruddy in the lamplight, and smiling.

'Good, you are awake. It is six o'clock,' he anticipated Jack's first question. 'Dinner time, in fact. Are you hungry? We would very much like you to be our guest of honour in the mess, but that sadly is not possible since you cannot get up. I will bring you your dinner on a tray, and – would you permit Hinkel and me to eat in here with you?'

'I should be very glad of the company,' Jack said.

'Thank you. We shall be with you very soon. But first,' he added delicately, 'I think you might wish to be attended by a servant.'

It was a particular kindness, as Jack had just begun to wonder how to address the problem. Altman left and a mess servant came in who, though he did not speak English, seemed skilled in caring for a gentleman confined to bed. Jack guessed he had been a valet before the war. He managed everything very skilfully, with the minimum of painful movement for Jack, and afterwards helped him to sit up, provided a basin for him to wash his face and hands, and brushed his hair for him. When they had put Jack to bed they had dressed him in a nightshirt, borrowed from heaven knew who, and now the orderly brought out of one of the drawers of the large chest in the corner a woollen jacket, which perhaps had belonged to the owner of the house, and helped him put it on.

Jack thanked him, and he nodded and went away. Soon afterwards two more orderlies came in and set up a table at the foot of the bed with two chairs facing Jack, and laid out the silver and linen. Then Altmann and Hinkel came in and sat down, and a mess servant brought Jack's tray, and served the officers at the table.

It was a good meal – better, he noted wryly, than they had on their side of the line. There was a clear soup with barley, pickled herrings and cucumber, a good stew of beef with potatoes, stewed apples served with a rather strange kind of cake, very pale and dry, and then cheese and biscuits. There was German hock to drink with the soup and fish, French burgundy with the stew, and finally port with the cheese. 'It is a habit I learned in Oxford,' Altmann said. 'Port is not much drunk in Germany but fortunately I was able to take some home with me when I left, and I brought a dozen with me to the front. It is pleasant to have someone to drink it with. The others all prefer schnapps or brandy – don't you, Hinkel? I am glad to see you have a good appetite, Lieutenant Compton. How is the leg feeling now?'

Jack had indeed been hungry, and had cleared his plate at each course. His leg was throbbing painfully, but the pain was not more than he could bear, as long as he kept still.

'Better when I don't think about it,' he said, and Altmann laughed, and translated for Hinkel, who had not caught the meaning.

Hinkel now said eagerly, 'You will forgive – are you that Compton of Sopwith Company, who won the Schneider trophy?'

Jack admitted it. Altmann looked pleased. 'We thought perhaps you were. I have seen you fly, you know, at Hendon and at Brooklands.' Hinkel said something in German, and he translated. 'The names of the pioneers of flying are all known to us, especially those who have helped to design new aircraft. We are more than ever pleased to have you as our guest.'

The conversation from there on grew warm and lively. Aided by the generous food and wine, as they talked 'shop' Jack was able quite to forget not only the pain of his leg but his situation. Hinkel's English seemed to improve with use, and with Altmann to translate the technical terms both ways, they all got on very well.

It was only when the servant came in with cigars that the conversation stopped, and when they had all lit up, a sort of restraint seemed to have come with the interruption. The night was quiet outside, and Jack asked at last, rather diffi- dently, whether they had any news of the day's actions.

'Ah,' said Altmann, with a rueful look. 'That is rather a sore point to raise. Hinkel and I guessed that you would ask at some moment, and we discussed what we should tell you.' Hinkel shrugged and looked away. 'I have to tell you,' Altmann went on gently, 'that it is fortunate for you that it was we who found you, and not anyone from the other side.' From this Jack understood he meant soldiers. There was always a faint hostility between the army and its air service, and evidently that was true in Germany as well.

'What happened?' Jack asked.

'There was an important attack on the line,' Altmann said, unsmiling now. 'It – it did not succeed. Your line held, though I believe there was heavy loss on your side.'

'Heavy loss on our side too,' Hinkel said tersely. 'Your infantry fight like devils.'

Jack's heart had lifted at the news that the attack had failed, but he kept his expression grave and said, 'I am sorry for your loss.'

'War,' said Altmann, with a shrug that said everything. When men went to war, some lived and some died. That was in the nature of it. He lifted his port glass. 'Though we are enemies, there is one thing we can drink to, at least. The comradeship of the air.'

They raised their glasses, and drank the toast. Hinkel said something in a low voice to Altmann, who answered him shortly, and with a faint look of annoyance. He turned to Jack. 'I am reminded,' he said, his mouth turning down. 'Though you are honoured guest of our mess, you are also prisoner-of-war. As you are, most unfortunately, incapacitated,' he bowed politely towards Jack's leg, which throbbed in response as he thought of it again, 'there will be no need to place a guard on your door, for which I am quite glad.'

'Thank you,' said Jack.

'For now, I am the senior officer here. However, our commander, who is absent today, will be back tomorrow, and I think then he will wish to remove you from here. It will be, most unfortunately, to a prison hospital.'

Jack could only nod, his mouth dry at the word 'prison'.

Altmann spread his hands in a little, anxious gesture. 'It is true that you need proper medical care. We have here no X-ray machine, no plaster-of-paris. The doctor tells me that your fracture is a difficult one and needs more than merely a splint, but we have here no facility. For this you must either be moved to a field hospital nearby, or much further to a military hospital. Perhaps first to the one, and then to the other.'

'To a military hospital in Germany,' Hinkel amplified. 'By train.'

'I understand,' Jack said, his throat dry. 'Thank you for telling me.'

Altmann seemed to search around for words of comfort. At last he said, 'It is a great pity you do not speak German. There are books I could lend to you, but they are all in German. Reading would help to pass the long boredom of captivity.'

In a little while they left him, and afterwards the orderly came to prepare him for sleep. Alone in the darkness, Jack thought again and again of Altmann's words. *The long boredom of captivity*. He was a prisoner-of-war. He must spend the rest of the war, however long it was, in a military prison, sitting idle and useless in a cell somewhere in Germany, while Altmann and Hinkel and all the rest were able to go on flying and fighting and living their lives, taking part in the great adventure, doing their part for their country and their ideals, stepping outside whenever they liked, breathing the sweet air of freedom.

Supposing the war went on for years and years? The Napoleonic wars had lasted a generation. He would die from frustration and misery. He felt a great ache of yearning for the sky, for the peace and freedom of it. To fly high above the earth, in the great, quiet exaltation of the air, to feel the wind on his face, to hear it singing in the wires . . .

And Helen. When would he see her again? Would he even be allowed to write to her? If the war went on and on, she would forget him, or at least learn to live without him. She might at last meet someone else she could like enough to marry. Well, if he was mouldering in a prison cell, it was right that she should. He would not want her life to end as well as his. But he regretted now, so much, that they had not married when they could, before he went away. Even if he had only had one day with her, it would have been worth it, for the precious memory. Weak tears rushed to his eyes and he swallowed them down. He saw her face before his mind's eye, smiling, heard her voice. But memory was fickle, he knew that. If he were imprisoned for years, eventually he would not be able to recall what she looked or sounded like. He would only know the great emptiness inside him that yearned for her and would never be appeased.

There was no possibility of escape, in the condition he was in. And by the time his leg was healed, he would be far away in a prison in Germany. Black bitterness closed down his thoughts, and he wished he had not managed to land the aeroplane, that he had been killed outright. At that moment it seemed a better alternative than the wasteland of tedium and mental agony that lay ahead.

Early the next morning, Altmann brought the squadron commander, Unterbergen, to see him. Unterbergen was a tall man, too tall for a pilot, with a lean, aristocratic face, and greying fair hair cut so short it was hardly more than a shining stubble over his head. He wore a monocle on a gold chain pinned to his lapel, from which Jack guessed he was an administrator and did not fly any more. He did not smile, but he spoke to Jack with a deadly kindness, the kindness one would address to someone about to be executed. It filled Jack with gloom. He would rather have been shouted at and threatened.

Unterbergen spoke good English, though not as good as Altmann's, and with a heavy accent. He asked Jack many questions, some of which Jack answered, and some of which he declined to, as politely as possible. Unterbergen accepted the refusals and did not press him. It was all very gentlemanly.

When he had finished with the questions, Unterbergen sat in silence for a few moments, evidently deep in thought. Then he said, 'I think your injury is painful?'

'It's – tolerable, thank you,' Jack said.

Unterbergen nodded, as if he knew perfectly well that it was almost not tolerable. 'We have not the facilities here to treat you,' he said abruptly. 'If the bone is not soon properly set, there may be consequences. The doctor says you may have difficulty later. Perhaps not walk very well, or with—' He appealed to Altmann for the word, and when it was supplied in a murmur, finished, 'With a limp.' He paused a moment, seeking the right words. 'An airman needs two sound ankles, isn't it? I believe it is as well that you know this, what the doctor says.'

Jack bowed his head and said, 'Thank you.'

'I am very sorry,' said Unterbergen. 'We will do what we can.'

'You have all been very kind to me,' Jack said. They left him alone. Not only a prisoner, but perhaps not able to fly again, when and if he was ever released. He sank into a black reaction. When the mess servant brought him luncheon on a tray, he could not eat it. None of the flyers came near him, and he supposed they were up – the weather was grey but the sky was not so low, from what he could see through his window, and there was a little breeze blowing. Soon it would be winter, and flying would be problematical in any case. He would have had leave, almost certainly. He would have gone home and married Helen. He stared at the wall and did not notice when the servant came in to remove his untouched tray.

He heard the flyers return at about four as dusk began to fall, heard the sudden cheerful noise as they trooped in downstairs, talking and laughing about their day's adventures. He remembered his own mess, Deane and Culverhouse always earnestly talking shop, Vaughan and Flint arguing endlessly, Bell, who was a self-taught pianist and could knock out all the popular tunes by ear, singing along in a strangled voice with his pipe clenched between his teeth. Last night – or, rather, the last night he had been there – Bell had been singing 'Ragtime Cowboy Joe', and Culverhouse had picked up two ashtrays and solemnly clopped them together for the horse's hoofs. When they came in, cold of cheek and watery-eyed from the sting of the wind, they would plump themselves down in whatever chairs were available and demand tea. He wondered what the German flyers had instead. He could imagine Altmann drinking tea, perhaps, but not the others. Did they have coffee in the same sort of way, or was that whole hot-drink business an English thing? He felt suddenly very lonely. But when a little later Altmann tapped on the door and put an enquiring head around it, he pretended to be asleep. He could not bear to talk to him, and hear the pity in his voice.

He must actually have slept, because he woke with a sense that hours had passed, and a few minutes later he heard a clock somewhere in the house strike nine. The flyers would be rising from dinner, he supposed, and seeking their evening's amusements. He became aware that he was very hungry, having eaten nothing all day, and that he needed to relieve himself. He had no bell, however. He must wait until someone came.

Soon after that he heard footsteps along the passage outside, and before he could shout out, there was a tap on the door and it opened to reveal Altmann again, this time accompanied by Unterbergen.

'May we come in?' Jack nodded, but before he could frame his request for a chamber pot, Altmann, smiling with what looked like relief, said, 'We have good news for you. At least, I think it is good news – perhaps the very best.'

Unterbergen lifted a chair from beside the wall, placed it by the bedside, and sat with a businesslike air. 'As I told you this morning,' he said, 'we have not the facilities for treating your injury. But neither of the alternatives that seemed to be before us pleased me.'

Altmann, standing behind him, said, 'When one is an airman, one has a fellow feeling, don't you think?'

'It is important that your injury is attended to so that you shall not be prevented from flying in the future,' said Unterbergen. 'I have been making some telephone calls.' He smiled suddenly, the first time Jack had seen him smile, and the effect was a transformation. Jack could not speak for the hope that suddenly pressed upwards in his throat.

'You have heard, perhaps, of Leutnant Wilhelm?' Unterbergen asked. 'One of our airmen?'

Jack began to shake his head, and then remembered. 'He came down two – no, three days ago, on our side of the line. It wasn't my squadron that found him, but of course we heard the story.'

'Just so. Wilhelm is prisoner-of-war – we have been informed of so much. And it came into my thoughts,'

Unterbergen went on, 'that we are not so rich in airmen we can afford to lose him. I thought perhaps your people feel might the same.'

Altmann positively beamed. 'The commander has been telephoning all day, with the result that an exchange has been arranged, you for Wilhelm.'

Jack's lips moved, but no sound emerged.

'Frankly,' Altmann said, 'our medical authorities had no wish to waste time on you, having enough of our own people to attend to. You had become – excuse me – a nuisance to us.'

Jack managed to smile now. He could see from Unterbergen's studied air of indifference that it had been he who had made the nuisance. Telephoning all day – yes, that was it. How kind! How very kind! 'Thank you,' he managed. 'I don't know what to say.'

Unterbergen waved it away, and stood up. 'There is not much time. The exchange is to take place tonight, under flag of truce, during those hours when neither of us shells the other. Your people are to send an ambulance for you, and I believe it will be here quite soon – within the hour. I shall leave Altmann to explain to you.' He clicked his heels and bowed, and went quickly away, as if to prevent Jack thanking him any more.

Altmann grinned down at him. 'I can't tell you how glad I am for you. Now, to the arrangements. I think it will be best for you to travel in that nightshirt – which belonged to the owner of this house who had left it behind, so perhaps he does not want it. But we will fold up your own clothes and they will go with you. In a few minutes we must take you downstairs on the – *brancard*?'

'Stretcher.'

'Just so. I shall never remember it – on the stretcher to be waiting in the hall when the ambulance comes. But is there anything you require first? I think you did not have any dinner.'

Jack explained his needs, and Altmann said he would send a servant along at once. 'And I will have them pack some food for you to eat on the journey.'

'Thank you,' said Jack. 'I shall never forget your kindness.' He offered his hand, and Altmann shook it firmly.

'I am sorry I shall not have more chances to talk with you,' he said. 'I suppose they will send you home, with a broken ankle? It seems you will be home before I will.'

'Yes,' said Jack, and thought of Helen.

'You have a – sweetheart?' Jack nodded. 'Lucky man. Well, and so I will say now not goodbye, but *auf wiedersehen*. When the war is over, I shall certainly come to England again, and then perhaps we shall meet?'

'I should like that,' Jack said. 'I'll buy you dinner.'

'At the Ritz?' Altmann said. 'That is very English, isn't it?'

'For tea,' Jack corrected. 'For dinner it must be Rules. That's the most English restaurant in London.'

'Rules it shall be, then,' Altmann said. They shook hands once more.

'I shan't forget,' said Jack.

After the attack on the 11th of November, the Germans withdrew to their trenches and the line settled down to the relative calm of intermittent shelling, sniping, and the occasional raid; but from information gathered by the RFC there did not seem to be any preparation going on for further big pushes. The promised Territorials were beginning to arrive, and the British commanders began cautiously to withdraw units to send them back for rest.

The remnant of the West Herts came out of the line at six o'clock on the evening of the 16th. They were not even called the West Herts any more. The generals had taken to calling these fragments of battalions by the name of the surviving senior officer, so they were referred to as Fenniman's Force. They numbered a hundred and eight and three officers.

They marched down the now familiar Menin road, passing a battalion of Territorial sappers going the other way, distinctive by their clean uniforms and full kit. They stared in some surprise at the West Herts as they passed, and there were one or two questions and answers, in the usual jocular manner of Tommies.

'Blimey, mate, where's your kit?'

'This is it, mate. It's called a rifle.'

'Where's the rest of your mob, then?'

'They're lying about somewhere – about six feet under.'

Ypres was being shelled again, and a large building was burning. The rear of the Territorials' column was twisting round to look at the red sky and the shell bursts.

'Cor, it's just like fireworks!' one new soldier cried appreciatively.

One of Bertie's men, Mitchell, heard the remark as he passed and said in mock-happy tones, 'Oh, you'll love it up at the front, mate. Ole Fritz makes sure you get lovely fireworks, bomfires, the lot. It's like Guy Fawkes' every night – only no cocoa.'

They marched to a farm seven miles behind the line, and were directed to a barn, which, as there were now so few of them, was big enough to accommodate them all. A hot meal of stew was brought out to them by a wide-eyed ASC unit, fresh from England, together with boxes of bacon for their breakfast. The corporal in charge was worried and apologetic. 'There isn't much here, sir,' he said to Bertie. 'It's all they gave me. You are the First Battalion, the West Hertfordshire Regiment? I hope there's going to be enough for all of you.'

'There'll be enough,' Bertie said grimly.

It was wonderful to be away from the front, away from the guns, knowing they would not be called on to stand-to in the black hour before dawn. The night, as it settled down around them, was magically quiet, with no sound but the pattering rain. After the meal and a cigarette, no-one felt much like talking, and by nine thirty everyone was asleep. It was the best sleep in months. Bertie woke only once, not knowing what had roused him. All around the men were sleeping like the dead, too deeply to stir or even to snore. Then he heard again what it had been – the high-pitched yapping and quarrelling of young foxes. It was the first evidence of animal life he had witnessed in weeks, and it went deep, touched a well-spring of something in him that he had shut down and denied. He wanted to cry. He had not known how much he had longed for ungouged earth, unshattered trees, the simple, natural life of birds and beasts – the green peace of the countryside in which he had grown up. He turned on his side and was almost instantly asleep, and dreamed of a clearing in a wood with a stream running through it, and a woman who reclined in the grass smiling at him, dabbling her fingers in the water. The stream looked so clear and cool and he wanted so much to go and drink and bathe himself, but his feet would not move. He wanted so much to talk to the woman, but though she held out a hand to him, and he saw her lips moving, his own did not, and he could not hear her words. In his dream he was deaf, dumb and immobile. He woke with tears on his cheeks.

In the morning they remained at the farm while Fenniman went to get further orders and information. The old woman there produced a dozen eggs and shyly offered them to Bertie and Pennyfather. Everyone yearned inexpressibly for eggs, which seemed somehow the archetype of fresh food and home-cooking. After a brief discussion, the men agreed to draw lots for them. Lewis, acting cook, fried them up with the bacon ration, and everyone gathered round the lucky recipients to watch them eat. It was perhaps a good example of how close they had become that each of the eggs was cut into fragments, and almost everyone in the barn had a taste – even if the merest taste – of civilisation that morning.

After breakfast Bertie went to enquire of the old woman if there was any work to be done, and she gratefully accepted the offer. For the morning the men drew water, cut wood, undertook a number of small repairs, cleaned out a cow-house, pulled turnips and dug over a vegetable patch. They were all immensely cheerful, not only because of their good night's sleep but simply because of the different nature of what they were doing. Bertie felt it with them. There were plenty of hands for the work, so there was no need for him to join in it, but he rifled the absent farmer's toolbox and spent a happy half-hour replacing the hinges on a shutter, chiselling out new rebates with precision and screwing the shutters back in place with a sense of absurd satisfaction in a simple task well done. He would have painted them afterwards, had there been any paint.

The midday meal of bully beef and biscuit was delivered to them, and the old woman produced an apple for each man from store. They were beginning to wrinkle a little, but they were as sweet as childhood, and the men devoured every scrap, pips and all. Soon after that, Fenniman returned, and called Bertie and Pennyfather aside for a talk.

'We're going to a village called Noordpeene, about twenty miles away, not far from St Omer. We'll go into proper billets there for a rest.'

'You mean beds, in houses?' Pennyfather asked in amazement.

'Just that,' said Fenniman, with a smile. 'Every luxury village houses can afford.'

'Baths, do you think? I can't tell you how I long for a bath. I'd swap an egg for a bath any day.'

'If you had an egg,' Bertie said. 'What happens afterwards?' he asked Fenniman.

'After that we'll be re-equipped, and we'll probably have to go back into the line for a time, but it looks as though things are quietening down up there. They're saying officially that the battle is over, and that they don't expect any major movement from the Germans until next year. So we're all going to get some leave. A week for the men and two weeks for officers. It'll be staggered, of course, but everyone should get home in December or early January.'

Pennyfather grinned with delight. 'I'll get to see my wife and boys. Wouldn't it be wonderful if leave fell around Christmas?'

But Bertie had seen something in Fenniman's face that was not wholly joyful. He met his eyes and said, 'What is it, Fen? Some other news? What happens after that?'

'From what they're saying now,' Fenniman said slowly, 'we're going to be split up. When we go back into the line after rest, we'll be put together with some other remnants, possibly the Worcesters, as a company in a mixed battalion. And then when the new Kitchener units start to come out, we'll be spread among them to give them a bit of stiffening.'

Experienced soldiers will be too valuable to keep together when so many raw recruits are being thrown into it.' He met Bertie's eyes. 'Do you know that nine-tenths of the BEF is gone – dead, missing or wounded? The regular army doesn't exist any more.'

They had known, of course, that the losses were heavy, but the statistic brought it home to them, and it was still a shock. Of the hundred thousand who had come out to France, ninety thousand were casualties. They were silent, their eyes distant as each of them thought of the fallen of their own small world.

'It's a damn shame to split us up,' Pennyfather said at last, indignantly. 'After all we've been through together!'

Fenniman shrugged. 'Can't argue with the army. But look here, I think we ought to keep this from the men. Don't want to spoil their rest period – or their leave. Time enough to tell them when it happens – do you agree?'

They nodded.

'As to us—'

'As to us,' said Pennyfather, 'we'd better make sure we enjoy ourselves at this Noordwhatsit while we can. The three of us – like the three musketeers.'

'Wine, women and song?' Fenniman suggested, with a grin.

'Well, wine and song, anyway,' said Bertie. 'And I tell you one thing – if there's a piano anywhere in the village, I'm going to sniff it out. I will play that Chopin piece if it's the last thing I do.'

'What Chopin piece?' asked Fenniman, and Bertie put his arm across his shoulders and told him about it as they strolled back to the barn.

CHAPTER EIGHTEEN

Helen had never been in a hospital before, and she found the experience daunting. Everything about it, the atmosphere, the repellent smell of disinfectant, the oppressive silence of the long, echoing corridors, seemed calculated to make her feel out of her place, humble, and apprehensive. She had been given directions at the front door, but got lost anyway, there being no signs on the walls with the usual helpful, pointing hands. There seemed no-one to ask. The occasional nurse scurried aloofly past in the distance and disappeared through an anonymous door, but she did not feel it would be right to raise her voice in this cathedral hush to attract her attention.

At last someone came out of a door and almost bumped into her. It was a tall woman in nurse's uniform. She had a hatchet face and a preoccupied frown, and the little red-edged shoulder cape of her uniform was heavy with medals.

Helen managed to croak out, 'Excuse me, could you—'

But the woman lifted a dismissive hand and said, 'Not now, dear,' and was already away into that rapid nurse's walk, picking up speed smoothly like a motor-car. Helen felt close to bursting into tears, like a maid being 'told off'; and this suddenly tickled her sense of the absurd. What could this woman do to her, after all? She raised her voice. 'Excuse me, I'm trying to find Horatio Martin Ward.'

The figure braked, turned, and the hard eyes surveyed Helen, trying to collate the evidence of her age, accent and clothing and come to a conclusion. 'You wish to visit a patient?' she asked at last.

'Yes,' said Helen; and, a little riled, added, 'What else?'

'I thought perhaps you had come to volunteer,' said the woman. Then she rallied. 'You are in quite the wrong part of the hospital. Quite.'

'I'm sorry. I got lost,' Helen said.

The woman almost smiled. It was a terrifying sight: Helen could hear the granite cracking. 'That is quite all right,' she said. 'Go to the end of this corridor and turn left. Through the door at the end, up the stairs to the next floor, through the double doors on your left, to the end of the corridor and turn right, and you will see the ward straight in front of you. Good morning.' And she was away again, this time with determination.

Helen managed to find Horatio Martin Ward, though she felt it was by the skin of her teeth, especially as there was no sign on the door. But peeping through the tiny square porthole in the door, she saw beds with men in them, and a table down the centre with vases of flowers on it, and pushed her way in. An intelligent-looking young woman with a red cross on the bib of her apron came to her and said, 'Can I help you?'

'Is this Horatio Martin Ward?' Helen asked.

'Yes, it is.' The girl had an upper-class accent, and she smiled at Helen's expression. 'Matron had all the direction signs taken down, in case the Germans invade. I'm not sure why knowing the names of the wards would be likely to help them conquer us, but Matron is a law unto herself. Who have you come to see?'

But Helen, with the eye of love, had already spotted him. She almost ran past the rows of neatly made beds, each with a pyjamaed figure in it, or a man in a dressing-gown sitting out beside it. Then she was standing at the end of the bed, at last, at last feasting her eyes on the sight of Jack. He was propped up against the pillows with his eyes shut, apparently asleep. His hair was cut shorter than she had ever seen it, and his throat looked tender and young above the open collar of his striped pyjamas. She had never seen him in pyjamas before – she had never seen any male creature except her little nephews in pyjamas – and it gave her a pang that was more motherly than passionate. Jack's face was pale and rather gaunt and there were lines of pain in it, and dark shadows below his eyes. His hands were resting on a book on his stomach – *Riders of the Purple Sage*, she saw, with a quiver of amusement. The hands looked the same, strong and brown and capable, but the bedclothes bulged in a long tunnel over one leg, and the juxtaposition of strength and weakness had her gulping against tears, realising all over again how she had nearly lost him.

She must have made a noise, for his eyes flickered open. He frowned a moment, as if he did not remember where he was, and then a slow smile of delight spread over his face. He held out a hand to her and she went round and took it. His fingers gripped hers tightly, and she obeyed the little tug on them and leaned over to kiss him. His lips were smooth and firm, and a bolt of love shot through her stomach.

She suddenly became aware that every man in the ward was watching, and straightened up abruptly, reddening. To be seen kissing a man in public! But the smiles she glimpsed before she sat down on the hard chair at the bedside were indulgent rather than ribald or disapproving.

'I was dreaming about you,' Jack said, keeping hold of her hand, 'and then I suddenly woke up and there you were standing before me. For a moment I thought I must still be asleep. It's so good to see you!'

'Oh, Jack,' she said, fighting again with foolish tears. 'Thank God you're safe. If I'd lost you . . .'

'I know, darling,' he said. 'I've thought the same thing, over and over.'

'How are you? Is it very painful?'

'It is a bit, but it's not so bad now I can keep it still. The journey home wasn't much fun, but there were hundreds far worse off than me on the hospital ship. Some of those poor fellows—' He dragged his memory away from the shattered wrecks of humanity he had travelled with. 'Anyway, the important thing is that I'm here. How is everyone? How's Rug?'

'He misses you. Every day he goes sniffing round every bit of the house and garden, in case he's just mislaid you somewhere. And whenever I get his leash out to take him for a walk, he rushes to the front door and then drags me down the street looking this way and that, to see if you're hiding anywhere. Poor old dog, he'll be so glad to see you again. Everyone else is fine. Mother's given up embroidery for knitting, though she's not very good at it yet. She keeps starting socks but she can't turn the heel so they always end up as scarves.'

Jack was smiling now, and she was glad to see a little of the strain going out of his face. 'Go on. How is your father?'

'He's very well. He devours every detail of the war that's in the newspapers, especially anything to do with the Royal Flying Corps. He's terribly proud of you, and has shocking arguments with his friends who say that aeroplanes are no use to soldiers. It's rather funny to hear him repeating the arguments you brought up that night at dinner as if they were his own. And Molly's joined a Red Cross class to learn first aid. She's terribly keen, but I rather suspect some of the keenness is to do with the doctor who teaches it. He is really rather a charmer. The only person who isn't enjoying himself is brother Freddie, who doesn't have any heroic part to play, and has to work longer hours because two of his clerks have volunteered. Poor Freddie! If this war had only come ten years earlier, he could have been a hero. As it is, all he can do is grumble, even though he knows it doesn't suit him.'

Laughing, Jack said, 'Oh, how I've missed your conversational style! I've enjoyed your letters, but it's not quite like having you here in front of me and seeing your wonderful expressive face. But tell me, beloved, how are you? You look tired.'

'That's just worry about you. I'm perfectly fine, otherwise.' Her smile disappeared abruptly, and her face was bleak for a moment. 'When I knew how nearly I'd lost you, I kept thinking how stupid I was not to have married you before you went away, when I had the chance.'

'I've been thinking exactly the same thing,' said Jack.

'When I knew I was coming down, and then when I thought I was going to be a prisoner-of-war, all I could think about was that we'd missed our chance of happiness together.'

Helen folded both her hands round his and smiled wryly. 'All for the sake of a silly wedding, meant to please other people and not ourselves. I could kick myself.'

'It was my fault, first and last,' said Jack. 'If I hadn't spent all those years on unsuitable women – what was it you called them? Pretty idiots.'

Helen shook her head. 'Let's not waste time on recriminations. I'm just so glad to be here with you now. How long will you have to stay in hospital?'

'From what they say, I will have quite a lot of pain for a couple of weeks, and that's best treated here. But once the healing starts and the leg settles down, I'll probably be moved to a convalescent hospital.'

'And when will you be sound again?'

'They don't know yet. It was a complicated fracture, and it might be three months or even six before I'm fit to go back to the war.'

'Six months!'

'It's not so bad, darling,' he hastened to comfort her. 'They're not saying I'll never walk again, you know.'

'Fool! I'm *glad* it'll be six months before you have to risk your life again! Oh, I know you won't look at it that way, but you have to forgive me for being a woman.'

'Forgive you!' He squeezed her hand again, and their eyes met in the kiss that propriety forbade.

'What will they do with you? I suppose they'll give you a ground job? But you'll be in England, that's the main thing.'

'Yes, which means we can be together. If,' he added, suddenly sober, 'that's what you still want.'

She gave a laugh that was half a sob. 'How can you doubt it? Jack, how soon can we get married?'

'I'll be in a wheelchair for weeks,' he warned.

'I don't mind marrying you in a wheelchair. What about when you get out of here? You said they'd send you to a convalescent hospital. If you're convalescent, couldn't you come home? Molly and I would look after you.'

'What would your mother say to that?'

'She suggested it herself. She said we could turn the morning-room into a bedroom for you, to save having to take you up and down stairs. And I could drive you about in the motor, and take you to hospital when you had to go for treatment. Would they let you, do you think?'

'I should think they'd be glad of the bed,' said Jack. 'If you're really sure . . .'

'I'm sure,' Helen said. 'I don't want to miss my chance again.'

'I won't be much use to you as a husband for some time,' he said, a little shyly.

'You'll still be all the husband I shall ever want,' she said, and to Jack her eyes seemed to be shining like stars.

Jessie was deeply distressed by the news of Jack's accident and injury. Like most people, though she accepted that casualties were a part of war, the reality of it had never properly impinged on her until it was someone of her own who was involved. And Jack had been her childhood favourite, her friend and hero. As they grew up, it was he who had been her confidant, and she could not bear the idea of his being hurt.

But when Helen had been to see him, she telephoned not only Morland Place, but Maystone too, and after a long, comfortable chat Jessie allowed herself to be convinced that it could have been a great deal worse, and that Jack would make a full recovery. Helen even offered her her own comfort, that six months away from the front was a bonus to everyone who loved Jack. She dissuaded Jessie from jumping onto a train at once, knowing that in his present state he would not be able to bear too much visiting, by telling her that as soon as he was released from the military hospital they would be getting married in a very quiet ceremony – 'No fuss and feathers,' Helen said, 'but you will be welcome to come. We can't set a date yet,' she went on, 'because we don't know how his leg is going to behave, but

I'm having the banns read so that we can be ready at any time.'

Jessie was comforted, and a letter received soon afterwards from Bertie relieved her mind of her other worry, for she had not heard from him since the beginning of the interminable battle for Ypres. He wrote that he was out of the line and safely behind it, and that he would be getting leave some time in December.

It was a sorry-looking battalion that came back for our first rest since we got to Ypres [he wrote]. Out of the thousand men, plus two lots of reinforcements, who came out to France, we are down to about a hundred, plus only three officers. The BEF as a whole has lost nine-tenths of its strength. A heavy price to pay, but that, I suppose, is war. I count myself very lucky. And the Germans have suffered even more heavily. We have held them off, no matter what they threw at us, and when the weather clears next spring we will finish the job. Everything has quietened down here now as both sides dig in for the winter and there will be nothing much doing for a time. I rather hope that we will be moved away from this part of the line as it is very low-lying and floods all through the winter, which will make the trenches very unpleasant. But we will go where we are sent, of course. Meanwhile I wait to hear when my leave will fall. As I will have two weeks, I shall have enough time to come up to Yorkshire for a day or two and see you, and all at Morland Place.

That was something to look forward to – indeed, Christmas, when everyone expected to be getting leave, was becoming more and more of a beacon. In the mean time, her life had settled down into a new pattern. Although some of her lads at Twelvetrees had left, with so much of the stock gone there wasn't a great deal of work, and there was no need for her to do more than supervise, give orders and answer questions. Most mornings she drove herself down to the stables, but she was always back for an early luncheon, and then dutifully spent her two hours on the bed, reading.

Outside of this occupation, she might go for a walk with Brach, visit Morland Place or the Cornleighs, occasionally go into York. Some evenings were taken up with writing letters, and wrestling with accounts; and besides all this, there was her war work to keep her occupied. Most ladies were knitting khaki socks, mufflers and balaclavas against the winter to come, but Jessie loathed knitting almost as much as sewing. Besides, having obtained her two Red Cross certificates, in First Aid and Home Nursing, she saw no reason not to get the benefit of them. At the first-aid class she had attended at the cottage hospital at Bickerton, she now helped the presiding doctor, demonstrating the bandaging and other techniques she had learned to new 'pupils' – the stout and earnest ladies of York who wanted to do something for the war effort. On another day she attended the Red Cross supply depot, which had been set up in a hotel in Bootham. Here other York ladies did their bit, by rolling bandages and cutting out pyjamas and shirts for soldiers. They did it so badly and wasted so much material that Jessie soon begged Uncle Teddy to send them one of his seamstresses to do the work, which left the ladies free to do what they did best – drink tea, chat, and impress each other with the nobility of their desire to serve their country. Tucked away in a quiet corner, Jessie helped with the administration, using the skills she had learned in running her business, and kept away from the gossip, which she found tedious.

Her favourite 'war work' was done at Heworth Park, a large house that the absentee owner had given up as a convalescent home for wounded Belgian officers. Jessie went there to help out one or two afternoons a week. The matron was a former military nurse, with whom Mrs Wycherley was acquainted, so though qualified nurses were often impatient of amateurs trying to help, especially when they were 'ladies', the matron made an exception in their case. They were not allowed to do any actual nursing, but as the men were convalescent rather than gravely ill, there were always little tasks to be undertaken. Jessie and Mrs Wycherley made themselves useful by running errands for the patients, serving hot drinks, lighting cigarettes, carrying trays at meal-times, writing letters home for those who could not hold a pen, reading aloud to those with eye or head injuries.

Most of all, Jessie felt, they were useful in cheering up these poor men, who were wounded and far from home, and who hardly knew when, if ever, they would be able to return to the native land that had been overrun, raped and pillaged by the Godless Hun. She talked to them, made little jokes, listened to their stories, played cards or dominoes with them. There was one poor young man in particular who tugged at her heart. He had lost his right arm to a shell, and was struggling with bitter patience to learn to use his left hand instead; but the hardest thing for him to bear was that he had not heard anything of his young wife and child for weeks. The town where he had left them was now in occupied territory, and the atrocity stories that filled the newspapers had left him fearing the worst. There was nothing Jessie could say to comfort or reassure him: she could only help him pass a little of the time that dragged so heavily, and write letters for him, because he said his left-handed writing was still illegible.

Most of the officers spoke English, which was a good thing as Jessie's school French was rudimentary, and though it was improving, they still had to spell out many of the words when she wrote to their dictation. Mrs Wycherley visited Heworth Park less often as other concerns took up her time, but Jessie continued to go as often as she could. She even shared her new-found love of books with them. She began by reading aloud to Lieutenant Dupont, whose eyes were bandaged and – though he had not been officially told – would never see again. But even the men who could have read for themselves liked so much to listen to her that now when she sat by Dupont's bedside, those who could leave their beds would gather round, and the rest of the ward would fall silent to try to catch her words. She was reading them *The Riddle of the Sands* by Erskine Childers, and had already planned the next three books she would take in.

So she was able to give a cheerful account of herself in her weekly letter to Ned, and skip over the things that went wrong. The cook, Mrs Peck, grew bored with the simple food she had to prepare for a manless household, and gave notice. Good cooks were always in demand, and she had found a better place, where her talents would be appreciated. Peggy, the senior housemaid, could cook well enough for Jessie's purposes, and with Tomlinson to help her, she and Susie, the under-housemaid, and the kitchenmaid Katy did the work of the reduced household without much trouble.

Gladding complained that Peggy's cooking wasn't up to his standards, and threatened to leave, but Jessie did not even hold her breath when the threat was conveyed to her. The sour old man would never go. He was comfortable, well-paid and had little to do. Tomlinson grumbled that it wouldn't have killed Gladding to offer to clean the silver once a week, now that Daltry was away; but Gladding would not even wash the motor, saying it was not a horse and therefore not his responsibility. Jessie had to pay a local boy to do it, and if she had hoped that the sight would shame Gladding into relenting, she was soon disabused.

Ned's letters to her were as regular as a heartbeat, but he had no great talent for expressing himself and they were rather formal, dull little essays. He wrote about the camp, about route marches and fieldcraft exercises, the weather, and the inter-platoon rugby match that he had captained. At the end of October the battalion received its horses and he sent for Compass Rose. The army was to buy her for his use. Jessie made the arrangements with the railway, and Gladding rode Compass Rose to the station one morning and put her on the train. After that Jessie did not think it fair to keep Hotspur up, all alone. She had one of the Twelvetrees grooms come and fetch him, knock off his shoes and turn him out. She suggested to Gladding that he now had plenty of time on his hands to do one or two little jobs in the house, but he stuck out his lip and said he had enough to do in his garden, and thereafter spent most of his days in the potting shed, smoking his pipe and reading the *Daily Mail*.

Dr Hasty had told Jessie she must not allow herself to get upset about anything, so she tried to ignore the situation; but she thought that if Ned had been home, he would have put Gladding in his place. It was not the only reason she missed him. Now that the bouts of sickness and dizziness had passed, she felt very well and missed their lovemaking. The bed, which had seemed delightfully spacious at first, now began to strike her as only empty, and on cold nights it was hard not to have his hot body to snuggle up to. She missed his company, too – missed having about her the one person who was interested in every tiny detail of what she did. Her mother had always been the other person she could tell everything to, but these days Henrietta was always tired, and seemed intermittently unwell, and sometimes when Jessie visited full of conversation, she curbed it at the sight of her mother's weary face.

At the end of November, as surprising as delightful, came a visit from Violet. Henrietta and Venetia were distant cousins and old confidantes, and they had planned from the moment their daughters were born that they should be friends. There was only five months between Violet and Jessie and, having characters and temperaments that complemented each other, they had got on well in childhood and grown up to be as close as their mothers had hoped. Since their marriages they did not see each other so often, but they kept up a steady correspondence, and every now and then Jessie went to stay with Violet for a taste of London life. Because of their different social stations, the visiting had always been that way round. Violet had never even seen Maystone Villa. But she came to Yorkshire in November on an errand for her mother, bringing Emma with her, and stayed at Morland Place, where Emma had long been a favourite. As soon as it was polite to leave her hostess, she had herself driven over to Maystone.

The friends embraced and cried a little bit – which was not normally in Jessie's style, but her secret pregnancy seemed to bring a well of tears closer to the surface for all sorts of emotions. When they had admired each other and said how well each other looked, and Violet's Pekineses,

Lapsang and Souchong, had made friends with Brach and settled down together by the fire, Violet insisted on a guided tour of the house.

'It's lovely!' she enthused. 'It's so neat and complete.'

'It's nothing compared with your mansions,' Jessie laughed, 'so you needn't be kind.'

'But I'm not! I really love it. It's the sort of house I always dreamed of when I was a girl. Don't you remember?'

'You wanted a white house with green shutters and a paling fence, like the doctor's wife,' Jessie said.

'Yes. I know yours isn't white and doesn't have shutters—'

'And I've a laurel hedge instead of palings.'

'But it's the *feeling*,' Violet said helplessly, unable to find the words.

'Well, I do know what you mean,' Jessie said. 'And I quite like my little house.'

'Only "quite"?' Violet said.

Jessie suspected that she had a very different way of looking at houses from Violet, and whatever she said could only disappoint. Violet had enjoyed planning the alterations to the London house, and was looking forward to doing the same to the country house one day, but Jessie had no interest in wallpaper, paint colours, curtains, furnishings and what-have-you, and could not imagine what difference knocking down a wall or putting in a window would make. To her a house was a place to be when you were not riding, or to shelter in when the weather was too bad to be outdoors. If it was reasonably comfortable, that was enough for her.

So she changed the subject. 'It's lovely to have you visit me here. What brings you down to Yorkshire?'

'Mama asked me to come and look at Shawes for her.'

Shawes was a house only half a mile from Morland Place. It was a Vanbrugh mansion, much admired by students of architecture for its purity. It was known as 'Vanbrugh's Little Gem', and was in all the tourist guides, though it was not open to the public, for it had not been lived in regularly for years. Venetia had inherited it from her mother along with the Chelmsford title, and had used it from time to time as a summer retreat, but it was rather too far from London to be convenient for a woman as busy as Venetia had always been.

'Oh, is she thinking of coming to stay?' Jessie asked. 'Mother will be so pleased.'

'No, it isn't that. In fact, it looks as though the war is going to keep her busier than ever. Papa says she is "retiring in reverse". They had been planning to give up most of their occupations and spend more time in the country, but Papa's so busy in the War Office, and now everyone wants Mama to be on their committees, and she and Papa complain that they never see each other any more.'

They had finished their tour and retired to the drawing-room, where Violet, divested of her sables and hat, was looking very decorative on the settle before the fire. Her black hair was drawn into an enormous soft chignon, and her white skin and deep blue eyes were enhanced by the violet silk of her gown. There were pearls round her neck and diamond and pearl earrings in her ears, and she was, Jessie decided, more beautiful than ever. No-one would ever guess that she was a mother of three. 'So what does your mother want Shawes for?' Jessie asked.

'Oh, she thought it might serve for a convalescent home, now that so many more casualties are coming through. There are just thousands and thousands from Ypres. It was a terrible business. Well, of course, you know all about it, what with Jack being hurt. I'm so glad, by the way, that he's safely back in England. Mother was terribly upset when she heard about him. She went down to the hospital to visit him – did you know?'

'No, I didn't. How kind of her.'

'Well, she was always fond of him – all of your brothers, of course, but Jack most of all. She told me she remembered so well how she visited Morland Place one time – years and years ago – when Jack was just a boy, and he explained to her all about aeroplanes and how man would fly one day. Of course nobody ever had in those days, and nobody really believed it was possible – but he did.'

'Yes, he never swerved from his conviction that someone

would invent an aeroplane one day,' Jessie said. 'It might so easily have been him. So did your mother say how Jack looked?'

'Rather worn and thin, but they're doing everything for him and, of course, he's not in any danger. But she said his broken ankle is more complicated than he realises and he'll be unable to walk for longer than he thinks. She didn't consider it right to worry him about it, but I don't mind telling you because I know you love him best.'

'But he will walk again?' Jessie asked anxiously.

'Oh, yes, but it might be some months. I'm afraid he's out of the war for the time being.'

Susie came in just then with tea and cakes, and conversation stopped while she laid everything within reach and then departed. Jessie took up the pot and poured, and all three dogs woke from their doze, eyeing the cake-stand with interest. Brach was too well trained to do more than lift her head and flare her nostrils, but the Pekineses sat up and unfurled their little pink tongues, their round, shining eyes travelling from face to hand and hand to face in case any signal should be sent about titbits coming their way.

Violet accepted a piece of Madeira cake and said, 'I must say, while I was very proud that Holkam volunteered straight away – and he does look so distinguished in his uniform – I was rather disappointed when he was sent to Horseguards and not to France. So many of one's friends went to France, and it isn't something one can boast about, is it, that one's husband is at Headquarters in London?'

'Surely people don't criticise him for that?' Jessie said.

'Not criticise, exactly, but they give one *looks*, you know. Everyone is so busy with the war effort and there really is a dreadful sort of competition as to who is doing the most.'

'Yes, it's the same here,' Jessie said.

'The oddest people are coming to the fore. The Suffragettes, for instance – well, you know how the Government was treating them last year. It was almost civil war. And then Asquith issued the general amnesty, and since then, they've thrown themselves into the war as if they were the ones who thought of it.'

'I read that the militants had given up campaigning for the duration of the war,' Jessie said.

'But it's more than that. They've joined all the committees and go out collecting for all the funds, and they're twice as enthusiastic as anyone else. Mrs Pankhurst and that dreadful daughter of hers – who used to hate men so much, and despised everything that men do – they never mention votes for women now. They're making speeches about how it's everyone's duty to defend England against the Germans, and claim that it was democracy they were fighting for all along! And they harangue the men for not volunteering fast enough, and call them all sorts of names. They've invented a sort of league, and they stand on street corners handing out white feathers to any man not in uniform, to say they are cowards. Mama says they've set themselves up as unofficial recruiting agents for Lord Kitchener. She says it must make Lord Kitchener mad because he dislikes all women, but Suffragettes most of all.'

Jessie laughed at that, but said, 'I wonder if some of them aren't rather glad of the war for letting them off their militant pranks. It must have been most unpleasant. It's probably a relief not to have to go on having oneself arrested and put in prison, then starving oneself.'

'I expect you're right,' said Violet. She put her plate, with the remaining morsel of cake, on the settle beside her, and went on, 'Of course, the Government's attitude to women hasn't really changed a bit. Mama was incensed when a deputation of women doctors went to the War Office to offer their services, and they were told that if they really wanted to help, they should go home and keep quiet.'

'Was your mother one of them?'

'No, Mama thinks she's too old to go doctoring, but everyone wants her to head their committee, because she's such a Great Name. I must say,' she added, with a little flush of eagerness, 'that it's rather exciting to have all these things going on, and to feel that one can be part of something as important as a war. I never cared much before about anything like that. You know, all I ever wanted was a husband and children. But now I'm on the Belgian

Refugees Committee and the War Hardship Committee, and – well, it's rather agreeable to be doing one's bit, as they say.'

'Dear Violet,' Jessie smiled. 'You're turning into a Modern Woman. Oh! Look out for that dog!'

One of the Pekineses – Jessie couldn't tell them apart – had crept up close to Violet and, finally overcome by the delectable smell of cake so temptingly close, had put its forepaws up on the settle and was reaching towards the plate. Before Violet could react, the dog had inhaled and the cake was gone. 'Oh dear. Bad Souchong! Bad dog,' she said, but without great conviction. Brach sighed deeply and rolled her eyes at such carryings-on. Begging was *not* allowed in Jessie's house, but the canine visitors were evidently treated more leniently than her.

'So tell me about the children,' Jessie said, when she had refilled Violet's cup. 'I expect you'll be going down to Lincolnshire soon. You're not usually in Town at this time of the year, are you?'

'No, but everything's different because of the war. Holkam is fixed in Town, and I can't think of leaving London with so much going on. I took Emma down to see them last Saturday-to-Monday, and they were all very well. Charlotte's hair is starting to curl beautifully now, and she chatters and laughs all day long. Emma's devoted to her.'

'Is Emma going to continue to stay with you? She's been with you for quite a while now.'

'She feels as I do, that London is the place to be at the moment. I'm delighted to have her for as long as she wants to stay. It makes such a difference to have a female companion.' She eyed Jessie a moment and said, 'It must be rather lonely for you here, with Ned away. You and he were always so close.'

Jessie nodded, and said, 'I had better get used to it, though. Once he finishes training he'll be off overseas.'

'Yes. Poor Jessie.' Violet reached out and laid a delicate hand over Jessie's. 'You are looking a little peaked, now I come to study you. Wouldn't you like to come to London with us when we go back, and have a little fun and excitement? It must be rather dull, stuck here in Yorkshire with nothing to do.'

Jessie laughed. 'Nothing to do? My dear girl, I've never been busier.' And she told her about her own war work.

Violet listened with increasing respect, and then said, 'Well, I shan't pity you for being bored, at all events! But you do look a little under the weather, all the same. If you ever do feel like a vacation, let me know. You know you're welcome at any time.'

Violet soon discovered that Shawes was not in any condition to house convalescents without a great deal of work. She and Emma stayed only a day or two, but Uncle Teddy managed to cram quite a bit of social activity into that time, begged them to stay longer, and urged Emma to think of Morland Place as her home whenever she wanted. Emma was rather torn, for she loved everyone at Morland Place, hadn't had half enough time to talk to Jessie, and was, as always, flattered by Polly's hero worship of her. But the call of Violet and London were too strong for her. Peter Hargrave and Kit Dawnay had gone away to camp, but there were plenty more young men, some in uniform and some not, and London was more madly social since the war had started than ever before. It would be foolish, she pleaded for understanding, to be anywhere else just now. Teddy chucked her chin and said she should enjoy herself while she was young, but that he hoped to see her next summer for a long stay.

When the young ladies had gone, everything felt rather flat by contrast. Jessie's war-work routine, though absorbing, seemed lacking in sociability compared with Violet's. She felt rather out of sorts, and therefore inclined to feel sorry for herself. There was nothing much to do at Twelvetrees, and she went more often to Morland Place, though still resisting her mother's regular urgings to move there while Ned was away.

At the beginning of December, Ned's commission came through, and he was gazetted second lieutenant. The commissions were published in the *London Gazette*, and Teddy bought dozens of copies to send to friends and family. Ned had his photograph taken in his new uniform, and

Teddy had it copied and framed so that it could take pride of place both in his own drawing-room and in Maystone's. The orders about Christmas leave had not yet been posted, but Ned wrote to say that everyone would get some time, though it would not necessarily coincide with Christmas Day.

Being more often at Morland Place, Jessie began to notice that her mother was really not well. She seemed not to have recovered from the tiredness that had marked her after the strain of coping with the chicken-pox, and after Violet's visit she contracted a heavy cold, which, though it departed after the usual length of time, left her lethargic and with a tiring cough. When she saw Dr Hasty on her own account, Jessie told him about her anxieties for her mother.

'She is a little run down,' he said. 'It's nothing to worry about, but I would like to see her rest a little more.'

'The trouble is, she'll never rest at home,' Jessie said. 'There's always too much to do, and she never could lie on a sofa and watch someone else do her chores.'

'And you're just like her,' Hasty said, with mock severity. 'You're doing too much, even though I warned you against it.'

'I take my afternoon rest, as you told me to,' she protested.

'Yes, and it's gone from two hours to not much more than one, according to that good maid of yours.'

'But I feel very well,' Jessie said.

'Feelings aren't always a good guide. You're in your fourth month, and it can be a delicate time. I really wish I could persuade both you and your mother to go away for a little while – take a holiday from everything.'

Jessie thought about it, and the idea suddenly had appeal. It was a long time since she had had her mother to herself, and the thought of spending time with her, time when they could talk and not be interrupted by servants or visitors, seemed delightful.

'But where could we go?' she asked. 'You'd never get Mother to go very far from Morland Place – and not for very long, either.'

'It needn't be for very long. I think a week of complete

407

change would work wonders. As to where . . .' Hasty considered. 'There's always Scarborough.'

'Scarborough? At this time of year? There'd be no-one there.'

'Which is just what I'd prescribe. I don't,' he said severely, 'mean you to be going to parties and balls and junkets. A quiet time – gentle walks, good food, bracing, clean air and, above all, nothing to worry about.'

'Scarborough,' Jessie said thoughtfully.

'Yes,' said Hasty, evidently warming to his own idea, 'and you'd be close enough for your mother to feel she was in touch, should there be an emergency – which I should be sure to warn your uncle there must not be. And I have a very good colleague in Scarborough – Dr Wren – who could keep an eye on you for me. I think it would do very well. Do you think you might persuade your mother to go?'

'You don't seem to think *I* need persuading.'

'You'll go for your mother's sake, like the good girl you are,' said Hasty, 'which is killing two birds with one stone. I'd like to see some roses in your cheeks, and the air at Scarborough would do that for you, and give you an appetite.'

Jessie smiled. 'I wouldn't put it past you to hint to Mother that she ought to go for *my* sake. Playing both ends against the middle.'

Hasty looked modest. 'It's what makes me a good doctor,' he said.

CHAPTER NINETEEN

Teddy was immediately in favour of the proposed trip to Scarborough. He suggested that Alice should go as well, always eager to secure to her anything in the way of a treat or benefit. But Alice looked her horror at the idea. There would be no-one there, she warned him; and it would be cold. She was no great walker, but Henrietta and Jessie would be sure to be striding out every day, in weather they would call bracing, and she would call Arctic. She was a chilly mortal and liked the assurance of the large fires and comforts that she had at home; she liked her own bed, her own cook, and the visits of her friends. And besides, it would not be a treat to her to go away without Teddy. Though she spoke as gently as always, she said enough to convince Teddy that she was not just being polite, and he dropped the suggestion.

He was for hiring a house for Jessie and Henrietta, saying that a private house was always more agreeable than a hotel, but Jessie took him aside and firmly quashed the idea. 'If we have a house, we'll have to have servants.'

'There's no difficulty about that. You can take as many from here as you need. They can go ahead and have everything ready for you when you arrive.'

'But think, Uncle Teddy: a house and servants, ordering meals, settling their routines – how will that be a holiday for Mother? She'll fall straight back into her old ways.'

He paused for thought. 'Perhaps you're right.'

'Whereas in a hotel there's no housekeeping, no servants

to chase after, no tradesmen, no bills to pay – except the one at the end.'

'Which I'll deal with,' Teddy said, on firmer ground. 'You don't need to think about that.'

Jessie smiled and reached up to kiss his cheek. 'Thank you. You are very kind. And I think a hotel will be much more fun. I haven't stayed in one since my honeymoon. It will be lovely to choose food from a menu in the restaurant, instead of having to think what to have and order it in, and then, when the time comes, find one doesn't fancy it after all.'

It gave Teddy another thing to worry about. 'Have you not been eating properly since Ned went away? Is that why you're looking peaky?'

'I eat plenty,' Jessie said. 'It's just dull work having to think about it.'

'But you are looking less bonny than usual,' Teddy insisted. 'Although,' he added, 'I can't say you look thin, exactly. You seem to have put *on* a little weight, if anything.'

Jessie quickly changed the subject. 'I wonder, should we go to Scarborough by train or in the motor?'

Teddy was all for the motor, until he understood that in that case, Jessie would insist on driving, whereupon he discovered all the unsurpassable advantages of rail travel. The matter decided, he undertook to arrange everything. All she would have to do was to choose what to have Tomlinson pack for her.

They travelled down on Saturday the 12th of December, seen off at York station by Teddy and Polly. Polly was torn between wishing she could go with them – for she was as eager for a change as anyone – and pitying them for having to go to Scarborough, of all places, and out of season. Her view of the town was coloured by her unhappy experience at school; but on the other hand, Lennie's regiment was in training camp there. On the whole she *was* inclined to think herself unlucky at not being able to go along, but her school did not break up for another week, and her father was adamant that she could not have any more time out of it.

As they settled back into their first-class seats, Henrietta smiled at Jessie and confessed herself excited.

'Me too,' said Jessie. 'It's lovely to be going away, especially with just the two of us. It makes me feel like a child again.'

They had decided not to take maids, as they meant to dress simply; and Jessie had reluctantly decided to leave behind Brach, who would not have been allowed in the hotel room and would not have been happy in a kennel. Brach was to spend the week at Morland Place, and when Jessie had taken her over the day before she had settled immediately into her old place before the fire with the other dogs, and hardly even looked up when Jessie left.

So there was nothing to worry about, and nothing for them to do but enjoy themselves. Teddy had booked them rooms at the Grand, the finest hotel at the 'Queen of Resorts', as Scarborough liked to style itself. It was a magnificent hotel, the largest brick-built edifice in Europe, standing on an elevated position right at the centre of the curve of South Bay. It had been completed in 1867, and was designed around the theme of time. There were four towers, one at each corner, to denote the seasons. It was built over twelve floors, to denote the months of the year; and there were fifty-two chimneys, and three hundred and sixty-five rooms. Jessie wasn't sure what to make of this information, but there was no doubt that the majestic building dominated the scene, and could not have been more comfortable or convenient. Their rooms were on the south front, facing the sea, and were large and luxurious, with a communicating door between them. The hotel had its own picture house, and down below a splendid restaurant with sea views.

As soon as they arrived at the hotel they were handed a note from Dr Hasty's friend, Dr Wren, welcoming them to Scarborough and begging leave to call on them that afternoon. And they were still admiring their rooms and thinking about unpacking their bags when a note was brought up, which had been left by a Mrs Gresham, whose husband was a Territorial officer and friend to Colonel Bassett, inviting them to dinner that evening.

'How very kind,' Henrietta said.

'I suppose so,' Jessie said, 'but I was looking forward to eating in the restaurant. I do hope we aren't going to be bombarded with invitations while we're here.'

'Oh dear,' Henrietta said. 'Do you think we may be? I didn't bring the right clothes for that sort of thing.'

'It's Uncle Teddy,' Jessie said. 'He thinks we won't have a nice time on our own. I'm willing to bet he's told everyone he knows in Scarborough – and everyone he knows who *knows* anyone in Scarborough – to invite us.'

'I suppose we can't refuse?' Henrietta said wistfully.

'Well, perhaps not this one – if the Greshams are particular friends of Colonel Hound. But I think we might say to anyone else who asks us that we mean to be *very* quiet. In fact,' she added, on a happy thought, 'I might ask Dr Wren to say that I *ought* to be very quiet, and then we won't offend anyone.'

Henrietta sent off a message to the Greshams, accepting the invitation and begging to be excused from dressing as they had not brought formal clothes with them; and a note came back expressing the Greshams' delight, saying that it would be quite informal with no other guests but family, and proposing to send a motor to collect them at seven thirty.

In the afternoon, when they were having tea, Dr Wren appeared and introduced himself, and was asked to sit down and join them. Jessie liked him at once. He was a tall, big-built man quite at odds with his name: the spindly little gilt chair he drew up to their tea table almost seemed to quail before him; but his voice was gentle and his manners were lively without being in the least rough. He did not quiz her about her health, only said that Hasty had asked him to look in on them, as if it were a social rather than a professional call.

'You'll find it very quiet here,' he said. 'All the summer visitors are gone and the Christmas visitors haven't arrived yet. But no doubt quietness is what you've come for.'

'Yes, and I hope we shall have it,' Jessie said, and explained about the invitation from the Greshams. 'I was wondering if you could order me to be quiet, so that we could avoid having to dine out every night.'

Wren laughed. 'You look extremely healthy to me, Mrs Morland, but I think I can see my way to helping you in a little harmless subterfuge. Though, really, you will disappoint a lot of people in Scarborough. We don't often have distinguished visitors at this time of year, and everyone will want to take advantage.'

He went on to tell them what things were especially worth visiting in the town, and then Jessie asked him about his work – he did a great deal among the poor, and attended the workhouse in Dean Road and several charitable institutions. She told him about her hospital visiting, and a lively conversation followed. When he rose to go, he said, 'Tomorrow is Sunday, and I dare say you will want to go to church. If you have no other idea, I should like to recommend St Columba's to you. It's the one Mrs Wren and I attend. It really is quite an imposing building, worth looking at, and the vicar, who is a friend of ours, gives a very good sermon. I'd be happy to call for you in the morning if you would like it.'

'Thank you, we'd like that very much,' said Henrietta.

'Good,' said Dr Wren. 'Then I'll call for you at a quarter to eleven.' He smiled and added, 'Mrs Wren was urgent for my asking you to luncheon after the service, but in view of your need for quiet I hardly dare mention it. We should be delighted if you would honour us, but I shall not press you.'

Jessie and her mother consulted with their eyes, and Henrietta said, 'Please tell Mrs Wren we shall be very happy to come.'

From what they had seen of Dr Wren, they thought that they would enjoy their Sunday luncheon, but were not much looking forward to the Gresham dinner, especially when a chambermaid of whom they enquired told them that the Greshams' address was in one of the 'poshest' parts of town, on Filey Road where all the big houses were. Their anxieties were not eased by the splendid motor-car and uniformed chauffeur that were sent for them, or by their first sight of Rosemount, a large modern house standing in extensive and wooded grounds, not far from the Spa in the south end of the town.

But the Greshams had kept scrupulously to their agreement not to dress, and welcomed them kindly, with every attention meant to put them at ease. Colonel Gresham was in tweeds, his wife in a plain dark dress with no jewels but pearls. The other guest, their neighbour, John Turner, who was a former county sheriff, was wearing a lounge suit. 'We said only family, but we are such old friends we count John as family,' Mrs Gresham explained. The others present were the Greshams' eighteen-year-old daughter Rosemary, and their son, Erskine, who was in uniform, on leave from the 2nd Green Howards at the front. He had been wounded at the Menin cross-roads – part of the interminable battle of Ypres – and was convalescing.

'We're so glad to be able to secure a little company for Erskine,' Mrs Gresham confided to Jessie. 'It's so dull for him at home with only us old folk. And Scarborough is a very elderly town in winter. You really are doing us all a great service by accepting our invitation. I do hope we didn't impose too much – and on your first evening.'

'Not at all. We're very glad to be here,' said Jessie, and by now she meant it. Despite the grandness of the house and the number of servants, there was no oppressive air of formality. Jessie sat beside Erskine Gresham, and was as glad of male company – especially a young, handsome man – as he was of female. She questioned him eagerly about Ypres. He did not know Bertie, but he knew of various actions of the West Herts and spoke of them with admiration. He was able to explain much more about the situation and the battle than Bertie could get across in the confines of a letter; but when she saw remembering it all was rather a strain on him, she changed the conversation to horses, which was a lucky choice, as he was a keen huntsman, and they had plenty to talk about for the rest of dinner.

Afterwards she talked to Rosemary Gresham, who was a lively and intelligent young woman, just then engaged in a long-running battle with her father, who did not want her to go to Oxford. She had won a place at Somerville – 'But

Daddy doesn't see why any woman wants a university education. I suppose it would be expensive for him, but then he complains in any case that I cost him a fortune when I'm at home, what with clothes and parties and tennis subscriptions and so on. So he might as well let me go. What do you think?'

'I'm afraid you're asking the wrong person,' Jessie said. 'I haven't any brains at all. I hardly even went to school, never mind university.'

'Oh, but I overheard some of what you were saying to Erskine, and you have a business all of your own, don't you?'

'It doesn't need a university degree to run a horse-dealing business.'

'I know, but the point is that you are *doing* something. I can't bear the idea of being one of those girls who sit about at home until they get married and then sit about in another home for the rest of their lives.'

'You sound like my cousin Emma Weston. She always talks about what she wants to do – though it's a different thing nearly every time. But she hasn't worried so much about having a career since the war started. I think she's having enough fun as it is – though she is staying in London,' she concluded apologetically.

'Well, it seems to me,' Rosemary said judiciously, 'that there isn't anything for us women in this war. The men go off and fight, and *they* have plenty to do. But unless the Germans invade – which is impossible in any case – there's simply no part in it for us. What does your cousin do in London?'

'Mostly she goes to luncheons and teas and dances and so on, where she meets handsome young men in uniform,' said Jessie, suppressing a smile at the disapproving frown that creased Rosemary's fair brow.

'Oh. So I might as well go to Somerville and get on with planning my life the way I want it,' Rosemary said. 'The war won't last long, and it won't make any difference to anything here at home, so why put off my plans because of it? I'm definitely going to talk to Daddy again tomorrow.'

Jessie silently wished her luck, and turned to a conversation with her hostess, who bred spaniels, and had a lot of interesting things to say about blood lines, to which Jessie could contribute her own experiences with horses.

All in all it was a very pleasant evening, and Jessie enjoyed the conversation and the company. Their social engagement the next day was very different. Dr Wren collected them from the hotel in his small and rattling Morris and took them straight to St Columba's, where they sat in his usual pew with Mrs Wren, who *was* as small and round as the name. The church was imposing and the sermon, as promised, interesting, and afterwards they went back to the doctor's comfortable but rather shabby old house, where they were soon joined by the vicar. He was an elderly bachelor, and Mrs Wren whispered to Jessie that his housekeeper was a shocking cook, so the poor soul liked to eat at someone else's table as often as possible. 'I like to get him here and feed him up when I can,' she said. 'And besides, it's a miserable thing eating alone, don't you think? It makes it seem hardly worth one's while to have the table laid. I'm sure he has a sandwich at his desk more often than not, rather than sit down alone at that great big dining-table.'

This rather struck a chord with Jessie, who had had difficulty for weeks in thinking of what to order for her own meals. She had eaten heartily last night, and now, faced with an excellent roast rib of beef, with Yorkshire puddings, and a gravy so handsome and delicious she almost expected it to sing as it was placed before her, she ate heartily again. She saw her mother look across the table with approval; and approved herself when she saw Mother accepting another slice of pink and melting beef and taking another crisply baked potato.

Apart from offering excellent food, the Wrens did not make any fuss about having guests, and Jessie and Henrietta felt comfortably as though they ate here every week, like the vicar. The conversation ranged from the local to the general and back again without pause, and Jessie found herself remembering the occasions she had dined with another doctor, Mark Darroway, and his family in London.

Darroway, too, did a great deal of free work. At the end of the meal, when Dr Wren got up and fetched the port (there had been quite a bit of getting up to fetch things throughout the meal – the Wrens evidently did not believe in ringing and twiddling their thumbs until the servant arrived – and there was no question, either, of the women leaving the table before the men) Jessie found herself again in conversation with him about his work and told him about Mark Darroway.

'He foresaw the war ages ago,' she said, 'and he told me the most useful thing any woman could do was to learn first aid. So you could say he is responsible for everything I do now, in the way of Red Cross work and hospital visiting.'

'And your aunt, you say, is a lady doctor?' Wren asked with interest.

'She's not really an aunt. She's my mother's distant cousin, so I suppose she's mine too, only at another remove. But she was one of the first women to qualify as a doctor.' And when she told Wren her name, he looked most impressed.

'But of course I've heard of her. She's done a great deal of important research into tuberculosis. And her mother was a pioneer of nursing and founded a great hospital. No wonder you're so interested in medicine. It must run in the blood.'

Jessie smiled deprecatingly. 'I'm hardly blood-related at all, you know. And her daughter isn't interested in medicine the least bit. Are your children doctors?'

Dr Wren laughed. 'No, my son went into banking, and my daughter married a farmer, so that scuppers my argument, doesn't it?'

They had a most pleasant afternoon, but as Dr Wren dropped them back at the hotel, he stayed Jessie a moment behind her mother and said, 'Having observed you for a few hours, I think you would be wise to refuse more invitations and settle for the quiet time you came here for. You look tired.'

'I feel pretty well,' Jessie said.

'But not thoroughly well? Yes, that's what I thought. I don't think there's anything to worry about, but no gadding about, a gentle walk every day and early to bed is what I'd prescribe for you, and you have my permission to quote me if any more invitations come. And – though I'm sure you won't need to – please call on me at any time if you have any anxieties or feel less well than usual. Hasty is a dear friend of mine and I've promised to keep a close eye on you.'

'Thank you,' said Jessie. 'But all I need is the sea air and peace and quiet.'

'Peace and quiet is certainly what you'll get in Scarborough in December,' Wren said with a smile.

The next two days passed quickly, despite their refusing several more invitations. They were happy to be quiet together, comfortable in each other's company. For entertainment, it was enough to be by the sea, which was different every moment, exhilarating to the senses. Jessie felt she could never be bored within sight and sound of the sea. There was a wonderful space and airiness about the South Bay at this time of year, when the sands were empty of people and washed clean by the tides. Many of Scarborough's attractions were closed, but they had enough to do. Henrietta's early-rising habits were not to be reformed for a mere few days' holiday, and as soon as she began moving around Jessie heard her and woke too. So they dressed quickly and went out for a walk before the town was properly astir. Then after breakfast they walked again. There was plenty to look at. There was the old castle, up on the green promontory that divided the North and South Bays. There was always some activity around the little harbour, with its busy fishing fleet. There were the resident artists, who preferred Scarborough in its crowd-free, winter guise, and were always to be seen setting up along the Foreshore or the Esplanade, painting the same view for the hundredth time in the hope of a different quality of light. And there were the gentlemen bathers, who swam every morning off the beach near the Spa, braving the chill of the North Sea no matter what the weather. Watching them plunge in gave Jessie a pleasant sense of contrasting comfort, and sent her to her breakfast with an appetite sharpened by their ordeal.

The weather was dry and cold, but dull, with the early-morning sea mists that were to be expected at that time of year. But the air was refreshing and invigorating with its smells of salt and tar and seaweed. Jessie liked to watch the seagulls wheel about overhead, and the little sanderlings running along by the water's edge like clockwork toys, always just avoiding the incoming waves, as if they were afraid of getting their feet wet. Sometimes Jessie and her mother talked, but often they were silent, walking or sitting by unspoken accord. Once Dr Wren went past, crammed into his little car, tooted his horn at them and waved. Once Jessie got into conversation with some convalescent soldiers who were taking the air on the Foreshore, where they were staying at the Royal Northern Sea Bathing and Convalescent Home. Some were Belgians, and she found that they knew some of her visitees at Heworth Park and were glad to hear news of them.

She and her mother had wondered whether they might see Lennie while they were in Scarborough, and on Monday afternoon when they were pottering about the shops, the battalion came marching through the streets, much to the excitement of the residents, who were very proud of 'their' regiment and always cheered them past. Henrietta and Jessie hurried to the edge of the pavement, and scanned the passing soldiers, but it was hard to tell one from another, all in uniform and with their caps shadowing their faces. But then Jessie cried, 'There he is!' and a moment later Henrietta spotted him too, and they both waved and called out to him. Under discipline, he could not wave back, but he glanced sidelong at them, and a self-conscious smirk tugged at his mouth. He was past and gone in a moment, but the one glimpse gave them fuel for conversation for some time, as they agreed that he looked well, and had put on weight and muscle.

'He looks a man, now, instead of a boy,' said Henrietta, almost sadly.

'Poor Polly,' Jessie said. 'Won't she wish she'd been here when we tell?'

On Wednesday morning they went out for their early walk,

and were returning to the hotel just before eight o'clock, pausing to talk to two of the convalescent-home soldiers who were out for their first, slow shuffle along the Foreshore. Jessie was standing facing the sea, and as she chatted to Captain Duclerc, she saw over his shoulder the shape of two enormous ships just appearing through the murk of the morning mist, grey on grey.

'Oh, look!' she said. 'Aren't those battleships?'

Her mother and the two officers looked round. 'Yes, they are battleships,' said Duclerc. 'But why are they so close to the shore?'

'It must be some kind of exercise,' Jessie said. 'Oh, there's another one.'

A third ship eased out of the mist in the wake of the other two. They cleared the headland and were steaming southwards, parallel with the shore and about a mile out. The leading ship was smaller than the other two, Jessie saw; and as she watched, the smoke from their stacks changed from grey to black as they increased speed.

Suddenly there was a crash, so loud that it made Jessie jump and bite her tongue. It was followed by a screaming noise somewhere up in the air and then another crash.

Then she realised one of the ships had fired, and laughed in shaky relief. 'I thought it was an enormous thunderclap,' she said. 'I suppose they must be on manoeuvres. What do you—'

But there was another tremendous crash, and this time she saw the flash of something like a giant firework exploding in the sky just above the castle; a third crash and she clearly saw a gout of smoke and debris leap up as whatever it was struck the Old Barracks up under the castle wall.

'They're firing at the castle,' she said blankly. 'Why ever would they do that?' And then, meeting Captain Duclerc's eyes, she saw them widen, as her own did, with realisation. 'It's the Germans!' she gasped.

It would never have occurred to her for an instant that the grey battleships suddenly appearing so close to shore were anything but British. The Royal Navy had ruled the oceans for so long that the safety of the sea was ingrained deeply in every English mind. As the ships belched out shell after shell from their huge guns, it was as though a piece of familiar furniture had suddenly taken on malevolent life.

Duclerc had heard shells before, and his reaction was swift. 'Run!' he cried. 'Take cover! Go, go, run!'

He had already turned away from the sea, but he and Lebrun were both lame and could hardly hobble. Jessie took his arm to help him. He tried to push her away. 'Leave us! Save yourselves!'

But she did not release him. 'You'll be quicker if you lean on me,' she said. 'Mother, run back to the hotel.'

Henrietta, though white with shock, went immediately to Lebrun. 'And leave you?' she said. 'Never.'

With the support of the women, the soldiers were able to hop along more quickly. Jessie cast a quick glance backwards over her shoulder and saw the grey monsters advancing steadily southwards. The first fusillade was over, and they were silent as they reloaded, but they were somehow more menacing for that. Would they get to shelter before the guns came opposite them? It was only a few yards to the convalescent home, and as soon as they neared the door, nurses came running out to take over.

'Come in and shelter here,' Duclerc said, but Jessie shook her head.

'No, we must go back to the hotel, pick up our things and get away. If the Germans are coming . . .'

'Yes, yes, you're right,' said Duclerc. 'Go to the railway station, take whatever train you can. Don't stay for your baggage.'

Jessie and Henrietta handed over their charges and hurried away towards the hotel.

'I do want to pack my things,' Henrietta said breathlessly. 'Surely we'll have time for that?' And her sentence ended in a little shriek as, with an appalling crash, the shelling began again.

Other people were coming out into the street now, looking bewildered, wondering what was going on. Up ahead, by the Spa, Jessie could see the gentlemen bathers staggering out of the sea and running up the beach to grab their discarded clothes. A woman rushed past her, clutching a birdcage in which a terrified canary tried to keep its grip on its perch. 'The Germans are coming! The Germans are coming!' she wailed as she ran. The words, rather than the sound of the shelling, seemed to penetrate the morning fog of those who had come out of their houses, and their eyes widened with shock. Soon they were running back indoors, and the cry was taken up and passed along.

Jessie looked back. The leading, smaller ship was racing southwards in silence, but the two larger ships were firing as they ploughed along parallel to the shore, raking the sea front with shells. The noise was appalling: the boom of the guns, the hideous high-pitched scream of the shell's flight, and then the terrible, tearing crash of the explosion. They were hitting buildings along the Foreshore Road now. She saw a shell rip into what she was sure was the convalescent home.

'Oh, God!' she cried out; and stumbled.

'Don't fall, Jessie! Please don't fall!' Henrietta's voice was high and unnatural, and Jessie realised she was gripping her arm so hard it hurt.

'I won't,' Jessie said, and suddenly her mind was quite calm. We won't reach the hotel in time, she thought. We must shelter somewhere. She saw the gentlemen bathers up ahead running from the beach now. Some went on running into the town; others crouched down behind the sea wall. With a screaming, splintering explosion, a shell burst into the glass frontage of the Olympia Picture Palace just behind them, and Jessie flung her arm round her mother's shoulders and without a word pulled her down to the ground below the sea wall.

The shells came shrieking overhead, aimed now at the Grand Hotel, which must be such an inviting target, perched up there, dominating the skyline. With her mother's head buried in her shoulder Jessie watched in horror as shell after shell tore into the building, ripping through the roof, the attic windows, the façade, blowing great chunks of masonry off the corners as easily as if it were made of cake. The glass of the restaurant's windows and roof was shattered, shards catching the light as they rocketed outwards. More shells, and more shells – would it never end? She saw a row of ghastly, gaping holes appear as guest rooms were torn open. Only yesterday she and her mother had stood here on the front and discussed which windows in that façade were their two rooms. Now with numb terror she saw those rooms destroyed. If they had not been out for their walk, they would be dead by now, she thought, her stomach falling away from her in sick realisation. If they had not been early risers, they would certainly be dead, blown to shreds like the remnants of the curtains that hung in tatters out of the ugly holes their rooms had become.

She could not count how many shells were fired into the hotel – twenty? Thirty? Fifty? But at last they stopped screaming overhead, as the ships moved on and the hail of destruction was aimed at buildings further south. Now was their chance, Jessie thought. They must get away. No need to worry about collecting their clothes – there would be nothing left of them. They must simply get to the railway station, as Duclerc had said, and leave before the Germans landed. Whatever train was in the station, she thought, they would take it, no matter where it was going. Above all, they must escape. She knew there was no time to lose, but for the moment she could not move. She was trembling all over, and her legs were like string. It was not fear so much as the noise. She never wanted to hear a noise like that again. She felt as though it had battered the bones out of her and left her a heap of jelly.

Her mother was trembling too. 'Mother,' she said, shaking her a little. Her voice came out hoarse and strange. 'Mother, we must go now. They've moved on – it's our chance.'

Henrietta lifted her head. Her face was chalk white and her eyes wide and staring. Jessie knew she must look much the same. Shells were crashing into the area of the Esplanade and the Filey Road, where they had dined on Saturday night, gouging great holes in the beach in front of the Spa where the bathing men had run across minutes ago, blowing up trees in the gardens behind the Spa buildings. But there were none now passing overhead. 'We must go – *now*,' Jessie said urgently.

Clutching each other, they staggered to their feet.

Henrietta looked towards the hotel, and uttered a little cry of fear. 'That was – there – that – our *rooms*!' she stammered. 'Gone. Our things—'

'Gone too,' said Jessie. 'No use going in. We must go straight to the station. We must get home.'

'God, yes!' Henrietta said fervently. Home. If the Germans came, they wanted to be at home. She had a sudden vision of Morland Place under siege. They had talked about pulling up the drawbridge, firing from the walls. Polly had wanted to pour boiling oil. It had been lighthearted, a game. No-one had ever believed that the Germans might really come. And what use would the fortress walls of Morland Place be against shells? In her mind she saw one ripping through her home like tearing paper, and her legs gave way under her. Jessie sagged under her sudden collapse, but managed to bear her up, and then they were hurrying, clutching each other, half walking, half running up the road past the hotel. There were bricks and glass and shattered wood everywhere, great chunks of cornice, half a grandfather clock poking up from a heap of rubble, two halves of a bed-head, split down the middle but otherwise undamaged, lying on its own in a clear space. Jessie glanced in through one of the holes as they passed, and saw the wallpaper of the room within shredded as though it had been clawed by a monster cat. What could have done that? There was nothing in the room at all but heaps of glass and matchwood. She couldn't now remember what the room had been – was it the writing room? She had sat there on Monday night to write to Ned, but the chair she had sat in and the table she had leaned on were indistinguishable, equally reduced to kindling.

Now the streets were full of people, all fleeing the menace of the guns. The sound of the shelling still went on further south, louder than any sound the people might make; and the grey sky was crimson here and there with the glow of fires. Jessie was reminded of something by the sight of people hurrying along clutching bundles, children's hands, the leashes of dogs. Someone had a cart piled with belongings, someone else had managed to pack a suitcase, which had something white flapping out of it where the lid had been closed on it. One woman carried a parrot in a cage; a small child clutched a terrified kitten to her chest. People were in whatever they had been wearing when the shells came, many of them in nightclothes, some half dressed. Jessie saw a man in a nightshirt and one boot hobbling along, with dabs of lather on his half-shaved face.

Refugees, she thought. That was what she was remembering – Bertie's accounts from France of the refugees fleeing before the Germans. And, just as in France, there was one sentence on the pale lips in the strained faces: *The Germans are coming!*

Now they were in Westborough, the main thoroughfare with the tramlines up the centre, which led to the railway station. As they passed the end of York Place a glance told Jessie that it had taken a severe beating – it looked as though every window in the street had been broken. But there was something else – a woman crouching beside an old man who was sitting on the kerb in his nightshirt. The nightshirt was grey and white in stripes, and there were scarlet flowers of blood blooming here and there on it.

Jessie halted against the drag of her mother's forward movement. 'Mother!'

Henrietta stopped, and looked. Their eyes met.

'I must help,' Jessie said. For what else had she taken her first-aid certificate? Henrietta swallowed her urgent need to get home and nodded. They turned aside out of the flow and hurried towards the couple.

The woman looked up as they approached, shock and terror distorting her face. 'My father,' she said. 'The glass. A bomb or something – bits came in.'

Jessie pushed her gently back and knelt by the old man. He was less shocked than his daughter, she thought. Perhaps he had been a soldier in his time. There seemed to be blood all over his legs, but the biggest flower was on his back. His face was covered with white bristles over a pasty pallor that was almost grey by contrast, but he looked at Jessie and spoke rationally. 'Shrapnel. I was just getting up. Bloody great chunks of shrapnel. Are you a nurse?'

425

'Yes,' Jessie said, thinking he would be less likely to object to her tending him if he thought she was. She eased his nightshirt away from his skin at the back and looked down inside it. There was a large gash, but there did not seem to be anything in it. She inserted her hand to feel, and the old man said, 'Hey!' in protest, but then fell silent. No, there was nothing in it. It was bleeding freely, but not spouting. He would need stitches, she thought.

'Let me look at your legs.' Under the blood there was a score of cuts, only one deep.

The woman kept on talking as she watched Jessie helplessly. 'I was making the tea to take up to him. George went off to work at seven. He's at the gasworks. Did they bomb the gasworks? I hope George is all right. I was just going to get Dad up and there was this bang, and stuff came in the window. A piece of it just like a dagger went past me. I was holding the tea caddy, making Dad's tea. Next minute it was gone. It was stuck to the kitchen wall with this dagger thing right through it.'

'Shrapnel. It was shrapnel,' said the old man, irritably.

'It only just missed me,' the woman said tonelessly, her eyes glazed. 'I was holding the tea caddy in my hand, and next minute it's nailed to the wall.'

Jessie pulled out her handkerchief – a good big one that she always carried out of old habit from her riding days – and bound it round the old man's worst cut. 'We must get you to medical help,' she said. 'Your cuts aren't too bad but some of them will need stitching. Do you think you can walk if we help you?'

'Course I can!' he said, but when they helped him up, he swayed and nearly fell. 'Ma legs is gone funny,' he said, bewildered by his own weakness.

'I hope George is all right. Did they bomb the gasworks, do you know?' the woman said.

'I don't know,' Jessie said. No use asking her where the nearest hospital or Red Cross place was. 'Better get him to the station,' she said to her mother. 'There's bound to be help there.'

Jessie and Henrietta got one either side of him with their

shoulders under his armpits, and started off, with the woman trailing behind them, muttering about the gasworks and tea caddies in a disconnected way. The old man tried to walk, but had obviously lost enough blood to drain his strength, and they were obliged before they reached the end of the road to hook their free hands under his knees and lift him.

He was a scrawny old thing but, even so, heavy for two women to carry. They were more than glad when they reached the main road to be accosted by a large, strong-looking man, who said, ''Ere, give 'im to me. Ah'll tek 'im. Coom on, old feller. That's right.' He heaved the old man up into his arms like a child. 'By 'eck, you're bleedin' a bit,' he discovered.

'He needs some stitches. We thought there might be a Red Cross place at the station,' Jessie said.

'Nay, that's in the Wesleyan Chapel, just back there a step. Red Cross an' St John's have tekken over t' basement for a hospital. We'd best get 'im there.'

It was only a few yards. Just as they reached it, a measured, rapid tramping behind them made Jessie turn her head, to see a platoon of Yorkshire Hussars quick-marching down Westborough towards the sea front. It was a cheering and steadying sight. Their officers were billeted at the Pavilion Hotel, opposite the station, and had obviously reacted to the emergency and sent off what men were to hand.

The little group hurried down the outside steps to the basement, and walked into a scene of organised chaos, as the doctors and nurses attended to the wounded who were walking or being helped in.

A Red Cross nurse came up and directed the helpful man to put his burden down on a chair, and bent over him. 'Is he a relative?' she demanded, and the man gestured help-lessly towards Jessie, who in turn pushed forward the old man's daughter.

'I'll be off, then,' said the helpful man, backed away and hurried for the stairs.

'We should go too,' Henrietta said urgently to Jessie. In the distance the noise of shelling, which had died away some-what, was growing louder again.

'All right,' said Jessie, and turned away to follow her. At that moment a woman came staggering down the steps, in her nightgown and with a red flannel shawl slipping off her shoulders. She was carrying a small child in her arms, and the child was screaming, his face covered with blood.

'Help me!' the woman cried. 'Somebody help me!'

Jessie looked round. Every nurse and doctor in the room was already attending to someone, the most urgent knot gathered round a badly injured soldier lying on a stretcher on the ground. There was no-one free to go to the woman. Jessie caught her mother's eye and shrugged. 'Come and set him down here,' she said to the woman. Much as she longed to go home, she had to do what she could.

Henrietta watched her for a moment, then looked round to see where help was needed.

The three German ships sailed southward as far as White Nab, and then the smaller one went on southwards while the larger two turned about and began to steam northwards, raking the town again as they passed. This time they raised the elevation of the guns and the shells fell further into the town, into the most heavily populated part behind the Victoria Road. In the chapel basement they heard the shells coming nearer, then screaming overhead, and the tremendous explosions, which shook the floor and rattled the windows, as they crashed into houses only yards away.

More and more wounded came down into the hospital, and Jessie, her sleeves rolled up now, helped where she could. One of the doctors saw that she was calm and competent and directed her to this patient and that. Some of the injuries were horrible – one woman was brought in with both feet blown off, and died soon afterwards; another's side was ripped open in a foot-long gash; a man was cut right across his face and left eye. It was a violent baptism into first aid for Jessie, who had only bandaged pretend wounds until now, but she was kept so busy she had no time to be afraid, or feel sick or faint at the sights before her. She only hoped no shell would land on them here, for they would never be able to get the wounded out. Other doctors had come in to help now, and she looked about for Dr Wren but did not see him. But she understood from what she heard that the main hospital was to the north side of South Bay, in Friar's Entry, quite close to where the Wrens lived, so she supposed he was working there.

The Germans seemed to be concentrating on Victoria Street, for the shelling went on and on. After some time two men in orderlies' uniform came down the steps, one supporting the other, who was clutching his arm, his face white with pain. A nurse went to receive him, and Jessie, who was bandaging a child's foot, heard her say that the arm was broken.

'He's the ambulance driver,' the injured man's companion said. 'What's to do now? We need someone to drive it. Can anyone here drive?'

Jessie tied the ends of the bandage and looked up. In the basement, apart from the doctors, nurses and the wounded, there were only women who had brought in children and were staying with them. 'Does anyone know how to drive?' the orderly asked again, and no-one responded.

She met his eyes. 'I can drive,' she said.

He looked at her doubtfully. 'Will you? I don't know how to, or I'd do it.'

'I can drive,' Jessie said again. She looked round for Henrietta, and found her nearby, listening. 'Mother, you'd better go to the station and try to get on a train.'

Henrietta shook her head, her lips tight. 'I'll stay here and help. Oh, Jessie – I know you must do it but, please, be careful.'

'I will,' she said. It was clear to her, as it must have been to her mother, that it would be a matter of luck, one way or the other, and that care did not come into it. The shells were still falling, but one had to do what one could. 'Come on,' she said to the man. 'Show me where it is.'

The streets were littered with debris, broken glass and discarded belongings. Everywhere people were hurrying, trying to get to the railway station, or fleeing the town on foot, on horseback, in motor-cars; or helping the wounded along, looking for help. Jessie found she could drive the ambulance well enough, and with the orderly to guide her she picked her way through the debris to Victoria Street and turned right. The shelling seemed to have gone further north now – there were no shells landing at this end of the road, at any rate. As they reached the turning of Belle Vue Street a policeman, his uniform covered with dust and his helmet missing, flagged them down.

'Got some badly wounded folks here,' he said, 'need to be tekken to th'ospital.'

A shrapnel shell had burst in the street, and a boy of eleven had been hit in the head and carried twenty yards by the blow. He was unconscious and looked close to death. A young man had been gashed in the thigh, leg and wrist by shrapnel as he had stood in his doorway, and an older man had been hit in the back as he ran home from work to try to get to his family. Willing hands lifted them into the ambulance, and the policeman climbed up afterwards to cradle the child. The orderly, whose name was Nairn, climbed up beside Jessie and gave her instructions as she drove to the main hospital. There they deposited their cargo, turned round and went back out into the town.

After the second trip, Jessie became aware that the shelling had stopped, and as a brief spasm of relief washed over her, she realised how tense she had been until then, expecting at any moment, in the back of her mind, to be blown up. Of course, it might only be a temporary lull, as the Germans turned round to make another pass, but she was grateful for the respite all the same.

For the next hour or more, Jessie drove the ambulance back and forth through the town, ferrying the passengers to hospital. The devastation was awful, ruined houses with gaping windows, bare roofs, collapsed walls and chimneys, torn rooms exposed to the outside air with their owners' possessions pitifully on display, broken and abandoned. There had been no more shelling, and the word was that the German ships had sailed on northwards after the second pass, but no-one took any comfort from that. They would be back, and this time they would land and march through the streets. The exodus of everyone who could flee carried on, and motor-car owners were ferrying people on a regular service from the centre to the outlying villages.

As they worked they heard stories of terrible disasters and miraculous escapes. John Turner, whom Jessie had met at dinner on Saturday, had had his house hit by three shells on the first pass. The postman, who had just reached his front door, was blown half-way down the drive and was found badly injured, the letters from his bag scattered all over the grounds. Turner's maid had been killed, her stomach ripped open and both her legs shattered by shrapnel. A whole family had been killed in Wykeham Street when their house collapsed after a direct hit; in another street an eleven-year-old girl, alone in the house, had hidden behind a sofa. When her mother managed to get back to the house it was a ruin, everything in the house reduced to matchwood, but the sofa, though its fabric was ripped and its stuffing blown all over the room, was still in one piece, and the little girl emerged from behind it white from head to foot with plaster dust but unhurt.

Rosemount, the home of the Greshams, had suffered from the same hail of shells that afflicted John Turner, and Jessie heard that Mrs Gresham and Rosemary had both been wounded by flying glass, though not badly. All the girls at Queen Margaret's School had been at breakfast when the bombardment started, and had run from the shelling, then marched across country until they reached Seamer and safety.

Jessie was driving the ambulance through Westborough past the railway station when a soldier wearing a white armband hailed her. As she stopped beside him, she saw to her surprise that it was Lennie.

Lennie came up to the window. 'I thought I saw you in the crowd the other day. What are you doing here?'

'The ambulance driver broke his arm, and I was the only person around who could drive,' she said.

'I meant, what are you doing in Scarborough?'

'I came with Mother for a holiday. The doctor said she needed peace and quiet.' Lennie grimaced at that. 'Are you hurt? There's blood on your face.'

He looked surprised and wiped it off with his forearm. 'It isn't mine. We were drilling in the station yard when all this started, so they gave us these armbands and sent us to help the wounded. I say, this is a lark, isn't it? We'd sooner be manning the trenches, you know,' he added. 'We ought to be setting up the defences for when the Germans come back. But orders are orders.'

'I saw some Hussars going towards the beach a while ago.'

'Yes, and I think they've got a machine-gun up at the castle. But it's not much. I hope they're sending in more troops. Who'd have thought the Huns would attack an unarmed town like this?'

'I must get on,' Jessie said. 'What did you flag me down for?'

'Oh, yes. I've got two old people over there, not badly wounded, but they're very shocked, and I think they should go to hospital. Can you take them?'

'Yes, bring them over,' said Jessie.

He and Nairn helped the old people in, and then Jessie leaned out of the window to wave to Lennie as she drove off. 'Good luck!' she called.

'Same to you,' he called back. 'Keep your head down when the shelling starts again.'

They stopped to take up a stretcher case, then headed for the hospital. Two orderlies ran out to take in the stretcher, and they were followed by Dr Wren, who started in surprise when he saw Jessie in the ambulance cab, and came hurrying over to her.

'What are you doing there?' he demanded. 'I assumed you and your mother had left long ago.'

'The driver broke his arm, and no-one else could drive,' she said simply. 'Someone had to do it.'

'Of course,' Wren said sympathetically, 'but you've done your part now. Let me find someone else.'

'I can drive, sir,' said one of the orderlies, a young man of seventeen.

'Very good,' said Wren. 'Take that stretcher inside and then come back here.'

432

'I'm all right,' said Jessie. 'And you need him here.'

'We can manage. You must get out of Scarborough before the Germans come back. Is your mother all right?'

'Yes. She's helping at the Red Cross hospital.'

'That's right by the station. Have the ambulance drive you back there, find her, and both of you get on the first train you can.' He laid a hand over hers, resting on the open window. 'I know you want to help, and I honour you for it, but your duty now is to that baby.'

'I feel fine, really,' she said. It occurred to her she hadn't thought about being pregnant since the shelling started.

'Make sure you keep it that way. Get home as soon as you can. I'm serious now.'

'All right, I'll go. Do you think I can just telephone Uncle Teddy first?'

Wren shook his head. 'No telephone calls allowed – they're being reserved for official business. And no telegrams, either.'

'Good Lord,' Jessie said. 'But they must know about it in York by now. Uncle will be frantic.'

'All the more reason to get back there as soon as possible,' said Wren, and this time Jessie agreed with him.

CHAPTER TWENTY

Robbie was the first of the family to hear about the bombardment. He was at his desk at the bank when a fellow clerk, Osgood, came in and announced in some excitement, 'I say, Compton, have you heard? The Germans have landed at Scarborough.'

Robbie looked up and frowned. 'Scarborough? No. How could they have?'

'It's true,' said Osgood. 'First they sent the German navy and bombed the town, and then they landed. A fellow was just in who saw someone who knew.'

'What fellow? What someone?'

'A customer,' said Osgood patiently. 'Mr Althorpe, if you must know. He met a man down by the station who'd just come from Scarborough – fled from the bombing with his family. *He* told him the Germans had landed – thousands and thousands of them marching up the beach,' he embroidered happily.

'But – good God! – my mother's there! And my sister. On holiday.' He scrambled up from the desk. 'They went on Saturday.'

'I say, I'm awfully sorry,' said Osgood. 'I didn't know you had people there. It might not be true, you know. These things get about just anyhow. Perhaps it isn't true. Probably just a story.'

But Robbie dashed past him without hearing. He went first to the office of his principal and asked for permission to telephone home. When he explained the matter, Mr

Laxton was all sympathy. Robbie telephoned Morland Place and spoke to Uncle Teddy, who promised to let him know as soon as he found out anything, and then he went back to his desk to chew his lip and stare blankly at the wall, unable to concentrate on his work.

At Morland Place, Teddy was frantic. He very soon discovered what Jessie had learned, that it was not possible to telephone anyone in Scarborough, which in itself seemed a confirmation of the story. He telephoned to various people in York, and bit by bit the truth was pieced together. The invasion story, it seemed, was untrue, or at least was an anticipation of what everyone expected, but the shelling of the town by German ships was real enough. The damage was terrible and there had been many casualties.

He learned that there had been attacks also on Hartlepool and Whitby, which suggested a large German fleet must be operating along the North Sea coast – and what could that be for but to facilitate an invasion?

'Well, if they come here, they'll find us ready for them,' he said to Ethel and Alice. 'Thank God I had the drawbridge repaired!'

Since the war began he had been working on his plans for defending Morland Place, and now he hurried to fetch them from his desk in the steward's room. He called Sawry and the senior servants to join the family in the drawing-room. 'In my absence,' he told the butler, 'and until Mr Robert comes home, you must be in command.'

'Yes, sir, of course. I understand,' said Sawry, looking anything but pleased at the promotion.

'I don't want the lower servants alarmed. Everyone must keep calm and do his part. If it comes to a siege we have plenty of food, but I don't anticipate the Germans will get this far for days. However, we must be prepared – exposed, as we are, outside the city walls. Simmons, I shall need you.'

'Sir?' said the chauffeur.

'I must drive to Scarborough and try to find the mistress and Miss Jessie.' Alice gave a little cry, at once stifled. Teddy took her hands and pressed them. 'I must go – you see that?

'I will be as careful as I can. Brown, I'll take my Purdeys with me, just in case.'

'Sir, let me come with you,' Brown pleaded. He had survived the *Titanic* sinking alongside his master, and did not want to lose him now.

'No, old friend,' said Teddy. 'We need every man possible here to defend the house, if it should come to it.'

He had Simmons drive him first to the railway station, in case his sister and niece had managed to get onto a train. There were huge crowds milling around the station and its yard. Some of them were evidently refugees, for they were unkempt and dishevelled, some with blankets draped over nightclothes. Many were carrying bundles of belongings hastily snatched up. One woman, looking dazed and bewildered, held a large Christmas cake clutched to her chest – in the heat of the moment it was the one thing she could not bear to leave for the Germans, with all that good fruit and marzipan and the thick icing she had only finished the night before.

Teddy could not see Henrietta and Jessie anywhere, and decided to find the station master and ask him what trains had come in, and what were expected. It took time to force his way through to the station master's office, but once there he was swiftly admitted and received with all courtesy.

'I'm trying to find out what I can, Mr Morland,' said the station master. 'This fellow here –' he indicated an engine driver standing by, cap in hand '– was in Scarborough station when it started. I was just asking him—'

The engine driver could not wait to tell his story. 'Three German battleships, sir, just appeared out of nowhere. It'd be about eight o'clock, sir, near as I can say. They fired on the town, sir, hundreds of shells. Blew it to bits. Everyone was running, trying to get away. Trying to get on trains. No tickets, most of 'em. The porters and staff were trying to keep order. I knew the driver of the eight twenty-five to Leeds, so I got him to take me up in the cab.'

'That's against regulations, you know,' said the station master, sternly.

'I've an old mother here in York,' the driver said defiantly, 'and I wasn't having her worry about me. Besides, if the Germans are coming, I'm keeping out of it. Well, when we got to Leeds, I hopped another ride back here.'

'Was the Grand Hotel hit, do you know?' Teddy asked him.

'Blown to bits,' said the driver. 'The first lot of shells was all along the front. They couldn't hardly miss the Grand.'

'Oh, good God,' Teddy muttered. He turned to the station master. 'Are the trains running now?'

'We've had one train in from Scarborough, and there were others to Pickering and Malton, as well as the one to Leeds. But the railway authorities have stopped any more leaving either way until they can check that the line is clear and not damaged. It wouldn't help anyone, sir, to have a derailment or an accident on our hands as well.'

'Then I shall have to drive,' Teddy said. 'May I use your telephone?'

'No calls to Scarborough, sir,' the station master said quickly.

'I know that. I want to call my nephew in York.' He telephoned Robbie and told him what he knew, and urged him to go home as soon as possible, as there was no man in the house apart from servants. Then he left and struggled out through the crowds to the motor-car.

The road from Scarborough was busier than usual, with a stream of motors, carts and even, as he drew nearer the town, people on foot, all in flight. The sight only made Teddy more agitated. The engine driver's words haunted him – the Grand blown to bits! If the shelling had started at eight o'clock, where had Jessie and Henrietta been? They were both early risers, he knew that, but perhaps on holiday, especially when Henrietta had been told to rest, they might lie longer abed. Or they might have been having breakfast – that seemed the most likely thing. He could not envisage Henrietta still in bed at eight o'clock. But having breakfast was just as bad, if the whole hotel was destroyed. Or nearly as bad – perhaps there was more chance of escaping from the restaurant than a bedroom. But escaping to what, if the shells were falling all around? Oh, why, why had he encouraged them to go? He had booked their rooms for them, and their railway tickets. He would never forgive himself. He crouched forward in his seat as if it would make the motor go faster, and prayed silently, 'Oh, God, please!'

Simmons spoke through the tube. 'We're nearly there, sir. Where would you like me to go?'

'To the Grand,' he said. It was the obvious place to start.

There had been no more shelling after half past eight, and news was filtering through that the ships that had done the damage had gone on north to Whitby. As time passed and the ships did not reappear, some of Scarborough's panic turned to indignation. Where was the Royal Navy? How could German warships be allowed to get so close to British shores unchallenged, do their terrible work and get away unscathed?

The flight from the town went on, but more calmly, with people stopping to collect possessions, somewhat comforted by the soldiers dug in along the beach and up on Castle Hill. At least if the Germans came now they would not be totally undefended. But the town – oh, the town was shattered! Street after street, smashed and ruined, houses, shops, churches, the town hall, the Grand – all the main hotels – the Floral Hall, the Spa gardens. How was it all to be cleared up, and rebuilt? How were lives to be put together again? Who would pay?

Released from her duty to help, Jessie felt a reaction as the ambulance drove her back to Westborough, as though all her muscles, tensed for a task, had abruptly relaxed. She felt limp and tired and, as she really appreciated the devastation of the streets for the first time, a little depressed.

The first person she saw as she got down outside the Wesleyan Chapel was Erskine Gresham, helping a man up the steps. 'Hullo!' he said. 'I'm surprised to see you here. I thought you'd have left town long ago.'

'I'm going now. We were going to the station earlier, but people needed help so we stayed. I've been driving an ambulance.'

'I say, good show!'

'How are you all at Rosemount?' Jessie asked, embarrassed by his admiring look.

'Not too badly. About thirteen shells fell around us, mostly at the back of the house, did quite a bit of damage. The mater and Rosy were in the kitchen trying to calm the servants and they got a few cuts from all the glass, but they're not deep. The guv'nor's more angry than shocked. He's taking it out on the debris with a shovel. Got everything under control, so I thought I'd come out and see if anyone in the town needed help.' He looked around, and an expression of concern came over his face. 'Oh, but I say, where's your mother? Here I am rattling on – she is all right, isn't she? I heard the Grand was hit, but they said no-one there was hurt.'

'It's all right, we were both out walking when it happened. Mother's down there, helping with the wounded. I'm surprised you didn't see her.'

'I didn't go further than the door. They asked me to see that chap up the steps and said they didn't need any more help. I say, have you really been driving an ambulance? You really are a topping sort!'

Jessie grinned suddenly. 'Yes, I am, aren't I? What a good job I learned to drive, as well as first aid.'

'I shouldn't think there's anything you can't do,' he said. 'We could do with you out in France.'

'When will you be going back, do you know?'

'My wound's about healed, so in another week or so. Probably immediately after Christmas. It's all quiet out there at the moment, but of course everyone needs leave so I'll have to relieve another officer. Perhaps your cousin, Parke?'

'Well, good luck when you go back,' she said. 'Keep your head down.'

He grinned. 'I will. And you too.'

Henrietta looked greatly relieved to see her, and had no objection at all to their immediate departure. 'Are you feeling all right?' she asked.

'Yes, I'm fine. Only tired. I forgot all about the baby while I was driving the ambulance.'

'I shouldn't have let you forget it,' Henrietta said.

'Don't worry. We're going home now.'

It was not quite that easy. The station was still thronged with people trying to escape, as well as being a central point for people wanting information and soldiers wanting orders. And at the moment, so the distracted staff had to tell everyone a dozen times a minute, there were no trains going out because there was some doubt about the safety of the line. The engineers were checking it now.

Someone shouted that the excursion station further down the line at Westover Road had trains going out, and there was a surging exodus that almost knocked Jessie over. As she clung to her mother for balance, Henrietta said, 'Should we go too, do you think? Is it true – will there be a train there?'

'I don't know,' Jessie said. 'Let's wait a minute until the crowd thins. I don't think I can fight my way through such a mob.'

And that was how Teddy found them soon afterwards. He pushed his way through to their side, and engulfed them both in a silent hug, his face white and strained. He had seen the damage to the Grand, and the gaping holes where once their rooms had been, and the staff's assurance that the ladies had gone out and not returned before the shells hit had only given him the most temporary relief. Outside must have been as dangerous as inside. Asking where the nearest first-aid station was, he had been directed first to the main hospital at Friar's Entry. Enquiry had been long and frustrating, but he had seen no sign of his loved ones, and had gone thence to the Wesleyan Chapel, where at last he had found word.

'I thought I'd lost you,' he said, and there was another long, silent embrace.

'How did you get here?' Jessie asked.

'Simmons is outside with the motor. I'm going to drive you home right this minute.'

'We're ready,' said Henrietta with relief.

'Where are your things?' Teddy asked. 'Oh – stupid of me. I suppose—' He shuddered. 'Thank God you weren't in your rooms when it happened. Our father always hated

Scarborough, Hen. I should never have let you come here.'

Henrietta shook her head at his illogic. 'It isn't Scarborough's fault. But I shall be glad to get home.'

At half past eleven in the morning the first official statement was issued by the Admiralty, and at noon a special cabinet meeting was convened at 10 Downing Street and the Prime Minister, Mr Asquith, was apprised of the situation by Mr Churchill, the First Lord. At one o'clock the Leeds Rifles, a Territorial regiment billeted in the dining room of Rowntree's chocolate factory in York, were marched down to York station to huge acclaim from the crowds, to go to Scarborough's defence. They were not able to leave for Scarborough until half past two, as it took time to assemble a suitable train, and the engineers were still checking the track. But as the light began to fail, the first of them arrived, and were set to clear the station of rubble until the rest of the battalion caught up. Persistent rumours that the Germans had landed meant the soldiers believed they were going to have a crack at the enemy straight off. When all had arrived they were formed up and marched through the town to dig themselves in along the sand. But the only ships that appeared were two British destroyers, cruising past in the gathering dusk on patrol.

By the evening more statements had been issued by the Admiralty and the War Office, and it was known throughout the kingdom that three coastal towns had been attacked. It was not, it seemed, a precursor to invasion. The Admiralty had expected something of the sort, a ploy by the Germans to try to divert British naval strength from the Channel. They were sorry, but they could do nothing to prevent it. Exposed towns on the east coast must expect to be bombarded, and must simply put up with it. The job of the Royal Navy was to protect England, not little bits of it. Such attacks, though deplorable, were devoid of military significance, and the Admiralty would not be diverted from its settled strategy on that account.

At Morland Place there was rejoicing that the missing had been restored to them. Brach almost knocked Jessie down in her joy. There was relief, too, that there was not going to be an invasion via Scarborough – though Teddy kept his plans ready on hand just in case. There was a telephone call from Ned, who had begged permission as soon as the news of the bombardment reached them at Black Brow to ring home. Fortunately, as the battalion had been out on an exercise, this was not until after Jessie and Henrietta were safely back at Morland Place, so his anxiety, which was acute, was short-lived.

He begged Jessie not to go home to Maystone that night. Uncle Teddy had already asked her, and she was only too glad to stay, with all the comfort of her childhood home and her family around her. They dined early, and after a short time in the drawing-room Teddy urged Jessie and Henrietta to go to bed. They smiled across the room at each other at his solicitude, but were not unwilling, after such a day. They walked up the stairs arm in arm, with Brach pressed close to Jessie's thigh, as if she knew she had nearly lost her. At the door of the East Bedroom – her old room – Jessie kissed her mother and said, 'Well, we survived.'

'With honour,' said Henrietta. 'Sleep well, darling.'

There was a fire in the grate, and a hot-water bottle had been slipped between the sheets, and Jessie hopped into bed and snuggled down with a sense of delicious comfort. Her mind flickered at first back and forth over the memories of the day, but she was very tired, and she was soon drifting down into sleep. She thought of her conversation with Ned, and how worried he had been for her. And she thought about the baby, and how any day now, according to Dr Hasty, she would be 'feeling life'. How strange that would be, to feel another living thing inside her! She decided that as soon as it happened, she would not hold off any longer from telling Ned about the baby. She had almost told him this evening on the telephone, but had stopped herself, not liking to add to his anxiety about her ordeal. Besides, she wanted to tell him face to face. She wanted to see his expression, and hear him say how . . .

She slept; and woke to a sense of unease. She lay in the darkness listening, but there was no sound. What had woken her? She shifted position, and felt wetness. Was the hot-water bottle leaking? But her feet weren't wet. And then a sharp, thick pain drove through her, waking her fully. Fear and dread came fast and cold and heavy to her mind. She knew what that wetness was. With trembling hands she reached out for the candle and matches, and let out a small cry as the pain came again. *Mother!* she cried in her mind. *Mother, make it all right! I can't lose the baby again.* The pain was cutting her in half. *Oh, Mother, make it stop!*

Jessie lay in her bed in the East Bedroom and wept into her pillow. The baby had been dead, Dr Hasty said, and that was why it had come when it did. It had not been her fault. It was nothing to do with driving the ambulance in Scarborough. She had not killed it. It had been dead already.

But even when she believed him, it was no comfort. She wept and wept, not noisily, but broken-heartedly. She would never feel it kick now. She would not see the delight on Ned's face. She had failed him – failed herself, failed, most of all, her poor baby. Her inhospitable womb could not sustain life. She would never give Ned a child – and now that she was sure of it, it was the thing she wanted most of all. The guilt of her secret thoughts of the past, her glad-ness not to be pregnant, gnawed at her now. But, most of all, there was sorrow. She cried and cried as though she would never stop, staring into an abyss of loss, her body aching and, oh, so empty.

She cried for two days. Dr Hasty tried to ease her mind, saying that there was no reason she should not conceive again. She would have lots of children. These things were unfortunate and upsetting, but they happened more often than one would think, and should not be viewed as an indi-cation of anything wrong. She heard him but did not heed him, and when the tears stopped, she sank into a deep depression.

Henrietta nursed her tenderly, repeating the doctor's assurances. She hated to see her brave Jessie reduced to such helplessness, her eyes red and swollen with weeping. But the depression after the tears was even harder to bear.

The white, suffering face so still on the pillow, the bleak eyes turned away, staring at nothing, hurt her far more, because there was nothing she could do about it.

There was no question of Jessie's going to Maystone at present. Tomlinson would have liked to come and nurse her mistress, but the house could not be left unsupervised, so she remained at Maystone and sent Susie instead, to fetch and carry for the sick-room. Brach stayed in the room most of the time, sleeping beside the bed, keeping one ear cocked for any movement or word. But Jessie could take no comfort from Brach. She was lost in a dark place.

Ned came on the third day. The battalion's leave had been set, and his days off were not due until after Christmas, but the news of the miscarriage had somehow filtered through the officers' mess, and there was great, though largely unspoken, sympathy for him. It was not a subject men could comfortably discuss, especially as he had never mentioned that his wife was expecting. The grimness of his expression did not invite comment, however well meant. But the following day one of his fellow subalterns, Venman, came shyly up to him and offered to swap leave with him, if the CO agreed. Venman was supposed to be having the 19th to the 23rd, but was happy to take Ned's days, if it would comfort him to see his wife sooner. 'We're all so sorry, old fellow,' Venman said quietly.

Ned thanked him bemusedly out of the shock that enveloped him. He had not realised there were such kind feelings towards him in the mess. He felt just a little comforted, accepted the offer, and gripped the outstretched hand gratefully. Colonel Bassett had no objection to the swap. Ned got up before dawn on the 19th, hitched a ride to York on a transport, took a taxi-cab out to Morland Place, and was there by mid-morning.

The first sight of him made Henrietta cry – she was always close to tears these days. 'Oh, Ned, I'm so sorry,' she said.

Ned looked pale. 'How is she?'

'She's taking it very hard,' Henrietta said, dabbing at her

444

eyes. 'She thinks it means she won't ever have a baby.' She hesitated. 'She thinks you'll blame her.'

Ned seemed to flinch a little at the words, but he said, 'I'll go up and see her.' His face looked so grim Henrietta almost wanted to stop him. This was not the easy-going, smiling boy she remembered. He looked like a soldier now, and it was not just the uniform or the haircut. His face was firm, his mouth set, and there was something in his eyes . . . She hoped he would not be too hard on her child, but she was afraid to interfere in case she made things worse.

Ned was shocked at the sight of Jessie, lying so flat and unmoving in the bed, her face pinched with suffering. He was used to her upright: strong, defiant, arguing with him, always wanting her own way. The anger he had brought with him without realising it ebbed away, and he felt only lost and hurt.

She did not look at him as he came in. Brach got up, ears flattened, tail swinging, and came to him, rolling her eyes up apologetically as she licked his hand – delighted to see him but hoping that whatever was wrong was not her fault. He caressed her automatically, but then pushed her away and went to the bedside. There was a penitential sort of chair there – the plain, hard, wooden sort that gets relegated from room to room and ekes out its final years in a spare bedroom. It fitted his mood to perch on it uncomfortably. He had no idea what to say to his wife (his wife!) – and it was evident she was not going to open the conversation.

'How are you feeling?' he asked her at last.

He thought she wouldn't answer, but at last she said, 'Empty.'

Her voice was as flat as the word, and the word upset him an unexpected amount. He had to clear his throat and blink back tears. He said, 'Much pain?'

'Not now,' she said.

There was silence, and a gulf between them.

'One of the fellows swapped leave with me,' he tried next. 'I have until the twenty-third.'

She said nothing.

The feelings surged up in him, and the words broke out. 'Why didn't you tell me?'

Tears filled Jessie's eyes with frightening readiness. 'Would it have made any difference?' she said.

What she meant was that she would still have lost the child – and then he would have been even more upset, having been raised to the heights of expectation only to be dashed as much further down.

But he didn't understand what she didn't say aloud. 'Yes, to me. I had the right to know. *Why* didn't you tell me? I was its father – don't I count at all?'

Jessie couldn't answer. She hurt too much to have anything to offer to his hurt. The tears rolled over and ran down her cheeks, slowly and silently.

Ned hated to see her cry. In his pain he struck out at her. 'I sometimes think you don't care for me at all,' he said, in a low voice. 'Not even to tell me! Do you *know* how I felt when I heard?' She couldn't answer. A sort of madness seized him. 'I don't think you wanted the baby in the first place,' he went on, lashing himself as much as her. 'Are you sorry you married me? Is that what it is?'

She wept, every part of her hurting, her empty body aching with loss, her mind hurting most of all. Brach, lying mournfully by the fire, lifted her head and whined. Terrible pain tore at Ned's heart, to see her crying, to see her so low and defeated, to have added to her pain, perhaps – but helpless in his own pain to help it. In his agony he *knew* she didn't love him, and that was the worst thing of all.

'I'm sorry,' he said, and his voice cracked. He was fighting tears too. 'I'm sorry.' He was sorry for everything, and did not know how to make anything right again. He reached for conventional words. 'Jessie, don't cry. I didn't mean it, I know you wanted the baby. Oh, please, don't cry!'

He reached into the shaking, damp bundle of her, and found her hand and squeezed it. Her crying seemed to ease a little, and his relief was enormous. He held her hand in both his and stroked it. 'It will be all right,' he said. 'We'll have other babies. Everything will be all right.'

He sat there for a long time, until Susie came up with

Jessie's tray, and to call him down to luncheon. 'I'll stay here with you, and help you eat,' he said. He went on eagerly, 'I'll feed you, shall I, like a—' He stopped. Clumsy, clumsy fool!

Jessie almost looked at him, swivelled her eyes towards him a little to say it didn't matter. 'No, you go down,' she said wearily. 'Talk to Mother. I don't want anything anyway. Please – go down.'

Little Susie bustled him gently away from the bed, and whispered that she would see Madam had something. And so, feeling like a clumsy interloper, a great brutal man in this fragile world of women, Ned tiptoed helplessly out.

The next day a calm reigned in the East Bedroom. Ned sat with Jessie for a long time in the morning and talked to her, mostly about the camp and the training and the battalion. The baby was not mentioned between them. He would have liked to ask her about Scarborough, but dared not raise the subject. It was a relief to him simply not to see her tears. She spoke to him, responded to what he said; when he asked how she felt, she answered that she had no pain and felt better that day. But her eyes did not quite meet his, and he felt she wasn't really there. They were like two people who had quarrelled and were being polite. The distance between them was necessary to keep their bruised surfaces apart, but it hurt Ned deeply, though he didn't know what to do about it. But it was better for her health, he thought, that she should not cry, and he comforted himself with that.

Hasty came and examined her, and pronounced himself satisfied. She was going on very well, he said, and would make a full recovery in a few weeks. She should go carefully for a month or two, but then could resume her normal life.

'And in – let's say – three months, you'll be able to start another baby,' he added. Jessie did not answer, her eyes like stone.

The days of Ned's leave fled away. One part of her felt sorry and guilty that she could not enjoy it, or help him enjoy it. It was awful to waste this little, precious time he was at home – and who knew when he would be able to come again? Not for months, perhaps. He had been gone since October and she hadn't seen him once in that time. But she had nothing to give him out of her emptiness, could do nothing but hide inside herself and try not to feel.

On the twenty-third, he came in the afternoon to tell her that he was leaving, because he had to be back at the camp by evening.

'Oh,' was all she could think of to say. She was sorry, but in a way she was relieved. She could not comfort him, and his presence only reminded her of her own sorrow and guilt. She had not meant to lose the baby; the bombing of Scarborough had not been her fault, and if the same thing happened again she would do as she had done, because it had been the right thing to do. But she remembered how she had not thought once about the baby all the time it was happening. She knew, illogically, that the baby had felt she didn't care, and had died for lack of her love. There was a part of her that did not want to exchange her old life for the new one of being a mother, and the baby had known. If she had wanted it with the whole of her heart and mind and being . . . Well, it was too late now. She felt, hopelessly, that there would be no more babies.

'I'm sorry,' she said, and it was 'sorry' for all of these things.

Ned only thought she meant she was sorry he was going back. 'I wish I could stay longer,' he said. 'I'll write to you.'

'Yes.'

'And you'll write to me? Often?'

'Yes,' she said, and, making an effort, 'I will, I promise.'

He leaned over to kiss her, and at the last moment she moved her head a little so that the kiss was on her cheek instead of her lips. 'Get well soon,' he said, his heart breaking. Her cheek was pale and cold, and her eyes were still turned away from him. But he had to go. His duty could not be denied.

When he had gone she lay down under the covers and thought she would cry again, but it seemed all the tears had been used up. She lay, her eyes dry and burning, and ached with misery.

* * *

She liked to have Alice to sit with her, because Alice didn't talk. She just sat across the room by the window, where the light was better, and sewed her endless lengths of fine embroidery. Alice had lost a child, and had been told she could never have another. She never referred to it even obliquely, but it was there between them, something in the silence that said, *I understand.*

On Christmas Day Jessie felt she must make an effort not to spoil things for the family, and said she felt well enough to come downstairs. One of the footmen carried her down and put her on the daybed in the drawing-room, where Henrietta had prepared blankets and pillows. Uncle Teddy was pathetically glad to see her downstairs, and hovered nearby trying to think of things to offer her. Polly viewed her with awe from a distance, as if she were a bomb that might explode.

Jessie tried to smile, but the smell of the Christmas tree in the corner was too poignant, and Christmas was too intimately involved with birth and with children. At four, rising five, James William was old enough to be fully involved with the whole delight of Christmas; Roberta at three and a half was beginning to understand; and even little Jeremy, at eighteen months, gazed at the tree, when the candles were lit, with eyes that shone with wonder. And there was Ethel being hovered over by Rob, who could not conceal his uxorious pride in her.

Jessie tried to smile and be gay, but it was all too much, and long before the Christmas geese were out of the oven, she had begun to shake with a nervous chill, and had to be hurried back to bed.

The attacks came, on and off, for several days, fits of shivering and sweating, accompanied by a black despair. In between she lay weakly, staring at the walls. She began to be haunted by the sound of a baby crying. Jeremy was the youngest child in the house, and he did not cry like that any more. It was the piercing wail of a new baby she could hear – the sound that tugs at the pit of a woman and can't be ignored. The first time she heard it she rang the bell in a panic, thinking that Ethel's baby must have come early.

By the time Susie reached her, she was shivering like a frightened horse. After that, the sound came at odd intervals. Sometimes she would strain her ears and it would resolve itself into something else entirely – the cry of a bird outside, the telephone ringing downstairs, the whining of the wind in the chimney. Once it was only the sound of Brach snoring softly by the fire. But often she could not find the source of it. It was a faint sound, almost beyond the range of hearing. In this old house, where there had been uncounted births and deaths, there were so many ghosts. The sound seemed almost to be coming from the walls themselves, like a manifestation of the grief that had soaked into them over the ages. It was as though the very fabric of the house was crying in a newborn baby's voice, to reproach her.

CHAPTER TWENTY-ONE

Dr Hasty said she could begin to get up for an hour a day, and she heard him dimly, without interest. She did not want to get up. The world outside her bed seemed hostile and uncomfortable, and she did not want to engage with it. Uncle Teddy was directing things for her at the stables, but she listened to his reports without hearing. Ned wrote to her, but she hadn't the strength to write back, and forgot what his letters said as soon as she put them down.

Robbie went to Maystone one day on his way home from work and collected an armful of books, all the ones Tomlinson thought she would like, with some fresh nightdresses. He brought back a bunch of snowdrops Tomlinson had picked for her from her own garden, to urge her to get well and come home.

'How sweet and fragrant,' Henrietta said. 'Smell, Jessie, how sweet,' she urged. Jessie sniffed obediently, but smelled nothing, and only sighed.

News came from the outside world. Frank's battalion was due to go abroad in March, but only on garrison duty to Egypt, to release seasoned troops for the front. He would have embarkation leave, and would come to Morland Place then. Jessie was vaguely glad it was so far off, so that she would be sure to be well enough for it, but most of her hardly cared. And Jack's leg was healing, though more slowly than he had expected, so he had held off on the wedding, and he and Helen were now thinking of a date at the end of January. Good for Jack, she thought, out of the daze that surrounded her.

The days were short, not light until eight and dark again at four, and she slept a lot. When she was asleep she had marvellous dreams. She could not remember them when she woke, but she knew they were lovely, and she clung to sleep as the one comfort in her empty world. She slept in great hungry gulps, shutting out the ache of her mind and body. Sometimes she thought that perhaps one day she would just not wake up, and the thought did not appal her.

She was woken from a dream one day by an unusual sound. She thought at first it was the phantom baby's cry, and shuddered under the covers. But gradually, as she scraped the cobwebs from her mind, she realised that it was someone playing the piano in the drawing-room. She could only hear it very faintly because of the distance, and then only because the door to her room had been left open. She struggled up onto one elbow and saw that the room was empty. No-one was sitting with her; and even Brach was not in her usual place by the fire. She must have nosed the door open and gone out, Jessie thought.

But who was playing the piano? Ethel had more or less given up, and it was not Alice's style, nor yet one of her pieces. Straining to hear, she thought she recognised it from long ago. Chopin. Something she used to play herself, years ago, she thought – a berceuse. It had been her 'party piece', for when she was called down from the nursery to show off to guests in the drawing-room. Her father had used to laugh at her, saying he pitied the baby that was rocked to her tempestuous thumping. She felt a fleeting pang of missing her father, who had so often laughed her out of her wildness. But it was good he could not see her now. It would have broken his heart.

The music went on, tantalising her out of her memories. Could it possibly be her mother playing? But the execution was too firm and sure. Was it a visitor? Or – was she imagining it? She reached for the bell cord and pulled, feeling suddenly alone and frightened. Everyone had gone away and left her, even Brach. She felt the familiar creeping approach of panic.

Susie came in, and at once it subsided. Susie looked guilty. 'Oh, madam, I'm sorry, I didn't know you were awake.'

Didn't know, because you went out and left me, Jessie thought resentfully, but all she said was, 'Who is that playing the piano?'

'Playing the piano?' Susie repeated blankly.

Did I imagine it, then? 'When I woke, I thought it was – you know – a baby crying,' she said falteringly. 'You – you can't hear it?'

'Oh, yes, madam, I hear it,' Susie said. 'It's the piano all right.'

Relief flooded her on that score, at least. 'But who's playing it?'

'I'm sure I don't know, madam,' Susie said, but there was consciousness in her face.

Why would she lie? Jessie wondered. But she only said, 'Go and find out, then.' Susie turned away. 'Help me sit up, first.' She felt so weak that sitting up often made her dizzy, but there was something about the sound of that piano that was nagging at her. Susie settled her against her pillows, and went away, with a guilty little backwards look. Shortly afterwards Brach came padding in, licking her lips ingratiatingly. 'And what have *you* been up to?' Jessie demanded. Brach smiled and waved her tail in pleasure at being spoken to, but Jessie said, 'You deserted me too, so don't pretend.'

There was a long pause, so long that Jessie was going to ring again, when she heard footsteps coming up the stairs. Not a maid's – not a woman's of any sort. It wasn't Uncle Teddy – she knew his tread. Not Sawry – he never made a sound. Not a servant at all. A big man with a firm, confident tread. She stared at the door, something like fear clenching her heart. The step was right outside. Brach was waving her whole hindquarters in anticipation – her nose knew who it was. Jessie almost cried out as a big shape darkened the doorway – bigger than human, surely? Something supernatural! Her heart pounded in her ears.

And then he crossed the room in a few swift strides and was staring down at her, smiling.

'Bertie!'

'Yes, it's me,' he said. 'Not a ghost. Don't be scared.'

'Bertie! Oh, Bertie!'

He sat down hurriedly on the edge of the bed to catch her as she flung herself at him. And then she was held in his strong arms, against his hard chest, the buttons of his uniform hurting her in a way that was entirely pleasurable. The roaring in her ears subsided. Her face was pressed against his neck, the familiar, loved smell of him in her nostrils, and she felt him kiss the top of her head, tenderly, as he had used to do years ago.

'Oh, my Jessie,' he said. 'I was hoping I'd see you, but they told me you were too ill. They said, "Wait and see if she wakes up." I was hoping and hoping you would, because I've only got a few hours.'

She answered him, and he had to move her face gently back from his neck to understand her. 'They should have woken me,' she said. 'Oh, Bertie, I'm so glad to see you.'

'I'm so sorry you've been ill,' he said. She saw in the shock of his expression how bad she looked. Tenderly he wiped the tears away from under her eyes with the side of his thumb, first one side, and then the other. 'My poor Jessie.'

'You're on leave,' she said, feasting her eyes on his face. It was so familiar, it was almost like looking in a mirror. He was thinner, more weather-beaten; the lines beside his mouth were etched deeper, and the creases at his eye corners were pale when he did not smile, where he had screwed them up against the sun.

'Yes, and I promised you I'd come up here when I got it. But I didn't get two weeks, only one, so I've only got this one day.'

'You're not going away right now?'

'Tonight. I have to be back at barracks tomorrow morning, for transport back to France.'

'Don't go tonight! Stay tonight. You can catch the milk train,' she urged, her eyes clinging to him.

'Does it mean so much to you?' he asked, searching her face. She nodded. 'All right, then. I'll stay tonight.'

Relief swept over her, and she sank back on her pillows. 'You look different,' she said.

'I'd like to say you don't, but it wouldn't be true.'

'Different, but just the same. Just the same old Bertie.'

'You must have been starving yourself,' he said sternly.

'I couldn't eat. Everything was – oh, you know. Dust and ashes.'

'Poor little girl. Would you eat now, if I brought you something?'

'I think I might be able to.'

'What would you like?' They looked into each other's eyes, and the thought came to them both at the same time. 'A boiled egg,' he said.

'With toast soldiers,' she completed.

'Like I brought you when you broke your silly arm, riding your father's stallion.' He laid his big warm hand over hers. 'And now you've been breaking your silly heart.'

'Oh, Bertie.' It was a sigh that came all the way up from the soles of her feet – but not an absolutely desolate sigh. There *was* comfort in the world, after all. The pain had receded just a little.

He smiled. '"Oh, Bertie", indeed. I suppose you want me to feed it to you, like I did then?'

'No, but I'd like you to sit with me while I eat. Oh, don't go away and ask for it – just ring. Bertie, you wouldn't really have gone away again without seeing me?'

'I tiptoed to your door twice, but you didn't wake.'

'I was having a lovely dream.' Perhaps, she thought, she had been dreaming about him; but she didn't say so. 'I heard you playing the piano. It *was* you, wasn't it?'

'Yes.'

'I thought so. I recognised your style.'

'*Unpractised* is my style at the moment. But I've been thinking about it for weeks now, at the front. I just had an irrational longing to play the piano. I felt somehow that if I could, I could bear anything.'

'Was it terrible?' she asked, in a small voice.

'It was – not nice. But we're soldiers, we know what to expect. No, it wasn't that, not the fighting, not even losing so many of my men. It was the destruction of everything around us that I hated – people's lives and people's houses and all the little things of everyday life we take for granted in peace. I suppose the piano was the essence of all that.'

'And was it that piece you wanted to play, particularly?'

'Yes. It kept running through my mind.'

'It's a piece I used to play when I was a girl.'

'I know. I learned it too, when I was a boy.'

They looked at each other and smiled, not because it was funny, but for pleasure.

Susie came in, in response to the bell. 'Susie, why didn't you tell me it was Captain Parke downstairs?' Jessie asked.

'Mrs Robert told me not to. She was afraid it would be too much of a shock when you'd just woken. She wanted it broken to you gently if you was awake.'

'How could you be a shock?' Jessie said to Bertie, her eyes on his face.

'A nice shock, perhaps,' he smiled.

Jessie ordered her boiled egg, and Susie looked impressed, and went away happily. It was the first time she had shown any interest in food since that dreadful night.

When they were alone again, Bertie said, 'Talking of shocks, I very much wanted to hear about Scarborough, but I've been forbidden to raise the topic. Would it be too frightful for you to talk about it?'

'No, not frightful,' she said. 'I'd like to tell you about it.' Without noticing it, he still had hold of her hand, and she felt safe there in the circle of firelight with him. Outside the day was dark and grey and the rain was beating past the window, but in here was all comfort. 'It was the noise of the shells that was the worst thing. I kept thinking that you would know all about that noise. It was terrible – unbearable.'

'Yes, I know,' he said.

She told him everything about that day in Scarborough, and when it came to it, she told him about losing the baby, too, and though she cried at that point, it was a gentle crying, not the tearing, awful crying of the first days.

'It's so sad,' he said. 'But you'll have others. The doctor said there was nothing wrong with you, that it was just bad luck.'

'When did you speak to Dr Hasty?' she said.

'Your mother told me.'

'Oh.' She thought a moment. 'Don't let's talk about that,' she said. It was not that she could not bear to talk about it, but that she did not need to talk about it, not now. It was just bad luck, he had said – not her fault. It would be all right. She could leave it be, just now. 'Tell me about your men, and the other officers. Tell me things you've done.'

So he told her a soldier's stories, her hand – surprisingly soft without its riding callouses – warm and alive in his. This moment could not last. Soon he would have to leave her, to go back to the front and the cold, bleak life of the winter trenches; but for now she was here with him, close and loving, and he had all of her attention and, he believed, a good piece of her heart. He would enjoy it while he could, to make memories to take with him when he left.

He told her soldier's anecdotes, of misfortune and comradeship and practical jokes, and when Susie came in with the tray she was astonished to find her mistress laughing, and the pinched, worn look almost gone from her thin face.

After Bertie's visit, Jessie began to improve. First she sat up; then she began to eat properly; then she was out of bed for an hour – feeling, the first time, as though all the bones had been removed from her while she slept. She staggered, pale and weak, to a chair by the fire, and sat there until it was time to stagger back. But each day she got up for longer and went further, and by the end of a week she was out of bed, only needing an afternoon rest on the sofa. At the end of the fourth week after the miscarriage she had herself driven over to Maystone to see how things were going on, and to collect some more clothes – for she was not yet ready to go home. Tomlinson was so glad to see her she almost cried. The next day she had herself driven to Twelvetrees to see Hotspur, who was so glad to see her Jessie almost cried.

Six weeks after the miscarriage Dr Hasty pronounced her fit to travel south for Jack's wedding. No-one was more pleased than Jessie that she would not be letting down her favourite brother. Physically she felt almost back to normal; mentally there was a scar, but she got along by never thinking of it. She was aware of a shadow in the corner of her mind that she must not look at, something which, if awakened, would threaten to engulf her. She knew that some time she would have to look, have to come to terms with it – but not now. When she was stronger, when the pain was further in the past, she would have to discover what she still felt about the baby, and herself, and Ned. But not now.

The wedding was to be a quiet one, but the Ormerods had invited all those at Morland Place, if they liked to come. Henrietta and Teddy were going, with Polly. Alice had pleaded off. Teddy knew she did not much care for meeting strangers, and assured her she needn't, that the Ormerods and Jack and Helen would understand. Robbie did not want to miss the wedding of his own brother, especially as Frank could not be there, but Ethel felt herself too large with child either to travel or to be seen in public, and he would not leave her. So it was just four of them who took the train to London early in the morning of the 30th of January.

They reached Fairoaks in time for a light luncheon with Mr and Mrs Ormerod, Helen and Molly, before the latter two went up to dress. Helen seemed wonderfully calm, but Jessie noticed when they sat down at table that her hands on the cutlery shook slightly, and she barely ate a mouthful of the poached fish and lamb cutlets that were put before her. Mr and Mrs Ormerod were too polite to reveal their feelings to comparative strangers, and the conversation was mostly about the war (Mr Ormerod) and the price of things being so shocking (Mrs Ormerod). Only Molly showed how excited she was, and chattered to Jessie in a low voice about her bridesmaid's dress and how no-one had ever believed 'old Helen' would ever get married, but that Jack was so nice and had promised that he would introduce her, Molly, to lots of brother officers so that she should never get into the same position, and how up until quite recently she had thought 'all that love business' was 'too grue' but now she quite thought she'd like to get married herself one day, if it was to someone like Jack. Jessie diagnosed a severe case of hero worship, but was able to agree with Molly with absolute truth that Jack was one of the nicest people in the world.

'He's so nice I think he almost deserves your sister,' she finished.

Molly stared a moment as she worked out the sense of that. 'But Helen's not anything very special,' she said in surprise. 'She's not bad, for a sister, and I like her of course – a lot – but she's not 'specially pretty. And she's awfully *old*.'

Jessie smiled. 'I expect Jack thinks she's beautiful, and not a bit old.'

'Yes, I suppose he does,' Molly said, and lapsed into silence over this puzzle.

The Ormerods' motor took the Morland Place contingent and Mrs Ormerod to the church, going back to fetch the bride and her father and the bridesmaid. Jack was at the church to greet them, in a wheelchair, but looking very tanned and healthy. His leg, still in plaster, did not seem like part of him.

When Jessie bent over to greet him, he kissed her tenderly and whispered, 'Oh, Jessie, I'm so sorry.'

She squeezed his hand. 'Don't talk about it. I'm so happy for you.'

He assured them that he was coming on famously, and already taking a few steps on crutches; but said they'd decided the wheelchair was safer for the church because it would have been too undignified if the groom had tumbled over and brought down the bride as they walked down the aisle. Jessie thought he seemed very nervous, but it was a nice kind of nervousness, and touched her very much.

As promised, it was a quiet wedding, with only close family – on Helen's side, her parents and sister, her brother Freddie and his wife and children, her cousin Mrs Hewlitt who had done so much to bring her and Jack together, and an aged aunt who could never be left out. In addition there were half a dozen female friends from Helen's past, half a dozen service friends of Jack's, and friends of them both from the sphere of aviation – among whom were the Sopwiths. In all there were about thirty people, which seemed a tiny group in the large church. The day was dark and dreary outside, threatening rain, and the candles inside shone the more brightly for that, glinting off the brass and silver and imparting a warmth to the colour of the stone. Seeing the men in uniform, she thought of Ned up at Black Brow – probably struggling through the sleet on an exercise – and of Bertie – somewhere in a trench in France, facing the enemy – both of them, like all those in uniform, ready to suffer discomfort and danger in order that she could enjoy this moment of peace and pleasure.

The organ struck up, the doors were thrown open, and Helen came in on her father's arm. The congregation most properly did not turn to stare, but Jessie could not resist a covert look sideways under her eyelashes as the pair reached her. Helen was dressed in cream silk georgette, a slender gown reaching just to her ankles, with the now fashionable 'V-neck', with an over-tunic of cream lace, which was draped and folded in two tiers over the hips, falling to points behind. She wore a small cream-coloured hat with a veil of fine spotted net, through which Jessie could easily see her face, glowing with rapture as she walked towards the figure in khaki, waiting for her at the altar. Jessie removed her eyes, feeling almost that she had pried on something private, and felt a warm wash of grateful tears that her darling Jack was so much loved.

After the service everyone returned to Fairoaks in a variety of motor-cars – Jessie, Polly and Molly travelled together with two of the young flying officers, much to the girls' gratification. At the house, Rug rushed up officiously to greet everyone and pass them on to the receiving line. Helen, with her veil back now, seemed in a daze of happiness, as though she hardly dared believe it was all happening. Jessie kissed her new sister-in-law's cheek and wished her happy, and then added in a whisper, 'I'll pinch you, if you like.'

Helen laughed. 'Is it so obvious?'

'I firmly believe you're real,' Jessie said, 'and I'll sign you an affidavit that Jack is, if you need one.'

Jack, seated beside Helen, caught at her hand and said, 'No whispering, there!'

Jessie stooped to kiss him, and said, 'I was just telling her how perfect you are.'

'Then she'll know you're lying,' said Jack, with a grin.

'Darling Jackie,' Jessie said. 'I'm so glad that you're going to be happy – and I know you will be. She's just right for you.'

'Much too good for me,' Jack said, with a look up at his bride that would have melted stone.

After that there was champagne, a handsome buffet, speeches, and a cake of pre-war magnificence, which Mrs Ormerod felt obliged to excuse by saying to Henrietta that she had bought the fruit and the sugar *well* before war was declared, and had been keeping it ever since. 'So I hope there won't be *any* talk of hoarding. But really, if one can't give one's own daughter a proper wedding – well, what is the war *for*?'

Afterwards again there was dancing. Jack and Helen had borrowed a gramophone and some half a dozen records from a friend, and while the older ones sat and talked in the background, the young people enjoyed themselves with the new dances. It was something novel to Jessie, who watched Molly with respect as she did the steps with insouciant skill, dancing with one officer after another. Polly hopped her way around in magnificent ignorance, stepping on toes so lightly they hardly noticed, and making her partners laugh so much she was never left without one.

Jessie did not dance. She sat with Jack, while he told her the full story of his crash, brief captivity and release. 'What will happen now?' she asked. 'You won't be going back to France?'

'Not for a while. I shan't be able to fly for months. But they'll find me a ground job until my leg heals. I don't know whether it will be instruction or back to designing. There's a great need for people in both areas. I shall still be doing my bit for the war effort, don't worry.'

'I wasn't worried about that,' Jessie said. 'I was just thinking Helen would be glad to have you at home for a little while, seeing you're only just married.'

'When is Ned going overseas?' Jack asked, his sympathy in his face. 'You must miss him so much – especially now.'

Jessie's eyes moved away. 'I don't know – nothing's been said. Not for months yet, though, I imagine.' She smiled rather tautly. 'Don't pity me, Jackie, or I shall start crying. Tell me more about flying.'

At about eight o'clock there was a wonderful surprise for the Morlands as the door opened and Frank walked in, in uniform, rather damp about the shoulders and head from the rain. 'I got a few hours off,' he explained. 'But it's been such a deuced long journey getting here, I'll have to leave again almost straight away. Still, I couldn't resist coming. Wanted to see you properly turned off, Jack, old man.'

Jack was reduced almost to tears by the pleasure and surprise of seeing him. Jessie felt similarly moved, especially at the sight of her middle brother, the quiet one, the intellectual, in uniform. Molly couldn't take her eyes off Frank, thinking him exceptionally handsome and *just* the right age, and managed to bring herself to his attention by being the one to fetch him a large glass of whisky and a piece of the wedding cake, after which he pretty well had to talk to her for a bit. Jack heaved himself, with help, out of his chair onto his crutches, and went for a short walk alone with his brother for a private chat, after which Helen joined them for a few moments; and then Frank had to leave, with tears and hugs from his mother and sister and a silent, emotional handshake from Uncle Teddy.

When he had gone, a mellowness came over the wedding party. The dancing was resumed and the gramophone records with waltz tunes came round more often. Even Teddy persuaded Henrietta to take to the floor with him. The bride slipped away to change, and returned in a neat tailor-made to take the groom away. Everyone crowded to the door, where Jack's motor stood waiting with the suitcases already packed for the honeymoon.

The rain had stopped, and a gibbous moon was sliding

in and out of the clouds, making the wet world shine and the faintly moving trees glitter. There were kisses and tears and good wishes. Jessie pressed her lips to Jack's cool, lean cheek and whispered, 'Be happy.'

Helen climbed behind the wheel of the motor, Jack was helped in at the other side, and they were off. Jessie turned back with the rest to the house, and found her mother beside her.

'I like Helen very much,' Henrietta said. 'I hope this war is over soon, so they can settle down together.'

'So do I. I can just see them, driving together and flying together and doing everything together. What a lucky pair they are.'

'It was a lovely wedding,' said Henrietta.

The clouds were clearing fast, and the gibbous moon, sailing clear, shone down on water, water and more water. The sheets and lagoons and meres of it seemed to join together under the moonlight to make an unmoving inland sea, broken here and there by the skeleton of a ruined tree, a broken fencepost, the remains of a hedge, a scrawl of barbed wire. Bertie could see his breath misting before him. It would be cold later – cold enough for frost, for thin ice to form over the shallower meres. But at least the rain had stopped.

In a place as low-lying as Flanders, a season as rainy as this had been was a disaster. There was nowhere for it to drain away to. The trenches were full of water, and their sodden walls continually slid and crashed inward in a morass of mud. Every day they bailed out and redug the trenches, propped up walls with wood, corrugated iron, anything they could find – work not just for the sappers, but for every man not on guard duty. Where digging down was hopeless they tried to build upwards, making breastworks and redoubts instead; but they had to fill the sandbags with earth, and the floods washed through them and they collapsed. They worked and walked and stood in water, and in its concomitant evil, mud. If they managed to get the water out of a trench temporarily, the passage of boots would turn the bottom into a thick, greasy porage in which a man sank up to his ankles, his calves, his knees. And then it would rain again and the porage would turn to soup.

It was heartbreaking work. The only comfort was that there was little activity along this part of the front, because the enemy, not far away in their own trenches, were in the same boat. Everyone was too wet and too beleaguered by rain and mud to pursue the war vigorously. In the spring – when the rain stopped – they would fight again. For now, they were just surviving.

Bertie paused to light a cigarette, cupping his hands round his lighter to conceal the flame, then carrying the cigarette as soldiers do, between finger and thumb with the glowing end hidden in his palm. Snipers were a law to themselves, and continued to be a danger even when everyone else had gone to ground. Even during the so-called Christmas Truce, there had still been the risk of being hit by a sniper in certain places in the trench.

He had got back to his men on the morning of the 31st of December, and had heard all about the truce from Pennyfather.

'It was uncanny. You could feel the atmosphere growing all through Christmas Eve. Nobody said anything, but the thought was everywhere so you could almost hear it – "It's Christmas. We don't want to fight." And then we heard the Germans singing carols. "Silent Night" was one we all recognised.'

One of the men had joined in, and then another, until they were all singing – not loudly or raucously, not to drown out the enemy, as they had sometimes done on the Aisne – but softly, reflectively, almost mournfully.

'They were singing *with* the Germans, you see,' Pennyfather said, wondering at the strangeness of it.

Then, in the morning, on Christmas Day, a German in his trench had shouted out, 'Hey, Tommee, merry Christmas!'

And so it had begun. The shouts of goodwill back and forth, and then the first daring, tentative step over the parapet into no man's land. One from each side, watched by tired men who knew, but hardly dared believe, that it was not a trick. The meeting in the centre – the shaking of hands, the slowly spreading smiles.

'And then they all went,' said Pennyfather. 'I couldn't have stopped them and, frankly, I didn't want to. I went too. It was like a dream. I met a German officer in the centre and we shook hands and I offered him a cigarette. He offered me a drink from his flask. All I noticed was that he was about my age, and looked just as muddy.'

The men began to chat and laugh. Photographs of wives and children were shown. Gifts were exchanged. Both sides had been sent heaps of Christmas delicacies by their grateful public at home, and there was chocolate and cake and biscuits and tobacco. Tommies and Fritzes swapped gingerbread for Cadbury's Milk Chocolate, *stollen* for Callard and Bowser's butterscotch, *wurst* for Christmas pudding. Someone came across an empty five-pound plum-jam tin, and started kicking it about, and soon they were playing football with it, twenty a side, thirty a side, and no rules. Football, the common language of the working man.

'I heard them saying to each other, "Never again. We'll never fight again. We won't shoot unless you do,"' said Pennyfather. 'The rain had stopped. It was very cold, and a bit misty, but nice. It was good to be alive.'

The next day, when the Germans did not begin firing again, everyone knew the holiday was to go on. Pennyfather thought it would be a good time to get out and retrieve their dead who had been lying in the mud in no man's land for weeks. The German officers had had the same idea.

'We met in the middle to talk about it and—' Pennyfather hesitated, as though, at a distance, he could hardly believe what he was going to say. 'We agreed the best thing was to dig a common grave and put everyone in it, from both sides. To share the work, you see.'

And so they did. The work went on for most of the day, and when dusk came they held a joint service, lined up on either side of the grave, the words spoken in both languages, simultaneously, over the earth where German and English dead lay together, side by side, in a harmony nothing more could ever disturb.

After that, the unofficial truce had continued, with each side taking the opportunity to do necessary repairs, improve the trenches, string new barbed wire and, most of all, to relax and rest. There had not been much visiting between the sides (though stories were already rife about goings-on at other parts of the line) but they all knew that no-one was going to shoot, and that if you had to pop out of your trench for some reason, you could do it with impunity.

'I thought at first that it was more than a truce,' Pennyfather said. 'When we said to each other, "Never again", we all meant it, and I wondered what would happen if I had to order the men to fire. Would they refuse? It would be mutiny. We could all be shot.'

'You could all be shot for fraternising with the enemy,' Bertie had said, more in wonder than disapproval. He could feel the atmosphere for himself. But as he made his rounds that day, he had realised that these men, the remainder of the professional army, were not fools, and they were not traitors. They knew that the war would start up again, and sooner rather than later. They knew why they were here to fight, and that the enemy was the enemy, no matter how much like themselves he seemed face to face. They bore no personal animosity to the wet, muddy men in the trenches opposite; but the war had to be fought and won. It was not mutiny they wanted, it was just a holiday. They were tired to death, and they needed to stop for just a little while, needed to be sane for a little while before the madness resumed.

It was New Year's Eve, and at about eleven o'clock the firing had started from the German side. Bertie had run out into the trench and crouched behind the parapet, trying to see what he could through the periscope.

Pennyfather reached his side. 'Is this it, sir? Is this the end of it?' he said rather breathlessly. The men beyond him fingered their rifles a little nervously, waiting for orders.

Bertie turned to him with a slow grin. 'Continental time,' he said.

'Sir?'

'The Germans are not on Greenwich mean time. They're

an hour ahead. It's midnight with them. They're firing straight up in the air.'

Pennyfather grinned, too, in understanding, and all along the line the men relaxed. Not yet, then. Not quite yet.

When the fusillade died away, there was a silence, and then a distant voice, echoing over the mere, shouted, 'Hey, Tommee!'

Bertie answered for them. 'Yes, Fritz?'

'Happy New Year!'

'You're an hour early!' Bertie shouted back. 'But happy New Year, anyway.'

At midnight, Pennyfather asked Bertie if they could return the compliment. Bertie went out into the trench with him, and watched without comment as the men fired into the air, and shouted a chorus of 'Happy New Year' to each other and to the Germans out there in the dark. When it was over and the men had settled down again, Bertie walked down to the end and risked a look over.

'Tommee!' came the same voice – an officer, he assumed, since he spoke English.

'Still here, Fritz, old boy,' he called back.

'Nineteen fifteen,' called the German. 'The year of peace, yes?'

'I will if you will,' Bertie shouted.

'What do you say?' Fritz did not understand.

'I said yes, old man,' called Bertie. 'The year of peace.'

He thought about that night now, a month later. The firing had begun again the next day. The men had had their holiday. They knew it couldn't last – and angry letters from Headquarters were buzzing up and down the line like hornets. Only the fact that the truce had been almost universal had saved the men from disciplinary action. But they knew they were safe, and they knew the generals knew. All the same, they were professional soldiers, and after their holiday they buckled down with barely a sigh and got on with it.

Not that there had been much action during that month. With the rain and the trench conditions it was all they could do to survive. There was no question of pushing forward.

Both sides were marking time until spring, when the all-out action would start again. The generals would already be planning their big offensive, probably for March. Bertie had heard that reinforcements would be coming out from England then.

The temperature had dropped ten degrees while he had been smoking his cigarette, and the frost was sparkling down through the air in a way that was utterly beautiful. He took the last draw and doused the butt in the water at his feet, then turned and squelched back through the mud towards his dugout, his ears burning with the cold. The moon kept him company, reflecting its face in the pools of standing water ahead of him. He felt oddly content.

Nineteen fifteen. The year of peace.